After the End:
The Journey

RJ Lynch

Two Hands Media—Mukwonago, WI
ISBN: 978-1-7345323-1-9
Library of Congress Control Number: pending
Title: *After the End: The Journey*
Author: RJ Lynch
Digital distribution | 2021
Paperback | 2021

This is a work of fiction. The characters, names, incidents, places, and dialogue are products of the author's imagination, and are not to be construed as real.

Dedication

First, I want to thank New Book Authors Publishing and Em Hughes for taking another risk on me. It means the world for you to stick with me. Now I want to dedicate this story to my mentors, for we are all lost on our journeys without the right people to guide us and give us a chance. Mike Chapes, Josh Buchholtz, Mike Johnson, Brandon Schlotthauer, and the late Mike Furlong; you all took a chance on me believing when no one else did, you taught me more than I could imagine, and helped me become who I am. I cannot put into words the role you all have played.

Table of Contents

Preface

Despite everything that I have gone through, it is amazing how much of a difference a year can make. A year ago, I was probably drunk off my mind taking home some woman making a horrible life decision. I had no responsibility as I had been given gifts for being a "hero." I was miserably happy. It is an odd phrase, but one that I know many people can relate to. The numbness that you feel. The emptiness that replaces the pain you were used to. The nightmares disappeared because I was too drunk to have them, most nights anyway. Yet, that relief you feel comes at a cost. You are not just numb to the pain anymore. No, you become numb to the happiness as well. You lose sight of what is essential and the important people. If only I had opened my eyes sooner, maybe things would have been different. Sorry, I apologize for the rambling, but I found it necessary to understand where I was.

Now, as I said, a year makes a difference, and precisely the few days that preceded the start of my journey changed me. My name is Rob Doran, and during the War, I was a part of a seven-man team that didn't officially exist. A team that accomplished feats that created legends across both battle lines. Though we were legends, I wish I had nothing to do with them, but I will get to that later. The one member of the team you should be concerned with is the most well-known, John Kore. John is a villainous snake, a monster to be precise. However, he is the closest thing I've ever had to a brother. Without him, I would never have survived the War.

That being said, there has always been a distinct difference between us. He has always been heartless and manipulative, working his own angles every step of the way. Yet, I never thought the man I called brother would threaten the people I loved and kill the woman who owned my heart.

The man I called brother stood next to me as I lay on the ground paralyzed by some drug he had concocted. From there, he raised his gun and shot her. Iris, the woman I was set to marry after a long wait caused by my own stupidity. I watched as she bled out, unable to help her as she took her final breaths. The worst part of it all was that he had planned it all.

I had fallen out of her life due to my antics. Though she waited for me, I was ready to die without her. That was until he brought us together again. He helped me find love again just to rip it away when it was still new. I hated him. Well, maybe hate is the wrong. The truth is I don't understand my feelings for him now. I understand him so differently now, and it is hard to express how I feel about him. I will let you come to your own conclusions on John. You will notice that he is evil, but life isn't as black and white as the fairy tales we tell our children.

Now that you understand me. I need you to understand why you are. Our world is in danger. John and Ascension are in a position to destroy what is left. It is beyond anything I could have imagined, and if you are reading this, I may very well be dead, or we won. Either way, you must know a few of us are against his power, but the odds are not in our favor. We are desperate soldiers living on a prayer, and if we are dead when you read this, you must rise. If you do not, it will not be long before his forces come for you. The annihilation we thought was avoided when the War ended is near.

Had I acted sooner? Had I not been the drunk I was a year ago, maybe I could have gotten ahead of all this, but I failed all of you. Now read this and understand what has led me to New Orleans and the cusp of a battle I don't know if I can win.

Part 1
Nowhere and Unknown

Early August, 10 A.L.A.

Chapter 1
Ghost Town

Before I begin my story, I want to clarify some things that may differ due to the separation of our peoples. Though our use of months has stayed relatively consistent, we have forgone the old B.C.E. and A.D.E. calendar for A.L.A. or After Los Angeles. With the first bombs of the War falling on L.A. on September 5th, we decided to start every year after that as 1 A.L.A. and henceforth. Along with that, many conversations will have a bit of artistic liberty.

The journey started back in the small Wisconsin city of Despartian, where John and I had spent most of our time after the War ended. I was a drunk, and he was slowly taking control of Ascension and beginning to spin his web. I didn't trust him because we ended our fighting days together poorly, but I ignored him more than anything. That was until people started ending up dead. Without my knowledge, he had recruited our old commander Gene and knife specialist Jackson to cause havoc across the city as the Eye and Jester. It was a ploy to draw me out. Whatever the reason is, he needs me for his plan. I thought the project was stopped when myself, a man with a metal arm named Ponleak, and my old doctor friend Anna brought the pair down.

Only for John to reveal himself as the mastermind and kill Iris while leaving Despartian in pieces. After that day, I took three weeks to retrain my body and collect information on where John may have run to. I needed those weeks after I realized that the only reason, I beat the elderly Gene was that it was part of John's plan. I could beat simpletons due to instinct that Gene had ingrained in me, but a man with skill would better me. I needed to be the old version of myself again if I had any chance of taking my revenge.

Revenge, I was blinded by it early on. The numbness I had felt weeks prior was replaced by a raging fire. It was a dangerous game to play and one that Iris had warned me against, but I felt again while no longer understanding how to control them.

The weeks of training led to an early stumbling block. John and his young niece Trisha were ghosts. Some whispers and rumors might have resembled them, but nothing solid enough to follow. I couldn't understand how the sharp-dressed devil that represented the only corporation left in the world and the black-haired monster with the complexion of a young goddess could just vanish. The two wore their individuality proudly and made no effort to blend, yet, they were gone without a single trace.

The only answer I could fathom arose from Ascension and the connections it had brokered for John. Ascension had dabbled in every endeavor they could get their hands on since John had ascended to the throne. The corporation had physical plants worldwide, and I feared that he may have used those connections to exit the country. I soon came to my senses when I realized that John would not have started this game if he did not intend to fight it himself. John wanted me to find him, he wanted to fight me again on his terms, but his reason still evaded me.

As the weeks dragged by and the few allies, I had turned up dead end after dead end, I began to grow disheartened. During the War, one of John's specialties was tracking our opposition. He had a nose greater than any bloodhound that gave us a distinct advantage during our fights in the densest forest between South America and Southeast Asia. This tracking ability of his also allowed him to cover tracks unlike anyone else. John wasn't going to be found if he did not want to be, and the only time he would like to be found would be if he was in complete control. When John is in total control, no one is safe.

After those grueling weeks had passed, the moment I was training for finally arrived. Whether it was chance or John setting a piece of cheese in the mousetrap, a lead far more promising than any of the prior ones emerged. The rumor revolved around a small town in Illinois that bordered the Mississippi River, an easy journey from his starting point in Despartian. More importantly, the city was home to an abandoned Ascension satellite factory. Now the name of the city no longer holds a place in my memory, but it is where the story truly begins.

I remember first rolling into what I couldn't believe was considered a town. Unlike the lively streets and hustle of daily construction I had grown accustomed to, there were just ghosts. Luckily, that was what I was looking for.

If memory serves me, it was right around August 5th. The sun had been scorching my skin the last few days, leaving me burned and miserable while sweating every ounce of water I took in. Making matters worse was the humidity. The wetness of the air glued my dirty clothes to my skin. The tightness of it made the heat unbearable. I hoped that along with finding John, I would also stumble on some supplies.

As I mentioned before, this town was barely that, to the point that I thought I was walking into an ambush. The city was poorly maintained as the buildings were turning into dust. Picture an old Western town where the buildings creaked and the wood planks that held the walls together rippled as the wind gusted. It seemed to be devoid of all life, and one last disaster would finally wipe the town off the face of the Earth.

It was a tragic sight that many people can relate to, but I often forget about it. Those seven years had left a scar on this planet that stretched across every inch of land. However, by the time I had sobered up enough to return home, Despartian had already begun rebuilding. Leaving me with only memories of growth rather than tragedy. Whoever called this place home was not as fortunate. They had to face a second calamity that should have brought them prosperity. John has a habit of upsetting the natural order of things you can say. To understand John's evil, you must understand history, not the one that has aged and become biased with the sentiment. No, you must hear how one domino fell into the other.

When the War ended, there was a void. Multiple voids of power, order, and technology, there was nothing but chaos. Some municipalities began reforming the best they could, but nothing connected them. Then a group of old greedy capitalists made a history-altering move. I hate saying capitalist as I was a profound lover of the system, but it is a term that describes them well. They weren't what I would classify as intelligent men but very opportunistic. Several of them had been C.E.O.s of renowned tech companies before the War. They took hold of the voids they saw, forming the company known as Ascension. A name they chose to represent ascending to glory or some fluff like that.

They started with the power grid, which had strategically been decimated throughout the War. To do this, they started putting up satellite factories across the globe. In theory, it was a perfect move, but as I said, these were not wise men, and they continued to fail, which would set them up for their fall. Despite the failures, these factories' presence created work for people that had nothing in the aftermath of the chaos. In the company's early days, the most significant thing they did was instill hope in those barely limping along.

I speak ill of these men who formed Ascension but looking back on it, they did something. I was a war hero who descended into drunken stupors. I could have helped give people the hope they were clamoring for, but in the end, it was them. Just another regret and failure I carry with me, but once again, I digressed.

Then the fateful day occurred, I have never been made privy to how he did it or what happened, but John seized control of the corporation. An intelligent businessman in his own right, and a better strategist, he made a move that saved Ascension while dooming thousands. Ascension had always allowed its workforce to stay in whatever city it wanted. However, with the lack of communication systems, no one could collaborate, so he changed that. John centralized the greatest minds from each satellite to five locations. They were a collection of pre-war metropolises and shadows that existed in my past. His chosen five were; Despartian, Memphis, New Orleans, Berlin, and Tokyo. Each city had been the site of a significant battle that directed the course of the War. They were what he deemed as the perfect locations for the rebirth of civilization. He was highly confident in his ability to turn the company around.

The problem was that by centralizing everything, he had closed over fifty satellites and stolen hope from thousands. In an instant, John should have become the most hated man globally, but he didn't, thanks to his own planning. Given the state of the world's communication network, news traveled slowly. A few bribes and intimidation tactics were enough to change the story to one that decreed the board members as the guilty party. While he was now the savior that would attempt to undo the damage the best he could.

He had maneuvered things perfectly so that he was always the light in the darkness.

Worse yet was how quickly he was able to turn public favor back to Ascension. The shift turned the five cities into thriving cultural hubs flourishing with success. Victories seemed to fall like dominos as the power grid was reestablished within weeks of the takeover. A takeover of ruined railroads revitalized the reconstruction of the country. A phone and telegraph network connected those who thought they would never speak to loved ones again with the power grid in place. The last part came with the catch of only being available to the richest and treasured individuals, but it was a start.

Transportation, communication, and power, all things that John deemed essential for the rebirth of our world. It was a glorious and quick success that made him the most powerful man in the world, but I question how fast it occurred. I will never know for sure, but I believe he had a hand in the failures of the board itself. Then he used them as scapegoats for the collateral damage that would occur, like that of the small town in Illinois I arrived in.

Now you are caught up for those of you who were unaware of how the world got into its current power structure. This brings me to the start of my journey and the rumor I followed. Unlike previous leads that tried to track the man, this one was different. This one scared me regardless of whether it led me to John or not, as it stated that one of the abandoned factories was up and running again. This time creating weapons. A terrifying thought as there is no counter to new weapons being built. Nearly all guns were collected by Ascension after the War and destroyed or tagged for tracking purposes, so the thought that new ones were circulating was a threat to the world.

Now back to the town, I walked down the single gravel road that ran through it, peering into every shambled hut looking for any life. There was no way that a place like this could house a weapons factory large enough to threaten anyone. The only possible weapon would have to come from the rats and mold littering the buildings.

After a bit of wandering, I came across an inn with the sound of life coming from within. Correction, inn isn't the right word. After taking a look inside, it would be more accurately described as a coffin. The patrons looked like mere skeletons as their skin seemed one size too small as it attempted to stretch across their bodies. Not a hint of fat or excess laid on their bodies. I watched as this collection of sunburnt mummies moved only in small increments, some barely lifting their glasses of water to their lips.

They had issues turning their necks to look at me. Like the town itself, they were dust with rotting foundations. I should have been devastated. I should have crumbled at sight, but there was just no empathy in those days. I was so consumed by my mission that I couldn't concern myself with the feelings of others. Unbeknownst to me at the time, I had become the man I was hunting. I saw people as pawns and insignificant if they couldn't help me. That dark place, it was...terrifying.

As I sauntered through the bar, I started to feel the icy stares land on my back. I tried to ignore them and avoid eye contact. I didn't want to risk the time that I would have wasted dispatching the mummies. I figured that the glares were only from men I beat during the War, but the more I walked, the more I could feel all eyes falling on me. They hated me as if I was a conqueror who was strolling through the land's he had just taken control of. The disdain I felt was something I had not felt in years; it was pure hatred that I couldn't fathom. Granted, I did not help things with the ego I was walking with, but that was not the initial cause of the hate.

"Why is a Desirable like yourself in the outer ring?" An old lady barked from behind the bar. There was a bit of defiance in her voice and spunk that was surprising for her ghastly appearance. She was only an inch or two above five feet with a hump in her upper back that took away some of the already diminutive height. Though she did have more meat on her bones than the others and something was different about her. Her eyes were different.

"If I ask the women of my life, I guess the consensus would be desirable, but I have never been called a Desirable before. Which leads me to the simple question; what are you talking about?" I joked, trying to defend myself against her accusations. The demonstration of my ignorance gave her pause for a moment. She looked at me once again before making her following comments.

"Ah, I see," she paused for a moment, scanning me over a few times, "Despite the appearance, you are not from the inner city. Sorry about the anger. You see, outsiders are rare in these parts." Her tone had quickly changed as she reached behind the counter to grab me a glass. "So, what brings a young man like yourself to our little paradise?" She asked, attempting to smile. I chuckled at her calling this place a paradise, but I didn't linger long on her sarcasm. I was intrigued by her mention of an inner-city. If John was going to be anywhere, that sounded much more his style.

"You see, it is a tale as old as time; a man loves a woman, man's friend kills woman, man wants revenge." I answered, trying to break the tension that still hung in the air, but the daggers only seemed to plunge deeper from their stares.

"That does sound like a German original from my youth. Not the cartoon fluff you probably grew up on, but I don't recognize it given the years I've spent out of childhood. Would you mind telling me who the characters are?" She replied, pouring some water into a pair of glasses. She handed me one of the glasses, and I gave her the photo of John I had.

"This would be our antagonist, much more of an evil king than a troll under the bridge. My sources tell me he might have a castle nearby in an old Ascension factory." I informed her, flashing the photo. She took the picture from me and analyzed it as she sipped her water. As she examined the image, I looked around the room again. The icy glares had disappeared as each patron had returned to murky drinks and scraps barely fitting a mouse. If I can tell you the truth, I think some of them might have been eating mice. It was quite a demeaning scene, not what anyone would consider civilized living.

"Your antagonist is quite a famous one, and as you said, he is a king. One that rules Ascension, if I remember correctly? How does this saint of a man turn into a beast, a spell, a curse, or something else?" She asked.

"He was. And to answer your second question, he became a beast when he took off the sheep's clothing." I told her.

"I see, he is the worst type of monster; he is a man. Well, that is quite troublesome. Now, I know he isn't with us, but he may be in the inner half with the Desirables. It would be natural, after all, for the wolf to run with wolves once he removes his disguise." She explained, wiping down the counter as if she was about to leave. In the moments after she spoke the word 'Desirable' again, I could feel the tension in the room rise again. Whoever these people were, they were the reason that the small tavern looked at me in disgust. I understood that the term created anxiety in the patrons, but I didn't have the time to be sensitive to these people's fears during those days.

"Alright, lady. Who are these Desirables, and where can I find their encampment!" I demanded. Our game was fun for a moment, but now I needed answers. There was a lead, and I couldn't mess around anymore. I needed intel so that I could end the sadistic game I was being forced to play.

When she mentioned the Desirables, the room grew cold. When I said the name, they began to turn hostile. I could hear snarls squeaking from their lips, and I moved my hand to the staff that I had acquired from Gene during our battle in Despartian. I didn't want to waste my time fighting, but I would end it quickly if that was their choice.

Before the patrons or I could make a move, the old woman grabbed me by the arm and pulled me into the back where we would be alone. It was no more than a blink of the eye, but by that time, she had tossed me into this new room and bolted the door behind me. It was clear to me now that the frail old woman I had first seen was not as brittle as she acted. Once in the new room, she straightened out the hump in her back and stood tall. I looked at her closer. Then noticed the muscle that hid beneath her sleeve, along with a fire in her eyes. She wasn't from this town initially.

"You bloody inconsiderate chump! I know that you can't be so dense!" She yelled with her hands waving in the air.

"I don't have time for this, tell me what I need to know, and I will be out of here!" I hollered back, refusing to back down.

"You are a bloody fool. Do you realize that you are in a world without main characters and side characters? This isn't some story where only a few lives matter. Those are real people out there! Those people are traumatized by that word, and its use is only accepted by a few! I use it out of necessity; you used it out of ignorance and with a loud boast knowing it angered them when I said it!" She lectured as if I cared at the time.

"Of course, this isn't a damn story, but I don't think you realize the gravity of the situation." I pointed out, trying to calm myself down. She bit her lip for a moment as if my words were punches to the gut.

"No, you don't understand the bloody gravity of the situation. You have those eyes fixated on a single thing...revenge. By the way, you walk, the way you speak, and how quickly you were ready to fight, I can tell that you were a great soldier. Hell, you might even be good enough to fight John in the right headspace, but you were just tossed around by an old lady, you hothead." She explained with her voice level lowering.

We stood around silent for a few moments afterward. I needed to calm myself down, and she was prepared to wait for me, though I didn't understand why. She could have just kicked me out of the inn and let me find the inner city on my own. There was no reason for her to be in this room with me, but here she was. Not only was she standing there with me, but she was also calling me on my crap. I was growing curious as my temper subsided.

"Why are you here?" I asked her at last.

"Because you have a big bloody mouth, and I want to protect those citizens." She answered.

"No, why are you in this town? You are from somewhere else, yet you are starving yourself for mummies." I pointed out. She chuckled as her head dropped. She realized that whatever act she had been putting on was blown at this point.

"Maybe you aren't that stupid after all. I'll tell you, but first I want to know what is your plan if/when I tell you about the inner city?"

"The outline is quite simple; sneak into the city, find the factory, track down John, and defeat him while cracking any necessary skulls along the way." I outlined for her. She was not impressed as her hand quickly rose to her forehead.

"I prayed for help, and I was sent an idiot. That is not a plan. You have a series of goals and ambitions. More concerning, they are goals of a man that is desperate with pain etched upon their soul. I fear that if I let you go, you may do more harm for this town than good." She surmised.

I stood silent after her last comments. I couldn't really argue with her as there wasn't anything untrue about her analysis. I was relying on brute strength and my training with no care for any damage I did. If I had screwed up, then torment might have been unleashed on the people of that inn, but I didn't give a damn. My path was set, and it was a dangerous one.

While I stood silent, I could feel her peering into my soul with her eyes. She gazed into my blue eyes with her emerald eyes. I tried to dart mine away, but no matter how hard I tried, she kept finding my gaze. I just couldn't hide from here. Then she asked the big question, "What did he take from you?"

"I already told you what he did. He killed the woman I loved, the woman I was about to marry. The man that I called brother stole my life and peace of mind. He forced me to fight my greatest mentor, and then he shot Iris! He didn't just take from me; he ripped my world away from me." I replied with a trembling hand. As I looked upon my own hands, I could see Iris's blood dripping from my fingertips again. I could see my world slipping through them as I lay on the ground, powerless with nothing more than tears draining from my eyes.

She watched as I struggled to regain control, standing silent with those penetrating eyes made from emeralds. Then, at last, she made the poignant comment that is all too often asked at moments like this. The question that people like me hate answering is, "Will killing this man make things better? More importantly, is it what either your mentor or loved one would want?" My eyes darted towards hers, holding back the anger in my heart the best I could.

I had heard the whole *revenge doesn't solve anything speech* a hundred times. When you are at war, you have two options. You carry every death as a burden in need of revenge, or you accept that in war, people die and that the other side is just trying to stay alive as much as you are. The first one is often bred in cooperation with the dehumanization of the opponent to create perfect soldiers. Gene had a different philosophy. He wanted us to remain human and hold that piece of our soul that is lost when killing others. I knew from those past speeches that revenge never accomplished anything in the long run. However, the way I saw it, John was different. My goal may have been revenge, but ending him would be beneficial to everyone.

"You can save your breath, old woman. I really don't care what you have to say! My journey may be one destined for damnation, but I already live a form of Hell! I'm just trying to move forward. Now tell me how to get to that factory you spoke of!" This woman tried to force me into deeper reflection, but that wasn't what I was here for. I wanted shallow gain, which left little room for meaning beyond myself.

"Anger rarely leads to success, but I can tell that I won't get through to you until you have your answer, so I will tell you the story. Then I will tell you about myself." She began before my interruption.

"I don't care about the history. I just want a map and a quick rundown of my opponents!" I hollered as I dismissed her offer while trying to regain my composure.

"Shut up and listen!" She ordered with a point of her bony finger. I snarled, but knew better than to argue at this point. "This city quickly jumped on the Ascension phenom, which led to prosperity that we thought would be impossible after the War. People were cheering and happy again. Some smiles had not been seen in seven years. Then he took over, and things changed. The factory was closed, and we spiraled, except for the Desirables."

"You see, it was John who created that term when he personally visited the city and gave the factory to an outsider. This outsider was a cruel man, and under John's direction, he separated the town by strength. The strongest men ran to join him in prosperity, and the most beautiful women were dragged to the other side of the wall they erected to divide us. This wall was used to keep the rest of us out as he raided our homes, stealing supplies and young women. And on their side of that bloody wall, there is one rule: if you are stronger than someone else, you do what you want. Making it a safe haven for criminals supplied by a fully functional weapons factory." She told me. The last part of her explanation forced my head to perk up.

"So, the factory is fully functional?" She nodded confirming my greatest fear, "He has to be there then. He is planning his next move from within the factory. How do I get there?"

The old woman paced around the room for several minutes. I grew anxious in the silence. I wanted to end this quickly despite an aching hunch that warned me that things wouldn't be simple even if she hurried her thoughts.

"It is a simple trip, but I need you to make me a deal." She informed me.

"What?" My agitation was perking up again.

"Tone and patience," she paused to ensure my cooperation, "You are right to a point. I am from here but only recently returned. I have a bigger plan in motion, and if you charge into the city, I need you to leave the gate open. Don't ask why. Just do it, and you might find help."

"Sounds easy enough. Iris always said I had a habit of leaving doors open anyways." I joked.

"Funny. So the gate will be about two miles east of here on top of the hill. Usually, two to three well-armed guards are at attention, but you should be more than enough for them. Once you are inside, the factory is in the heart of the city." She explained while drawing out a rough sketch for me. She also placed another markdown inside the city. However, I wasn't sure why yet.

"Deal, I'll leave then," I informed her, just for her to stop me in my tracks.

"You'll go in the morning. I need to make preparations for my own plan." She commanded.

I was not pleased with her demands, but it was growing late. My stomach growled like a bear recently woken from hibernation. I decided that it would be best to wait. She prepared a bed for me in the back room we had hidden in, along with the best meal she could throw together, given the lack of supplies. Her kindness was surprising but strategic as I would have been useless had I died because I was undernourished.

Chapter 2
The Strong Will Prosper

The following morning, I awoke before sunset after a rough night. The whole time my mind had been possessed by the face of that devil I pursued. Every time I went to close my eyes, I either saw his face or that of Iris. I missed those intoxicatingly innocent sapphire eyes and the angelic flow in her blonde hair. I cherished those images of her, but at the end of every dream, the nightmare reality that I knew returned. Her kind, lively eyes would be replaced by those of a dying woman. That is why even now, I often find myself waking when the bats still scour the night, and the rooster sleeps. It is not an existence that I enjoy, but maybe it is the punishment I deserve for all the evils I perpetrated.

I searched the bag I had brought with me and changed into an outfit that did not reek of sweat from the sun's scorching gaze. Once ready, I grabbed my staff and started to sneak out of the old inn. I had hoped to avoid conversation, but it wasn't a luxury I would receive.

"You slept awfully." The old woman stated as she cleaned some glasses while the oatmeal on the stove started to boil ever so slightly.

"Didn't expect you to be up," I grunted while I sheathed my staff just off my left hip.

"Not with all the yelling you did during the night. Besides, I have to start breakfast early for the town's people."

"Have fun with that. I'll be off." I waved as I headed for the door.

"You are a bloody idiot, aren't you?" She cackled.

"What did I do this time?"

"You never questioned the extra mark I put on your sketched map." She explained.

"Okay, what is the mark for?" I asked this time around to appease her.

"That is the location of Mother Althea's brothel. She is an ally in the city and if you need her, give her this medallion." She suggested as she slid a small medal to me. I looked it over, flipping the medal between my fingers. It was shaped like an old-fashioned pan flute made out of sterling silver.

"You said she runs a brothel?" I clarified.

"Yes, and I'm sure a guy like you will have no problem finding it. Now get out of here before the townspeople arrive." She ordered, shooing me away.

The old lady might have been wise but had zero sense of distance. The hike was the farthest mile I had ever trekked. It took me a solid hour to make my way just outside of the city walls. As I stood just outside of the field of vision for the guards, I thought about what I was about to do. Yet, I don't think I understood how reckless I was at the time. I was prepared to march into a city based on survival of the fittest to face an army supporting a man that was already my equal or better. I was talented, but still only a single man. I want to say I understood that at the time, though I didn't care. I only genuinely understand now how much of a risk I was to the city's I entered. John had already torn apart one city to draw me out and showed no signs of mercy when it came to any others.

I say that John didn't care about destroying a city as if he was the only one, but that was our squad. We were a collection of extraordinary men with a talent for destabilizing governments. It didn't matter if it was a country or a small town. If there was a power structure, we knew how to throw it into chaos. We were a controlled plague.

If I lost control, I could destroy this town. Once my mind was clear of the little hesitation I did have, I found bushes to hide in while I calmed myself down. From there, I observed the gate and the guards around it. The first thing I noticed was the makeup of the wall. The wall was sturdy but made up of scraps that the inner city likely stole from the outer city, which explained some oddly deteriorating buildings. That being said, even for a patchwork job, it was large and uncrossable without risking my life.

After taking a small lap, I concluded that the only way in was through the two guards that stood in front of the gate. These men were heavily armored in pitch black bullet-proof armor with crimson lining for the stitchwork. I could tell by the outlines of their armor that had each had a small handgun and blade hanging from their waist.

They were better equipped than I, but I knew that I would be better trained even before talking to them. That may sound arrogant, but when you have fought enough battles, you can read your opponents before the match is ever fought, confidence is earned. I had sized up their stances and could tell that they had only been trained for a few months. I smiled as I approached them, knowing there was only one option, and the plan was being made up as I went.

"Halt! Only our raiders and the guest of the mayor are allowed to enter. Now state your purpose, grunt!" One ordered as he started to reach for his gun!

"Well, gentlemen, since the end of the War, I have been looking for worthy opponents to face. I have traveled to several cities only to be disappointed by what they offered. Now I want to test the best this city has to offer, but in front of me, I just see more weaklings," I antagonized with a jolly smile.

Based on what the old woman had told me about these people, they were all ego. If I pressed the right buttons, I could throw them off balance. If they were off balance, I could take them with little effort. It didn't take long for my comments to work their magic as the two men grew agitated. I could already see my opportunity arise. The one who had first questioned me drew his weapon and placed it firmly against my temple. A classic intimidation tactic for a weakling. He hoped that he could scare me. He wanted me to run. He thought he was tough for holding a gun. What he didn't know was that I had never turned my back on a fight, nor was I going to start now. He was also unaware that the battle was over as soon as he moved within a few feet of me. A gun against my head was a terrifying one for most but a position of power for me.

"You said you see weaklings. What about now?" He asked with an egotistical smirk. I'm sure this was a trick that worked for him in most cases, but I am not a typical case for these men.

"Still weak, but now I see you as cowards as well. Now bring me a true warrior who will test me, or get out of the way." I ordered, pressing my head into the muzzle. Though he tried to hide his fear, I could feel the quiver of the weapon. He had become complacent after dealing with the outer city's compliance. His partner started to shake at the sight of a man who dared them to shoot. I had missed the feeling I had that day. Your blood begins to boil, the heart pumps faster and faster until it falls silent. The movement starts to happen on its own as all senses fall in line with the present moment, and soon after, the fight begins.

"Interesting last words. Then again, if you dance for us, maybe you can see another day." He joked despite his hand shaking. He glanced at his partner, who was chuckling at the idea. I was not quite as amused, so I used the opportunity to make my move before he turned jumpy. With his head turned, I swiveled my own which caused him to stumble forward as I grabbed his wrist and twisted it. The first man let out a yelp. His ally went for his own weapon, but with control of the arm and gun of the first I placed a bullet in each kneecap. That immobilized him. I followed that with a jab to the first one's throat, causing him to double over.

The second man continued to scream as he reached again for his weapon. I placed another kick to his head, knocking him out. The other I left conscious. I had him pinned to the ground with my knee driving it into his chest. There was a part of me that was releasing my anger out on this poor man. I could feel his sternum crushing beneath me as I had no mercy.

"If you two are the best there is to offer, it might be time to move on. You are not even worthy to shine my shoes." I smirked as I knocked the first man out.

As I stood up, I saw that the gate had already been opened and a new man was standing on the other side. He had begun a slow clap with a grin stretched across his face. Hanging from his mouth, a cigar hung with smoke puffing out at a constant pace. This man was different. His armor was the same, but he reeked of the stench of battle. His gloves were crimson-colored and had been stained by blood from multiple sources. His most distinguishing feature was an eyepatch that rested over his left eye. His demeanor was that of a grizzled veteran like myself. If I had to fight him, he would have been a much sterner test. That being said, I needed to get past him. John was somewhere beyond the wall, and I had to find him.

"I haven't seen anyone with those types of skills for quite some time. It was impressive, stranger. Impressive enough that I might let you in my city if you finish the job." He started with a giant puff of smoke.

"What do you mean by 'finish the job'?" I asked, trying to maintain some form of innocence.

"Kill them, and I'll let you pass. Men like this have proven too weak to guard a gate, making them merely a waste of space. Time for new blood." He finished, sliding a hatchet to me.

I picked the weapon up. It was a simple device made for butchers. One I had always found the use of as barbaric. However, following orders, for now, would be easier than trying to fight him as well. Besides, if I was set on revenge as I was, I had to be alright with killing again.

Maybe I should explain what I mean by being alright with killing again. After the War ended, I swore to never kill again. You see, for those of you who have spared the experience, it takes something from you. A little bit of your soul and humanity are ripped away. It leaves you changed every time. The trauma it causes psychologically is brutal to put into words. Especially the first one. When the body drops and the blood spills, you remember for a moment that you killed a human being. That person was a friend, a parent, or someone's child. It is a hard thing to accept once and harder to go do it again and again.

That is why I swore it off and became the drunk I was. It was my way of coping, and I hoped to never do it again. Before that day, I killed these monsters that John had created, but they had lost their minds. I was able to justify it as mercy, but these guards. I moved mercilessly. I did not hesitate as I wished I would have. I acted in a way I don't want to describe, and merely the memory scares me now. That moment is where I was probably at my lowest as I was the monster that I had always feared.

Once the men were dead, I remember looking up at the man whose grin now stretched from ear to ear. His cigar barely stayed in his mouth as he approached me. The way he looked at me and the bodies was eerie. It was the look of a cold-hearted devil who enjoyed the killing and its effect on the person killing. He was a psychopath, and there wasn't a doubt about it.

I met him in his approach and handed him his hatchet back. "Welcome, child of strength. You are worthy of entering my city. Follow me." He ordered. As he led me through the gate, I dropped a small piece of metal I had found into the mechanism, jarring it partially open as the old woman had asked. Even in my low spots, I was a man of my word. Besides, I was curious what she would do with access to the inner city, given the people living in the outer city.

He led me into the inner city, where my stomach dropped almost immediately. As I had been warned, they had turned the place into a sanctuary for tyrants. It lacked rules and structure outside of the philosophy etched into signs all around: 'Only the Strongest Prosper.' Every man I saw had bruises or broken bones. Blood dripped from knuckles and wounds. Then there were those eyes, those hollowed-out eyes from soulless corpses etching their look on what soul you may have. It was the eyes of the women that I speak of. In a city like this one, the women often suffer as it becomes difficult to defend themselves. They watch themselves or others become victims of assault, killing, or rape. They become brutalized to the point that they lose control and hope.

Though I had grown a hardened heart, their soulless gaze caused my heart to ache. I wanted to help them, but I could not destroy this alone. Despite my earlier arrogance, I understood now how horrifying the city really could be. There would be no allies in the city outside of this Mother Althea I was supposed to make contact with. Worse yet, if I turned the city on itself, which could be done, it would only bring suffering on those who had suffered far more than they should have.

While my mind wandered, the strange man continued to lead me deeper into the city. Now with a second cigar to replace the nub the first had become. Before I even realized it, I was already deep into the heart of the city. He led me to what I can only describe as a small park. There a mass of people gathered. They were hollering louder and louder as the sound of a drum began to echo. I feared that I had fallen into a trap and I was merely a pig being led to slaughter. The thought grew far direr when I realized that these men were the toughest in the city. While the others I had seen looked beaten, these men were pristine with rippling muscles, granite jaws, and eyes like lions on the hunt. These were the best who had been allowed to prosper. The rest were trying to be these men.

I tried to remain calm and act ignorant to the worst possibility as he led me deeper into the crowd. Each of them let the stranger pass with space but would quickly squeeze in on me, which forced me to aggressively push through them. I was not going to back down now. Nor could I run as it would have only ended in disaster. At last, we reached the eye of the crowd where the stranger signaled me to stay put as he moved forward. The drum had intensified until he raised his hand, drawing silence from the mob around us.

"Good morning, gentlemen! I would like to apologize for the delay in our morning activities, but a pressing need called me to the outer gate! Do not fear the delay netted us a new soldier. One unlike any that has joined us before! This man here is Rob Doran, a legend from the War, so welcome him our way!" He shouted. I don't know what was more disturbing, that he somehow knew my name or that I was welcomed with boos that drowned out my own thoughts. He raised his hand again to speak. "I know this isn't what you came here for! No, you want to see if anyone can dethrone the Cairo Butcher! So, come meet your maker, boys!"

He drew his hatchet again with the proclamation, still fresh with blood, and antagonized the crowd. The primitive drumbeat began again as the crowd jeered. The name Butcher rang a bell deep down in my memory. Initially, the name wasn't enough to recall the memory, so I watched what happened next. The first challenger charged at him with a spear, giving him a significant advantage had he not closed too quickly, but alas, he did. The Butcher sidestepped the hothead, delivering a blow to the spear itself, shattering it in the man's hands. In an eye-blink, he followed that with the removal of the man's right hand. The challenger cried out in pain, retreating back into the mob. Not an ounce of sweat glistened on the Butcher.

A second man that stood behind the Butcher started to unsheathe his weapon slowly. He was too slow. The Butcher had heard the metal. He spun himself around, grabbing the blade of the broken spear off the ground. Then, he threw it into the second man's shoulder in a fluid motion, dropping him to a knee. In a single leap, he reached the man, kicking him square in the jaw and shelving him instantly.

He was brutally efficient. As I watched his actions, my memory slowly returned to me. He had known me because John and I had arrested him during the War quite early on. His name was Jack Schroeder, and he had received the only court-martial during the War. Should there have been more? Yes, but if that doesn't speak to this man's twisted mind. I don't know what does.

The rumor that led to the court-martial process was that he would seek out innocent civilians to cut them to ribbons with his lucky hatchet along with killing enemy soldiers. That should have been enough on its own, but we were short soldiers. We needed to win that war at any cost. It shouldn't have come at the price it did, though. The final straw that sent John and I after him was when he struck down his soldiers who tried to stop him from killing fifteen women and children at a school in Cairo. They failed, and apparently so did I when I only placed him in cuffs that day.

I had tried to forget him, but it would appear that fate would allow me to undo the mistake I made many years ago. A few more unremarkable fights occurred with predictable outcomes. Jack didn't even stop smoking as he humiliated the challengers one after another until none more wanted to risk their lives. Losing a contest like this had twice the normal consequences. Not only did you lose an appendage, but you became weaker, meaning that the hungry dogs roaming the city could now pounce and take what little you had. The reward was kingship, but the risk was certain death, even if it wasn't immediate.

"Good effort today, boys! I actually broke a sweat!" He growled, wiping his brow, covered in the blood of other men, "Actually, no sweat, just your blood. Gwahaha!" He sheathed his weapon and approached me again with a great smile. I faked a smile of my own, trying to appease him for now. There was still much I needed to know before challenging such a willing opponent.

The fake smile seemed to work as he grabbed me by the arm, laughing. The crowd had already begun to disperse by this point, but as he began to lead me again, they parted like the Red Sea. I could not yet tell if they respected him that much or feared his capabilities. An important distinction if I wanted to leave the city alive.

"Shall we grab a drink at the compound?" He asked.

"Soon, but I was told to go see a woman by the name of Mother Althea for a good time first," I answered. It was now or never with her. Once I was inside his compound, there would be no going back.

"Mother Althea...oh yes. That is Mother Whore's real name. Your reputation precedes you. Follow me." He replied, leading me down one of the back alleys.

It took us a few minutes before we reached an old brick building that shined in the late morning sunlight. Some frills and extras were over the top for the modern-day design. A group of men lined up outside a large ruby red wooden door with golden handles. The building that was hidden in the shadows managed to capture the heart of the city. Jack knocked on the door, calling for its opening. I deduced that the king was never denied access, as it opened just enough for the two of us to enter.

Once inside, I had to readjust to the new light sources. While outside shined bright, the brothel instantly hit you with the shadows and dim lighting. My eyes were shocked by the sudden change. They forced me to rely on my other senses, the most prominent being the smell of perfumes that mixed together to create a piquant aroma. I felt like I had been thrust into the arms of a woman, face pressed firmly in her bosom just from the smell that filled the air. The aromas were accompanied by giggles around me.

As my eyes adjusted, I saw how close I was to her bosom and the sources of the giggles. A young blonde with chocolate eyes stared at me as my own had fallen upon, well, let's say, an ample chest. If I am being honest, I was just happy that I was not ogling. Not too bad anyway.

"Go find, Mother!" Jack ordered as he patted my back with a smile. As the young girl ran off, I began to search the balcony that overlooked us and the door. About eight other women were strung across its ledge as they stared at me with a hunger and flirtatious grins that I honestly missed. Though I was dedicated to Iris, a man's urges occasionally reappear, mainly when his soul burns hot with emotion, be it love or hatred. A balancing act that has led to the ruin of many men.

Just as I had started to absorb my surroundings, I saw her. A woman with charcoal hair and a clingy teal dress that accented her every curve. Her eyes were a shamrock green that made any man feel lucky to be in her presence. Her brow was beginning to show her age, but she had maintained youth later into life than most. The only thing that gave away her actual age was the grace she moved with, accompanied by mannerisms of control that are only developed through time. A gold chain hung from her neck, but it lacked the decoration that had once hung from it. She smiled with only her lips as her hand reached out to me. I kissed her bronzed skin with a tenderness that I had not shown in weeks.

"Mother Altea, I presume," I said while removing my lips from her hand.

"I am. Now may I ask, who has summoned me and disturbed my girls before our daily opening?" She asked, drawing her hand back to her side.

"My name is Rob Doran, and I was told to give you this once I entered the city," I replied, slipping her the coin the innkeeper had given me. She took it and began to turn it over in her hand to check its validity. After a moment, she smiled, showing a few teeth this time.

"Jack, I believe our guest has earned a private meeting with me. It will only take a few minutes." She instructed, taking me by the hand. She led me down the main hall to a back room. It was pitch black inside, aside from a few candles that lit our way to an old mattress with silk sheets. She pushed me down on the bed as she headed towards a table in the corner.

"Remove your shirt." She instructed with quiet assertiveness. I was taken aback by the sudden demand and calm displayed as she poured something into a pair of glasses.

"This is not why I am here, Madam." I protested as she handed me the cup. Once again, she flashed the closed-lipped smile as she began to drink from her own cup. She sat behind me, starting to undo her own blouse. "I'm sorry, ma'am. I am dedicated to my recently passed love." I tried to stand only for her to firmly grasp my shoulder.

"I understand, but there are certain appearances we must maintain." She informed me, removing her top layer to display breast barely contained by a thin lace bra.

"What do you mean? By all appearances, we are alone." I asked, sitting back down as I took a sip from the cup. It was just water, which made me wonder more. What was all the ceremony about?

"It only appears that way. All the rooms in this house have a one-sided mirror where the guards or Jack can watch the girls for suspicious behavior. You see, Jack protects this place and our girls in exchange for information. We use our womanly ways to extract intel that he uses to stay in power. Even now, he watches us." She informed me by holding her mouth to my neck to hide it from the mirror in front of us.

"So, what is this really about?" I asked as I removed my shirt to cover my own words. With my shirt removed, she began to lather my body with oil on the nightstand next to her. I was surprised at how nonchalant she was while oiling my body. The scars that covered my body often scared people away. The toughness was not easy on hands as delicate as hers, but then again, I saw all the other men in the city. I saw the missing limbs and how Jack treated challengers. She probably saw worse over the years. More impressive than her lack of surprise was how well she handled herself reciting crucial information to me while hiding her lips.

"Normally, the combination of what I would sneak into the drink, the incense, and oils coax information from our targets before bedding them. In our case, I will sensually massage you as I explain what is happening. When it is your turn, I will wrap myself around you to hide your mouth. They only have sight, protection I insisted on for the safety of my girls." She explained, moving in front of me. While she massaged the oils into my chest, she used one hand to guide my head into her chest where the clasp of her bra was.

"What is that medallion?" I asked, using my mouth to undo her bra as she had hinted at.

"That piece completes the necklace I wear and is the symbol of rebellion. Once I wear the finished necklace outside of this room, all the oppressed of the city will know that freedom is coming." She said, her hands moving across my aching body as we each would move to kiss the other's shoulder or neck.

"What is my part? Why did the innkeeper give it to me?"

"If I were to guess, she saw something in you that made her believe that today is the day, or maybe it was the appearance of that other stranger at the factory. Whatever it is, understand this. We are both using you as a distraction. Jack is obviously obsessed with you, and I am going to tell him you are plotting to destroy him." She told me, moving behind me, hands pushing on my skin. I knew that the stranger she spoke of had to be John, or at least that is what I had to believe.

"That won't be hard to do since the last time I saw him, I arrested him, but won't that hurt my chances of entering the factory. More importantly, won't that threaten my chances of seeing the stranger who is my real target?" I asked, leaning back for a kiss. This line of questioning clearly surprised her as I saw her eyes hesitate and her hands cease.

"Luckily for you, that is not his style. Jack likes to play with his targets and act smarter than he is. Once he discovers your intentions, he will bring you to the factory to toy with you. Once inside, you will need to hold his attention. If you do that, my girls will begin the assassinations. Then Gina will lead a force through the doors you presumably opened for her." She explained, regaining her rhythm.

At last, I understood what was going on. I was the distraction for a coup d'etat. In the end, I did not care about their side objectives as long as I reached John.

The problem is a plan like that has several disadvantages. All stemming from a lack of control. I'm sure that they had been tracking and analyzing their opposition obsessively, but one deviation could mean disaster. It becomes even more treacherous when you add in a third party. They were lucky that I was as talented as they were hoping. I could distract anyone for quite some time, but if John was there. It was unpredictable and relied too much on what they couldn't control. It is a plan for the desperate.

"Though your plan sounds flawed, I will play along for now. Just stay out of my way. That stranger and I have personal business to handle." I clarified, nibbling on her skin just hard enough to make my point without hurting her. We each looked into one another's eyes to confirm our mutual understanding.

After the massage, we redressed in silence. We had shared more than enough information, and now it was time for business, and our business was not one for the faint of heart. Betrayal and murder are not tasks that should be taken lightly, yet in a matter of minutes, we had finalized the overthrow of a city's established order. She led me out of the room with little contact, where Jack was waiting patiently for me with what I could only assume was the fourth cigar since I met him.

"Done already? Well, she is a professional, I guess." Jack commented.

"I didn't want to waste an extra hour of your time, so I opted for just a massage." I smiled as he laughed at my insinuation.

After my comments, Mother Althea walked to a corner of the room and motioned for Jack to join her. Knowing that she had accomplished her mission Jack followed the command. Even though I knew what they were discussing, my body still shivered at the thought of them talking in private. She told a man I had just watched beat five men in minutes that I planned to kill him. If there was even a slight miscalculation, then I would die on the spot without ever seeing John again.

She had hidden her face behind a fan, but I could still see him. His eyes continued to dart in my direction as his jolly grin began to fade. I grew more nervous but had I run, I would have destroyed both dreams. She peeked her eyes over the fan and reassured me enough to help me hold my ground. As their conversation wrapped up, I saw the smile return with his approach.

"Quite a fighter and a lover you are, Rob. Mother Althea had quite a glowing review of you." He smiled, trying to hide his newfound knowledge.

"Thank you. I do aim to please the ladies. Now I think we should go find some food." I suggested.

"I agree. Let's head to the factory and grab a drink." He commanded with a wave of his hand.

Chapter 3
Tyrants Fall

During the walk, we passed more of the desperation that I had seen at first. Beyond that, the city wasn't anything unique from a normal slum. Jack and I spoke about the city and Mother Althea. He had far more interest in her than I anticipated. He informed me that she had just shown up one day and coaxed her way into the position she was in now. He was also insistent on talking about how impressed he was that she could handle the things she did at her age. She was just shy of fifty, not that it mattered. The way he talked about everything was bland and lackluster. He tried to put everyone and everything down. Meanwhile, if something related to him came up, he spoke with his ego.

However, he did tell me something useful. He talked about the origin of the factory. It was initially a power tool factory that he converted when he took command of it. Despite his openness on some facets, he was particularly vague regarding who gave him its authority. Not really a surprise as John picks his leadership parties carefully. He ensures that he is never connected to anything that could ruin his future plans. An illegal weapons factory would qualify in that context.

When we arrived at the factory, I found it relatively unremarkable. It looked abandoned from the outside. However, this appearance of hollowness was only a mask quickly tossed aside after some observation. The smell of gunpowder filled the air, and I could hear the rumblings of the machinery inside as soon as Jack shut up. The curious site was the yard outside filled with old shipping containers that looked like they had recently been refurbished.

It is hard at times like that to separate the feeling of excitement and nerves. When you enter the heart of the beast, your body becomes unsure of how to act. The real test becomes whether you move forward or run. Maybe I should have run, knowing that odds were heavily weighted against me. Still, I was too arrogant to think it was beyond my capabilities. I could say that my deal with Mother Althea moved me forward, but it wasn't. If it hasn't been clear yet, my one-track focus on revenge was all that moved me.

As we passed through the corridors, I took note of anything important. I needed to know how to navigate through this building when being chased with weapons. You know the typical thing you do walking into any building. On top of that, I was also trying to figure out how to cause the most damage. This would accomplish two goals: the distraction the ladies needed and upset John's plans. Then, at last, we arrived at an office that overlooked the massive complex.

"So, what is your pleasure, Rob?" He asked as he opened a cabinet behind his desk. Poison, I wondered? No, that would be too quick, and Althea said he preferred to torture his opponents. He wouldn't have wasted his time walking here just to poison me.

"Usually, blondes or brunettes, but I'll drink anything as long as it is expensive enough." I joked, looking at the cabinet with a variety of bottles. It was quite a collection. Jack smiled at my joke though he was not laughing as he was before. I saw him reach past most of the bottles and pull out a bottle of scotch with a label that was mostly worn away. All that was left on the bottle was a twenty-five. He had spared no expense.

"I respect your honesty and have been looking for a good reason to drink this bottle. I had sent it back directly from Scotland during the War." He gloated with an odd grin.

"Interesting, I don't remember any battles in Scotland." I pointed out. He chuckled at my comment.

"You seem a bit confused. I never said I was there for a battle. It just housed the most intact prison that was near Cairo." He explained as he sat the glasses and bottle on the desk.

From there, he began pouring the drink into the glasses that were not made for something so elegant. He handed me my glass and watched closely. He was still trying to figure me out even after hearing about my 'intentions'. I played my part from there, laying some lines about the nose and look of the drink. I even tried to remember some tasting notes to describe it. It was all just a show, and he knew it. More importantly, I knew he knew it, but we had begun our game of chess. This was the best tasting scotch I ever had during a game of chess.

As we dug into our glasses, he described his acquisition of the bottle in more detail. After John and I had seized him, he was placed in an encampment in Scotland. That didn't last long when some radicals freed all the prisoners, including him. Jack had a blast in the chaos and did the honor of killing the warden. Then he took the man's scotch. I will never understand how devils like him find luck at every corner.

"So, what is with all this kindness?" I asked as the liquid slowly disappeared.

"New opportunities and unexpected gifts." He cheered, clinking my glass. I smiled at his odd phrase, but deep down, I had to worry about what was happening outside the factory. More importantly, I could hear the machinery behind me. The machines were working at full force, and I worried about what John could be planning to do with shipping containers and new guns. Given the size of the building, if this thing was working at total capacity, he could arm a small army in only a few weeks.

"Everyone likes gifts, but what are you talking about?"

"Well, I recently had an old friend drop into town, and I've been unable to get him the perfect present. He has done so much for me, and I wanted to make it right. Then you walk into town planning to kill him and me. Can you believe my luck? Gwahahah," he laughed. He wanted to see some form of emotion, but I kept calm at that moment.

"I see that Mother Althea told you some things. Not completely true things, but close enough." I replied, leaning back in my chair. I continued to sip my glass just to dig under his skin further.

"Then why not tell us the truth." A familiar voice hissed. I turned around to see John sitting in the shadows. He had been there the whole time without a word, so close, and I had no idea. My blood boiled to the point where I broke the glass in my hand. It looks badass in the movies, but I wouldn't try it. Luckily, I only sliced my hand partially.

"I could, but it will be far more enjoyable to rub your face in it once I bring you both down." I boasted, regaining my composure.

"Cocky prick, aren't you!?!" Jack yelled, slamming his butcher ax into the table! Despite all his efforts, he couldn't draw any emotion out of me. John was too overwhelming for me. No threat he could make mattered more than my revenge. Especially when it was coming from a man I had already defeated.

"Not cocky, you idiot. He knew that this was a trap. He played you and doesn't fear you." John replied. "It would appear that your unrequited love wants you dead. You are a moron and a useless pawn, it seems."

It was nice to know that John was an ass to everyone, not just me. Besides, I hoped that I could use his own attitude against their relationship. John started to creep closer as I tried to calculate my next best set of moves. However, I had to think through every possibility knowing about John's unpredictability.

"I didn't know we were doing the whole saying each other's thoughts thing today. I figured after you killed Iris that the cutesy stuff was over," I said.

"You're right, that did feel a bit out of place, but you may only have a few breaths left. I didn't want you to waste them on his idiotic statements." He began as he paced his way around the room. "Now I know that you don't care about Jack, and neither do I, but I need this factory. And every factory needs a manager."

"Hold on, I'm more than just a manager handling complaints!" Jack interrupted. John never liked being interrupted, but he stayed strangely calm. He turned his attention from me to Jack and sauntered over to his ally.

"You are what I say you are. My friends freed you, and I gave you this city, don't think I can't take it away from you like that!" John snapped as he clamped down his other hand on Jack's shoulder. "Don't ever interrupt me again!"

As he turned towards me, I could see the disdain in both their faces. Hate is what united the two of them, which on the best days was a delicate partnership. Jack was clasping his fist tightly, trying to hold back a swing. Apparently, he wasn't that much of an idiot after all. I had observed his fighting during the early scrum and surmised that he stood no chance against John in a straight fight. They both knew it too.

"Are you two done bickering, or should I come back in like an hour?" I taunted while guards filtered into the room.

"Sorry about that, Rob. I know time is valuable for both of us. The reason I brought you here is that it is time to take our game off pause. The world is about to enter its final stage of evolution, and I need you. I need my only friend to follow me to the end of the world one last time to decide its fate. To do this, you will follow me down the Mississippi River, finding my influences along the way. Then the next time we meet, I will ask you a question, and your answer will decide the fate of this world. Now I have to leave, but don't worry, Jack and his friends will keep you occupied." John smiled as he put extra venom on that word friend. Though his smile felt genuine, it raised emotions that I don't fully comprehend. It wasn't the love of a friend I once had, and it wasn't hate for the man who killed Iris. It was somewhere in between in that sweet spot of passion with no label.

"You think you can get away from me again?" I grunted through my teeth as he walked away from me. He turned around to say something but decided to simply flash that damn smile. Followed by a cough that consumed him for a few moments. Once he was settled, he shook off the cough and was gone. From there the guards began to tie me up. I wanted to chase after him, but I had a slightly more pressing need with Jack standing over me with his butcher ax.

"It is time to pay for ending my campaign and trying to kill me." He said as he motioned for the other guards to start beating me. Punch after punch fell on my body. I did everything in my power to hide any signs of pain. I wanted them to believe that they were nothing to me. I was biding my time, but it was not easy when men tried to break your ribs. "I was hoping that you, of all people, would see my vision to build a world based on strength, but you are too focused on revenge. Together we could have taken down John, but you have to destroy everything he touches, even me." He took a seat as he watched the guards continue to wail on me. At last, one of their blows drew blood as a cut formed above my left eye.

I would not be capable of holding out much longer if they continued at this pace. My ribs were going to crack soon, and the internal bleeding would start. If I did not escape their clutches, I would never reach John.

"Build a world based on strength? That is all the world has ever been, and it destroyed us. That is what created John in the first place, and now we need to create something else! We need something better!" I argued in the free moments between punches.

"Strength is the only way to survive and the only way to rule. Why don't you get that?"

"Simple the strength that people have always ruled by is simply borrowed strength. It is borrowed strength that is then transferred or taken away. When that happens, a vacuum is created, which creates struggle. This struggle breeds hate, despair, and death. The only way we can survive is if the cycle ends." I argued.

"You are a naive fool. I thought that you would be different. After I saw you chop the guards to pieces, I thought you would be different." Another few punches rained down before he waved the guards off.

"I may be naive, but at least I'm not ignorant," I replied. I could see his brow twitch.

"I think it is time to kill you! Men!" He shouted, and the guards drew their weapons.

"Do you want to know the real problem I have with you?" I asked, trying to buy time. I was starting to think Althea had failed, so it was time to make my own moves.

"Why don't you tell me?"

"My problem," I started before spitting out some blood, "is that you talk about having all this strength, but it is all John's. He gave you this city. If it wasn't for him, you'd be sitting in a hole wasting away knowing that I had kicked your ass once before." I taunted. He withdrew his hatchet again, motioning for his guards to release me.

"Well, let's see about that. I think you'll find my strength is quite real after all." He claimed. It took me a minute to stand up as the injuries were worse than I'd like to admit. My nose was broken, and the laceration above my left eye was aching. It wasn't prime fighting conditions, but I could take him. I was reasonably confident about that.

As soon as I was standing, Jack came for my head. Forcing me to duck quickly, only losing a few hairs in the process. I rolled to the right and cleared one of the guards holding my staff at the time. As the guard hit the wall, I unfurled the weapon and prepped myself. Jack swung again. This time I caught the hatchet with my own weapon stopping it just inches from my face. It was so close that I could smell the blood that had stained it earlier that morning. He continued to press harder, but I held him at bay until, at last, I pushed him back. He charged again, swinging wildly. Unaccustomed to an equal opponent, he was left off-balance. While I continued to move freely like a flag in the wind avoiding every blow.

This technique only infuriated my opponent further. He had grown used to straightforward fighting and forgotten how to fight a battle of wits. He swung, and I spun, kicking him in the rear with a taunting blow. I wish I could say it was easy, but I had to hide winces with every strike. Then moved past the pain quickly as he swung again, this time going for my legs. I avoided the blow by jumping onto the desk. I grabbed the glass he used earlier as I spun off of it during another avoidable strike. As he stood hunched over the desk, embarrassed, I heard him scream. This time I ducked and countered by hitting him in the face with the glass.

That blow stopped him in his tracks at last. It had not only shattered the glass, but I could visibly see his ego shatter. I had opened a large gash across his face. Stretched from his ear to the middle of his forehead. Quite a wound, and it began to bleed profusely soon after opening. He gripped his hatchet tighter, and just before I thought he was going to lunge, he ran out the door. I was shocked by the cowardly behavior. I expected him to be a blood-hungry beast that would strike harder, but instead, I had a dog with his tail between his legs.

I wanted to chase after the wounded pup, but the last few guards grew a pair of balls despite their leader's display. It was not their brightest idea and was made worse when one tried to pull a gun. As soon as he made an attempt, I was on top of him, twisting his arm and stealing the weapon. In the process, I flipped him to the ground and kicked another guard in his knee, buckling it instantly. A third tried to swing a blade at my head, but a simple duck and chop to the throat dropped him. The last knew he was overmatched and turned to run. I shot him in the ass. I was never a fan of guns. Even when I was at war, there was something too impersonal. If I wanted to kill someone, I wanted to feel the kill; I wanted to feel like I was losing something as their life faded. I never wanted it to be easy, and at times guns could make it too easy.

I walked over to the table and grabbed the bag that I had brought with me, but before I could throw it over my shoulder, the first guard had locked me in a headlock. I moved my right hand between his arms and my neck to create a slight separation. Then I reverse headbutted him, breaking his nose instantly. His teeth had carved a cut in my head as well during the blow. As he staggered away, I drew my staff from my bag and swung it straight across his face, likely breaking several more bones.

As I winced and coughed up a slight amount of blood, I failed to notice the man I had kicked across the room earlier had regained consciousness. The only thing that alerted me to his presence was the click when he pulled back the hammer of his gun. I spun around instantly, knowing I couldn't waste a moment. He was still sitting on the ground, but he was too far away from me. I had no other options. I had to do whatever he said.

"Drop the weapon!" He ordered.

"Come on, buddy, you know that it isn't worth it. I sent you flying, your boss running, and I took out the other men in seconds. If you miss, you'll end up pulling your own foot out of your mouth." I threatened to try to talk my way out of it. He looked around for a moment, but his resolution stayed strong. It was the calmest hand I had seen in the city, and to be honest, I was proud while slightly terrified.

"Death is my only option here. Jack will just make it far more painful than you can imagine." The young man stated.

"If you think this is the right move, then I can't stop you." I nodded, closing my eyes. His resolve was firm, and I was out of options. Fate would have to make the decision now.

I closed my eyes tighter and wondered if that would be the end of my journey. Struck down by a lowly grunt, quite anti-climactic, but a fitting end to a man consumed by revenge. Obviously, it wasn't. As fate would have it, the moment he pulled the trigger, the building shook, sending me to the ground and the bullet whizzing past my ear.

As the building shook, a tile rattled above his head and fell square onto him. He was knocked out cold, and our battle had ended. I didn't deserve that form of luck. I should have been dead for being careless, but fate had other plans. Maybe John and destiny were intertwined in a manner that I had no grasp of. As much as I wanted to contemplate the meaning behind it all, I counted my blessings and ran. I tried to find John, but given the delay, I knew he was gone. I chose instead to follow the blood trail left by Jack's dripping forehead.

As I followed the trail, I found panic consuming the factory. There were enough guards to stop me, but everyone was in a frenzy trying to exit the building. I hadn't located the source of the rumblings yet, but with the smoke filling the halls, I had a hunch about what it could be. Mother Althea had pulled off her end of the deal with the innkeeper. I wasn't sure how they did it, but I was happy to have no opposition as I cruised through the building.

After twisting through several hallways, the blood trail finally led me to a boiler room in the back of the building. The door was slightly ajar, and a light flickered inside. I had not processed it earlier, but the explosion had sent the electrical grid into disarray. I pushed the door open with my staff and prepped for whatever Jack had planned. It was a pitiful look inside. The once-mighty Cairo Butcher stood holding a young woman with his hatchet to her throat. Blood dripping off his eye patch.

"How did you pull this off? You weren't even here a day, and yet you've undone years of hard work!" He screamed, gripping her tighter. I couldn't make out her face, but it was clear that she was young. Her hair was rustled and unkempt, but it glimmered in the light.

"Jack, calm down and let the girl go! This is a fight between men, not one worthy of a hostage. Or are you really the coward I thought you were." I taunted. I stepped lightly, watching his moves closely, knowing that taunts were a dangerous game at this point. The pride-filled man from before was gone and now I dealt with an unhinged animal.

"Fight between men? Is that what you think? From what I saw and heard; this is all about women like this! My top generals slain in a brothel, an army rising within my city against me, and undesirables spreading throughout the streets! She is as much involved in this as you and I!" He yelled as the blade neared the young woman's throat!

"Put her down, Jack, and let's finish what John started. He brought this fight to your doorstep, and you can either go out as a coward using a woman as a shield or like the soldier I think you are." I pleaded, trying to convince him to release her. There was a twitch growing in him, and his every move could be the end of her.

"You keep calling me a coward, yet you are the one who brought an army from outside this city!"

"Jack, I came here to kill John. I don't care about you; I only care about this girl for the sake of my conscience. Those people were created by your iron fist; your power search created people who loathed you. You created people who want justice against you. More importantly, they want to take your strength away." I admitted as I could see his grip on reality fading.

"Don't lie to me! Weaklings like them can't do this on their own! This was your doing! It had to be!" He asserted with doubt in his voice. For a moment, his head dropped, and the woman stomped on his foot. He released a yelp which I answered by throwing my staff at his head. It connected squarely, knocking him backward. Once the woman was free of his grip, I charged in tackling the staggering man to the ground.

Once I was on top of him, I worked my way to his back like an Olympic wrestler. Once there, I locked in a hold, trying to finish the man who I had let live years ago.

"Run!" I yelled to the woman once the hold was locked in. It was at that moment I noticed that she had already fled. Good for her, I thought. She did not owe me anything, and I didn't want her help in this instance. This man had facilitated John's escape, and he was about to feel the rage boiling in my stomach.

Jack began to wiggle his way out of the hold. And, I tried to re-secure it, but he was far more potent than I first anticipated, which allowed him to break free. He scrambled to his feet while I kicked up. He might have given me his best, but I had barely even started. I grabbed my staff off the floor and twirled it a few times. He gripped his hatchet and gritted his teeth. Then I antagonized him by flipping everyone's favorite finger. Sometimes you do stupid things, and considering my shape, I needed him off balance. As I thought, this worked its magic, and he charged. He swung a couple times, and with a smile, I parried the swings.

Jack had let anger cloud his vision, and at that point, it was time to toy with the overconfident waste of skin. He would swing, and I would use my staff to knock him off balance. Then I would spin around him and hit him in his ass. That was followed by another angry swing, and this was repeated for five minutes or so. At last, he was panting with hands-on knees.

"Done already? You would never have lasted long with Mother Althea. She would have eaten you alive." I smiled; my body was loosening back up from the beating at last. It was time for me to begin my own attack. First, I swung at his head, knowing he would duck. With his momentum already moving one way, I moved to a leg sweep which lifted him off the ground. Once he was in the air, I swung down on his stomach, drawing blood from his mouth instantly. He tried to roll to his knees, but I kicked him in the ribs sending him to his back. This time I followed by placing my boot on his throat.

I was in firm control at this point, but I wanted to play with him some more. I needed someone to suffer; that was all I knew. I was going to make him suffer. It was at this point that I noticed the smoke filling the room. The factory was burning, and it would only be a short time before the place would blow. Knowing my time was short and energy would be better spent elsewhere, I knocked him out. From there, I ran from the building. I didn't need to be the one who killed him, but I didn't need to help him either.

Chapter 4
Mother's Charm

Once I was out of the factory, I found ruins and chaos. A group of much more able-bodied men had joined the undesirables and had sent Jack's men running. With no leadership, their intimidation advantage shrank. I met a couple of the guards along the way and did my part to send them packing.

It must have been a short battle as the time between the explosion and my escape was not long. My struggle with Jack only lasted a few minutes, yet they had overpowered a city built on power in less than half an hour. Whoever this innkeeper was, she had connections to pair with a brain.

I continued walking through the battle zone streets for some time, finding no signs of John. I hoped that he had been caught up in one of the fights, but nothing. Just meaningless squabbles that were settling themselves out. Just before I exited the city, I was met by Mother Althea, the innkeeper, and the young woman.

"You were worth the gamble, I see." The innkeeper smiled. Compared to before, she was now standing with particular pride that did not fit her surroundings. She was covered in clothing built for war and carried a mace heavier than most people could manage.

"It would appear so, but you could have warned me about the Mother Althea treatment." I chuckled. Both of the older women smiled at the comment. They didn't need me to say more.

"So, did you find the other man?" Mother asked.

"I did, but he escaped while Jack had me pinned," I explained.

"Where is Jack?" the innkeeper asked. I just motioned my head towards the factory that was detonating from the inside. The fire had hit the ammunition depots and was consuming the building. I could see the disappointment on their faces. Like myself, they wanted to administer justice.

"He will no longer be a problem, trust me on that, but now I have to leave. John is on the run, causing more trouble, and I have to chase him south." I explained,

"He is gone, Rob. You just freed a city from oppression. Come celebrate with us; Gina, my daughter, and I will make sure you are well prepared." Mother Althea stated with a smile.

"So, the mystery innkeeper has a name. I thought Mother mentioned it earlier, but I wasn't sure she meant you." I said, changing the subject for a moment as I looked to the newly named old woman.

"I do indeed, and there is more I still have to tell you. That is why you should join us for the night." Gina proclaimed, grabbing me by the arm.

As the fighting de-escalated, the roars of battle turned to cheers of victory. Burning buildings turned into bonfires filled with dancing. Food that escaped these people for so long now flowed in abundance. I watched mummies eat food that they had not seen in years. The weakened members of the inner city found nutrition that had been beaten from them. It was an atmosphere of happiness. The sun was setting on the battlefield while full stomachs and dancing lifted spirits. Even I began to relax for a while as we all danced. I shifted from Gina to Mother to any other woman or man that asked for my hand.

However, my sense of enjoyment did not last long. In the back of my mind, John's smile kept creeping its way back in. I needed to move on. Around midnight I left the lovely young woman I had been dancing with and went to grab my gear. I filled my bag with food and placed my staff safely within. I threw my bag over my shoulder and disappeared into the shadows.

My absence did not go unnoticed as Mother Althea chased me down an alley. "Where are you going? The party is just getting started."

"I have to move on, Althea. There is more going on than just what is happening in this city."

"That is far truer than you know." She slowed down for a moment and hung her head to think through her subsequent response.

"What do you mean by that?"

"John was posted in Despartian, so I'm going to assume that is where you are from." Mother started as her head rose slightly.

"That's right. I take it Gina told you who I was looking for."

"I always knew who he was. It is hard not to, but back to my original point. I've heard that Despartian is different and lacks the unrest that most of us face. In fact, more places are like this to some degree than Despartian, mainly because of John and Ascension. However, there is a group that fights for a better world. One that is free of his influence. This group is led by a man named Pan. Now his group operates mostly in the shadows, but his highest officials carry a pan flute medallion." She explained, handing back the medallion I had given her before.

"I take it that this really doesn't belong to you?" I asked. She shook her head and motioned it back towards the campfire.

"I don't exactly know where Gina sits in the hierarchy, but when in doubt, using her name and your deeds here may help you. His forces are not always the kindest to newbies, but hopefully, that can save your life." She told me.

"That explains the rest of the forces, but what is your part in all of this?" I asked, trying to dig deeper into the world that I had ignored for so long.

"Outside of Pan, there are other groups that help protect the innocents, and one of those is called the Asters. It was a crew formed by myself and my sister, who is now down in New Orleans. We are spread across many cities in the country. We work in the shadows doing work like I do here. Brothels that collect information and hide defenseless women from the brutes that run rampant in cities all over."

"I'm going to make things better," I whispered just loud enough for her to hear.

"I thought all you cared about was revenge for your beloved?" She asked me. She was right. That was my mission, but there was just something that made me say I'd help.

"It is all I care about, but if I can help exquisite women like yourself from time to time, I think that would be alright," I replied, lacking a better response.

"I haven't been called exquisite in quite some time, Rob. Is that your form of flirting?"

"I just call them as I see them, and that massage was otherworldly. Even a sane man would be tempted by it." I smiled back.

"So, Rob, are you a sane man or an insane one still lost in grief?"
She asked, creeping closer with an inviting smile. I could feel my
heart race as she approached. Althea had this look in her eyes. It was
a warm and comforting gaze that drew you in.

"Depends when you ask, but I will say that at the current moment,
I'm a little bit of both," I told her as I crept closer to the point where
there was no space between us. She was just short enough where her
forehead rested at the height of my lips.

"It has been a while, hasn't it, Rob?" She whispered into my ear. I
nodded slowly, remembering the massage she gave from earlier and
the gentle touch of her skin. "Then I'll make sure to take it gently on
you." I smiled at this as I grasped her close and pinned her to the
wall. From there, we wasted the rest of the night finding a bed in one
of the crumbled buildings. It was a rash decision fueled by liquor
and the celebration, but I don't regret it.

The following morning Mother Althea was up before me and
woke me from my slumber. It was a surprise, but I guess she wanted
to have one last discussion.

"That was quite a night," I remarked as I tried to roll out of bed. It
took me a few attempts to work through the soreness from Jack's
beating, but it rose eventually.

"It was, but I guess I didn't have to take it easy on you." She
replied, and I chuckled. "But before you whisk yourself away, I have
a few last pieces of advice for you."

"And what would those be?" I asked as I reclothed myself.

"If you are to beat John and help people, you have to let go of this
burden you carry. As we exposed our souls last night, I could feel
the pain you carry, aching through every scar as my hands moved
across your body. The death of your loved one broke you, but you
were cracking long before that." She began, grabbing her own
clothes.

"You don't know a damn thing," I replied with agitation. She was
right, but this woman who had only known me for a day calling me
outdrove me irate.

"You're right. I don't know, but I was broken long enough to
know when I sleep with a person who has a fractured soul. You can
grow again, Rob. You can find peace again that isn't solely
dependent on killing John." She explained as she now rose to look at
me eye-to-eye. I wanted to hide my gaze but knew that it would be

pointless. She already knew everything she needed to. I looked at her one last time. Memorized how her top clung to her curves and how her hair hung in a mess. Then I turned to walk away. I didn't want to reflect and dig into what she was saying. I wasn't ready for it yet.

"Before you leave the city, stop by the brothel. Inside you will find a man in a leather jacket that will place a symbol of the Asters on your body. Use it correctly, and you will find help in nearly every city you enter." She told me as I walked out the door. I left her and whatever conversation she wanted to have behind. I was a child running at that time.

I made my way to the brothel as she had ordered, where I found a bearded man with hair to his waist. He took me inside, where he sat me down and placed the tattoo on my shoulder. It took an hour and a half to finish but was well done given the short notice. I covered myself up quickly and headed for the exit. I hoped that I would have a clean escape, but Gina was waiting at the door.

"What is it now? Mother Althea already took up a considerable amount of my time." I commented as she stood stonewalled.

"So, I've heard. Don't worry, this will not take long. First, I know that Mother told you about me, so if you find yourself in St. Louis, knows my commanding officer is stationed there. She is a fierce woman with a heart of gold. Truthfully you remind me of her in a lot of ways. So all you will need to do is tell her that Gina sent you. If you need to identify her, look for a pan flute-like this," Gina instructed as she revealed a pan flute tattoo, "Second, take this bag of supplies we prepared and note." She handed me a large duffel bag and a letter with my name inscribed on it.

"Thank you." I nodded as I left the city for good. I turned one last time and then pushed the events from the previous days out of my mind.

Once I had put some distance between the city and myself, I pulled out the note. It was in a tattered envelope, with my name written in bold cursive. The message was from John and read as follows:

Dear Rob,

I told you that you would make it out. Unless this is Jack, but I highly doubt that. I mean, what kind of idiot names himself the

Butcher, so scary. A name like that is for someone whose real name is Sal. Sal's probably overweight, near divorce and wishing he was, and he likely has the meat sweats. Oh, how I find the meat sweats detestable. I digress, though, as I know that it is Rob who is reading this. Well, I guess you are wondering why I would take the time to write to you? Why would I do everything I am doing? Well, the truth is you need to know a few things before our next meeting. So, without further ado.

When I was a young man, I was born into a small, poor family. It was composed of myself, my parents, and my older brother. Now my brother was a complicated man. In fact, he was a detestable loser with early signs of psychopathy. As for our little shack, we called home. That was located in Overtown, Miami. A place that was called Colored Town during Jim Crow and was not kind to our light-skinned family.

Despite the poverty and being ostracized, I stayed reasonably sane with my tendency to be a perfectionist. If I did everything right, I figured I would climb out of that Hell hole and the demon, known as my father, who acted as our tormentor. Speaking of my father, he was a professional boxer. No, he was a professional loser who took out all his losses on his sons. I didn't like my father, but I did everything I could to appease him so he wouldn't hit me. My brother, on the other hand, was always in a fight with dad. Sometimes I swear my brother intended to poke the bear. Things only got worse as the years dragged on, and when my father caught him torturing a squirrel, it terrified me. I wasn't sure what scared me more at the time. My brother's actions or my father's beating.

A few years later, I would get my answer when Clark, my brother, and I were playing basketball in Reeves Park. I think I was eight or so at that point. We had a good day until two kids from his class suddenly showed up and started heckling us. As you can imagine, my brother didn't take crap from our dad, so he wasn't going to take it from two kids. He started to fight them, which led to the two of them whaling at him. I should have let them kill him. It would have saved Trisha a lot of trouble, along with the others. I apologize, Rob, but I stepped in using my father's training to fight back. He wanted his favorite son to be a famous fighter, and I was too much for the boy I had been fighting. I pushed him into the hoop when his head bounced off the hoop stand and then the asphalt on his way down.

I wonder if you remember the first man you killed because I remember the blood. I remember the distant look in the poor boy's eyes. His friend was in shock. Especially when my psychopath of a brother struck him from behind with a brick to the head. I had killed the boy by accident. He meant every bit of his kill. Then he looked at me and told me it was for my own good, but there was no remorse in his eyes that day. What was even scarier was how quickly he acted when he needed to make their bodies disappear.

The bodies were found, of course, but we were at the bottom of the suspect list. The case went cold, though I do think a pedophile was caught in the process. That is something, I guess. That day, I got away with my first murder, and the day I saw my brother start to slip.

This might not have been what you were expecting to read, but this is the start of my story, and once you read my last letter, I hope you will understand. I hope that you will conclude what I have, but I will leave you with what has been said until then. Stay on track, Rob, and you will find out more.

See ya next time Rob!

After I finished reading the letter, I stood with it for a moment. I had known John for years, yet he never told me he had a brother. I didn't even know about any family until I heard about his niece Trisha. On top of that, to learn that he had killed at such a young age was tragic. I did remember my first kill, but to feel that when you are only eight. It had to be life-altering.

I took the letter and folded it in half to tuck it away for the rest of my journey. Out of all the messages he could have left, this is the one he wanted to give me, which meant it was part of the game he was playing. Secret factories, bands of rebels, and cryptic letters were how I started my journey. Not exactly an average start, but it would end up being par for the course. With that, I headed back on my way, unsure what else would be waiting for me.

Part 2
Walk in the Woods

Late August, 10 A.L.A.

Chapter 5
Just Bear with Me

I followed the stars south for a couple of days, sporadically stopping for a day to focus on training. Jack may have fallen quickly, but I still felt out of shape. I was missing something, an edge that would determine my battle versus John. I wasn't sure what that looked like, but I was obsessed with finding it during my training. Every morning I followed a strict bodyweight regimen and practiced for two hours with my staff, yet it didn't truly feel like I was training. Yes, I was in fabulous shape, but something was different, and it wasn't until later that I understood what was missing.

A week into this routine, I determined that I was utterly lost. Since the War, the Earth had started reclaiming the land, sprouting trees at astonishing rates, and expanding many state parks. On top of this, the idea of signage no longer existed. Maps had been redrawn by catastrophe and left no one to create them. Things weren't the same as they had been, but the world was returning to its new normal. At least the scenery was beautiful this time of year. It wasn't full autumn yet. However, the leaves were just starting to change. Such beauty is the microcosm of the cycle of death and life.

I may have been lost, but I did enjoy the valley that I was wandering around in. I decided that the only way to become unlost when one has no guide is to keep going. I worked my way through the forest, looking for a clearing to rest. Despite the bravado, I generally demonstrated my body was beginning to weaken. For ten years, I fought some form of war, either real or inside myself. The fighting was all I knew, but it had grown quite old. I was growing old. All the scars were beginning to cumulate.

Further, into the woods, I plunged until I found a decent clearing at last. Once there, I made a small shelter and built a small fire. I began cooking some of the food I had left and settled in for the night. Hoping to have a good rest again, which would be my first since Althea. Laying down under the shining stars to stare into the heavens, I couldn't doze off. Comfortable and exhausted, yet my mind wouldn't shut off. Part of my restlessness was John, that part was prominent, but it wasn't just him. I had spent years trudging through forests, specifically those in parts of East Asia, making me quite comfortable sleeping in them. Unfortunately, it also left me uneasy about them. Stampedes of Asian elephants, snakes attempting to cuddle, and tigers lurking for food. Not to mention living in territory filled with people wanting you dead puts everyone on edge. To this day, sitting in the woods stimulates all the memories and places me in a state of high awareness.

Each time I attempted to close my eyes, I saw only the darkest images. On occasion, John flashed that grin; in other instances, I would see elephants rampaging. I searched my bag for something unique that Gina had slipped in it. I pulled out the unmarked bottle of what turned out to be rum. I opened it and started to chug the cheap aged rum. I was yearning for my mind to settle, but my mind only moved faster no matter how much I drank. Then, at last, I passed out.

Several hours passed, and I slept alright. It was a drunken sleep where I tossed and turned the whole night. The most unsettling part happened around three. Around that time, I heard rustling coming from the bushes, followed by a low growl. Even in that state, I quickly snapped up, grabbing my staff and rising to my feet. Immediately I realized how drunk I still was. My steps were uneasy while balance faltered.

As I tried to balance myself, I saw a hungry black bear gazing in my direction. That little bit of drunk I felt quickly dissipated at the sight of the beast. I began to back up slowly, trying not to disturb the beast. As I retreated, the beast started to sniff around my campsite. He stuck his nose into my bag and removed all the food I had left. Once he had finished off my rations, his attention turned to me. He approached ever so slightly, revealing its slim figure. That being said, it was probably around 400 pounds on what could have been a 600-pound frame.

On top of that, my stick was no match for his claws if he turned violent. I don't know a lot about bears, but given how small he was for his frame, I assume something was wrong with him. He was starved and desperate. Usually, I wouldn't have been a target, but he needed any and all nourishment that he could muster at this point.

As he grew closer, I could feel my heart beginning to jump out of my chest. In my life, I had seen men at their most desperate as they tried to survive. An animal of this sort was something entirely different. Even at their lowest points, mankind has higher thought to contend with. This bear only had survival as a concern. He was not unpredictable like man, but his ferocity could be unlike anything I'd ever seen.

As I stood thinking, he approached me until he was within feet of my position. I had hoped that the beast would decide to take the easy food and run by avoiding confrontation. I was proven wrong quickly when the beast began to charge. Using what little sense I had, I rolled to the side to avoid the initial strike. In return, I swung my staff, striking him across the face. I was satisfied at first when the bear staggered. However, he turned back to me with a roar that could shake a man from his head to his toes. He was far more desperate than I had imagined, as a blow like the one I gave often would have scared a black bear away. He wanted me dead while I lacked the tools to kill the beast. At that point, I had to convince him that I wasn't worth the effort, but that would be a challenge giving the look of starvation plastered over his face.

Once the bear decided to stand its ground, I knew that offense would be my only option. If I let him regain his senses, I wouldn't stand a chance. My first move was to hold my staff at its very end to maximize the length of it. It would reduce the force I could apply and slow each strike down. However, it kept me away from the creature's mouth, and that was of utmost importance. I kept aiming for his eyes, trying to blind them. This seemed to work for a time, but he caught on fast. After a while, he lowered his head to the ground. Taking his snout and eyes out of the firing zone. The thick skull protected the beast as he continued to move closer to me.

I could no longer slow the beast down with my blows. While he was at the advantage when it came to pure brute strength. If he continued his path, I would be caught in a matter of moments. I could no longer fight the beast, making my only option to run. The bear's vision was blurry from the early blows giving me the perfect opportunity to run.

I've always been on the faster side, but it only took the bear a few seconds to gather itself and run me down. I was pinned against an old oak with the hungry beast drooling next to me. At this point, I was convinced that my journey would be over. At that point, I had to chuckle at how fate's middle fingers seem to work. I closed my eyes as he growled once more, covering me with saliva.

In the end, you are supposed to see the thing that you desire most. I expected to see Iris, yet in this instance, I saw John again. I'm not sure what a psychoanalyst would say about that, but it was unsettling. I wondered if he was what I desired most. I asked if I had forgotten who I was.

The next thing I knew, I heard a whooshing sound followed by a whimper. I opened my eyes and saw the bear running away. Next to me was a spear stuck in the ground. Friend or foe, I was not alone in this forest. More importantly, they were a friend at that moment in time, ensuring my survival once more.

"Who's there?!?" I called as I reached for the spear in the ground. As I pulled it from the land, I kept my eyes on the bushes. I was looking for any sign of a disturbance that could hint at the stranger's location, but everything was silent. Until finally, an old man came sauntering out of the brush line. The first impression was an extremely lackluster one, to say the least. He was a bit shorter than I am and lacked any hair. He was probably in his late fifties, given the wrinkles of time that had engrained across his brow. The only thing that impressed me was the strength I could see in his movement, but it shouldn't have been enough to scare the bear away. Once he neared me, I noticed the strangest part about him. A glaze covered his eyes. My savior was blind.

"Don't make me regret saving you, boy. Old Paw-Paw has grown mighty hungry in recent days." The man said at last. Now that he stood within feet of me, he seemed to stare through me with his glazed-over eyes. Despite his lack of sight, it still felt like he was looking deep into my soul. He had no concept of how I looked, yet I had a feeling that he knew more about me than almost anyone before him. After a moment of silence, he stretched his arm out and snatched the spear out of my hand. Once he did that, I expected him to say something, but instead, he turned away to begin his march home. I was left awed.

"Come now, I have a place for you to sober up and sleep." He commented as he motioned for me to follow him. Now I'm not one for going back to strange old men's homes, but let me tell you, I've never had one scare off a bear for me either.

"I'll follow you if you give me your name first," I replied, trying to gain something before I followed him.

"Your generation always lacked manners...Don't you know that it is impolite to demand a name before first supplying your own? Especially when the other person is offering hospitality." He instructed! I was surprised by his response. I couldn't tell you the last time anyone spoke about manners. I mean, he was right, but still. I felt a tad guilty at that point. The man just saved my life and offered up his home, yet I was trying to make demands. Not exactly a stellar impression to make.

"My apologies, it has been some time since I have met anyone with class. My name is Rob Doran." I replied, following him through the woods. I wondered at first if he heard me, as he didn't respond. He just continued on with his trek. As we went, I began to wonder if he was actually blind. Every move was precise. He avoided every branch and sharp rock that even my eyes almost missed. His mastery of the woods seemed to be superhuman.

"It is quite sad how the War robbed everyone of basic manners. Makes me glad that I moved into the woods to live alone." He commented as I caught a root with my foot. "Careful, these woods are unforgiving for idiots." I don't know if it was his laugh or comment that cut deeper.

"I'm not an idiot," I argued, wiping dirt off my face.

"Not very convincing coming from a man who got drunk in the woods, nearly eaten by a bear, and is wiping literal mud off his face." He pointed out as his laugh echoed.

"Fine, you caught me at a bad time, so what is your name? Now that my name and stupidity are well established." I replied, only to be interrupted with a rock sailing at my face.

"Don't you ever shut up, kid? It is truly distracting and makes it difficult for me to navigate. I see with all my other senses, particularly my hearing, and if I can't hear my surroundings, I might trip." He claimed. After this outburst, I decided that it wasn't worth pestering him any further.

His name really wasn't going to make that much of a difference in the end, so I did what he said, I shut up. We traveled for about a mile into the woods, where there was an old wooden hut. It seemed to be constructed from the wood in the forest and was dated just before the War. Based on my initial glance, it couldn't have been more extensive than 300 square feet. Amazingly, the hut appeared to be in near pristine condition. There were a few rots in the logs, but it was nicer than what most people in the world have today.

He led me into the hut, where I was quickly greeted by an intense odor. It wasn't a smell that I minded at all, but one that would make sleeping difficult. This strange old man loved meat apparently, smoked meats especially. Now I'm sure you'd love to hear me talk about anything else outside of the meat. Unfortunately, given that he was blind, he did not have a single light source outside of what came in naturally from the sun or moon. I couldn't tell you anything else about the interior.

"I'll light the fireplace before you trip over anything. It will make things a bit hot in here. Still, you people disadvantaged with sight tend to become uncomfortable in total darkness." He explained in a condescending tone. Just the way his voice curled when mentioning sight was unlike anything I had heard before. I was taught to use all my senses to their fullest throughout my career, but he found my reliance on sight too strong.

In what felt like only a minute, the room was lit up. He had found his way to his fireplace and started a small fire. As soon as the room was lit, I noticed all the clutter. Every square inch of the walls was covered with arrows, spears, knives, and fresh kills. The ceiling had ropes strung across it holding butchered meats and vegetables. There was an old-fashioned refrigerator unit and barrels containing food. The only furniture in the center of the room is a hand-carved rocking chair with some pillows and a lumpy couch.

"So, noisy one, why were you out there taunting Paw-Paw?" He asked, sitting down in the chair

"Taunting? I was taking a nap when he stumbled into my camp." I defended myself.

"Don't tell me you're dull and stupid. I meant, what brings you to these woods?" He asked this time. I don't know if I've ever seen a blind man roll his eyes, but let me tell you, he rolled his eyes.

"I'm looking for someone but had to take a quick nap to continue on," I answered, being sure to stay vague. Even though this man had been so kind to me, I still couldn't trust him. Especially when your objective is to find the most powerful man in the world and kill him.

"Well, lucky you. You found someone, ya fool." He laughed, rocking the chair back in the process. It was the first time I had seen him smile since we met. It was a pretty delightful and cheerful grin. His teeth were white and shining as his smile filled the room.

"Hospitable and funny, I see, but now I'm looking for someone in particular. An old friend of mine." I explained, trying to hide my irritation with his joke.

"A friend of yours, you say. Well, I bet if he is as stupid as you, then he was Paw-Paw's lunch. Maybe I should have finally put him out of his misery and checked." He joked again as he grabbed a piece of meat from the ceiling and began to eat it. I was not amused with his constant assertion that I was an idiot, but it is hard to argue when you were nearly a late-night snack an hour earlier.

"Are you agitated enough yet, or are you going to keep avoiding the truth? Currently, you and the truth remind me of middle school kids at a dance avoiding the opposite gender like the plague. It is quite a useless ploy you are attempting." He insisted with a smirk drawn across his face. I should have known that a man keens on hearing would pick up on my intentions to avoid a real conversation.

"So, you want the truth?" I snapped back. I wasn't sure why I was yelling at that point, but he had upset me.

"No, I want peace and quiet, but I made the mistake of saving you! Now I'm hoping to have a conversation that is actually worthwhile and not just a waste of my time!" He replied, matching my intensity.

"Why are old men so insistent in knowing everyone else's business?" I asked, trying to calm myself down. He scratched his bald head for a moment before he answered.

"I don't know. Maybe I'm just bored of sitting here farting and eating. Maybe it's because I saved your life, and I want to make sure it wasn't a mistake." He shrugged as he let go of a touch of gas right on cue. Laughing the whole time.

"You are quite odd, aren't you," I commented. I just couldn't figure him out. There was something about him that I felt I could trust, yet I barely knew him. Then again, he was insufferable with his insults.

"I'm blind and living in the woods on my own. You are going to need something better than *odd*. Now, how about you give me a real answer, and this conversation can move on." He negotiated.

"Fine, if it will get us closer to ending this talk. I am searching for an old friend of mine. He killed someone I cared about deeply, and now I want revenge." I admitted.

"You're special, aren't you, kid? And I don't mean special in a good way either." He said in a stale tone of voice. His delivery walked that line between seriousness and sarcasm. Truthfully I couldn't tell you which one it was at this point.

"What do you mean by that? I tell you the truth, and you call me special. Why?" I asked him as I tried to figure out his point.

"Easy. You are still only telling me part of the truth, but now you have reached the point where you think that you are telling the full truth." He clarified.

"Alright, you have my attention. What do you mean by the full truth? Revenge is revenge, isn't that enough?" I asked as I tried to figure out his point.

"Okay, we'll try this a different way. Why are you the one chasing this man?" He asked. I thought he was senile at this point.

"I told you he…." I started before being interrupted.

"No, you still aren't getting it. I don't care about what this man did. There are thousands of men doing evil things every day. I want to know why YOU are chasing him. Why not let anyone else do it?" He clarified. I felt a little clearer about his question, but it felt like we were talking in circles.

"Why me? Because no one else has a chance against him. Nor does anyone know how evil he is." I claimed, questioning whether or not I really could stop him given our history.

"He must be some form of the demon if only one man can stop him." He chuckled, leaning back in his chair. He clasped his fingers together and began to think as he waited for my subsequent response.

"No, he is a man, if only barely, but the blood he has spilled is on my hands. He is my responsibility, and I am the one he has taken the most from." I told him with a lowering of my head. Had I only intervened sooner, then I could have saved so many lives.

"Alright, Captain Ahab. What you describe isn't revenge. It is called obsession. You no longer seek just revenge. You are trying to satisfy an itch, one that will never be scratched the way you are going." He commented as the floorboards creaked.

"Are they not the same thing?" I asked.

"To an idiot they are, but despite my jokes, you don't strike me as an idiot. Revenge is righting a wrong someone has committed against you. Obsession is being controlled by it. It is when revenge becomes deadly, and you become so blinded by your target that you lose sight of your real goal. If you wanted revenge against this man, you would do whatever you could. You would bring an army to his door. Instead, you are so obsessed with the idea of doing it on your own. You claim you are the only one capable because you can't stand anyone else taking your glory, catching your whale." He lectured. I bit my lip for a second as I processed what he said. I wondered if he was right. There were people that would have followed me, that would have helped me. Yet, I was alone. I was obsessed with John, but that wasn't the only thing.

"I can't let him hurt anyone else," I whispered. I thought it was only loud enough for me to hear, but I was wrong.

"Ah, so there is the truth I was looking for. It is fear that drives you." He smiled as if he had just reached some revelation. As he said that, I noticed a tear forming in my eye. I wasn't sure how long it had been there, but it sat in my left eye, just waiting to fall. I tried to wipe it away, but it returned almost instantly.

"No, it is an obsession. He doesn't scare me." I insisted.

"I doubt he does. It is hard to scare a man who doesn't fear death, but you are afraid of loss, which you cannot control. You aren't on this journey alone because you have to be the killer. You are doing it because you don't want to lose anyone else. Instead, you want to kill him or die fighting alone." He analyzed.

"How did you know I didn't fear death?" I asked, changing the subject slightly.

"Because Paw-Paw had you pinned, but never once did I hear you beg. Not once did you yell for help. Instead, you accepted your fate. That is not an easy thing to do." He explained.

I sat for a few minutes in the silence, trying to wrap my head around what he had said. The things he mentioned all felt the same to me, yet different. I thought revenge and obsession were one thing, yet there was a difference there. I figured my fear was an attempt to protect, but in reality, it was the one fear that I still had. John had taken so much from me already I was afraid of what else he could do.

"How do you get revenge without giving into obsession, and how do you get past the fear?" I asked.

"The answer is the same to both: you let people in. People may die if revenge is your true goal, but they may die even if it is not. The most important thing is to realize that you cannot stand on an island and succeed. I promise you that your target isn't doing this alone. And maybe that is your answer. Take from him instead of letting him always take from you." He said.

"I don't know if anyone has ever suggested the eye-for-an-eye approach." I chuckled.

"That is because we get stuck in this idea of right and wrong. We think there is a right answer, and revenge cannot be it, but here is a fact I've learned. All we can do is what we think is best. If killing this man is what is best for the world, who am I to stop you? But if you come to this conclusion on your own, you are more likely to be wrong. When you stand with others, they help you see a collective truth that will combat your own. Then whoever is the victor will be the justified and righteous one while the other will be the evil wrongdoer." He said.

"That is a lot to digest right there," I commented as I worked through his words. I thought back to that little town and how he was right. I stood with a group that saw John as evil, and we fought his ideology with our own. Will that town be better off in twenty years? Who knows, but as a collective, we concluded that it was for the best. Maybe I did need some help.

"It is not easy, to say the least, so I think it would be best if we each slept and thought on it." He smiled one last time.

"That would be good, thank you." I nodded back. We chatted for about 10-minutes more on just small things as we each slowly fell asleep for the night.

Chapter 6
The Blind Leading the Blind

The morning came quicker than I had hoped, as it always does. The sun shone through the windows. The birds were chirping, and I found the old man had already left me behind. I was a bit disappointed. Despite his jabs early on, I had found him to be quite interesting. He had left some of the jerkies out for me that I ate quickly but cautiously, given the raging hangover that I was fighting at the time.

I threw my empty bag on my shoulder, secured my staff, and exited the hut. The minor excursion was over, or so I thought. Outside the cabin, the old man was sitting cross-legged in the grass. At first, I thought he was meditating with how still he sat, but once I approached him, I noticed that his hand was stretched out with nuts sitting in it. The local squirrels were crawling over him, eating out of his palms. He was entirely in tune with nature, unlike anything I'd seen since I met the monks in Japan.

"Finally sober?" He muttered, scaring the critters away. I had tried to sneak by but clearly failed at it.

"Getting there," I replied.

"Good to hear, now go fill your bag with food and come sit. Do not be shy. I will never go through everything that is in that house. I am not long for this world and do not wish to waste it." He ordered. As instructed, I filled my bag and quickly joined him. His comments made me curious.

"If you have more than enough food, why were you out in the woods?" I asked, planting my butt firmly on the ground.

"Some would say destiny, but I am not one of those fools who believe in things like that. In truth, I was taking a walk through the forest and allowed myself to hear the call you made without saying a word." He told me in his typically cryptic tone.

"You allowed yourself to hear the call?" I repeated.

"Yes, that is what I said. Let's not go back to stupid you by repeating everything I say. You see so many people walk through life looking towards their futures, their pasts, or they look towards their destiny. Even in movies, you see heroes looking for something until the day comes when they are summoned to this mythical destiny. Life doesn't work that way. When you sit and become present in the moment, you discover that where you are is where you are needed. Let's use you as an example. Was this John you muttered about in your sleep evil before?" He asked.

"He was," I replied.

"And you did nothing?" He assumed.

"Correct," I said.

"And where were you?" He asked.

"I was in Despartian with him. More importantly, I was stuck in the bottle." I told him.

"You may as well have only mentioned being stuck in the bottle as the first part was a lie. You were not in the city with him. You were stuck in the past. Had you been present, you would have known that you were needed in the now. People needed you then, but do not dwell on this. That is a lesson to learn, not a mistake to live with. If you do, you will miss the current needs." He lectured. I was starting to understand his point.

"Then what are the current needs?" I asked.

"I don't know. Only you can answer that question." He commented. At that moment, I felt him staring through me. He was trying to help me dig into last night's revelations. What did I need to do at this moment to fulfill my goals, to fight my fears, and to avoid losing myself to obsession? I felt that I was at the point where I couldn't go back anymore. I couldn't just forget about John and the things he did. Yet, I thought there might be a better option where I could be the man Iris loved. Indeed I could have justice, but in a way that would make her proud.

"I think I need to keep moving forward," I said at last.

"Why?" He asked.

"Because that is the only direction to head. I still want revenge, but that is just where the wind blows for now. It may change." I replied

"And so the idiot can learn." He smiled.

"Slowly, but I do every now and then," I told him.

"Then I will talk slowly as well." He said with long pauses in his voice.

"Is that your way of saying you want to tag along?" I asked.

"I have nothing better to do, and I think that life with you will make my last bit worth it. Especially if I get to be a teacher again." He informed me as he rose to his feet at last. "Besides, you've already taken all my food. Hahaha!"

"So, what is the plan?" I asked.

"To follow you, so where were you headed?" He asked in return.

"John told me to follow the river south," I informed him.

"Then south we go, but we take each step listening to the world. If destiny changes along the way, it changes. Saying that, I know there are some places south of here that need your help." He said. I nodded my head and smiled. Even though he couldn't see my gesture, I knew he understood what I was doing.

He then went over and grabbed a bag off the porch that was already packed. I had been played by this old man, but I was okay with it. I wanted to let someone help me again. I had gone so long without a mentor that this was going to be exciting and hopefully insightful. The old man seemed to turn into a spring chicken as he started down the road. Then, at last, I remembered the most crucial question.

"Hey, what is your name?" I asked.

"Oh. Didn't I tell you yet? The name is Mark, and I'm beating you by a mile already, come on." He goaded. I chuckled at his confidence and quickly caught up with him. Once I caught up, he played the old man card again. He acted like he was frail, handing me the bag while he would grab for his hip. I should have known that he would be a hassle, but there were some laughs in there as well.

Part 3
City of Despair

Early September 10 A.L.A.

Chapter 7
Leopard Skin

The first few days passed unremarkably, with little helpful conversation. I think I relayed my tale about Despartian and the city in Illinois. He told me about the forest and Paw-Paw. Apparently, the bear had contracted some disease a few weeks ago, causing him to lose weight rapidly. Mark was convinced the creature would not last long naturally, and he had been struggling with what to do. Paw-Paw had been lashing out, but Mark couldn't bring himself to kill the old bear. Now that Mark had left, it would only be a few days before the bear would become one with nature again.

By the fourth day of walking, I started meditating with him. He insisted that we stop and sit for at least fifteen minutes every few hours, not an unreasonable demand from an old man. At first, I thought it was for rest, but I quickly realized that he did not sleep. He wanted to center himself. Which he claimed helped him enjoy what life he had left. On the fourth day, he finally instructed me to sit next to him after he had finished his own session.

"I told you I'd be your teacher, so sit, boy. You haven't slept soundly for who knows how long." He ordered. I had accepted him as my teacher, making arguing a useless proposition. Besides, I had grown tired of the restless nights. If what he spoke of could cure me of John's haunting image or Iris dying, I would give it a whirl.

"Let's take a moment and start off by just closing your eyes and breathing...at first, just notice the rise and fall of your chest or stomach at the natural pace you enjoy." He began as I tried to follow his commands. I did as he said, just allowing myself to breathe and attempting to relax.

"You might find your mind wandering or tension existing in places it doesn't belong at that moment. I want you to take a deep breath and find centeredness in this. Now take some time and breathe." He commanded in the softest tone I had heard yet.

As I sat, I felt my mind wandering all around. I thought of John, of Iris, of all my other friends in Despartian. My mind went in every direction until I heard his voice say, *breath.* At that moment, I took my breath and let my mind calm down. Continuing to focus on it, I noticed the tension that was spread across my body. I hadn't seen it, but my hands had tightened. I was holding a fist to fight an enemy that wasn't there.

"As you breathe and find that inner peace, turn towards the present moment. Turn into you and your body. You may even notice the world around you and the sensations you feel from it." He cued as I stayed seated. Though my mind wandered, I noticed the drifting start to lessen the longer I sat. Now my mind slowly started to listen to the world around me.

"What do you hear?"

I heard the birds chirping in the trees and the rustle of the leaves as they left.

"What do you smell?"

The smell of the flowers hung in the air and the stench created filled my body with each inhale.

"What do you feel?"

I felt anxious. I was angry every time that John appeared in my visions. I felt conflicted when I saw Iris. Love, fear, anger, and so much more. I felt like I was alive.

"Now, stay with these feelings. Allow yourself to feel how you are in this moment and then breathe."

I sat in silence and allowed myself to feel everything that I had buried. I could feel my body crave the need to cry, and his voice soothed me further. That is when I screamed. A yell that I don't ever remember calling before. I saw her, I saw her holding my hand, and all I could do was scream to stop myself from crying.

I rose to my feet and started to walk away as he sat there. He said nothing as I ran into the woods just outside of his view. I gripped my chest as I could feel my heart pounding faster than ever. My breath which had just been so controlled, was now controlling me. Then I slipped down to lay against a tree. It was then that he finally came to stand next to me.

"What was that?" I asked. I had done meditation when I was younger but had never felt anything like that before.

"That was called dealing with trauma. You never cried for her, did you? You never cried for you?" He explained as he stood over my hyperventilating body.

"I cried when she died," I told him.

"Crying at the moment isn't dealing with it, Rob. You spent years in the bottle denying a past. Running from issues instead of facing them. Then you became obsessed with revenge because if that is all you can think of, you don't have to feel the pain." He lectured. "You can deny it, but your reaction said everything. I made you feel what your body and mind have craved to feel. You were forced to feel again, and you were terrified."

I wanted to run from what he was saying. I tried to yell again, but that would have only proved his point farther. I had never dealt with the pieces of me that I lost at war, and I hadn't taken time to cry over Iris. I never took time to mourn her loss. I just trained and fought. It was not the meditative experience I expected, but apparently, one I needed.

"Can we try that again?" I asked. He sat across from me and nodded his head.

"I want you to start with something different this time. While you breathe, I want you to look around you and notice your world, the sights that you see, and where everything is." He instructed. I looked around and noticed the trees and a few birds flying back and forth. I saw him sitting there cross-legged and at peace. He was breathing at his own pace. I turned slightly and saw the giant maple tree that I was leaning against. For it to grow that size, it had to have existed for generations. Surviving disaster after disaster.

As I looked around, I just continued to breathe until, at last, he told me to relax my eyes. I let them fall closed as my stomach rose with each inhale and fell with the exhales. This time my mind did not go to Iris or John. Instead, I saw the birds in the trees. I heard their wings flap and the leaves rustle. Instead of feeling the emotions I had before, I let my body feel the cold dirt under me and the roughness of the tree against my back. From time to time, my mind still wandered, but this time I not only looked towards my breathing but the world I had seen before my eyes closed.

He continued to cue a few more things over the next few minutes, but the experience stayed the same. I had found a little bit of peace.

More importantly, I found my way to peace and how to turn away from Iris and John.

"On your next set of breaths, allow your eyes to open and your body to awaken." He instructed. I was sad to see the peace go, but there was also a bit of relief when my body finally woke up.

"That was much better." I smiled. He laughed at my remarks with his loud belly laugh.

"Well, it couldn't get much worse. So what made this one different?" He asked.

"Instead of going straight to John or Iris, I thought of the birds in those trees and let that anchor me. I still saw them, but I did not feel the same emotions." I explained.

"Then it worked as I had hoped." He confirmed with another smile.

"Hm?" I uttered.

"You need to deal with your emotions, Rob, but there is a time and place for it. So I wanted you to experience a meditation that was based on the present moment. I wanted you to see the world around you and let it become central in your mind. That way, you could see that being present is possible. You just have to learn how to control your attention." He explained. From there, he rose to his feet and assisted me to my own.

"So, what now?" I asked.

"Now that your mind is a little clearer, it is time for your lesson." He explained as he walked into an open field.

"I thought that was my lesson," I stated as I followed him

"It was, and it wasn't. That was to prepare you to learn. This next lesson will help you grow stronger. Now I want you to close your eyes and listen again." He ordered with a sterner voice than before.

"Alright, but what is the point of this?" I asked as I followed his orders.

"I want to prepare you in ways that you have never experienced. Now, earlier you talked about the birds you saw, I want you to see how many you can hear. There are four trees directly behind you, with several birds squawking around in them. I want you to listen to their voices and tell me how many there are." He commanded. I wasn't sure what he was getting at, but he had already provided one epiphany, so why not hope for more.

As I stood in the center of the clearing, I began to listen to everything around me. I heard the wind blow, the grasshoppers creak, and the birds squawk. At first, I could not differentiate any of them. They were all birds, and the exercise was stupid, but I wasn't about to say that aloud. Then I tried to do what I had done during meditation. I began to focus on one sound at a time, using my breath to calm myself. It took a few minutes, but I could finally tune out the other sounds and focus solely on the birds. At that point, I just had to count. One, three, six, and seven different sounds I heard.

"There are seven birds in the trees," I answered while slowly opening my eyes. I expected a proud grin but only received a blow to the head from a small branch he had found.

"Close, but you are off. You rushed through the process a bit, but at least you tried my way." He told me as I rubbed the new bruise forming on my skull.

"Why did you have me do that? What was the lesson here?" I asked.

"Turn around and look at the trees. I want you to tell me how many you can see fluttering around." He instructed this time. I did as I was told, counting only four within direct sight though the fifth shook branches rapidly, giving me a strong hunch but nothing concrete. Three fewer birds. If I was counting enemies, I would have been quickly overpowered for my miscalculation.

"I only see four of them. I would have missed several of them," I admitted.

"That is the lesson I want you to learn. Over the years, you have become reliant on the easy sense. If you want the revenge you seek, you will need to become more than you are now. You will need to see what you can't see. Now come on, there is a city that needs you." He explained, finally starting to walk again. I thought about what he had said for a moment, and it excited me. John and I had trained together for nearly a decade learning all the same tricks. He was a few years older than me, giving him a slight upper hand, but otherwise, he knew everything that I did. I needed something that would surprise him. This might just be it. Though I did have to clarify something with him.

"How many birds were in the tree?" I asked. He picked up a rock and threw it at the trees, scaring the birds out of the trees without a word.

"Twelve birds. Six of them are small sparrows, three are wrens, two woodpeckers slid in, and a hawk was resting by himself." He detailed. As he spoke, I counted and cataloged each one. He had not only counted each one but nailed the type that they were. My jaw nearly dropped.

"How?" I asked, stupefied.

"Simple as I once learned to identify the unique characteristics of a face, I have learned to listen for the unique sounds. Whether it is the tone of a bird's chirp, the heaviness of a man's step, or the grind of machinery. Everything has something that makes it different. It might sound supernatural, but it is the same concept as growing used to sights. You see, you always hear people claiming that everyone in a certain group looks the same when they are never exposed to that group. However, if you spend enough time with the other group, you see that no one, not even twins, looks the same. Once you hear enough sounds, you notice that it is different as well. Unfortunately, you won't reach this level for a long time, but we can get close." He affirmed.

"Fascinating. What else can you do?" I asked, trying to contain my smile.

"Try and hit me." He commanded.

At first, I stood aghast by the command. I was a well-known soldier from the War, and he was a blind man. Sure he had scared a bear with a spear, but now he was unarmed. After my hesitation had passed, I went for a simple jab, but in an instant, he spun on his foot, sending me flying due to my own momentum. Adding insult to it, he struck me in the back with the stick again. He began to laugh as I rose from the ground.

"Why did you do that? You told me to hit you." I protested.

"I said to try and hit me. As a man who has been with women before, you should know that just because I tell you to do something doesn't mean I'm going to make it easy or pain-free." He laughed. I did not find it nearly as humorous. Then he asked the big question, "Did you learn anything?"

"That is an easy one. Stop listening to you and avoid the stick." I claimed as he swung the stick again. This time I was able to avoid the blow.

"You aren't exactly wrong, but you aren't right either. I'll tell you what I learned. A fully-abled man who is supposed to be a hero can get himself beat by a blind old man and a stick." He laughed again, trying to insult me.

"The first lesson was fun. This one seems like you just wanted to insult me!" I yelled! Mark sat on a nearby rock and clasped his hands to think for a moment.

"You don't understand that this is all one lesson." He began at last, "The birds were meant to teach you how far you can still go. Part two was to show how little you actually know, but the main theme is arrogance."

"Calling me arrogant now?" I said, shocked by his explanation.

"Yes, I am. Years of battles have dulled your senses of caution. You think that winning a hundred battles prepares you for the next hundred. Just look at the last few months you described to me. They are littered with losses yet, you think you can go straight for this vicious man who has proved to be your better. If you continue to fight as you always have, people will continue to die. And we both know that is what terrifies you the most." He explained. Self-reflection is always tricky, no matter how old you grow. I was forced to see what had become of me over the last few years, and I didn't like what I started to see. I had always denounced the title of hero, but I still carried myself that way.

"What would you have me do?" I asked. Though my words were filled with spite, the spite was not towards him. He was just the recipient. In truth, I was angry at myself for not seeing that I could not take John on in my current state.

"The first step is to embrace your failure. The second is to grow from them. A simple adage that carries a vast amount of weight. You are a great fighter. I could sense that about you from the moment I met you, but even the greatest men have weaknesses to work on. Ones that your enemy is willing to exploit, and we are going to work on those. The main thing is to just listen." He lectured.

"Okay," I answered with no better answer to give him at the time.

"That is enough teaching for now. We are closing in on St. Louis, a city of pure chaos. That can be said about most cities in our current world. Still, once you start hearing the stories from the people within its boundaries, you will understand what I mean. I ask that you listen to the stories and act as your heart tells you to. John may be the future goal, but let the present guide you and prepare you for what you believe to be inevitable." He ordered, taking me through the last few trees.

"No matter what happens, thank you for bringing me this far," I said.

"Don't thank me yet kid, there are fates far worse than being eaten by a bear." He smiled. All I could do was nod my head. I knew that someone walking the path I was rarely ever ended up in a place of good fortune. At the very least, I knew that it would come at a high cost. I thought I had avoided that by leaving everyone behind in Despartian. Both Pon, the man who aided me in Despartian, and Anna, the most incredible doctor friend a man can ask for, begged to join me on my journey, but the city needed them. Anna was the city's calming presence to survive the hardships left after John killed Iris and brought Hope tower to the ground.

Meanwhile, Pon could act as an agent of justice. He didn't want to work within the newly formed police force. Instead, he could serve as the vigilante that operated in ways no officially run entity could.

I left them because it was good for the city and for the reasons that Mark had flushed out when we first met. I had just lost Iris, and I was terrified of losing them as well. When I told them they could not come, I said it was for the city and that they would get in the way. The plan was to unleash my full fury and burn whatever stood in my way. Something impossible with friends around that could be burnt. That was John's second victory over me. Not only had he taken my loved one away, but he made himself the only focus in my mind.

As we approached the city of St. Louis, I thought back to some early memories I had of the city. I visited the city in my youth and could remember how beautiful it was. Like many, I found the arches to be a magnificent accent point. Now, as I stood looking at the city, I saw the cost of war. There was nothing but the remnants of the eloquent city. The arch stood as a skeleton of itself. It had been stripped for material during the War and then again during the rebuild. The buildings that once towered were flattened or burned to ash as easy targets.

The city was not unlike most, but once I grew closer, I started to see what Mark was talking about earlier. Outside the city, walls stood men and women addicted to the War's deadliest side effect.

Since the beginning of time, there has been a race to create the perfect killing machine, whether it was an actual machine or the man wielding it. During the last war, the desire to create super soldiers only intensified. Governments followed by the loosely established factions wanted nothing but the best to claim territory for themselves.

The 'super soldier' race created intense drug trials that reportedly are responsible for 10% of the deaths during the War. A number that is by no means a small percent given that some countries were obsessed with driving the number up and ruining themselves in the process. They injected drug concoctions into their populace that should never have existed. One of the most famous stories came from the Middle East, with fifteen men fighting off two hundred for three days. The drug used seemed perfect until the third day when all fifteen men died of brain aneurysms. After that, the position they fought for valiantly was conquered in a mere hour.

I can't speak to what Unity, the side I fought for that tried to keep the U.S. as one during the first half, did during the War as I never asked. I wanted to believe the side I fought for did not stoop to that level. I know it is a hopeless fantasy, but I needed to feel something after seeing all the lives it cost. After freeing hundreds from testing facilities, I had to think my own people weren't destroying lives. After I saw the bodies and brains turn to mush, I needed humanity to prevail. Do not take me for a fool though, there are nights where I think of my generals' depravity and shudder thinking of what they did.

The aftermath was a percentage of the population addicted to drugs that were no better than cocaine or heroin. The worst of these is infamous throughout the land as it was also the closest thing to the race's success. The name of this drug is Leopard Skin and arose from labs in Southeast Asia, where I spent most of the second half of the War. That drug is why I spent so much time in that area, in all honesty.

Skin is a highly addictive and dangerous compound that would never pass an ethical review board in its original format. This, however, is not what placed it into infamy. That happened when some genius took the pill form and liquified it. When the drug is injected directly into the bloodstream, it creates an entirely different response but similarly deadly results.

The original pill form interacts with the body more slowly and acts as a steroid on steroids. The body doesn't tire, and it blesses the user with strength ten times what should be possible. When it is injected directly into the bloodstream, it acts as a mix of heroin and steroids. The user is flushed with a rush of euphoria and strength but also becomes easily agitated. A very dangerous combo for those around the user. If I recall, the initial numbers indicated that taking the drug in the liquid form resulted in a coronary issue, such as a heart attack, every tenth time. Odds make it one of the deadliest drugs in existence but reportedly create a high, unlike anything before.

Detecting this as St. Louis' problem was quite simple. Those who have taken the drug show quick signs of their addiction. The first thing that happens is your skin starts to develop dark spots across the body, which was the source of its name. The high they experience is so intense that they rarely notice them and become near zombies. Each person sees and experiences it differently, but one man once told me that he thought he was God when he was on the drug.

Once the drug is clear and the withdrawal sets in, the dark spots remain while they slowly begin to itch like a thousand bug stings. From here, their insides start to feel as if they are turning into a melting pot. This is a precursor to one of the most straightforward symptoms: fever. Though the fever rarely grows warm enough to kill the user, it makes sleeping impossible. That first step into withdrawal is also the first towards madness.

Once the fever begins to subside slightly, the body starts to itch worse than before and constant ticking from the legs. If the body is not secured during the withdrawal process users, have been known to scratch their skin off or break bones from erratic kicking. This doesn't even dig into the psychological trauma that occurs. The mind begins to slip into madness, and the user tries to do anything they can to regain control that is no longer their own. If they do not take another hit, they beg for death, or I've heard some want you to remove their skin. I have seen people survive withdrawal, but I have seen more lose their minds forever. Even those who take it "properly" rarely come back from the edge they are pushed to.

On top of this, the dark spots can become infected, I don't know how as I am neither a doctor nor a user, but once they are infected, the grotesque smell permeates. It is a foul odor that I could have gone the rest of my life without smelling again, but as if fate had destined it. Leopard skin was once again in my path.

"I know you told me to be present so I can see where I am needed, and I can see what is needed. Unfortunately, this is not a job for me. I'm a punch and kick kind of guy. This job requires a more delicate touch." I informed the old man as the two of us stood at the edge of the city to see groups of folks preparing to die from their withdrawal.

"One thing that has amazed me about you. You have this habit of saying things that are true and false at the exact same time without knowing it. You may not be able to punch addiction in the face, and you can't even cure these people through force. However, the one thing that can save them is love. Those who love and are helping these people are in danger, and you can protect them. Now come and listen." He commanded. With that, he led me over to a man who sat against a wall shivering. Mark placed a blanket that was in his bag around that man and held him close.

As Mark held the man tighter, his eyes turned to me. The eyes told his whole story before he even began. I wondered without his sight how Mark could feel what I felt. The emptiness of his soul, the broken body, and the lack of will. Without seeing it, I don't understand how he could truly comprehend what I already knew. He was a classic Leopard Skin user with arms dotted in puncture wounds. Patches of skin were scratched off, and the fever was intensifying. He was in pain, and in days he would have to decide to live or slip silently into the abyss that called for him. Out of pity and curiosity, I sat next to Mark to hear the tale the man had to tell.

Once I was seated, Mark whispered something into the man's ear. The man seemed shocked by whatever Mark had said, causing a tear to form in his left eye. The man looked at me with a quiver on his lip, and I knew whatever was to come was not going to be pleasant for him to relay, yet at the same time, he knew he had to say it.

"My name is Josh," he began. He had to pause his story every few moments to catch his breath, "I am a veteran from the civil war portion of that disaster, and the War took everything. During the battle of St. Louis, I became severely injured. I wish it was the worst of it, but the opposing commander pushed things to a monstrous degree. We had fortified the city to the point that there was no way his army was getting in without heavy losses. Despite this, he pushed for several days until, at last, his men retreated from the boundaries.

"We thought it was a victory. There was even a celebration, but then Hell began. Barrels flew into buildings releasing a gas upon impact." He paused at that phrase, and the tears began to flow. The memory was fresh to him even though the War ended years ago. I tried to urge him to skip this part of his story, not only because of the pain it caused him but because I had heard it before. Chemical warfare was banned, and the commander he spoke of was a target. My team hunted the man down, and his head was somewhere that this man didn't need to know. Despite my urges, he didn't skip a detail.

"Gas-filled the city, and people kept dying one after another, and if you didn't die, you were left useless, like me. Those of us who managed to survive escaped as quickly as we could to the nearby woods, where we hid until reinforcements helped drive the commander out of the city. The rumor said that ghosts of our city caught up to him, but I doubt his evil was ever punished."

"Once they had been driven out, I found myself crippled with permanent lung damage and the rubble of my city. We thought things would be fine after that as the Civil War neared its end, but Hell was still coming for me. I grew happy for a time when my wife and daughter came to live with me from our small town just east of here. That happiness lasted for the rest of the War, then they moved in.

"They call themselves "The Family." They modeled their regime after a classic Italian mob and turned the ruined city into a trash dump. They started with small organized crime, and then they brought that bloody drug into our streets. I can't confirm it, but I know they were the ones that flooded the area with it despite its origins in Asia."

"Once our city was filled with junkies that couldn't fight back, they started ruling us with force. They enlisted an army from somewhere. A bunch of thugs that they bribed with the riches they had from before the War and drugs they were peddling. Any of us that resisted were instantly beaten down. Unable to deal with things, my wife started taking Leopard Skin until it killed her. Once she was dead, the gangsters took my daughter, Kristin. I don't know if she is dead or alive, but I have grown tired, and my body is giving out, so I decided to inject the drug and go out on a high." He finished his story, and his eyes began to close.

The emotional toll of the story had exhausted him to the point of near collapse. People rarely realize how hard it can be to talk. When a story is told much like the one I relay to you, we are forced to relive the moments. If it is a joyous moment in our lives, we can feel the love it brought. If harmful, it causes the person to relive well traumatic trauma. This man was so overcome by the memories that he passed out after telling us the tale.

Mark helped lower the man to the ground, placing his head on some soft ground around him. While I absorbed the story, I looked at the city I had once known. The grass and trees were starting to creep towards it as weeds grew from the rubble once roads. The addicted and withdrawing were wrapped in blankets, barely holding on to their lives. A few of the barrels used as fire pits showed the markings of the gas that once filled them.

Mark tucked the man into a more comfortable position and turned me towards the inner city. Most of the collapsed buildings had been cleared away, but pieces of rubble still littered the ground. As we started to walk, I felt myself looking towards the ground constantly as I avoided shards of glass and rusted nails. I wasn't sure if this was from the War or from the rebuild. Whoever was in charge of the rebuild had done or poor job. Buildings were missing pieces of their walls or had patches of random wood. The thin crowds seemed to wander aimlessly through the streets. Most were better off than the addicted, but they still had hopelessness in their eyes.

I can criticize John for his evil, but at least he did ensure that Despartian looked like a city again. Not just a collection of half-buildings and huts that now made up St. Louis. As always, Mark's ability to avoid every obstruction was impressive. Even the few children who played in the streets could not catch him off guard. He claimed that this was practice, but it appeared superhuman.

The deeper we traveled, the more crowded it became. Every now and then, there would be someone with a smile on their face, but it was rare. There were far more beggars than smiles. In between my observations and feelings of pity, I wondered why he wanted me to hear that story. I had heard ones like it a hundred times and thought I'd listen to a hundred more after it. If he had a purpose, it was not one that I could fathom at that moment. I felt terrible and wanted to do something, but there was nothing I could do. Even now, I wonder if there was a plan or the next moments would all be pure happenstance.

"Okay, I heard the poor man's story now; what do you want me to do about it?" I asked once I was caught back up again.

"That is up for you to decide, kid. You are a full-grown man learning to listen to the world and react accordingly after absorbing it. In the meantime, I am going to go find a beer. That story was depressing." He answered with a mischievous grin.

"You're kidding, right? You bring me all the way here. You have me listen to that story and have nothing else besides announcing your decision to drink. Where is that wisdom you were bestowing earlier?" I shouted at his nonchalance!

"You are an irritating little runt. I brought you here so that you could learn how to listen and be in the moment. It was to teach you how to not always focus on what you have lost or what you pursue. Yet, here you are, living in the past again. He told you a story, so what. I can tell you a hundred of them. All that matters is what YOU do with the information. What I am doing is getting a drink, so you can either follow me or do whatever you want." He informed me as he tried walking away again.

I continued to argue with him for the next few minutes, but nothing penetrated that skull of his. Though if he told the story, I'm sure he would say the same thing about me because he kept trying to tell me the same thing over and over again yet was too dumb to realize it. Instead, I was more focused on understanding the story. I was worried about his safety despite how he navigated the city better than me.

After what felt like an hour, though I'm sure the actual time was much shorter, we arrived at some hole-in-the-wall pub. He had let his ears lead him to a brick building likely built in the 20th century that had been maintained well over the years despite the abuse it absorbed. The miraculous appearance of the building was quickly ruined by the smell that poured out of its walls. Stale beer filled the air bringing in barflies that only added to the toxic nature of the air. It was a true shame, given the beauty of the exterior, but I had been in that situation before and couldn't blame the patrons.

Inside the bar, I was reminded of the outer city. It was dark and dingy, the place that hope went to die. The people inside mainly were leopard skin users or survivors. The dark spots never disappear; they only lighten up once the drug has entirely left the system, making recovering addicts easy to spot in a crowd. Don't get it wrong, some had other problems, but the drug was destroying this city like it was destined to. It was a pitiful sight knowing that all of them were on a one-way trip. The drug destroys everything it comes into contact with within the end. These people were just trying to drink that inevitable reality away. Even the recovering addicts had a shortened lifespan based on the research we had found on the drug.

We sat at a pair of bar stools resting at the bar. I started looking for all the exits out of habit while Mark called for the bartender. There was something odd about some of the patrons, but I couldn't put my finger on it. They were different from most of the customers. The look of despair did not drape across them in the same way. Unfortunately, Mark was too loud for me to hold my focus on any one person for long.

"Bartender, I would like two of your cheapest beers!" Mark said as he motioned for the head of the bar. The man strolled over to us, frustrated by the old man's impatience.

"I can do that, but you have to pay upfront. Too many junkies have tried ripping me off." He informed us in a garbled voice. I could see him trying to size both Mark and me up. He seemed ready to turn towards me when Mark pulled a silver necklace from his pocket. The bartender took it from him and began to study it in depth. He placed two bottles with ripped labels in front of us after the silver had been authenticated.

"This necklace will get you a few drinks, especially with my anniversary coming up soon. I'll keep your tab open until its worth is used." The man explained as he pocketed the necklace.

"Thank you, my dear sir. I greatly appreciate it." Mark responded as he handed me a drink. After that, we made our way to one of the few open tables and took our seats.

"So, where did you obtain that piece of jewelry?" I asked, hoping that I would get some form of history or story with it. Blind men tend to have little use for objects of decoration, but his answer was not what I had hoped for.

"Let's just say one of my birds brought it to me. Now I'm going to enjoy my drink, so shut up and listen. Maybe you'll hear something interesting." He commanded as he began working on his drink. It was at that moment that I started to understand what all of this was about. The man's story was one piece of the equation. To truly appreciate the mission, I needed to see what else was going on in the city. I needed to obtain a little more information.

I leaned back in my chair and began to listen to the stories being told around me. I tried to follow each conversation, but people were boring. Most talked about their families, their addiction, or the way the drug was ruining the city. None of which led to any kind of helpful information. That was until I picked up something from one of the groups that struck me as odd.

"The boss isn't going to be happy if those two aren't found." The first stranger said.

"No kidding. Knowing the boss, once he finds out somebody screwed up, they will lose his head if they haven't already. Honestly, I'm just glad I wasn't the one in charge of the prison last night. The one girl has been giving us trouble for months." The second replied as he took a shot of his drink.

"I'll drink to that. Now have you heard any updates?" The first asked in response.

"Rumor has it that they are searching the eastern sectors of the town. I heard that there is a resistance group in that area that would give them shelter." The second replied.

"Not surprised that sector has always been troubled. I wouldn't be surprised if our guys burned everything to the ground. It would be simple to scatter those scumbags and reveal the missing girls." The first chuckled.

"The problem is those girls would die and slow progress for a while. The boss hates that even more, but I guess the other girls would work." The second explained.

"Hm, that sounds interesting, don't you think?" Mark remarked, finishing his beer.

"Quite interesting indeed. Was this the plan all along?" I asked, noticing the beer in front of me was gone.

"Once we start living in the now, we begin to become one with the world around us. Learn how to react to its changes instead of allowing its changes to force our hand." He smiled, completely ignoring my question.

"Well, now that something is interesting going on, let's head east and see if it helps out," I said, beginning to rise from my seat.

"What is this 'we' you are talking about? I am a feeble old man who can't see. This journey is for young men who are punch and kick guys." He told me. He waved the bartender down for another drink as I stood shaking my head.

"But…" I tried to protest before he raised his hand to my mouth.

"That necklace should get me three more drinks, and I am not wasting it, kid. It has been months of dryness out in those woods. Now go before you miss all the action, you little pest." He commanded. I could not figure him out for the life of me. I even started to think he was a tad bit insane, but I was at least beginning to learn not to argue with him. I left the old man at the table and started making my way towards what I assumed would be the east side of town.

I traversed the city, trying to figure out why people lived there at all. Every street corner was littered with addicts and chaos. Josh had spoken of a group called The Family, yet I could see no attempts to control the disarray. Most mobsters I had come in contact with were obsessed with control. Not only would they flood the city with streets, but they should be heavily combing the streets to protect their bosses' interests. I kept my eyes open for the Aster Women that Althea had spoken of. However, the city didn't even seem to have brothels for them to exist within.

The east side of town was even worse than what I had seen up until that point. Buildings were falling apart all around me, but this part of town was where the epidemic started. When the drugs began to spread, it was evident that they tried to abandon the area. Buildings were torn to pieces. All that they in the wake of the chaos was will and a bit of duct tape. A few skeletons still lived in the area, but all of them were on the brink of death. Some of them were probably dead.

The poor skeletons were suffering from the rarest and most painful form of leopard skin withdrawal. If the spots begin to rise, it is a sign that internal bleeding has started and other blockages. It is at this point that the sufferer knows there is no turning back. Death is days away at this point, and for most that I have talked to, death is welcomed. They have hit acceptance at this point.

I may have arrived at the location the men had been talking about but could not find trouble anywhere. I feared that I had missed the excitement along with my chance. That was until I found five men off, let's say, suspicious character. They were dressed in black and gray military fatigues with black bandanas covering the lower half of their faces. None of them carried firearms but were equipped with blades and nightsticks. I assumed that these were the guards I had expected to see throughout the city, or at the very least, they were a poor attempt at a rap group. Now my initial plan was just to observe them as I looked for the women the men had been talking about, but then one of them forced my hand.

The man that was leading them started digging around in his coat until he found a small sphere. Even from my poor positioning, I could tell that it was a homemade incendiary device. The plan was a simple one from what I could deduce. They were going to burn the east side to the ground and draw out their targets or eliminate them in the process.

The original plan I had was calm, rational, and well-thought-out. It lasted 30-seconds once I saw that device. It may not have been enormous, but a well-placed one would start an immense fire with the state of the sector. If they had more, the area would burn quickly. I needed to keep it off the buildings and on the asphalt streets where the fire wouldn't spread.

I crept towards the group, trying to stay in their blind spot. Then once I was within striking distance, I drew my staff and knocked the device from the leader's hand. The device exploded while in the air. As I hoped, the flames that sprouted from it stayed away from the wood and only caught a few of the guards' clothing. This scattered them for a moment. I rolled out to find a solid position for their counter. The group leader was taken aback by my quick action, but unfortunately, his men recovered quickly.

I had assumed that these guards would be like Jack's, untrained thugs. This was a miscalculation on my part. In fact, these men showed signs of actual military training. Everything they did had a purpose and was precise. They were trained to move as a unit instead of individual fighters, making them a challenging obstacle.

Nevertheless, I could hold them off, thanks to my experience in situations like this. I would knock one back with my staff, kick a second, then disrupt the third's footing, and I repeated that over and over again. My advantage was my speed which none of them could compete with. Not only was my body faster, but I could mentally plan out my moves at a rate they could barely process.

There is a fatal flaw to speed, though. It rarely knocks the target out and is energy-consuming, making it challenging to sustain. The armor the men wore protected them enough to drag the battle out, putting me at an extra disadvantage. When that became obvious, the scale tipped in favor of the numbers. I put all my heart and anger into the fight, but eventually, their backup arrived to put me on my knees. I wondered what they would do at this point. Would I be a prisoner or a dead man before the night day was out?

I did not have to wait for the answer. Out of the shadows, a group of individuals came to my aid. They outnumbered the guards, and the rough training of these new fighters evened the fight out.

They used sticks, pipes, and chains for the battle. Which generally is not an effective assortment given each guard's equipment, but the new men made due. I tried to help out my saviors the best I could, but these men were trying to kill each other, and that was a fight I did not want any part of. After about twenty minutes or so, the dust settled, with the fight concluding. Most of my saviors remained while a couple of the guards were left badly injured and running. In the wreckage that was the east side, new bodies filled the streets with blood while the last remaining flames from the fight died out on the concrete, unable to find something to grip on.

During the scuffle, I had hoped that these men were on my side. It hadn't crossed my mind that they had no reason to trust me, which was soon proven. While I was looking at the miniature battlefield, they struck me over the head with a pipe. Just like that, I was out cold and at their mercy.

Chapter 8
Reunion

The next thing I knew, I was in a room being splashed by a bucket of arctic water. I hadn't felt something that cold in many winters. My body was nearly forced into shock. Every muscle constricted, and had the chains not held my arms up, I would have flung into a ball. I've never understood in all the times I've been captured why the water is always that cold. Just for once, I would have liked lukewarm water.

Awakened by the water, my mind tried to reorient itself. At first, I found it nearly impossible as my sight was affected by the cold shiver. As I slowly returned to reality, I was shirtless and hanging in a dark room. A door opened in front of me as a dark figure approached with a click of each step.

"Gentlemen, please let my friend go. He is an ally." The figure ordered. The voice, it froze me more than the water did. It was the voice of a ghost who had died a long time ago. The men released me as she had ordered, and as I fell to my knees, I was still left in silence. "I don't know if you have ever been speechless before, Rob." The ghost chuckled as she grew nearer to the light.

I couldn't believe my ears. Even when they said my name, I thought it was a mistake. Her footsteps grew nearer and nearer. Until at last, my eyes told the same story as my ears. A ghost with a heart-healing smile. I felt my body start to cry as I rose up from my beaten position.

"I know I have been seeing things recently, but you weren't the dead woman I thought I'd be seeing Dani." I smiled with the tears rolling.

I don't know how to accurately describe Dani to someone who hasn't met her in person. What words do you use to describe someone that Da Vinci could not recreate? What do you say about someone that would leave Shakespeare unable to write? What words accurately describe the woman who was the second most important person in your life after your fiancé? Iris was an angel, and Dani was as close as one could be to matching her.

I can describe her outward appearance, yet that feels cheap, given that it is her least astonishing aspect. Her hair was a voluminous onyx color that shined in the light. It looked almost silky and was tied in a ponytail. As I scanned down, my eyes fell upon the milk chocolate eyes of hers. They can draw you in and bring a man down with a single glance. Then there is my favorite part of her complexion, the smile that sparkles like diamonds. That grin balanced innocence, confidence, and comfort perfectly.

I'll keep the rest simple for the sake of decency. Her shoulders were broad and capable of carrying the weight of the world on them. Her chest was not prominent, but her powerful legs and the relatively large caboose more than compensated. The dancer in her was evident in these qualities.

Her physique is easy to describe, but there is so much more to her. She is strong both physically and mentally as there was no challenge she couldn't face. There was a part of me that believed she could face an army all her own. Especially given her brains. She wasn't a top-tier strategist, but her I.Q. sat somewhere near that genius-level though her modesty would never admit it. The most essential part when trying to understand Dani is her heart. There is only one person in this world that I have met that is kinder. Only one person is a better friend than Dani. That was her best friend, my fiancé, Iris. Other than that, no one could comfort quite like she, and I had always been happy to know such an exquisite woman. It had been over ten years to that point. She and Iris were younger than I was when they entered college. Dani soon became like a little sister to me, and then one thing led to another. Eventually, I found myself dating Iris. Life was perfect, if only for the blink of an eye.

"That is the Rob I know." She started, "Unfortunately, I don't have time for cute wit. I need your help. And I apologize for the manner you were brought here." As she finished her sentence, she revealed a pan flute tattoo hidden by her hairline. It would have been invisible if it hadn't been for the ponytail.

"It isn't the first time," I assured her as I rose fully to my feet.

"I don't want to know. Just come with me for now." She commanded. I just nodded my head. Whatever she needed to discuss required privacy, and further conversation in that cell would have been a waste.

As we walked, she explained that the guards did not know who I was and that it wasn't until she was doing her rounds that she discovered the mistake. Her men were trained to take prisoners when possible and ask questions later. It was easier to chain a man-up early than to trust him with no evidence.

Once we reached the new room, and it instantly screamed that it was her quarters. It had been ten years since the War started, yet she held onto a lot of her younger self only with a few additions. She had pictures littered around. Some of her family, her old boyfriend, killed in Despartian's raid, and a photo of Iris and her. Then there was the new life she led that infiltrated the room. Battle plans coupled with the city's layout were scattered across her desk, and weapons hung near the doorway. Lastly, I saw the cross hanging above her bed. A symbol of an institution that I never truly grasped, but something pivotal for her and Iris.

"So Gina told me to find you if I needed help, but it seems that you found me first." I started, trying to break the ice a tad.

"I guess the rumor is true then. You were the catalyst to that mess. I guess I shouldn't be surprised." she replied, walking to the dresser that my belongings rested on.

"No, you shouldn't be, but I am. She called you a commanding officer, you." I stated as she handed me the shirt and staff. As she did that, I could tell that she was noting the scars that covered my chest. A look of judgment I had grown accustomed to given the freak show that was my scarred skin. I dressed and started looking for something to drink.

"I could see how that would shock you. I have grown quite a bit since our last conversation," she answered in a formal tone that I had never heard from her.

At that moment, she let her raven hair fall to her shoulders. This brought my attention to a scar on her left shoulder that ran all the way down her back. My first instinct was to ask her what had happened. I had spent many days in the past trying to help and protect her. Just before I opened my mouth, I was able to stop myself. Even back then, she was constantly reminding me that she didn't need my protection. I knew this, but she meant too much to me to not at least be there if she needed it. Now she was stronger. I could tell by the way she ordered the men around and swaggered around the room. This was not the girl I knew ten years ago. Besides, I have no right digging into someone's past with the way my own back looked. I couldn't even remember where half of the mine originated.

In an attempt to distract me, I started to search the room. I wasn't really looking for anything, just trying to discover the new Dani. I was pleasantly surprised by a bottle of tequila that sat in one of her cabinets. Not something that was her style back in the day, but I could enjoy this new side of her. I pulled the bottle out and poured two glasses. Dani smiled as she watched me prepare the glasses. She helped by grabbing a container with ice.

"A very valid point." I said, handing her a glass in exchange for the ice, "Now, what is it that you need from me." At first, she wanted to reject my offer, but after a little good ole fashioned peer pressure, she took her glass and joined me in the midday drinking, or maybe it was night drinking. I don't know how long I was out for.

"It is ten in the morning, Rob." she clarified at last. There was a moment where I hesitated after hearing the time, but that hesitation didn't last long.

"Okay, then we aren't day drinking. We are just sampling what you have." I chuckled, "Besides, I have seen you do kegs and eggs before, so don't judge the guy who was out cold for drinking in the morning. Stop stalling and tell me what you need."

"To the point today, I see. A bit odd for you, but I guess you have changed too, huh?" She remarked, taking a drink from her own glass. She leaned against a table in the corner and waited for my answer.

"In ways, I can't even describe," I answered, lowering my voice.

"Well, anyway, I'm looking for help. This city has been unjustly conquered by a vicious group known as The Family. In response, I have been working to bring them to their knees. Unfortunately, I have had little success up to this point. Recently, my plan was to let myself get captured so that I could infiltrate their facility. Not hard, but when I went for my escape, I couldn't help as many people as I wanted. After that failure and what was the near-disaster in the east district, I think it is time to enlist some help." She admitted as we each worked on our glasses. I must admit that I liked this new Dani. When she spoke, there was both a directness and fire that brought power to her words. That or the morning tequila wasn't as easy as it used to be.

"Bringing down evil dictators. Brings me back to my younger days. Now is there a plan?" I asked in an attempt to gain clarification.

"Of course, there is a plan. You're not going to like it, though." She sighed, already anticipating my reaction.

"Great start to your pitch Dani. If that's how you were going to lead things off, you might have wanted to let me reach my second glass." I snickered. I could see that she was trying to find the right words, but nothing was there. At last, she grabbed one of the maps and brought it over to me.

"I need you to deliver me as a prisoner to this compound." She answered, at last, pointing towards a spot in the middle of nowhere. The mere mention of the plan had me pinning my ears back out of anger. Nearly dropping my glass.

"That is an idiotic plan, Dani!" I yelled. I did not want my disinterest in the plan to have a single doubt. I may not have known much about this mob she tried to bring down, but I knew going into a prison run by them a second time would be an unwise decision.

I waited for her response, but she stayed silent. She wanted her following words to bring calm to my soul, knowing that my buy-in was critical to her plan. She walked over to a nearby table and sat at it. She left her drink behind, showing that this was time for business.

"Come sit with me, Rob." She invited in a softer tone than before. She waved me over, and I joined her in leaving my drink behind. It was too early for it, after all.

"I know I'm not going to like what you have to say, but I will entertain it for now," I said. She flashed a small smile, trying to disarm my combative nature, but I was not in the mood for her games. I needed reasons, not just a smile.

"I take it that from your mention of Gina that you grasp that the two of us are part of something bigger, correct?" She asked. I nodded my head and motioned for her to continue. "Good, that should save some time. My job is to create a resistance group in this city and fight back against The Family. A simple plan that I'm sure you are familiar with. I started it about five months ago, and progress has been slow." She started. She took a moment for any questions, which I obliged.

"Why is this city so important to your people?" I asked.

"Rob, you should know as well as anyone that in war it isn't the city. It is about strategy, and right now, this place is important to our enemies. The leopard skin epidemic you've seen consuming the city was a strategic release that has now spread to the surrounding cities. We are interested because this is patient zero and where the drug is created. If we want to stop the spread, it has to be here." She explained. I could sense the desperation in her voice with every word she spoke.

"Okay, and what is being done?" I asked to dig deeper.

"Well, it has been impossible to penetrate the facility where the drug is kept and created. That was until we found out they were capturing women, so I got captured." She paused for a moment. I saw her reach for the scar I had noticed earlier and wince at the memory.

"Looks like the first trip didn't end well," I stated as I watched her rub her shoulder.

"No, it didn't go particularly great, but I did find answers. I discovered why they were taking the girls, how to smuggle out a few, and most importantly, that the method was far too slow. I decided to escape, which led me to a few hours ago when we found you. I knew that if you could get me inside that, you could also help me figure out how to bring the compound down for good." She explained at last. Her plan was flimsy at best. Truthfully, I wasn't sure there was a plan.

"I noticed that you never told me what they are doing to the girls inside the compound nor what the plan is once you're inside." I pointed out as I leaned back in my chair.

"I didn't tell you because you don't want to know," she answered sharply. She made it seem like her avoidance of my questions was my fault.

"Dani, don't act like you are protecting me from the information. You are protecting your interest, knowing I'll say you're an idiot if I know everything!" I yelled again, rising from my chair! I figured that she would stay down, but she grew to hold eye contact with me the whole time. She had always been strong-willed, but this was a backbone that I had never seen before.

"I don't know what I was expecting. You might have been a war hero, but deep down, you will always be the coward I always knew.

I'm going with or without you." She informed me. Her voice was calm, but every vowel had venom laced on it.

"Not if I stop you," I smirked. She did not appreciate my confidence and, in a blink, went to strike me with her left hand. I was shocked but quickly deflected it. She followed that with several more blows that I blocked. Eventually, I wrapped her arm around her own neck and had her in a choke. With zero waves of panic, she placed her foot on the chair and flipped us both, overusing it to push off.

Once on the ground, our flight didn't stop. She went for a few strikes and jumped to her feet first. She tried to sweep my legs as I rose, but it was a move I had seen many times before, allowing me to avoid it. On our feet again, her blows turned into more kicks with the occasional punch mixed in. I was still incomplete defense mode, not wanting to hurt her. My main goal was to turn it into a grapple where I could move without fear of doing damage.

At last, she made a mistake leaving her base weak. I closed quickly, pinning her to the table. I held each arm in mine with her back firmly on the table.

"Yield!" I ordered.

"You first." She grinned, looking down at our feet. I did the same and saw her left leg stationed between mine, ready to kick a particular area. "I know you really love that area of real estate."

"You wouldn't," I said. She just looked at me, and I let go, not wanting to go through that at this point.

"There, maybe you'll stop acting like a big brother that needs to protect me. I have learned how to do that all on my own." She protested with a pant.

"It isn't like that, Dani," I argued, trying to catch my own breath.

"You say that, but it is the same thing every time with you, Rob. You are so afraid of feeling the pain that you put everyone in a crystal casing that you need to guard at all times! We are adults who can handle ourselves!" She explained.

"Maybe if everyone would stop dying or getting mystery scars, I wouldn't have to protect them!" I yelled back.

"Sometimes, I forget how much fear is hidden under that bravado you boast." She claimed, calming down for a moment. I forgot to mention Dani's most irritating trait earlier when I was flaunting her virtues. She has always been willing to call me on my bull, even if it wasn't well-timed. That word fear was now becoming far too familiar when describing me.

"This isn't fear. This is me trying to talk sense into that stupid brain of yours." I replied, offended by her response.

"I...I know you always have the best intention, Rob." She sighed, "But sometimes you can be over the top. You have been a part of so many bad plans that worked. The odds, in this case, are not inconceivable. I just need you to support me this time. I need you to move past that fear for a minute."

"I can't lose you too!" I yelled with tears of frustration. She had no answer as I stood for a moment. I didn't have the right words after that. "I can't lose you again, Dani. I just found you again and the thought of losing my best friend. I don't know if I'm strong enough for that."

As we stood there, I thought of the talks I'd had with Mark in the woods. I thought about my days sitting on the bridge up in Despartian, where I thought about jumping. Miserable, alone, afraid, and not wanting to feel better because I didn't deserve to be alright. I was trying to move past that but seeing the person who knew me better than anyone made me think about it again.

"I'm sorry I wasn't there for her, for you," Dani claimed as she put a hand on my shoulder.

"Had I been there for you before, maybe you would have been there for us." I whimpered out.

"Well, be there for me now, Rob. I can protect myself, but I need you to save people." She smiled. She walked behind me and draped her arms over my shoulders, hugging my neck. I weakened my stance for a moment as I felt her embrace.

"I know it is your mission, but I can tell you love this place. Why?" I asked, trying to understand it all.

"I love them because it is what they deserve. So many people have been robbed of that fundamental desire. If we spread it, maybe we can prevent another disaster like Finis Temporis." She replied, letting go momentarily.

"I used to think that, but I fear that as long as we are here, man is damned to repeat itself," I told her. I once had hope for the betterment of man, but the things I have seen have broken me.

"You have grown cold, Rob. I know that losing Iris hurt, but we can't give up on everyone just because of a few devils that walk among us. I miss the man that used to live every day just to see others smile. There is more to this than just losing Iris." She pointed out.

She was right. It wasn't just the disappointment in her eyes as they slipped into nothingness. It wasn't just about the failure to see John's deception. It was everything leading up to that day. It was how I avoided her after the War. It was sleeping around in a city where we each knew everyone. It was failing her as a lover that was more disastrous than her death.

"There is, but to put it simply, I failed Iris. I let her die, and now I'm not going to let you die as well." I insisted. I could tell by the look in her eye that she didn't believe that that was all I had to say, yet she didn't push. She knew that I wasn't ready to talk about my deeper troubles at that time. Instead, she decided to take my words at face value.

"You didn't fail, Iris Rob. You were beaten by a man that was playing a game you didn't know existed. Now you know, and now you have me. Between the two of us, there is no way that the Family can stop us." She assured me.

"I want to say you are right, Dani, but there is so much going on these days I don't know what to believe anymore," I explained.

"Trust me, I have learned that the hard way with my new position. However, I promise to believe in you if you believe in me at least once." She told me. I still wasn't quite sure but figured that I would at least hear what other details she might have before dismissing all of it.

"How about this? Give me more details about your plan, and I will consider it." I bargained.

It wasn't much assurance. Yet her eyes lit up with those simple words. As her smile grew, she realized that she was penetrating my thick skull of mine. If she worded her subsequent sentences correctly, she knew that she had a chance of pulling off this longshot opportunity. If she was suicidal, at least I could try and prevent a complete disaster. She unfurled the maps and began to break down the details.

The facility that they were using was a few miles outside of the city limits. It was used as a maximum-security prison before the War. Apparently, the Family executed the last few prisoners held within the walls and decided that the 20-foot-high walls made from pure stone would make for an impenetrable fortress. I had broken into more potent complexes, but not with this lack of supplies or men.

Once she was done breaking down the essential details, she started to dig into the finer points. The building was split into four different blocks. The first one was the reception area, where prisoners were inspected and sorted into groups. She still wasn't going to tell me what these groups were, but fighting and pressing the issue any longer would have been pointless. Above the reception, part of the building, are the bedrooms that housed the Family's top members. Then, two towers on either side housed the prison cells and the leopard skin manufacturing labs. Those were the target areas that needed to fall. Then, at last, there was the fourth building that she did not identify. I had to push deeper about it.

"So you have detailed every part of the facility except for this building. Why is that?" I asked. Her eyes avoided mine for a moment as I could see the uncertainty.

"Honestly, I have no idea what is in that part of the facility. They dragged me through every other corner except for that one. It is protected by two large steel doors and several guards." she detailed. I could tell her tone and mannerisms, she was telling the truth, yet it still felt like she was hiding something. She had speculation about the room, but nothing concrete enough to be sure I deduced. At least they weren't substantial enough for her to worry me about them.

"Based on your descriptions and what I can deduce from them. The facility can only be destroyed from the inside or from a complete siege. Given the state of the city, I doubt there are enough bodies for a siege. Which is why you want to go back in, but what is my part in this?" I asked after breaking down the discussion to that point.

"So the plan so far is that you will act as a bounty guard to deliver me to the fortress. I could go on my own or under a guard's control, but if you deliver me, you can talk your way into a position of trust. Using that trust, I need you to explore the facility, looking for weaknesses and key targets. After about eight hours, I will make my escape. I'm going to assume that my old route is being guarded, which will make this a hairier mission. However, I don't want you to help me. Instead, I want you to destroy whatever you can while I run a prison break. If we succeed, the Leopard Skin production will be halted long enough for me to bring a branch of the rebellion to St. Louis for a siege and overthrow of the Family." She insisted with less confidence than I expected. She knew as well as I did that what she proposed was not a plan but a series of goals that led to a larger purpose. There were no details or certainties. She wanted me to join her as I was the only one able to ad-lib enough for this to be a remote success. I wanted to protest immediately but chose the higher ground.

"I don't like it, Dani. This is a foolish plan, but I might help you. First, I want to talk with my traveling companion." I insisted. It was the first time I had thought of Mark since Dani had me captured, but even if he was just an excuse at the time, I did value his input.

"I'm going to assume that the old man who walked in earlier today belongs to you, doesn't he? Welp, he is probably waiting for you out these doors." She said with a wave of her hand.

There was no way, I thought. He couldn't be this good, could he? I rose and opened her doors to see the old man sitting in a chair across from the entrance. I knew he could hear the whole series of conversations, yet he acted surprised when I exited the room.

"Done talking with your girlfriend?" Mark asked. Both Dani's and my own face turned red at his phrasing. Luckily, he couldn't see that, and I could put an end to his absurdly reasonably quickly.

"And it's good to see you aren't belly up at that bar Mark." I chuckled, thinking back to how I last saw him.

"Glad you missed me. Though I can't say the same about you." He replied with the slightest snicker.

Now our banter continued for a good five to ten minutes, but boring you with that would be pointless. Just know that we tried everything to get under each other's skin yet failed at every turn, only getting a laugh in return. Dani wanted to have me take it easy on him due to his blindness. I informed her that he is far thicker-skinned than his appearance suggests. I also mentioned his affinity for hitting me with a stick. She thought I was being dramatic but did not question me any further.

"Well, enough of that you coot I need to talk to you." I finally said, trying to end our attempts at wit that would have been handled better by masters of the silver tongue.

"Not now. I thought of another lesson that I want to teach you. Then we can have your useless conversation." He ordered, grabbing my hand.

"What do you mean by lesson? I thought you were busy being a pain in the ass." I argued as he pulled me away from Dani without a word. I was concerned that she did not try to stop him, but I told her that I was still deciding.

"I was, but then my tab ran out, so I figured you'd be interesting again, you little snot." He laughed. He yanked me down the hallway. Leading me to some small room quite the distance away from Dani's. Where he proceeded to throw me into the darkness.

"Okay, now that you've pulled me away from the girl, what is the plan?" I asked. Mark remained silent as he grabbed a stick from the corner and began to tap it around in an irritating manner. I called at him again, but the man who could hear anything now played deaf. The room was poorly lit, to begin with, when he hit the lights off.

"In our first lesson, I talked about your arrogance and need to be present. Now I want to teach you how to use all of you and about your new strength from complete presence." His voice echoed through the darkness. Without another word, he swept me off my feet, placing me on my back.

"Alright, so what is this lesson?" I groaned while rubbing my head.

"You see, I want you to hit me in the darkness, but the only way to do that is to truly listen." He commanded as he continued to stroll through the room.

The order and task were simple in theory but nearly impossible in practice, given the circumstance. I begged him for a little more instruction but only received blows to my thighs and back for my effort. He wanted me to put the pieces together on my own. My first step was figuring out how he could see so well. I understood that his hearing was beyond top-notch, yet he thought I could do the same.

As he continued to talk through the room, I tried to work through what he could be doing. What sounds existed even in the silence, I pondered? I had to be present. I needed to hear beyond the base sounds. Unfortunately, I was being struck repeatedly as I tried to listen. Strike after strike fell upon my body. They were light but annoying, especially when he continued to bother me about listening as if I wasn't already.

Then out of the nothingness, I heard something that I didn't expect. It was the movement of the air. The vents in the room creaked as the wind passed through them, and as Mark's stick swayed, it cut through the air. It was the faintest of sounds, but it was there. Now I had to track it. I had to separate the slight sound of his stick from the vents and basic air creaks.

I kept my mind focused on that idea as I looked for anything that was distinguishing. Taking several blows in the process. Then, at last, I picked up on something. There was a hitch whenever he drew it back. Before he struck, he pulled the stick around, and it snapped ever so slightly. It wasn't much, but it was all I had. It took me a few tries, but then I was finally able to avoid it.

"Well, for an idiot, you picked that lesson up fairly quickly. Now can you hit me?" He taunted, retreating into the shadows again. I waited for him to strike me, but there was nothing. Not even a slight wave through the air. I thought about staggering around like an idiot with my hands outstretched but thought better of it quickly.

There had to be something out there. I could hear the movements in the room. Hell, I could even find the walls that creaked. Yet, he was standing in utter silence. I started to wonder how he could find me in all of this. I was merely standing, standing, and... breathing. Could that be the answer, I wondered? Could something so minuscule be the key to his abilities? I had to try, so for several minutes.

Nothing. I couldn't track his breath and was out of leads.

"How can I hear when you do nothing?" I shouted in frustration!

"The breath was a good idea. Yet you are still impatient. You are practicing a new skill that will take more time to master regardless of your thoughts. Now pay closer attention this time." he informed me. As soon as he spoke, I knew that he was right on top of me. I reached out yet found nothing. I couldn't even find him when he was that close.

"You are good, old man. I will give you that. Time for round two." I pleaded as I realized that I had given up too quickly. I had rested on my skills too long and had not truly pushed myself in years.

"Take your time. Your stumbling has been far more entertaining than listening to the rabbits...I'll say frolicking together." He answered. This time his voice was farther away. Without a sound, he had distanced himself in mere moments. I smiled at my own incompetence. This time I let my mind go completely quiet. I became immersed at the moment, knowing that it was the only way to hear a sound that didn't exist.

As I fell into a trance-like state, I began to become one with everything. I took deep breaths letting my heart slow down, and my breath came to a near standstill. I let my mind just go from sensation to sensation, trying to hear each one individually and name it. Before I could find him, I needed to listen to the other sounds. The floor, vents, people walking outside the room, and much more I let go in and out with each breath. As I named the sound, I, at last, heard the cue I searched for.

I couldn't believe the momentarily muffled sound of a slight inhale. Not only did I hear him, but I could locate him. He was direct to my right. I lunged a few steps and stopped to listen again. This time I picked up on the sound quicker. He moved slightly, but I was getting closer. I repeated the process over and over again. Each time the process grew easier until, at last, I had cornered him. I grabbed his arm and felt like I was winning.

"I told you that it would take time. A little more practice, and you might just have a shot at pulling this off." He said as he turned on the lights. As soon as I regained my vision, I saw that he had led me all the way to the exit. I thought I was in control, but in reality, he was still in the lead role.

"Was this a lesson or just another game?" I asked. I understand his intentions now, but I was exhausted with games. John was playing with me, and I didn't want to deal with Mark in the same way.

"You seem a bit snippy there. Is there something we need to discuss?" He asked.

"No." I started as I shook my head. "The end of this lesson just reminded me of something John would do. Leading me to his goal while making it feel like my ideas.

"This man has truly damaged your view of life," Mark remarked. I nodded my head at the observation. "This wasn't meant to be a game. It was meant to show you how strong you can be when relying on yourself and using the moment as your greatest strength. The finale was to show that we always find our way out of the darkness when we take a moment to listen."

From there, we took a seat, and he had me recite the tale that Dani had explained to me. At first, I wondered why I was doing it since I knew he could hear from outside the room. Yet, he stayed silent throughout the story, and after I finished, he remained silent to think it through. I hoped that he would have some profound wisdom, yet nothing. He just sat and stared at me. Meanwhile, I had to think about the story myself. Until at last, he spoke:

"Do you care for this girl's safety?" He asked.

"I do," I answered.

"Will she stop if you don't go?" he followed with.

"No," I admitted with a slight bow of my head. I knew where he was going with this, but it wasn't something I wanted to hear.

"Then why are we having a discussion about this? If you go, you could lose her. If you don't go, you certainly will. The odds of avoiding loss are higher if you help her with her plan. Even if it is a stupid one." He told me.

"Why is it that when I have a bad idea, it is just a bad idea, but everyone else is only logical?" I mainly asked rhetorically.

"Because you are an idiot. Now go and help your girlfriend." he laughed, knowing the term would trigger me.

"She isn't my..." I started before he threw his stick at me. I dodged it while he just laughed, knowing his mission was accomplished.

"Doesn't matter, you fool. Find her, take care of the mission, and then we'll move on to our next step." He explained as he started to push me down the hallway.

He had pushed me along until we were in a section of the base with no one. I use the term "base" lightly. Dani's rebels had turned an old bunker from the War, that was little more than a hole, into a hidden fortress. It had been stripped of all tactically relevant material as was often demanded of our forces. However, the foundation allowed Dani to modify it for the newest soldiers.

The bunker was a steel monstrosity built about fifty feet underground based on the dimensions. During the War, I spent a lot of time in bunkers like this one. They were constructed quickly and placed in odd spots to gain tactical advantages. They were designed for quick use and then to be abandoned. However, these rebels had heavily modified it. They remodeled a wing solely for leopard skin rehab. It was unlike anything I had ever seen. Even before the War, rehab centers that were actually treated were rare. Addiction was always treated like evil instead of a disease that people could recover from with some basic human decency. It was admirable but a futile attempt. Nearly all leopard skin addicts died a gruesome death, whether while on the drug or during recovery.

Regardless of the futility of it all, it helped me understand why Dani was so passionate about these people. It was touching to see her care for people that we're fighting so hard to better the world that had given up on itself. Dani was giving these people everything because they had earned the right to have someone fight for them, and I had to wonder if I could hold the same kind of fortitude. I wondered if I was capable of such unselfishness when my eyes were clouded by my pursuit for John. Then I took my walk through the medical wing.

Only a handful of nurses were far outnumbered by the patients they had to care for. It was heart-wrenching as I watched them work. I could see the exhaustion in their eyes as they plunged into the depths. The withdrawal process for the drug was a harrowing experience for the user, and those who tried to care for them had to be saints. As the addicts fell into madness, fought off extreme fever, and attempted to claw through their own skin, these people with little training tried to ease their struggle.

Their methods were kind, but there was little that they could do. The nurses or, more likely, volunteers took shifts as they tried to tend to the different patients. Some sat with those strapped to the beds to prevent the scratching, others spoke to patients trying to stave off the madness, and a few placed wet clothes on those who suffered the worst heat illnesses. I wondered if they were actually helping people this way or just making themselves feel better. I had never heard of anything increasing survival rates, but then again, people so rarely cared. Even before the War, people blamed the addiction on the individual and took the stance that it was their duty to crawl out of the dysfunction.

"Don't look so awestruck. The patients don't like it when people stare at them." A fast-paced voice said from behind me. I looked over my shoulder to see a tall string bean standing far too close to me. When I turned around fully, I saw a pair of eyes that brought joy to the soul despite eternal tiredness that strained my own. His caramel eyes with the bags were accented by the fair sepia brown complexion. As I looked closer, I noticed that he was more than just a string bean. His clothing hid a lean muscular build that helped him command respect. He reached out his hand and flashed a smile that shined brighter than any movie star.

"Your facility?" I asked, meeting his hand with my own and a smile that tip-toed pathetic.

"Yes, and no. My idea Akia's resources and gumption." He smiled. I wondered who Akia was for a moment, but I assumed that Dani had taken on a false name once she joined the rebels. I only wished she could have mentioned it in all the details she had laid out to me.

"Well, regardless of who's it is, it is quite spectacular. Not just to build a rehab facility like this, but to fill it with such kindness and compassion is rare. Had we only been able to fill the world with people like your nurses and volunteers, we would have avoided that disaster." I explained as he walked me through the facility.

"The way you speak it reminds me of Akia and her former husband." He replied. The Dani I knew was far too heartbroken to look at a man for months after her boyfriend's death. If there had been such a man to break through the wall she erected, I had to know more.

"Former husband, you say?" I asked, looking for more details with the raise of my brow. I thought I knew Dani, but maybe the years had truly changed her. It had been obvious to her that I had changed, so why would I doubt things had happened to her as well. Yet, a name change and new husband is more than turning into an alcoholic. It is a complete character shift.

"You heard me correctly, but if she didn't feel the need to tell you about him, then neither do I. That sort of subject can be quite sore. Outside of that, I will answer any question you have." He informed me. Interestingly, he was so hesitant to tell me about Dani's apparent ex-husband, which I deduced to mean that he was no longer of this world. With that being the clear case, I figured that learning more about the stranger and his lab was more prudent.

"I can appreciate that type of loyalty, and the Akia I knew before the War would as well, so I'm sure she still does. That is why I'll respect your decision. Even though I didn't ask for your name yet." I stated with a bit of shame on my face. I would have introduced myself, but it was clear that he knew who I was in all this and didn't feel like wasting our time.

"Thank you for respecting that, Mr. Doran. And you are right; we never shared names. I've just grown accustomed to people knowing mine, so I rarely speak it. I am Evan Emem, the head doctor of this facility." He clarified at last as he led me through it.

"May I ask where you got the idea for this facility?" I questioned while we descended deeper into the rehab center. I was pretty anxious to see what it was all about. I needed to know if this fight was truly worth having. Though Mark had pointed me in the direction, I still needed to feel the purpose of the suicide mission Dani proposed.

"As you can imagine, being a man of color before and during the War was quite a challenge. Injustice flourished with people like me being treated less than human. The fullest extent of this was felt in the drug war that ravaged my communities. I wanted to make a change when I began my studies. Little did I know that during the War, I would serve with an Arab doctor by the name of Rafal Hakim that shared many of my ideals. We often spoke, dreaming of a facility like this where people have treated as human no matter the circumstance, with the central focus being love." Evan explained as he peeked into each room that we passed.

Every time he did, a volunteer flashed a smile back and showed parental affection towards their patients. It wasn't an exact science, nor were they trained. It was just groups of people sharing the one thing that connects all life, love. In some rooms, he would join the nurse and patient, leaving me at the doorway. I was convinced that he would be leading countries or corporations in the days before the War with the way he worked a room.

"Did Hakim teach you your bedside manner as well?" I asked. That name Hakim rang a bell somewhere deep in my memory, but it would not be answered until months had progressed.

"No, that is something I picked up on my own when I figured out the ultimate goal." He replied, pausing at the end.

"The ultimate goal," I repeated, filling the void he left with his abrupt stop in thought.

"Yes, the ultimate goal. You may refer to it as the meaning of life, but I prefer the goal rather than coining it as meaning. You see, I discovered during that vicious War that time is precious and time with people is an even scarcer commodity. I discovered how separated we had become through technology and the pursuit of stuff. So I found that the only real, meaningful way to live was to be here with the people in their present form. We too often live either fearing the past or the future. In doing so, we could never be happy." He told me.

"Living in the present, that is something I have been told a lot about recently, but what do you mean by 'their present form?" I asked.

"Let's take two examples." He started, pausing against a wall to prepare his speech, "First, we have a date. She is perfect in every way, and there is a spark between you two. Yet you know little of her when she tells you that she was a prostitute who had been with a hundred men. Many men have run from this scenario. However, her past is not who she is. The woman she is now is perfect for you, and that is the woman that deserves your love. If you get past the first trap of her past, you then start to question her future. Can she stay faithful? Does it matter? The question will only cause tension and drive her away as you punish her and yourself for something that had never happened. Instead, you must live with the current version of her.

"Second, let's take an ex-inmate who was shot by mistake. He spent years in prison for assault. When he was released, he got a job, a family, and a new life altogether. Life was perfect until he was shot, reaching for his I.D. The officer thought it was a gun during a traffic stop sign he blew out of anger. He had not done anything wrong in over ten years outside of one speeding ticket, yet some will justify the death as he had been a criminal. Does that matter? He had done his time. The eighteen-year-old version of him made a mistake that he paid for. When he was shot, he was more productive for society at twenty-eight than most. He was even going to become a lawyer as soon as he could. Should he have been given a free pass for what could become? No, it is far too uncertain. Should he have been killed for his past? No, because that was not him. He had flaws like all of us, and the only man you are dealing with is the angry man who blew a stop sign, not the criminal or the lawyer, just an average Joe." He told me. Though the second example sounded far more personal to him than the first.

It was an exciting thought, yet I felt like something was missing. His view was for the idealist. There had to be more. Living with someone in the present sounds excellent when you meet a stranger, but what about people you know? What about people like John, who had killed and done the worst deeds imaginable? I wanted to ask him about this, yet this simple ideal seemed to be pushing him forward through the darkest days of today. I could not bring myself to darken his dreams.

"That is quite a thought, and I'll have to think long about it," I told him, not hinting at my other thoughts. I wanted his ideal world to be actual, but there is much more complexity to life.

"It is quite a different take, and I can imagine you'll need time on it, but back to this place. You see, that mentality is what I focus on around here. When a new patient comes in, we do not care what brought them to this point, nor do we care what they will become. All we see is a person in pain that needs help." He explained.

"Noble," I said.

"Noble, yes. Easy or successful, not always. St. Louis had always been my home, and I hoped that I could help my city. Unfortunately, the Family had a firm grasp, and I didn't have the resources to stop people from dying in the streets. Though I did my best, my hopes were fading. I nearly gave up." He explained. At last, he opened the door to a room where ten healthy young folks stood. They each had hope in their eyes, and all that was left were faded marks that signified the leopard dots.

"You were going to give up before Akia arrived," I stated, acknowledging what he was ready to say.

"Correct." He replied.

"What exactly did she do for you?" I asked this time.

"When Akia arrived, it was just her and her husband. They had this map that led to this base, and soon after, she brought in some reinforcements to protect our operation." He explained.

"Quite the stroke of luck," I said, wondering if she had always intended to help them or if that initial arrival was just a scouting mission.

"I don't think luck had anything to do with it, but these people need hope, so I always tell them that she was an angel sent by God." He remarked as he smiled at some of his patients. Each one lit up when they saw those teeth shining. These people loved him.

"If it wasn't luck, what was it then?" I asked, knowing that he was probably correct.

"A map to a base and armed forces was too convenient. I think whoever she works for needs this city, and we had the misfortune of being caught in the middle. But regardless, she had kept us safe for a year now. And in the last year, she stopped our men from rushing into a foolish rebellion, as well as helped me achieve my dream." He asserted while shaking the hands of some of the patients that were recovered.

I looked around the room at those who were recovered and couldn't believe my eyes. I had never seen so many of them walking and acting normal at once. I wondered how successful this operation actually was. "So, what are their chances with you?"

"Normally, the survival rate of leopard skin addicts is around 10% once they enter withdrawal. About 60% would return to the drug, and the other 30% died or found their minds toasted. However, my treatment plan has that survival rate up to about 35%." He informed me.

"That is quite a remarkable feat given the fact that the drug sacrificed future life for present power," I commented as I looked at the addicts in recovery.

"It has been a difficult task, but every life saved is worth all the sacrifices we make." He boasted with a puffed-out chest.

"Honorable, but a bit foolish if you ask me," I said.

"Well, good thing we didn't ask you for your opinion." Evan retorted. He led me back out of the room to an open corridor that looked over the rest of the bunker. Though the rehab facility and the rest of the medical facilities made up most of the bunker, there were still some key features. The quarters were small, but they had enough room for beds and a scrap-filled kitchen. The training room was a little more than a room with some straw dummies and sweat-covered walls.

"You're right you didn't ask, but I must wonder what happened during the War to make this your dream?" I asked, looking over the ledge.

"As I said, I was a doctor in training when the War broke out. Specifically, I was studying to be a vascular surgeon who was at the top of my class. Not something easy for a man of my skin. My life was good until those pigs, calling themselves the Reverters, came for me. I was successful and outspoken, which was their ideal target. I was fortunate that Unity was nearby with doctor Hakim who saved my life. From there, I fought to protect those that saved my life, especially from the chemical warfare used against this city." He explained. There were a few more details he told me, but none that I would feel alright sharing. Nor are they details that will shed any more clarity on his character. Just know that he lost much in the War.

"You are a fool, but sometimes the world needs its fools to give the rest of us hope," I mumbled. He chuckled at my honest assessment.

"So, does that mean you are going to help me and be a fool as well?" Dani asked from behind us. Her voice shocked both of us as her silent approach hid her well. This time she had her hair in a mess and a set of ragged clothes on her body. She was ready to be a prisoner regardless of my answer.

"Akia," Evan said before I could speak.

"I guess it does." I smiled. Though she wouldn't admit it, I could feel her excitement.

"Good to hear. Now, Evan, you are in charge while I'm gone, and if neither Rob nor I am back within the timeframe, I gave you, execute plan ignis." She instructed, removing a black robe from a pack she was carrying.

Without another word, she led me to a spot just outside of the city. Two horses were fully packed and ready for a long journey. Outside she slipped a note to Evan and shooed him away. Leaving just the two of us. She explained the last details. Handed me the key and handcuffs for when we neared the facility. I still had my reservations, but the only person who can help a fool some days is a fool. I just happened to fit that bill expertly.

Chapter 9
Stronghold

We began our ride across the plains. A silent ride for the first few miles, but my mind began to wander. My conversation with Evan had raised so many questions that I wanted answers to before we each risked our lives fighting the Family. I had to know what had changed in Dani.

"So Dani, or should I say Akia, what have I missed over the years?" I asked. As I looked at her on horseback, I could see her body tense when I brought up her new name. She didn't want to talk about it but knew that our ride would be too long for her just to talk around my questions the whole time.

"I should have known Evan would open his big mouth, so what do you want to know?" She asked grudgingly.

"How about we just start from where I last heard you were," I suggested.

"And where is that, so I have a starting point?" She asked. I knew that I had already pushed her too far, which was odd because she and I had never kept secrets. She was the first to know about my crush on Iris. Also, the first one, I asked about the proposal and then everything in between. Conversely, she had confessed all her moments of vulnerability to me through the difficult days.

"The last thing that I had heard, you were in a battle somewhere in West Cambodia. An ugly battle by every standard and one that was considered a great failure. The records showed that you were considered M.I.A. and presumed dead." I told her, thinking back to one of the darkest days of my life. Even as I spoke the words, I could feel the knives digging into my soul. I had listened to the reports and never looked for my best friend. Regret is not a word I use lightly, but yeah, I made a mistake that day.

"Missing in action and not a single person gave a damn. Isn't that something? All the people I loved that fought in the War, but now a single person came for me." She scolded with her voice rising. Though she refused to look at me, I could hear the pain in her voice.

I wanted to make excuses. I wanted to give reasons why I failed her the way I did. The War was at its peak, and the drug race was just starting. Leopard skin was just entering our vocabulary, and as one can imagine, something like that takes priority. My team was tasked with hunting down labs to destroy them forever. If any of the drugs entered the War, it would have been a disaster. It would have changed the entire dynamic. I needed to be behind enemy lines to maintain any hope that the War would end quickly. I wanted to list all my excuses, yet that is all they were.

She was well aware of the fact that excuses had never stopped me before. During the ransacking of Despartian, I rushed back to the city as quickly as I could. I broke rank once we had captured Minneapolis despite it being my plan to capture the city at the cost of my home. Yet, when I received the message about Dani's disappearance, I did nothing. I had changed by that point. I had started to become the man I feared. I had started down my path to becoming the monster John wanted me to be.

I will not bore you with all the details, but I still remember the day vividly. Not because it was anything memorable. No, it was pretty regular. After three days of destroying a small lab in the Vietnamese jungles, my team returned to our ally's base. I was handed a letter. I figured it was from Iris as she was the only one that was given full access. That was the only one except for Dani's commanding officers. When she entered the front, I had made a deal to have him keep in contact at all times. The sun was shining, and birds frolicking in the sky. The others at the camp were celebrating, yet I stood with a letter that felt like an obituary.

If I am being honest, I could have left. I could have gone looking for her. I had discussed things with Gene, and given my reputation, he was entirely behind me. Even after our next orders came in, he still gave me permission to leave. Yet, I didn't. I sat on the fence about it until John started talking in my ear. He spoke about probability and chance and what it meant to be a soldier. Most importantly, he asked how many lives I would sacrifice chasing down what was most likely a corpse.

I gave up on her because I was no longer her friend at that point. We were both just soldiers. I was just the perfect soldier that would do anything to win the War. I accepted her fate too quickly. That decision cost me my last bits of humanity. I shut down my emotions at that point and fell into a haze that I would only escape a few times before the rise of the Eye.

Looking at it now, I wondered how much John had planned out. I don't think he planned this part, but I think he wanted me to lose that part of me. He always talked about making me more like him. I believe that talking me into abandoning Dani was his way of doing it. I spoke about her and Iris endlessly. He knew she was one of my weaknesses.

"I gave up on you," I whispered. I wasn't sure what she wanted to hear, but I needed to say something before I fell into the trap of self-pity.

"You did, but apologies are pointless, Rob. We cannot change the past." She explained. I said nothing. I merely let my head fall to my chest in recognition of my mistake.

"You are right, we can't change it, but that doesn't mean I can't apologize for my mistake," I told her, knowing there were no words that would make things right.

"I do appreciate you trying." She sighed, unsure herself what else there was to say.

"So after I left you, what happened?" I asked.

"Let me take it one step back. I was severely injured during the battle, and each side thought I was dead when I was bleeding out. As I lay in the jungle mud, I started praying that at least the enemy would find me and finish it. I was not that lucky. The battle dragged on for a few hours while I writhed in pain until one of the sides was forced to retreat miles away. It was at that time some local rebels found me and dragged me away."

"I didn't realize it, but being near death saved my mind and body. The rebels wanted to use me as male soldiers do at times. Still, the doctor needed me to recover for his experiments. He thought that if they had their way, I would have given up. A very accurate assumption."

"So I was imprisoned in a little hut with a group of other captives. Some were allies, some were our enemies, and others were just unlucky civilians. While I recovered, the doctor experimented on the other captives. He was trying to make a drug himself to protect the community from the War. Once I discovered his intention, I thought

I could persuade him to allow me to be a mercenary, but he didn't trust me. Do you know why he didn't trust me?" she asked semi-rhetorically.

"No," I replied.

"He didn't trust me because he wanted to protect his village from us as much as all the other sides. I became a soldier to protect those who couldn't help themselves. I transferred to the Asian front to liberate as that was the message we drove home, yet it was a lie. We were just concerned with winning at any price. Even if it meant burning down villages that were just trying to feed themselves." She preached. When she said that, I thought of Pon's home that my team burned to the ground with children inside to flush out the enemy. She was right. We didn't care about collateral damage.

"You can't take the blame for the mistakes our superiors made," I argued.

"Are we still talking about me?" she snapped back, catching my weak choice of words.

"Does it matter? I have lived with the regret my superiors have, and it has been years of Hell. There is no reason for us to live that way eternally," I explained. I was trying to hold a conversation with her, and the voice in my head again. Not the scenario I wanted.

"I don't regret the things I did. My only regret is not realizing that I could have stopped at any time. They would have called it deserting, but is that not better than deserting your soul in some jungle in the middle of nowhere." She responded with a softer tone than she had held up until that point. I could tell that one was directed towards me. However, it would have been far more poignant a couple of years ago.

"Let's get back to your story," I suggested riding a little bit faster so that she couldn't look at my face.

"I never stopped telling my story, but I will recenter it for you. As I sat waiting to become the next experiment, I made a promise to myself and God. If I were freed that day, I would devote myself to truly fighting for the helpless. I would not take commands that I did not have a say in. I would never follow blindly again. Instead, I would look for true paths to freedom. Like divine intervention, Pan arrived that day. Without a shot being fired, he had me released and the farmers armed to protect themselves. He also left them an officer to train them and fortify defenses." She informed me as she caught back up.

"I take it that is where the idea for the tattoo came from," I observed.

"Yes, it is. Pan is the shepherd of peace. He knew that the War would leave ripples that could end humanity permanently. Hence, he created his herd to help humanity find peace. For him fighting is just a means to him, and because of this, he never glorifies combat. He is different and lets each commander figure out how they will accomplish peace in each territory." She explained with a smile that I didn't expect to see again for some time. Just echoing his name and purpose had revitalized her. It had given her something that even my failures could not dampen.

"So, Pan is the man in charge of these rebels that I have heard so much about?" I said in return. Before I had finished, I could tell my words offended her as the new smile turned to a blank face again.

"We aren't just some band of rebels. What Pan did was organize a secret army that was spread throughout the world! This army is capable of lashing out against those who promote chaos, prey on the weak, or try to promote tyranny!" She exclaimed. The way she spoke was different. I wanted to ask her if this army was secretly a cult. It made me wonder how that girl I knew from over ten years ago could become this. Then again, confinement and reflecting on one's purpose in life does things to the mind.

"Fine, you are an organized army," I admitted to calm her down a tad. "Now that we have that clarified, how does the name change and husband sort into this mess? I figured that you'd never love again after your loss."

"The name is merely a cover given to me by Pan. It means firstborn and is reserved for me as his highest-ranking female. I use it with those that do not need to know the full truth. My supposed husband was my main aide for this mission. Even someone in my position is not supposed to travel alone, and a fake husband is a perfect cover. Unfortunately, he closed in on one of the Family members too quickly and was punished by crucifixion. They paraded him through the streets to set a vicious example." She explained. I could feel the guilt she had over his death.

"I'm sorry," I told her, pulling my horse alongside her.

"For what?" she asked, lifting her head again.

"I was too slow," I informed her in an attempt to shoulder some of the burdens.

"You may act differently, but deep down, you really haven't changed, Rob."

"Not the general consensus, but please explain," I suggested, a bit confused by what she meant.

"I mean, you may sleep around and get into stupid fights, but it is for the same reason you would annoy people to death in your attempts to be helpful." She explained with a slight grin growing across her face. The look and speech made it seem like she knew something that no one else knew.

"Are you going to tell me what this mythical deeper motivation is?"

"You feel unwanted." She said with a straight face. I was going to protest until she continued, "You think that you have to be the best soldier, the greatest lover, the one who can shoulder the world's problems. All because it is only then that you think people need you. It is only then that you think they'll want you and, in turn, love you. When we already love you."

Her words struck a deep chord that I didn't know existed, and I didn't have an answer for her at the time. She had not seen me in years, yet it felt like she was dissecting my deepest feelings. It felt like we had never been out of communication and that she knew me better than I knew me. I wished Mark would have been there for another lesson. Since he wasn't, I did the mature thing...I ignored her comment and sped up my horse. She didn't want to talk about her life any more profound, and I didn't want to take an inner look at myself, so the remainder of the ride was mostly sat in silence.

That was until she suggested we stop for lunch. I agreed to dismount with her and snack. Once off the horse, I found that I was walking a bit bowlegged. It was quite the sight, and my ass was on fire from the long ride. Little did I know that the little excursion was a trap to convince me to talk. "So now that you heard my story, why don't we dig into yours. I promise that I won't try to analyze you any further."

I didn't believe that last sentence one bit, but it was only fair. I forced her to talk about a life-altering moment. Plus, I was the one that had abandoned her on those battlefields years ago. The least I could do was tell her about what had happened after that day.

"My story is a simple one: war, drunk shenanigans, serial killer, dead wife, and now I travel with a cranky blind old man," I replied with as little detail as possible.

"But why are you here? The Iris, we both, know would never want you wasting your life chasing her killer down... She would tell you to go find something new and let revenge die." Dani pleaded as she leaned against the nearest tree. There was truth in her words yet ignorance. She only had half the story, and it showed. I felt like she was downplaying the trauma to a humiliating extent.

"I can't let revenge die! If I do that, there is no justice, and if there is no justice, I don't think I can be happy again."

"Why?" She asked with a concern written across her face.

"Because if she had loved another man, she would be alive right now." I tried to explain.

"Don't you dare say that again. Iris loved you. You made her happier than anyone had before. Now I might not have been there, but I promise you she was happier to die in love with you than to live miserable with anyone else," she lectured.

"But that's the point. She died all because of some game."

"And you can't kill yourself over it. To do that would be to ignore and forget her feelings for you."

"But she should be alive, Dani."

"And so should millions of others, but like you said, we can't carry the burdens of others."

"You're twisting my words."

"Am I? I think those were your words." I wanted to respond. I wanted to yell, but I knew I wasn't angry with her. I was still in turmoil over my decisions. Both Mark and Dani made me look inward and face the demons that I thought were simple enemies to fight. It wasn't something that I was prepared for, but I had to face it to truly honor Iris. I took a breath to calm back down.

"When did you get so wise," I asked?

"Well, I'm pretty sure that part of that was what you told me after the man I loved was killed." She answered, creeping closer.

"When did I get so wise then?" I chuckled back.

"Beats me. It never really made sense to me either," she laughed, "So what will make you happy?"

"Well, I'll be happy when he is dead," I argued with a grind of my teeth.

"Come on, Rob, we had a breakthrough there. Don't ignore it. You know that revenge doesn't breed happiness. It only creates pain and a feeling of nothingness."

"You may be right if it was any other man besides John, but he has to die."

As soon as I mentioned his name, I could see her mental gears begin to grind. She had heard he had been shot and died, so I had to explain the whole ruse. As I expected, no one else knew that John was the true villain behind what happened in Despartian. I dove into the dark details of how Trisha lured me into a trap and how I had been paralyzed while Iris died just out of my reach. While I told her the whole story, I could feel my chest tighten. As I reached the last details about Iris, I nearly collapsed. Every time I uttered her name, my body began to convulse. It was like I was reliving the paralysis again.

I had to pause after the story to regain my composure. Dani tried to comfort me, but no amount of kind words or hand-holding could help me. Eventually, I returned to normal, but it delayed our process longer than I want to admit. Once I had recovered, we began talking about John.

"This is dire news, Rob. Pan and I were working under the assumption that our biggest target was out of the way. We thought things were going to be simpler." She groaned, finally grasping the severity of the situation.

"What is Pan's part in this?"

"I guess we should start with what you know."

"Well, I know that John is the head of Ascension and everything that is connected with it. He was behind a weapons factory in Illinois. And most importantly, he is the biggest dickhead that you'll ever meet." Dani rolled her eyes at the last comment but chose to move past it.

"That is a good start, but there is a lot more to it. The weapons factory is only the tip of the iceberg. Any town that has a dictator-like setup, including this one, was supplied and backed by Ascension. They are like a virus that spreads from one area to the next, infecting the world and shaping it in his image."

"And if Ascension is behind it, then John is the virus's manufacturer." I figured as my mind twisted around over the thought.

"Yes, and we thought that if he was dead that we could get ahead of things and eradicate their influence. In reality, we were lulled to sleep."

"But once again, what is Pan's part?"

"Simple if Ascension is the disease. Pan's forces are the cure that free cities from their grip and destroy whatever method they used to control the area." She explained. Though her words were news to me, I was not surprised by the tale. I knew John was working multiple angles at all times, but now I wondered what his main goal in all of this was? If he really wanted the world, he wouldn't have brought me into the fold, so where would I really fit into all of this? There wasn't anything I could contribute to a man who had the world in a vice grip.

"I guess I shouldn't be surprised that he is behind this city's demise, especially after your friend Gina and I took down their weapons factory.".

"This is troubling news, but we need to take care of this city first. Then worry about John. Can you focus?"

"More so now that I know about their connection to Joh." Though keeping her safe was still my number one priority, John just made this a more compelling case. Unfortunately, I needed to tell Mark he was onto something with the whole being in the present thing.

"Good, let's ride then," she ordered! I was starting to like this confident new Dani.

The ride wasn't much past our resting spot, yet it was far longer than my ass wanted to sit. Once we arrived at a location just a mile away from the facility, we tied up the horses. There were a few trees to hide us as I changed into the robe she had for me. I hid my staff, and she put her hand in the first cuff. Then turned around to have me place her in the other one.

"You know this reminds me of a lovely Valentine's night just after the War ended." I smiled, securing the cuff.

"I don't want to hear about your affairs away from Iris." She told me, turning around.

"Who said I wasn't talking about a night with her," I chuckled. Her lips puckered a bit as she shook her head at my comments.

"Anyways, don't forget the plan. You are under the clock, which means no going rogue." She reminded with a look that would kill a lesser man.

"Funny, I was just thinking the same thing. Hahaha." She did not find my comment as funny as I did. Instead, she leaned back for a moment and placed a kiss on my cheek.

"Thank you." She whispered as we began our march towards the facility.

"Wait until we are sitting next to your bed with a glass of tequila before you begin thanking me," I whispered back.

We started our stroll, and my mind just started to wander. The walls grew more prominent as I thought of everything that could go wrong once we were close enough. I imagined bullets raining down on us like a late spring dousing. Their men would outnumber us and would cut us down before we could act.

All I could see was death. All I could see was us walking with Iris again. At least I wouldn't be alone, but if we died... I choked up at the thought, and my muscles grew rigid. I closed my eyes to find the moment as Mark had suggested, but the first thing I saw was the fleeting light in Iris' eyes. It was the same as before Mark had started, which irritated me further.

Dani must have felt my tension as she reached back with her handcuffed hands and squeezed mine. When her hand made contact, I was awakened from my darkness. I saw her in front of me and the slight shake that plagued her own walk. I held her hand tight before letting it go, just to reassure her that I would be there no matter what.

The walls above us were littered with armed men all attentive to our moves. However, there was only one that stood at the gate itself. I approached him with Dani now in tow. I wanted her behind me in case things went south.

"Stop strangers! Name yourself and your business," the guard shouted! His hand hovered over his weapon but let the men above him do most of the intimidating.

"My name is unimportant to fools like you, and I am bringing you back your prisoner!" I shouted back as I tried to deepen my voice into something more intimidating. Dani nearly started to laugh at the attempt, so I dropped that act quickly.

"Well, if your name isn't important, I guess I can just take the prisoner inside." He replied, stepping towards us.

"I would let you, but you already lost her once, so I think it would be best if I handled the transfer," I smirked, refusing to react to his advances.

"Oh, aren't we a smart one. Guess we'll have to take her from you. The boss doesn't like strangers." It was when he said 'we' that I noticed the second guard in the shadows. He slowly crept from his shadowy corner. I chose not to respond to this proclamation, hoping that my silence would goad him a bit more. As I figured, their next move was to draw their weapons to intimidate me.

"You may want to recheck your list. I'd be under the 'let them in if you like your life' category." I responded with a devilish grin growing. My taunt worked as the first man lunged within my reach. Usually, I would have just put them on their backs before they could blink, but I had to improvise for this fight. Not only did I need to beat them, but I had to maintain my grip on Dani, so it didn't look like she was there of her own will.

The first move was to back off for a moment so that the guards and Dani were within a single movement of one another. Once they were, I kicked the guard's knee and turned Dani around. I used her arms and chains to choke the guard. Throwing her arms around his neck and crisscrossed her arms to tighten the chain. It wasn't the most comfortable position to put her in, and her eyes told the whole story. While this happened, the second man stood in a bit of shock.

"So, do you want to make the same mistake, or will you let us in?" I asked as the first stopped kicking. The guards on the wall did not move as they were ordered only to act on command. The second man was far less cantankerous. All it took was a slightly murderous tone and the eyes of a monster to scare him into being a good boy. I'm not proud to admit that my impression might have been a bit too convincing as the man's pants seemed a bit...damp.

I had hoped that once we were inside that things would be easy for a few minutes. It wasn't, but it never hurts to hope that life will work out at least once. The atrium he led us into was filled quickly with guards that had far dryer pants.

To be precise, I believe about fifteen guards were surrounding us in that cement silo within seconds of the door opening. Each made had some form of melee weapon, mostly clubs or knives. Thankfully no one had a gun at that point. I started to create a strategy if things went poorly, as I knew that one on fifteen is not an ideal circumstance. The saving grace was that none of them looked sure of their conviction. Each one had at least a slight shake in their boots. Unfortunately, there was a glaring issue in every scenario. Dani was still in cuffs. I couldn't help her and fight at the same time. I needed her plan to work.

I grew tenser as each man began to approach us. They were circling us like a group of lionesses stalking their prey. This put heavy pressure on my shaky acting abilities. I needed to act like a selfish bounty hunter while walking the boundary of still being me. Convincing them, I was just in it for me while keeping Dani safe for the moment would push my limits if we fought.

The men had circled about as close as I was comfortable with when they all stopped. Not a word or sound was made yet. They could all feel the presence of the man I finally saw. He was a tall, sleek man dressed in a violet button-up shirt and black dress pants. His skin was glazed like an actor paid to look his best despite a pale complexion.

Chapter 10
Riccardo De Luca

I watched him descend the spiral staircase, unsure if he ever touched the ground. He held onto the railing with one hand while he passed his other hand's gangly fingers through his jet-black hair. He approached with a meticulous grace that reminded me of a jaguar strolling across the land. Despite the thinness of his hands, his grace was matched by a youthful strength that would make most men his age jealous. Despite the elegance, he mostly looked and moved like a spoiled brat that never worried a day in his life. He scanned up and down a few times, removing a coin from his pocket while he looked. He passed the coin between his fingers with a clunk every time it passed over the gold rings decorating his hands.

"Knocking out one guard and intimidating another while a plethora of guards had you in their crossfire, just to enter my stronghold. That is either the bravest, dumbest or most dedicated act I've ever seen. The former and latter are highly respectable, but I am often met by the burden of the middle one. So, which did you commit?" He asked with a confident sneer in his voice. His tone was eloquent, with emphasis placed on odd syllables. I intrigued him, and in truth, he was something himself. I let him pass the coin between his knuckles twice more before answering.

"That is for you to decide."

"Is it? What makes you say that?"

"What would you say about a deer that crosses a busy road?"

"Hm, I'd say it depends on whether or not it gets hit...I like you." With that, he paced for another moment looking at me and my cargo. I waited until his eyes stopped moving before I spoke again.

"So are you the end of the line or just another loud-mouth between me and payment?" I asked, trying to match his arrogance with my own flare. I clearly hit a nerve as he stopped fiddling with the coin.

"Liked you...let me rephrase my comment, you plebeian." He hissed this time around. He tried to act dignified, but I could tell he was what I thought. A brat that was given far too much control.

"Jury is still out on you. So can I talk business with you, or do I have to go through you?" I replied back, trying to ignore his insult at the end.

"A big mouth, but given your prize, I'll tell you that my father is still the boss. However, people like you can talk business with me."

"And who are you?"

"Riccardo De Luca, the heir to this family and the man who is ready to hang you by your family jewels." He threatened with a step closer. This brought his men in closer as well.

"Well, Ricky, let's cut to the chase. I dragged her a long way here and want a fair price. Otherwise, I'll go talk to daddy." I mocked. That one may have crossed the line as his smile grew wide while Dani's eyes filled with fear.

"At this rate, fair will mean you walk out alive." He explained, gliding towards Dani.

"Better men than you have made a very similar threat," I responded, trying to get the attention back on me, but it didn't work as he grew closer.

"I assure you there is not a better man." He replied in a pompous tone as he wrapped his hand around her neck. At first, I thought he would just choke her a bit, but the stick I had seen lifted her off the ground. I was shocked by the display of strength. Knowing what I did about leopard skin, I feared that he had used it in its original form. Once my fear of the drug subsided, my eyes turned towards Dani.

Watching her struggle, I wanted to lash out and bring him down. Dani's eyes called me off, stopping me before I could act. We couldn't risk the operation now. I had to find a way to make a deal with this man, despite him knowing how to push the right buttons.

"Maybe you are the one who should be careful if you harm my prize," I informed him to explain my hypersensitivity. I figured that he saw my fist tighten and couldn't afford to give him an edge in this.

"How do you know that she is a prize anyway? How do you know that she isn't just some piece of trash?" He asked as he threw her down like the garbage he was talking about.

"Easy, when I found her, she was knocking out several of your so-called guards. Which means she must have some type of importance to you." I told him as I laughed at the others that surrounded us.

"Maybe they were just doing their jobs." He smirked as she coughed to regain her breath.

"Do you just enjoy wasting both our time?"

"You're right. Arguing now seems pointless, so what is your price?" He finally asked as he wiped his hands off on one of the guards.

"How about a job?" I told him, shocking everyone in the room, including myself.

"Hm," he hummed. He took a step back to think about the offer for a moment while Dani used every non-verbal cue she could to yell at me. 'Don't be a hero,' her eyes said over and over again, but she wanted me to improvise, and I was doing the best I could.

"You know it would be a win-win," I added, trying to sway him even though I could read his intentions to accept.

"How is this a win-win proposition?" He asked with his eyebrow lifting.

"Well, on your end, you get a fighter that is 10x any of the other guards you have."

"And what do you gain?"

"I get a place to live and influence that I don't have on my own," I explained, hoping that he wouldn't look any deeper. I hoped that he would just like his end of the bargain.

"We both know that you are trying to blow smoke up my ass, but I'll play along if you can prove that 10x claim." He whistled, and his guards approached me.

Now that Dani was safe from them, I took the opportunity to go all out. I hovered my hand behind me as I waited for them to approach, and then when one was within striking distance, I whipped out the staff. I nearly knocked the closest man's jaw off with the strike. I spun into position as my eyes went on high alert. A few were behind me, but most stayed in front of me. Understanding that I was at a disadvantage, I struck first, going at one behind me as the rest collapsed in on me. I kept my feet moving as I hit each man. A few of them could land blows, but I could move fast enough to keep the impacts minor.

I put a few more of them on the ground when one grabbed me from behind. I dropped down and flung the guard over my back. Launching him into the men in front of me and then I struck at a few more. As the minutes passed, the fight turned sloppy, but I was in firm control. I broke one man's arm and shattered another's leg. I went for weak spots and kept them from moving as a unit. About 10 minutes passed when the last man finally hit the floor.

My breath was heavy, and my knuckles were bruised. Bloodstained both my staff and clothing as I stood in the middle of the fallen men. I heard a slow clap as my eyes finally came to a rest. I turned to Riccardo as he smiled at me.

"So you will take the deal?" I asked.

"After one last thing."

"What more do you need to see?"

"The girl needs to be punished, and I cannot think of anyone better to do it." He explained as he unhooked a whip that rested on his belt. As he handed me the whip, my eyes turned to Dani for a moment. I didn't know if I could do what he was asking. I had been on the receiving end of numerous whippings like this, and just thinking about the pain it would cause, Dani nearly froze me.

"How many?" I asked, barely avoiding the hesitation and hiding my reluctance.

"Fifteen lashes should suffice.

I took the whip from his hands reluctantly. The whip had been used recently as blood was still soaked in, and a piece of skin had attached itself. I could feel my stomach dropping as the guards ripped the back of Dani's shirt. I knew what I had to do and that I couldn't just fake it. If I was not practical, I would fail his test. I looked at her kneeling on the ground, back fully exposed except for a thin bra strap clinging tight to her body. I saw her back decorated with a few scars, precisely one large one that stretched from one shoulder to the next.

I hesitated for a moment while the whip dangled from my hand. That first blow was the toughest for me. I aimed the whip just parallel to her spine. I wanted to avoid the spinal cord and sensitive scar tissue the best I could. Unfortunately, it was still a strike to the back, and no matter how much I softened it, it drew a flinch as she was forced to hunch over. My own soul died a little bit with the blow, but unlike Riccardo, I paused for a moment to focus and to let her brace herself.

I attempted to be as precise as I could be but still found myself missing the mark. I could see it in her shiver, but she was able to maintain composure. While my heart tore at the pain I inflicted, I tried to shake it off and return to my assignment. The next one caught more of her lower back. It was less painful, but it knocked the breath out of her as she fell to her hands for a moment. She was assisted back up by the guards, and I went for the next strike. The blow landed right against her rib cage, and she shrieked. I wanted to avoid the one area at all cost, and I caught it on the fourth blow.

While she cried, Riccardo began to laugh at her pain. I wanted to turn and lash him across the face, but I had come too far. I needed to maintain my composure. Eleven blows, eleven more shrieks to work through. The fifth lash was routine as it can be, but then the sixth crossed her spine. I could see the nerves jump when the whip gripped her skin. This one drew blood. It dripped to the floor, puddling beneath her slowly.

Despite Dani's strength, this was a brutal display. I struck her the seventh time, and blood launched at us. Riccardo grew excited by the sight. The blood dripping seemed to focus him, almost making him stronger. The next three blows were fired rapidly. This reduced her recovery time, but also my ability to do profound damage. He forced me to slow down the last five so that he could enjoy it, and I grinded through each one. I don't remember any of them. Just the aftermath of her nearly passing out on the ground. She was conscious, fighting the pain the best she could. I shook as I handed the whip to Riccardo, who licked the bloody end as he rolled it back up. I was sick.

"I'm impressed, but I realize that I never got your name." He started as he paced away from her broken body.

"You can call me Alaster," I told him. I don't know where the name came from, but it felt right coming off my tongue.

"Disappointing, I was hoping for something cool like Razor, Killer, or John." He smiled. I wondered if he knew more than I thought, but I wouldn't fall for it regardless.

"John is a stupid name," I remarked, nearly laughing at the suggestion.

"You are right about that. I think you are going to fit in around here just fine. Come with me so we can talk specifics." He ordered. As he escorted me down the halls, his guards began to clean up the mess that was Dani. They dragged her off to her cell while he led me around.

"So, what is it that you'd have me do?" I asked as we continued down a hall towards what I assumed was the triangle part of the building I'd seen on the plans. Despite being talkative earlier, he just made awkward small talk that didn't answer my question. I wanted to repeat my question but realized he had his own agenda.

Eventually, after touring most of the triangle-shaped building, he took me to a large set of metal doors with three men standing outside of them. He knocked five times in a 2-1-2 pattern. As soon as he finished, the doors opened to reveal a room that could only be described as a source for nightmares. One of the silos on the map had guards plastered across every inch and barrel upon barrel of Leopard Skin in both forms. Any free space in the warehouse had boxes of guns and other weapons ready for shipping. Off on the side sat old trucks prepared to be loaded with the supplies. The product that filled that room could turn half the country into one large St. Louis. I know Dani didn't want me to pull anything stupid, but if the two of us left the facility with this room intact, none of it would matter. Regardless of whether this equipment was for John or anyone else. The only thing that could come from the equipment would be destruction.

"Have you ever seen anything more beautiful?" He asked.

"Well, there was this girl in Brazil that moved her hips in a way that I can't even describe." I laughed, trying to hide my discomfort. He didn't share my sense of humor, so I continued my part of the conversation. "What is all of this?"

"This is the future. The one that will have me sitting on the world's throne." He told me, grabbing one of the blades out of its crate.

"I feel the people of Ascension may have an issue with your coronation." I hoped he would tell me more about his connection to John, but that wasn't exactly the case.

"You sound like my father, so afraid of the boogeyman that you give up on your own ambitions. A shame, really, but that brings me to your part in this." He grinned. I will admit I only listened to about half of his plan at this point. I was tuning in and out, listening for the main points but trying to plan out my move simultaneously. It was hard counting all the guards with the noise he was making. I was shocked by how open he was and the hints that he was dropping. I had only met him, and he was oversharing. It made me wonder what trap I was walking into.

"That was a lot to take in, but if I understand things right, your father is standing in the way of your 'coronation,' as I called it." I inferred from the babbling he was doing.

"Correct. These men guard the warehouse for me while my bedridden father is kept clueless of its exact contents. But he has been growing curious and demanding recently, leading me to fear what he will do if he discovers this place." He explained with a long gaze set upon the equipment.

"So what is my part then? If you are so willing to talk about this in the open, you must have the guards on your side." I questioned, looking at the guards that surrounded us. Not one flinched when I talked about getting rid of the head of the house.

"There is truth in that, but not everyone is loyal, and I'm not fully sure who is. On the other hand, you have no connection to my father, and I see the ambition in your eyes. You will be rewarded for your part." He assured me.

"And once again, what is my part?"

"At dinner, my father is left alone in his room with only a pair of guards. That is when you will end his reign and make me a king," he whispered as he led me out of the room. He was a bold man; unfortunately, his boldness was reckless and would give me a perfect opportunity to strike. I wish I could relay the plan to Dani, but I had to act on this chance to create chaos.

"How long do I have before dinner?"

"You should have about five hours. If you don't strike, then you won't have a better chance." He explained as we returned to the main entrance.

"Trust me, I will keep to the schedule. I just need you to guarantee that this door will still be welcoming to me." I demanded before leaving.

"It should be, regardless it wouldn't be the first time you entered without an invite. Now go and prepare by yourself. I don't need anyone discovering our plan as it will make the last seconds of your life quite long." He threatened, closing the door behind me. I didn't trust him even in the most literal sense of the word, but it was something. All I needed was a plan for the rest.

Chapter 11
It's Not That Easy

I headed to the spot where Dani and I had tied up the horses. The whole way, I thought about Riccardo's plan and tried to remember every detail of the few parts of the compound. The triangle aspect of the building was the entrance and main building. One silo contained the storage, but the other two I was still unsure about.

It wasn't until I reached the horses and let my guard down that my body finally reacted in the way it had been craving. I threw up several times. I was just sick over what I had done and allowed myself to become. It may have been an act, but it churned my stomach to the point that it broke completely. I care for Dani too much to hurt her that way. To know that I was capable of that, even if it was just an act.

After my stomach was empty, I could start to concentrate again. I had five hours before I had to bring down the storage facility and kill the head of the Family. It seemed like a perfect scenario, but De Luca was set to die in five hours while I would have to wait for Dani to make her escape hours later. That had been our deal, and after the beating, I didn't want to rush her. My attention was split into three, with far too much time between everything for me to control it all. I had never been more envious of John in my life. He had a knack for this type of situation and knew what string needed to be pulled at what time.

I wondered if Mark knew what he had gotten me into. He had seemed so confident that things were going just as he had predicted. Still, that warehouse and Riccardo's ambition is not something anyone can plan for. He had told me to listen to the moment and be here. Yet, this isn't what I wanted. I didn't want to be the hero that Dani and this city needed. I wanted revenge, and that is it. I planned to kick the asses of various thugs. I figured I would have to sneak into some bases, but overthrowing an entire family that ruled a city by their might. That is something else. It requires a team and supplies, which I didn't have, besides the fact that I was much younger and less broken the last time I helped bring down a government. I was convinced that I was going to fail Dani.

"Don't forget to breathe, kid." Mark's voice called from a distance away. I thought I was hallucinating until I saw him and Evan riding up to me. Each man had a bag strapped to their shoulder as they rode up to me.

"Why are you two here?" I asked in shock. Both men dismounted and approached me.

"Dani has always left me behind as part of the backup plan. I have been a good soldier for some time now, but I couldn't stand back this time. I decided to accelerate Plan B. I'm going to be a part of the plan instead of just the guy in the background." He explained with his contagious smile. He handed me one of the bags, which was far heavier than I had anticipated.

"What's in the bag?" I asked, hesitant of what this plan was.

"Explosives, lots of them." He cheered. My eyes grew large as I nearly dropped the highly unstable bag.

"You don't know it yet, Evan, but this is exactly what I needed," I informed him with a bear hug.

"Alright, what is the plan?" He asked while Mark stood back, holding his bag tight. He shook his head as Evan asked his question. I said nothing.

"I told you that this wasn't our moment," Mark informed Evan without hearing my answer.

"You need us, though." Evan pleaded, knowing my silence was a confirmation of Mark's assessment.

"Mark is right. I can't sneak you guys in without making things worse." I explained as I placed my hand on his shoulder. I could tell that he wanted this badly, but I couldn't help him like he helped me.

"I know, I just wanted to be a part of this. I thought that helping people in that lab was my calling, but what Akia is doing seems more important. It feels right." He claimed.

"You love her, don't you?" I asked. I could tell by how he said her name and the light in his eyes that she was special to him. It worried me how quiet the old man was, but I hoped that it just meant that I was on the right track.

"I didn't know at first, but yes, I do. She doesn't feel the same way I've asked, but I still can't squash my feelings." He admitted, seemingly ashamed of what he said.

"Akia can be confusing, Evan, but I can say this. If you truly care for her, keep doing what you are doing. She knows better than anyone that she can't heal them like you can, so she fights. Yet if she could, I know she would want to have your gift." I assured him. It wasn't my place to speak for her, but I know I would have loved to have his gift. Killing is far easier than healing, and I have always been jealous of those that could heal like him or Anna.

"What can I do?" He asked, regaining his composure.

"Be here again in about eleven hours. That building will be on fire, and the prisoners will need help as Akia releases them." I instructed. He nodded his head, accepting his role, and remounted his horse. Mark walked with me for a moment before speaking.

"He loves a woman who won't even give him her real name," I muttered once we were far enough away.

"The heart doesn't care about names, just connections and his connection with a woman who doesn't exist. It will hurt him, but he will find others as long as he allows himself to open his heart again." Mark explained. Though his words were about Evan, I felt like they were also supposed to be a lesson.

"I don't know if I can do it," I told him.

"We have held only a few lessons, but I have seen them already shape your actions Rob, so let me impart one more on you. The idea of trust and faith." He said as we sat down.

"I have never been a holy man, Mark, and I don't think that will change today," I explained, refuting his term faith.

"I don't need you to believe in a religious text, but I need you to trust that we live in a kind universe." He explained despite my objection.

"Have you seen the world?"

"The way I see it, we are still here, Rob. If you focus on nothing, but disaster you become cynical. However, if you start to have faith that this world is just. If you trust that things will be as they are supposed, then what is there to fear. You create anxiety inside yourself before an event occurs. Yes, the event could end poorly, but it could work out. You have to have faith that things will be kind so that you can open yourself up to the changes that are all around you." He lectured.

I did not fully accept what he was saying at the moment, but there was truth in there. As I walked up to the gates, I never imagined the scenario that occurred. I only thought of the worst ones possible. I created tension and fear that only I was responsible for. If I let go of the need for control for a moment, maybe I could do this, and a surprise would occur again. Even if I failed, at least I would have done everything within my power. I bowed to him as I took his bag and assisted him to his horse. They confirmed that they would return to help in eleven hours however they could, but nothing would happen until the building was on fire.

The pair of men rode off to gather help as I stared off into the distance where the fortress was. Mark believed I had all the skills needed to do what was necessary, and now I had the equipment. I still wasn't sure about his idea of faith, but I had to give it a try with everything else we did.

While Evan and Mark rode off, I finalized my loose idea of a plan. De Luca had given me away into the warehouse even if he didn't want me there, and with all the leopard skin sitting in it, a decent enough spark would burn it all down. However, I knew my best option would be to bury everything in the rubble of the tower. If I could place the explosives in the right spots, I could drop the building on itself without bringing the prison down. Now all I had to do was wait until it was about an hour before the dinner. At that time, I would sneak in to start my plan. I played against the tree our horses were tied to and tried to catch up on my rest but found myself unsettled, so I decided to try that meditation thing again.

My mind began to wander back to the good days. Well, good is a strong word, as I recalled the day Dani told me she would enlist. I was proud, of course, but also a nervous wreck. The day she told me I was in the week between my initial training with Gene and my deployment. I went to war to protect those I loved, and now one of them was off to war herself. I tried to convince her to stay. I even included horror stories, but as always, she was stubborn. One reason we have gotten along so well. And despite my nervousness, I was proud of her because she had grown from being a scared twenty-year-old to a woman who wanted to protect people.

I don't know what would have been best for her. Had I convinced her to say, she would have likely perished when Despartian was ransacked. Knowing Dani, she insisted on fighting back, which would have cost her without proper training. At least when she was captured, she had a chance. Then again, maybe she wouldn't have died. Like Mark said, I needed to believe that her capture was the best thing to happen.

After I found peace in my decisions, I was finally able to rest. I let my backrest against the tree as I fell into a trance. It was a peaceful rest, probably one of the last good ones I can recall. I dozed for several hours and woke up just before I needed to leave.

When the hour for my move finally arrived, I made my way to the facility. I brought as many of the explosives as I could and the loose outline of a plan. The guards cared very little for my presence this time and even acted submissive. Looking at them, I realized that each of them was terrified. Whatever Riccardo did, he did it with fear. He had made death and torture a regular part of their lives. Now, none of them would even shed a tear if their boss died. I didn't have to overthrow a fortress; all I needed to do was spark chaos and let it drive his men away.

I reached the metal door that guarded the warehouse when the guards tried to engage me. The guards at the gate wanted to intimidate, but they backed down quickly. As soon as I stepped at them and stuck my chest out, they were terrified. I could see one had bruising all along his neck and wondered what Riccardo had done to break this man. I wanted to reach out, but they simply backed away. I knocked on the door in the 2-1-2 pattern and entered the silo. As I entered the room, I looked back and thought of the beaten guards. I had only gotten this far because their boss was an abusive monster, and now I was going to drop a building on them. I shouldn't have been in that room, but no one wanted to question the man their boss had personally walked through the building. Though the guilt ate at me, I had to move past it. I had only glimpsed at the architecture before. Now I had to quickly deduce where the maximum damage could be done without risking discovery.

Based on the age of the building and the damage it had sustained during the War, I needed to take out at least four of the main beams. Then a few on the barrels to start an inferno. Leopard skin in its liquid form is highly flammable. Which I discovered in the mountain ranges of South East Asia. After my team found four acres burned around a storage facility.

I crept through the warehouse waving and smiling with the guards that filled it. I tried to look natural, but placing C4 that will crush the people you are chatting with is a tad difficult. The first four went smoothly as I hid them at the back of each pillars' base. The barrels were a little more delicate as I had to sneak around them without knocking any over on top of hiding the devices. I placed them at the base of a few barrels as I kept my eyes moving from guard to guard. Everything was set, and they all had timers to go off, plus a remote detonation if I convinced Dani to leave sooner than planned. I couldn't believe how smooth it had gone. I started making my exit when I was finally approached.

"What are you doing with the leopard skin?" A young guard accused as he pointed his weapon at me. He may have been able to bellow a loud question, but he had no confidence in his stance. His weapon was shaking the whole time. If I were to venture a guess, this was the first time he had tried anything like this.

"You don't want to be here, kid," I assured him, trying to defuse the situation. I had come too far for everything to fall apart. I didn't need some stupid kid to ruin everything with a pointless fight.

"It is my duty to be here." He replied, steadying himself.

"Duty? How old are you, kid?" I asked him. He didn't like me asking questions and raised his weapon again. He may have been inexperienced, but he wouldn't be intimidated, so I pressed the issue. I grabbed his shaky hands and threw him down to the floor as quietly as I could, pushing his own weapon against his throat. "I'll ask one more time, how old are you?"

"I'm seventeen, sir." He replied as I relaxed to let him talk.

"Seventeen, and you think you know what duty is." I scolded. I felt offended by his comments for whatever reason. I didn't like the thought that this child was talking about something so personal to me.

As I waited for his reply, I looked around for the other guards. His accusation wasn't loud, but we were still in the open. I had to find someplace to move the conversation if it continued. I saw what looked like a small closet out of the corner of my eye and hoped that I could get him to it.

"Don't you dare scold me." He snarled with a tone he didn't have when he pointed the gun at me.

"Why not?"

"Because you know nothing about me or this place." He replied. I wondered if I had these guards pegged wrong.

"Then how about we talk about it in that closet over there," I suggested, still holding his weapon to his own throat.

"Do I have a choice?"

"Of course, I could kill you and just hide you in there instead," I suggested, but he didn't like that choice. He begrudgingly agreed to lead the way. I kept the weapon at his back while we slid to the other room. Once there, we continued the conversation though I did lower his weapon slightly to let him speak freely.

"Tell me, kid, why is it that you are so loyal to these scumbags?" I asked him.

"These men are the only brothers I have left."

"Quite an unfortunate family."

"Not my first choice."

"Then why?"

"It was join them or die. And I didn't want to die." He started to whimper. I could tell that his story was another tragedy marked upon this Earth, but I didn't have time.

"You know I understand that kid, but I can't let you get in my way," I told him as I prepared to kill him.

"Can you at least tell me what you are doing, so I know what will happen to my brothers?" He asked. It was a simple demand, but one I didn't have to oblige. However, I felt this urge to answer him.

"I will blow up this building and put an end to the De Luca's empire."

"Noble of you, wish I would have been brave enough." He said with a new look in his eyes. One that spoke of regret that surprised me again.

"What makes you say that?" This boy was something different. It wasn't logical, and it went against all of my training, but I was starting to wonder if I could trust him. I wanted to hear his answer.

"I mean, these brutes have made so many of our lives miserable, but they have been the only thing keeping us alive. Regardless of their brutality." He explained with a look in his eye that showed that he was telling the truth. There was a mix of pain, depression, and hopelessness. "It isn't the De Luca's that you're loyal to, is it?" I asked as I ultimately lowered the weapon.

"No, they aren't."

"Who are you really protecting?"

"When Riccardo 'enlisted' us, we came in as a group, and the other men I fought with are my family. And he has a sick tendency to punish us all if one of us fails, so I couldn't fall here." He opened up about.

"What if I could save you and your friends instead of killing you here?" I asked him as my wheels started to turn.

"How?"

"By beating the De Luca's." I smiled. He just shook his head at my response. "I'm being honest, kid, but I will need your help."

"What do you need?"

"I need you to get all of your friends out here so when the fighting starts, I have fewer to go through."

"That won't be easy to do. Some of them are even more terrified than I am. They think the Family is untouchable."

"If they don't believe you that a savior has come, tell them their sign will come soon as the head of the De Luca family will be dead with Riccardo next on the list."

"You are going to kill Mr. De Luca?!?" The boy asked, barely keeping his voice contained.

"Yes, which leads me to the second part. I will need you to get me this box once they imprison me." I instructed as I pulled a small palm-sized box from my pocket. He took it from me and turned it over a few times.

"What is this?" He finally asked.

"My escape."

"And how do you know I won't turn you in?"

"I don't, but there is something in your eyes that tells me you want the hope I am offering. Now take this, tell your friends, and meet me soon. Just don't shake the box." I ordered as I slid open the closet door. He placed the box in his pocket and left quietly. He turned around for a moment to look at me. We shared a glance, but that was it. I was putting a lot of faith in him, but I needed to. I didn't have any other option.

With my staff in hand, I headed off to the head of the Family. I stalked my way through the main compound, doing my best to avoid any conversation. As I crept, I started to reflect on my poor decision and what Dani's reaction would be. I hadn't even gotten the kid's name, and I trusted him with the most intimate details. All he had to do was squeal about one part of it, and I would be finished. Guards would be doubled, bombs defused, and I would be executed. I had just added a wildcard into an already unstable situation. In other words, I did the exact opposite of what my nemesis would have done. It didn't matter, though, whether he turned on me or helped me. I needed to execute the next stage as if things were going as planned. If I was distracted when I went after De Luca, things would not end well regardless of the kid's actions.

I reached the top floor without any resistance, as Riccardo promised. Unfortunately, he did not tell me which room was his father's, leaving me to check each one. The first one was clearly that of Riccardo's sister. Her room was organized, pink, and filled with the most expensive decor. There wasn't an inch of the walls unoccupied by some stupid canvas. I left the room quickly after sizing it up. The next room I checked turned out to be Riccardo's. It was a dark room filled with nothing but books and different whips spread across the walls. I thought I saw blood, but the shiver already running down my spine did not permit me to look any closer. After Riccardo's room, I found their mother's quarters. She did not sleep with her husband, and though there was no advantage to searching it, I was a bit curious what it might contain. The room was plain except for all the pictures. She had captured her family at their happiest, but Riccardo was in none of them. None of them except a single headshot from when he was about ten. He was smiling in it, which seemed to be the only reason to keep it. His own mother knew that something was off about him.

I left her room and at last arrived at the final door. I expected that there would at least be a guard out front, but nothing. I reached for the door when I noticed it was already cracked open. I tried to push it, but all I heard was a thud. Blood began to seep under the doorway, which I responded to with a harder push. This time I barged into the dimly lit room. I couldn't pick out all the details, but I knew there was someone on the bed as well as guards scattered across the floor. The body of one is what was blocking the door at first.

I drew my staff and approached the bed slowly, unsure of what had happened. Each guard only had one wound. Whoever had killed them was precise and methodical, not wasting a single motion. It had the makings of some of the greatest assassins in history. As I grew closer to the bed, I started hearing the gasp for air. I ran to the bedside and found Mr. De Luca bleeding out as he tried to hold any air he could. Unlike the guards, he had been stabbed numerous times. Each wound meant to deal the maximum amount of damage without killing him instantly.

"Who?" He tried to ask as he coughed up blood. I stood over him as this man who had broken this city lay in his own blood like a broken mess. This man brought his family to this city and destroyed it for his own vanity. He was a sad mess, but I felt nothing for him after what I had seen.

He tried to repeat the question, but he could only muster a few gargles. At that point, it would have been merciful to kill him, but I didn't. He deserved every bit of this suffering, so instead of ending him, I investigated the room. I paced around the room, looking for anything that would point to what had occurred. He tried saying something, but his voice was buried in the blood.

I found a safe that was broken open and papers scattered everywhere. I looked through the documents finding nothing that would point to what happened here. I slinked over to his desk, where other documents were shredded and moved around. I opened one of the drawers, which contained a note. I pulled it out as it had familiar handwriting. It was addressed to the old man and inside read as follows:

Your son dies for his ambitions, or the Executioner comes for you.
  ~John

I crumbled the note and threw it on the ground. It explained what happened here but raised even more questions. John has rarely concerned himself with the ambitions of others, so I had to wonder what Riccardo was planning that could draw his attention. On top of that, I wondered who this Executioner was. John has always preferred to take care of things himself due to his trust issues. The fact that he sent someone else to take care of this was worrisome.

That means there is an enemy out there capable of taking out several guards in one strike and has the trust of John.

I wanted to keep looking, but I had to get out of there before I was caught over the dead man. He coughed a few more times, and I decided to make sure the job was done. I grabbed one of the guards' knives and stuck it in the old man's chest to finish the job. Then I walked out. With the deed done, I exited the room quietly. That did not matter as a plethora of guards soon surrounded me along with their boss. Riccardo was as predictable as I had figured, so as of now, trusting the young man looked like the right move.

"I give you a job in the organization, and this is how you repay me." He commented, just dripping sarcasm. A few of the guards headed into the room, and the next thing we heard were gasps, with one of them running out of the room moments after entering.

"Sir, everyone is dead. All of his guards and Mr. De Luca himself, it looks like he was stabbed. I'm so sorry, sir." The guard informed Riccardo. Riccardo lowered his head momentarily then just shook it as if he was surprised. His arrogance was hard to watch. Even the other guards didn't seem to buy the act either.

"Take him into custody, boys. This man is dangerous, and I'll take care of him later." He ordered, wiping a fake tear from his eye. I chuckled for a moment and surrendered peacefully. It was nice to have my opponent play into my hands. I wondered if that is how John feels all the time. As we started our march to the prison, Riccardo waved his men back to speak in private.

"I hope that you understand that someone was going to take the fall here. People know about my ambitions, and if there was no other suspect, I would become one, and that cannot happen. But I must ask, how did you do it?" He asked me with a grotesque smile strung across his face. He wanted every brutal detail as if it would satisfy him in some way. I was disgusted.

"I didn't. Someone else was there before me. I merely just put him out of his misery," I explained.

"Right, playing innocent isn't going to work with the guy who gave you the order." Riccardo laughed as we continued to the prison cells.

He tried to engage in some niceties the rest of the walk, but I gave him nothing. I acted the way I should after killing the boss. With his blabbing, the walk seemed longer than it should have, but at last, we arrived at the prison block, which was mostly empty, outside of the girls that Dani was trying to free. I walked by each cell, looking for her, to see how she was doing, but she was nowhere to be found. Then, at last, we arrived at the most heavily guarded cell. There sat Dani on one of the cots inside. Riccardo opened the cell door and threw me in with her. She didn't make her emotions obvious, but I knew she wasn't happy. He waved goodbye to us, and she responded with a weak punch to my arm.

Chapter 12
Burn it Down.

"I took all those whippings, and this is how you repay it," Dani stated as she tried to move gingerly.

"I am sorry, Dani," I told her as I sat on the cot next to her.

"I know." She sighed with a large exhale.

"Let me see," I suggested. She rolled her eyes at first, but when I nudged her arm, she finally obliged. She lifted her shirt so that I could see the scars that I had left. Most of the bleeding had stopped, and luckily the guards had cleaned some of her wounds. I didn't understand why, but clearly, they needed to keep the scars from getting infected.

"They look worse than they feel." She told me, trying to comfort me when I should have been comforting her.

"I wish there would have been some other way, but there is a plan. We just have to wait, and you need to rest." I suggested while she lowered her shirt back down.

"Care to share?"

"Not really because it will only rattle you up, and I need you calm right now."

"At least tell me how you ended up here." She ordered with a vein popping in her forehead from my assertion that the plan would upset her.

"My first job was to kill Mr. De Luca, and as you know, I always finish the job." Her eyes grew wide as she processed what I had just said.

"You killed the head of the Family?" She asked, trying her hardest to keep her voice low and emotions contained.

"Technically, I finished him, but some assassin got to him first."

"Did you see this assassin? And who sent them?"

"No, I didn't. They must have gotten out before I got there. And John was the one who sent them."

"Now that is interesting. I wonder why John wanted him dead."

"According to the note, I found it was for not killing Riccardo."

"Riccardo? What does John care about...I mean, what does that mean for us?" She asked with her wheels turning. I didn't understand it either, but she now knew what had happened.

"I don't know, but we have a few hours, and we are both going to need our rest. So let's table this until later." I suggested as I could see her eyelids slipping. Unlike me, she was not able to rest the last few hours. I assumed the pain was excruciating, but she had to figure out how to sleep through it.

"But there is so much we still need to do." She said. This was the most anxious I had seen Dani in decades.

"Trust me, Dani, sleep is more important right now." She tried to push the point, but I kept rerouting the conversation until she understood my desires. I went to the other cot, and I at least fell asleep. As I slept, I could hear her shifting several times, so at least she tried to sleep again.

As I napped again, I began to think about Iris and John. I was walking down the streets of Despartian with Iris by my side. It was a classic winter day out with her. Flurries slowly fell from the sky, and the snow crunched with every step that we took. Lights were strung across the trees and buildings as the city prepared for the upcoming holiday season.

She loved that time of year. The joy in the air and a feeling of hope matched the energy she always had. I had always had mixed emotions in the winter as I always hated the cold and snow. On the other hand, Iris's birthday was in the winter, making it a beautiful time.

We walked through the snow while I thought about how lucky I was to have an angel by my side. Her flowing blonde hair and glimmering blue eyes made me weaker than a gingerbread man. She was my everything, and as I watched her interact with the faceless strangers on the sidewalk, my heart began to ache. I didn't understand why until a little later on.

"Isn't it beautiful out today?" She smiled as she moved through the streets.

"It is, and it is all I have ever wanted," I answered as I grabbed her hand, and she squeezed mine tight. As we continued to stroll through the streets, I twirled her around, and we began to dance in the snow.

I am not much of a dancer, but I gave it my best. She laughed at my flailing attempts. As she spun and I shuffled my feet, I smiled like I had never smiled before.

"It is amazing that this is the life we could have had." She sighed as the laughing and dancing finally stopped. I was caught off guard by her statement. We were having a lovely time, and then it just halted.

"What do you mean, Iris?"

"You avoided me for years because of some guilt you carried. Had you just talked to me, we could have had this. Despite all the pain in the world, we could have had some small piece of happiness." She said, walking away from me towards another man crouched down on the sidewalk.

"Iris," I muttered as I tried to walk to her but found my legs unable to move. As she reached to help the stranger, he stood and shot her! She slumped to the ground in an instant as her blood stained the pure white snow around her. I tried running to her, but with every step I took, I got farther away, and all I could hear was the laugh of the man who shot her, the man who now looked at me as I ran helplessly, John.

"Iris!" I screamed, waking Dani and me up from our slumbers. As I sat up in my bunk, my body was shaking and covered in sweat. I continued to gasp and shake as I tried to calm down, but the thought of losing her again was just overbearing. Just when I was about to start hyperventilating, I felt a hand massaging my back. I turned to Dani sitting next to me, trying her best to calm me down. Luckily, the guards had been on patrol, and she was able to bring me back to Earth before they heard anything.

"It was just a nightmare. It'll be alright." She said, trying to soothe me as her hand moved in small circles across my back. Her eyes were soft, with some of her ebony hairs covering her left eye.

"I'm okay," I assured her as my breathing returned to normal and the shaking stopped. Despite my assurances, she continued to sit by my side. She understood the content of my nightmare and wanted to make sure I was going to be okay.

"We both know that is a lie, but are you willing to talk about it?"

"Not yet. Not until we make it out of here."

"You know you can talk to me, Rob." The way she said my name. It reminded me of those days when I was with Iris. The calmness and love that filled their voices. Though it was a different type of love, they both cared for me. I knew this and wanted to tell her everything, but there was a job to do first. I couldn't let my emotions and my struggles affect our heads.

"I know Dani, but this isn't the place. The guards will be back soon." I reminded her while shooing her back to her own bunk.

"Promise we'll talk afterward."

"I promise, Dani." I smiled while I let my head fall back to the bed. I started to practice the breathing that Mark taught me earlier and hoped it would stave off the nightmares for at least some time.

Another hour or so passed when a knock came at our cell door. Once my eyes were clear, I saw the young man standing in front of the cell holding the box I had given him earlier. I sprung off the cot and ran to the door. I was shocked that he was actually there. Dani was hesitant, trying to figure out what I was so excited about.

"Glad to see you." I smiled as he unlocked the door.

"I almost didn't come." He replied with his head bowed.

"Who cares about almost, you are here, and that is all that matters," I assured him. Dani slowly approached from behind me, unsure what was going on.

"What is this?" She asked at last.

"Our escape plan." I smiled as I took the box from the kid and slid it back into my own pockets.

"Okay, and who is he?"

"Well, he's...hey kid, what's your name?" I asked, at last, realizing I made this kid critical to my plan without even knowing his name.

"Thomas."

"This is Thomas Dani, and he is a guard that wants the De Luca family to fall just as bad as us."

"Rob. Life isn't this easy." I knew she was right that usually, things weren't this easy, but just this once, I thought that I would trust it and not question a blessing standing in front of us.

"Just trust me." I smiled with my handheld out to her. She grabbed it as I pulled her along. She moved gingerly but was gaining some mobility and strength back. She was not limping as bad as before. Thomas led us down a nearby hallway with Dani looking around for guards, but there was virtually no one to be found to both our surprise. The view we did see were easy to avoid.

"Where is everyone?" Dani asked before I could open my mouth.

"When I first started telling my friends that a savior had come, they laughed, but once news spread that Mr. De Luca was dead, they finally believed that the nightmare would be over." He explained, cracking open a large metal door. Inside the room was the armory that housed my staff and a few weapons for Dani.

"Thank you for assisting Thomas, but I have to free the rest of the girls trapped here," Dani commanded as she secured a small handgun to her hip.

"Dani, Thomas will go with you, you'll need all the help you can get, and in the meantime, I will take care of Riccardo," I instructed. She was not happy with me bossing her around. Still, she realized that she couldn't do it independently in her condition.

"What makes you think that you can find Riccardo in this place?" Dani asked, tossing weapons for the other prisoners to Thomas.

"Plug your ears for a second." I grinned. She gave me a look as she followed my order. I pulled the trigger to the explosives out of the box and pressed the remote detonator. The building shook as the explosion could be heard echoing through the halls. By now, the whole warehouse was buried underneath itself, and Riccardo was either dead or throwing a tantrum.

"I could kiss you." Dani smiled as she put the pieces together.

"You can thank Evan for not listening to you."

"What do you…?"

"We can talk when it's all done; now go," I ordered as I ran towards the main building.

The lights were beginning to flicker from the detonation. The power was in complete disarray while I made my way towards Riccardo's rooms. I was hesitant to leave the two of them alone, but they would be better off if I could create enough distraction during my search for Riccardo. I reached the door to the main complex, closed my eyes, and took a deep breath. I didn't know what would be on the other side, but I knew it wasn't going to be easy.

I kicked the door open and was greeted by a multitude of guards all ready to kill me. They never stood a chance as I fought for people important to me while they fought for an abusive master. They raised their weapons, and I extended my staff.

I clashed with the first man. The mere force of my charge sent him flying backward. Then in a blink, I struck a second guard with my staff, knocking out several teeth in the process. These men were thugs swinging wildly in the air while I was moving with precision that they were not prepared for. They did land some glancing blows on occasion, but nothing to deter the haymakers I was delivering. I ducked under a swing and rose with an uppercut that dislocated one man's jaw. I dispersed their resistance quickly as I handed out a few broken jaws, snapped legs, and dislocated shoulders. They called me a demon as I moved, and they didn't stick around long once they understood our skill discrepancy.

After dealing with the weak ones, I started to head towards the remnants of the warehouse. As I got closer, I realized that the explosion had done more damage than I had anticipated. The lights had been disabled in the central column with it only enlightened by an occasional flicker. I could hear the crackling of the fire starting to roar louder. It would move to the main facility soon, but I needed to focus on finding Riccardo in the veil of darkness.

While climbing the staircase, one of the last guards blindsided me. He bloodied my nose, but that was it. I put his head into the drywall and left him to figure out whether pursuing the fight any longer would be in his best interest. With the last annoyance out of the way, I continued the climb. Higher and higher, I moved until, at last, I heard him.

"Is that you that I hear climbing the stairs?!?" Riccardo yelled with a crack of his whip! Based on the sound of his voice, he was on the floor above me. This nightmare would soon be over.

"Karma is coming for you, you sadistic monster!" I yelled back as I heard him crack the whip again.

"Oh, it is so good to hear your voice. I really wanted to kill you myself!"

"Funny, I was going to say the same thing!"

I climbed the last few steps, questioning why I was doing this. Dani and her fellow prisoners were safe by now. The storage facility with the leopard skin was obliterated, and the man in charge was killed. I didn't have to go after Riccardo. John wouldn't kill the old man just to let the pup live, yet I kept moving forward.

Once I stood on the top step, I stared down the long black hallway. My vision was restricted to no more than a few feet in front of me. The only sound was the cracking of his whip. He wanted to intimidate me, but neither of us could see the other. I walked down the hall, muffling my steps the best I could so that he couldn't locate me. Then to my surprise, I was struck across my shoulder with a piece of leather. He nearly knocked the staff out of my hands. I leaped backward as I tried to figure out how he had struck with such accuracy. I hoped it was dumb luck until a second whip struck me. This one was different as it had metal barbs on the end that tore skin as it pulled away. I screamed as my left shoulder was left raw.

"Did that hurt you, weaker creature?" He taunted. The third strike barely caught my core, ripping some skin off my ribcage. A more precise blow could have put me on the shelf for some time.

"That is quite a trick you have there. Maybe you could catch me up." I grunted, trying to apply pressure to the wound on my ribs. I wasn't bleeding much, but my shirt was starting to stick to my skin.

"I could do that, but where would the fun be? It is more entertaining watching you struggle physically and mentally." He taunted with a clinking laugh. I heard the metal clank ever so slightly to my side and was able to raise my hands to block it before it tore across my face. As my arms hung bloody, I continued to back up as it was the only direction that I thought would be safe. Until my back reached the railing. This was when the lights flickered for a moment, helping me avoid the next blow while revealing the goggles he was wearing. I assumed they were archaic versions of night vision goggles that he had probably used for hunting. Unfortunately, I was now his blinded prey.

As I puffed, I could hear Mark yelling at me. He kept telling me to concentrate and silence my mind. Following his orders one more time, I let my mind go blank. No more stimuli were clouding the moment. Mark had me ready for this, and with my eyes closed, I listened to the world. I raised my staff as the next strike caught my hip. I flinched as he laughed at my failures. He didn't realize that during that blow, I heard the whip crack in the air. All I had to do was listen and react.

The next blow only caught my back ever so slightly as I had dodged most of it with a spin. I may have lost an ounce of flesh, but I was ready now. Next time I would react faster, and Riccardo would be nothing. I inhaled deeply, and as my exhale fell from my mouth, I heard the whip drawback. The metal clanged the floor as he cracked it. His wrist began to snap forward, and I was clear of the whips' path. It hit nothing but the railing.

"How did you do that?" He questioned as his confidence was fading. This time I refused to answer. I wanted him nervous and talking so that I could find him quicker to end the fight. He attempted to hit me again, but the crack revealed the location fast enough to avoid it. Another couple of strikes missed, and he was flustered. Now he was tiring himself out and forcing himself to breathe heavily. I didn't need the sound of the whip. I knew where he was.   He yelled some obscenities at me as he tried to strike again. However, this time I didn't just avoid the whip. I pinned it down with my staff. He wanted to pull it back with little success. I was stronger than him, and outside of the loss of blood, I had little fatigue. I swooped down to grab the whip myself and pulled him towards me. He stumbled towards me as I swung my staff. Catching the prick across the face in the most satisfying of manners. His goggles broke while he released a defeated grunt. I grabbed the bludgeoned man and began to stroke his face with my bloodied hand. Then I started to hit him once for every strike he made me give Dani. There was no longer a clear distinction between my blood or his on my fist. After the last strike, I threw him to the stairwell, where a little light poked through the darkness.

"Why did you do this to me? I get freeing your little girlfriend and killing my Dad since I told you to, but what is with all the extra stuff? Why blow up my factory, kill my mother and sister in cold blood, and ruin me?" He gargled as he spat blood from his mouth and removed his broken goggles. He tried to crawl his way up the railing, but I stomped on his foot to hold him where he was.

"I've learned that some men just have to fall. Even if they are not a problem for me now, it is better to take them out before they become dangerous. You are one of those men. Now, I'm sorry your mother and sister died in the explosions, but bombs have no direction or mercy." I told him as I stood over the beaten man.

"They didn't die in the explosion. They were stabbed just like my father was!" He yelled, pulling his foot free of mine! This was news to me as it meant that whoever was going after the De Luca's was still in the building. I had to handle Riccardo quickly as this new player was likely John's assassin, who would be trained in a manner far more efficient than Riccardo. I was ready to leave him for the debris until the arrogant twit spat blood on me, and I reacted poorly.

I went to beat him to a pulp when the building began to shake, dropping some of the ceiling on us.

The falling cement broke our platform, dropping both of us down a flight. The fall nearly killed him and sprained my ankle while pinning me beneath some concrete. My staff had fallen a few feet outside of my reach. The half-dead man began to cackle between the splurges of blood.

"Well, I may die here, but at least I get to take you out first!" He cheered, using the rail to rise. As he leaned against the railing, he pulled a small pistol out. He limped closer to me and pulled the trigger. Nothing, but a click. The gun must have misfired, I thought, until he tried it several more times with the same result.

"Those are no use whenever myself or John are around." A deep voice explained from the shadowy hall. Both of us turned to see a dark figure walking down. I knew that this must be John's assassin dressed in a flowing black cloak with a pitch-black armor set. Under the drawn hood rested a mask that covered the assassin's face. As the figure grew closer, Riccardo froze. He tried to use the gun again, but nothing. He threw it at the figure who caught it and threw it back at Riccardo's bloody face. Knocking him against the rail, back now turned to the assailant while I could do nothing.

"Who are you?" He quivered while trying to regain composure. The figure did not respond; it only tilted its head and drove the blade through his heart. As Riccardo's body began to slump, the figure removed the blade and pushed Riccardo over the rail. After the display of mercilessness, I started using all my energy to push the stone off my leg. Once free, I rose to meet the killer, trying to put all my weight on my good leg.

"Who are you?" I asked, hoping these would not be my last words as well.

The figure said nothing as they approached me slowly. Their shrouded figure grew closer and more menacing with each step. Riccardo's blood dripped from the blade. I grabbed my staff as I prepared for a fight I wasn't sure I could win.

Even though there was no structural damage at the time, my ankle felt like it might as well have been dislocated. Meanwhile, my opponent was utterly fresh. My only grace was that the figure was much smaller than I first expected. They were not tiny but far more petite than one would imagine, given the body count, I already attributed to them. He spun the blade around in his hand a few times, just standing there, staring at me with those shrouded eyes. I felt my hand tremble like he hadn't in years. There was just an aura about the figure that I couldn't place.

"Who are you?!?" I yelled one more time. Still nothing, so like a fool, I charged in recklessly. In response, the figure grabbed my staff and flipped me down on the steps. He followed that up with a blow to the ribs I damaged weeks prior. Then as I tried to fight back, he turned me around and placed tiny needles in my shoulder and an old bullet wound. I tried to fight, but he was faster and seemed to know what I would do before I did. Then, at last, he looked me in the eyes as he placed tiny needles in my gut. I could tell they were looking into my soul, but the old Hannya mask they were wearing made it too dark for me to see theirs.

I fell to the ground, unable to move. I looked at the needle placements and noticed they were all at pressure points. Not only was this figure an expert fighter, but they had a medical background that could temporarily paralyze without killing. Whoever this was, they would be a problem the next time we faced, even with two good ankles.

"I am the Executioner, but John needs you alive for Operation Reset." He whispered before knocking me out.

Chapter 13
Dance Again

The next thing I knew, I was back in the bunker under St. Louis. As I started to stir, I realized how much pain I was in and how little movement I could muster. I wiggled myself to an upright position despite it all so that I could gauge my surroundings. At first, I wondered who pulled me out of the burning building, but I knew it had to be the Executioner. Like he had said, John wanted me alive. He wanted me in his game, and no one else could have found me in time to pull me from the wreckage.

From there, it appears that Dani's forces must have found me and brought me to her room instead of the main infirmary. Once my eyes adjusted, my ears began to pick up on the snoring coming from the corner. Mark had passed out in the chair next to the bed.

"Wake up, you, old man!" I yelled, startling the blind teacher. He fell out of the chair and had to recompose himself.

"Hey, that is mean. Not all of us get to sleep a whole day away." He answered by getting back up on his chair.

"A full day! Did everyone else make it out alright? Did they...we win?" I asked, trying to figure out what I had missed.

"That is why you are here, kid. Dani and that boy found you lying in a grass field just outside the building. The boy then carried you all the way here. Quite a kid you found." He grinned. When a knock came at the door. Mark called for the knocker to come in as the door opened.

"So, I heard some commotion coming from the room. Does that mean someone is finally awake?" Dani asked as she entered.

"Yeah, the little punk decided to wake me from my nap," Mark answered as I chuckled. I think I did more than just wake him up, but I'll keep that our secret. "I think I will leave you two alone now. I want to finish that dream I was having."

"No, you can stay, at least until she is out of her lecturing phase." I joked, although only Mark laughed as he left the two of us alone.

"What did I miss?" She led with. I figured it would be the lecture first, but she was far more concerned than I anticipated.

"I don't know. It was the assassin that killed Mr. De Luca. He finished off the whole family and then knocked me out. I'm assuming from there he must have carried me."

"Why do that?"

"I don't know. I think John still has a plan for me."

"That is terrifying." She shuddered as she grabbed the cloth of her pants. She knew the severity of the implication as much as I did. Nothing good could come from anything John was involved in.

"And what about you two? Did you find everyone?"

"We did. Once you blew the building, the guards lost their will to fight, and we saved everyone. Thanks to you and that kid. I don't know how to repay you, Rob."

"Friends don't have to repay one another. They just do things because they care."

"Still, how does some tequila sound?" She asked as she went to search one of her cabinets. She returned with two glasses and a vase-shaped bottle. "This bottle of reposado tequila used to run around $100 before the War, and I bet it is one of the few unopened bottles in the world. Shall we change that?" she asked, opening the bottle. She knew what I liked, and this was the perfect thing for the mood.

"I'm not sure you can hang with me, but let's see what you can do, Dani," I answered as she filled up each of our glasses. I took a quick whiff of the tequila, and it was beautiful. There was a hint of caramel, and on first taste, I found a richness in the finish that I can't describe. It had been a long time since I had something this expertly made. I missed that kind of taste. As I enjoyed mine, I looked over at Dani, who was leaning against the footer on her bed, and sipped her own glass.

"This is good," I commented after a few sips.

"That's good to hear because we have to finish this bottle tonight. I'm not keeping it after I leave here." She announced with a swirl of her drink.

"What do you mean by, leave here?"

"That is part of my duty with Pan. As one of his head generals, I go from city to city, organizing rebellions, starting the fights, and reestablishing order. Then I leave so that I can go to the next city that needs my help. St. Louis is no different, and although the plan moved faster than I anticipated with your arrival, it is just about time to move on." She explained drinking a little more from her cup. Though she was trying to comfort me and my injuries, I could see the restrictions in her own movements. Evan had bandaged her uptight.

"Don't you need your rest?" I asked, alluding to the damage I inflicted.

"I will once I'm back at the main base. Evan is good, but he is not what I need. Besides, my wounds will be safe for my journey. He ensured that."

"It's because he loves you, you know."

"I do, but to quote something you used to say before the War took your smile, 'what's not to love." She laughed, calling back to the days with her and Iris.

"I take it that there isn't a mutual feeling."

"He's just another face to fill in my dreams." She said as she finished her glass.

"A 'face to fill my dreams'?"

"Yeah, it's something that Pan says a lot. Basically, the human brain doesn't create faces. All it does is take the hundreds we see throughout our lives and place them on the background characters of our dreams. Now some move forward for a time, but then they can disappear just like that." She replied, snapping her fingers to emphasize the point.

"What about the main characters?"

"Well, that depends. When you are like the two of us, the main characters are the faces that haunt us. Those that we lost are burned into our memory, and we want them to be real again so badly that we create subconscious stories to give them life again."

"Pan certainly is an interesting man. What else can you tell me about him?"

"Good try, Rob, but I know when you are fishing. I want you to meet him without any previous notions in mind." She filled her cup and mine as she finished her explanation. I played innocent at the accusation, but she was right. I wanted information on this mystery man so that I could have a leg up. "Besides, do you really want to talk about work? Because I want to catch up."

"Catch-up." With that, we began talking about the old days. Exchanging stories and laughing the whole time as the bottle's volume plummeted. Some of the people and things we talked about I hadn't thought about in years. Stories that I could only share with her or Iris. The ones that brought an instant smile to my face. Hours passed like minutes once the good times started to roll.

Each of us had demons nagging at our heels so often that it seemed rare to just enjoy the fact that we were still alive. As the night started to wind down and the bottle dropped to below half, I no longer felt pain. My sprained ankle and patches of skin had seemingly healed through the beauty of self-medication. It was apparent that Dani's wounds were also growing painless. A falsehood that would at least bite me once I sobered up.

"Well, the bottle is...the bottle is almost empty." she slurred, setting the bottle on the table one last time.

"Eh, girlie ya didz itz."

"Shad up." As she replied, I attempted to stand up. It probably took three attempts, and once I was standing, I moved like a newborn giraffe.

"Sitz. Sitz, no, wha you doing? You stand, no, I stand. Neither us stand, Rob. What you look for, dude?" She asked as I looked through her cabinets, "No more. I see four of you."

Despite her objection, I continued to search through her cabinets. I don't know why there are a lot of holes I can't tell you about from that night. The amount of alcohol should have done to me what John and Riccardo failed to do.

"No drink. No, I want...wan...Music!" I answered as I turned to the other side of the room and made my way to a small counter with a CD player sitting on it. As I stumbled over there, Dani rose up to see what I was doing. I placed a CD in the player and started it up.

At first, there was a love song with a slow melody playing. I'm not sure how I looked once the music began to play, but it couldn't have been pretty. This was confirmed by Dani's laughter.

"Danz?" I asked as I held my hand out for her. She shook her head at first, but I continued to insist. It was not ideal for my ankle, but I finally got her to meet me standing up. From there, what we did wasn't dancing. It was swaying back and forth, using each other to keep the other standing up. There wasn't grace or technique. It was just pure comedy. Had anyone seen us, they would have died, but we were able to embrace each other and just sway.

"Remember that las week?" I asked, trying to muster some audible words.

"I member doz left feet." She assured me. Just before the War started, I had Dani take me through a dance lesson. I wanted to impress Iris, and Dani was one of the best dancers I had ever met.

"Left feet?"

"You stepped on my foot many times. I iced a week." She joked, with her smile growing more prominent. She rested her head on my shoulder, and I held her tight as we swayed a little longer. We continued for four or five songs growing close. Eventually, we were cheek to cheek, rocking easily in one another's arms. We didn't talk much during the dance. Instead, we just let the music and our bodies do all the talking. The CD was a conglomerate of every genre with some of the best slow songs a person could burn off the internet. I don't know where she got it, but I assumed it was found in someone's home after the War.

We were holding each other so tightly, it felt like our souls were intertwining with the music stitching them eternally together. We were two rivers meeting to create a lake. Each of us has our own force, but together something more splendid, something far more stable and beautiful.

At last, the final song came on. A classic little country piece that sets a mood about mortality. When the singer started to belt those words, she looked at me with those dark caramel eyes. I looked at her with the uneasy ocean blues of my own. She wrapped her arms around my neck as our foreheads touched ever so gently. She initiated the kiss, but I didn't fight back. It was only a matter of time before one of us did. Given our relationships with Iris, we shouldn't have, but it felt right at the time. That moment likely only lasted a few seconds, but it felt eternal at the same time. That was until we each pushed one another away. The fantastic thing about kisses like that is that they are incredibly efficient at sobering both parties up instantly. When we looked at each other again, all we saw was the red that plastered our faces.

It took both of us a moment to realize what had just occurred, but once it struck Dani, she started to retreat out of the room. She stumbled a few times but made her exit as soon as she could. I wasn't sure what to say, but I tried to go after her. Shortly after, I tripped over my own two feet and fell. Despite the embarrassment from the fall, I still wanted to chase after her. I tried to stand back up, but I fell again between the liquor and pain returning to my body. It was such a stupid mistake that I couldn't even get closure on as I passed out.

Chapter 14
Stronger with Time

After I sobered up, I went to go find her. Though most of the night was blurry, that kiss was not something I could forget. As I limped down the hall, my head and ankle both throbbed. It might have only been a sprain, but dancing on it had done it damage. Of course, that didn't stop me as I limped around the base. I found Mark, who was in a much cheerier mood than the day before. He was sitting around eating, so I decided to join him. I hoped that the food would calm the hangover.

"Here, have some tea. I'm sure it will help with your head." Mark said as he poured me a glass of tea. I slammed the glass down faster than anything I had ever drunk before.

"Thank you, I needed that," I told him as I set the glass back down.

"I figured. After I ran into Dani this morning, I figured that you would be in even rougher shape." He reported while pushing his food around on his plate.

"Oh, good, she's up. I was hoping to talk to her. We didn't get to finish our conversation last night." I said, leaning against the table to stable my spinning head.

"She is up, but unfortunately, you two won't be talking. She left this morning." He informed me. At first, I didn't process what he had said.

"What do you mean she left?" I asked, even though I knew deep down what he meant.

"I mean, she gave me this letter for you and said that she had to leave the city. Her job was done, were her exact words." He clarified as he dug into his pockets. He handed it to me, and it read as follows:

Rob,

Last night was fun, and I'm glad we could relax after that mess with Riccardo. Unfortunately, things are complicated. I'm not sure how to process the whole night, which has made me doubt other things in my life. It has made me question my loyalty to Pan, and I think that I need to figure things out away from the both of you. I know that that isn't fair to you, but I need to do this for myself. I need to clear my head and figure out what path I want to take. Please rest up for a week and then talk to Evan, who has supplies for you.

Sorry for the quick exit,
  Dani

I sat there holding the note. I couldn't fully process the events, but if this is what Dani thought was best for her, I had to let her go. Truthfully, I needed time to figure out how I felt about it all. In a way, I felt like I had betrayed Iris's memory, but at the same time, it had felt right in some way. It was probably best that I figured it out myself before we talked, so I turned my attention back to John.

"So, what did the note say? Believe it or not, I didn't read it." I looked at him and shook my head.

"Basically, what she told you. Her mission in the city was over, and it was time to move on. She also told me to talk to Evan before we go." He didn't say a word. He could tell that I was withholding information, but Mark always knew when to keep quiet. It was a talent that I did envy. "I'll come to find you after I talk to Evan. Just stay out of trouble until then."

"Not yet, Rob. Go back to your room and rest. You may think you are superman, but you are wobbling just walking." He ordered.

"How do you know?"

"Clunk, slide, clunk slide. That's all I hear when you walk."

"I don't go *clunk*." I protested, knowing that he was right about everything else.

He was right. No matter how tough I thought I was, there was no way that I was going to get very far on my ankle. Even if somehow I miraculously caught up to John, the meeting would end the same way as the one with this new partner of his.

After my temper subsided, he led me back towards the bedroom that was now mine for the time being. I couldn't believe that Dani had just left. I noticed that a few things were gone, but there was still much of her in that room. It broke my heart to think that I was responsible for her leaving in such a rush. I sat in the bed to think for a while and put together my next strategy.

A sprain like mine would typically take 3-4 weeks, given the severity. Still, I had to do everything to keep it closer to that 3-week number. However, my acceptance of three weeks came under the condition that Mark would continue to train me in any manner he could. He was hesitant at first but figured out how to host sessions that were sitting or laying-based.

The next three weeks were a brutal test of my patience. Whatever John was working on, he wasn't going to wait for me to heal. Throughout my rehab, I managed to stay active, often challenging myself with push-ups, one-legged jumps, and handstands. If there was a way to circumvent Evan's recommendations, I took it. Meanwhile, Mark dove deeper into our training. He had me cross-legged and meditating in spurts of fifteen minutes for at least two hours a day. Expanding on the ideas that were instilled earlier, teaching more about the art of mindfulness, trust, and concentration. He hoped that it would help me see clearer as I continued my journey, but there were steps still ahead I had to take before I truly learned.

When I was allowed to walk in a boot, I assisted Evan in reorganizing the city. It was in chaos after the De Luca's were gone, and he needed help that I specialized in. We spoke at great lengths of what he would need to stabilize the city again, but there was something off in our talks. I don't know if he blamed me for Dani leaving, but he was never the same once she was gone.

At last, my final day in the city came. Before Evan would let me leave, he had to show me one final thing. He took me to the recovery room, where a man sat next to a young woman. It took my brain a moment to process the face of the man in front of me now. Like the last time I had seen him, I had thought his soul was gone. It appeared that the body was just refusing to give up. Now there was a spirit to match the undying body. A smile that distracted the eyes from the Leopard Skin dots that riddled his body. It was Josh, who I had met when I first arrived.

He nearly died that day we spoke, but Evan's men found him soon after we separated. They brought him to the facility making little headway until his daughter returned home with Dani. She was the one that finally explained what the De Luca's were doing with the girls. Apparently, Leopard Skin works best when a mixture of A- blood and high amounts of estrogen are used. All the ladies that were captured were chosen because they matched the criteria. However, their saving grace was the rarity of their blood type. The De Luca's couldn't afford to overtrain them as it would set their operation back weeks. I had spent so many years fighting the drug over in Asia, and I had never seen this development. I wondered if it was something that John had discovered or who would have figured it out.

I wanted to make the goodbyes quick, but Mark encouraged me to take my time with it. He wanted me to embrace the feeling of success and the happiness around me. I tried my best to enjoy it, but deep down, I just couldn't. My mind always returned to what was still to come. Ever since the Executioner had beaten me, I was in my head about having two opponents that could go toe-to-toe with me. On top of that, I had started to wonder how much leopard skin was exported before I destroyed it. John had this operation going for months, and I refused to believe that he had left it all for the De Luca's to use as they pleased.

Once the goodbyes were complete, Mark and I headed to the outskirts of town, where Evan had prepared a boat for us under Dani's final directions. I use the term boat loosely. It was barely sturdy enough to hold our supplies and us, then every time a wave crashed against it, water seeped in. Momentarily I wondered if Dani wanted to see me die by suggesting that I use this thing on the Mississippi. Then again, I had no other option. Traveling on foot would take too long, and I needed to head south faster.

After my initial hesitation, I started to load the boat up and assisted Mark into it. Despite his ease on land, the water was not nearly as comfortable for him. It took a minute to help him settle in, and once he was, I threw my last bag in. Just before I jumped in, Thomas rode upon us.

"Come to say goodbye?"

"That, and I wanted to say thank you. I had given up on having any form of normal life, and then you showed up. Not only am I now free of Riccardo, but Dani left me this recommendation. Apparently, some of Pan's forces are coming to the city soon, and I am supposed to leave with them."

"That is exciting, but I know this kid. There is no such thing as a normal life. There is just living and dying, but I recommend doing things that promote the former more than the later." I suggested. Despite the wisdom behind my words, I could still hear Mark chuckle at them. I don't think he believes I practice what I preach.

I was happy for the kid as we all need to have a purpose in life. However, I also understood the route he was now destined to travel on. It would not be peaceful or normal by any means, and he had to understand that. That being said, I did believe he could handle the rode just as I knew that Dani believed in the kid as well.

The only thing I wondered about was what this Pan was really like. I had heard his name so many times now but knew nothing substantial about him. He was becoming a mystery that I would have to solve. If I didn't, I would be at another disadvantage as I knew that somehow he was a piece in John's game. Not on John's side, but a piece on the board nonetheless.

"I wish we could have done more for you, sir, but this is all we had." Thomas apologized as he looked over the haul I was working with.

"Don't worry about it. A couple bags of rice and a rowboat will get us where we need to be. Trust me, I've worked with less." I smiled as I shoved off from the shoreline.

"I hope to see you again, and good luck." He wished as we started to float off into the distance. I did not reply. Instead, I gave him a salute and set sail onto the next adventure.

Part 4
River Ride

Early October 10 A.L.A

Chapter 15
Like Water

While we sat on the boat and floated, I watched the river flow. I have always loved the Mississippi and its majesty. No matter what happened, the river continuously flowed without a wavering moment. It had a strength that I had always admired during my years living next to it. I watched the water move along the shoreline and pass below us. It crashed into the shores and retreated. I could put my hand in the water, breaking the surface, and it flowed around my fingers as well as through them. Never did it have to wonder where it was going. It just moved where it needed to. Then I watched the lily pads near the shoreline. Depending on the current, they would move in or out, yet despite their tenderness, they never broke.

I looked over at Mark to ask him about the things I saw, but he had decided to take a nap which left me alone in my head. I decided to clean my weapon for the first time in weeks instead. As I began to work on it, I noticed something stuck in the unfolding mechanism. I yanked at the obstruction a few times until it popped out. A letter with my name on it. On the back was a stamp made from blood. John did enjoy his theatrics. It read as follows:

Dear Rob,

I miss the old days. You know the ones before I shot the woman you loved. They were so pure and wonderful. At least I thought meeting you was a blast or was that just because there were a few explosions in that first mission. Who knows?

Thought I'd see how you were doing. I know this seems out of place, but it is boring not having you around to toy with. I know you are following the plan the best you can, and I appreciate it, but there is just something about having you here. I do wish we could have worked things out, Rob. I hope I could make you see that what I am doing is best. And more importantly, I wish I could fulfill my destiny as a death bringer with you by my side, but you have always cared about the lives of others. Admirable, but it will cost you, my old friend. With the end nearing for us, I will teach you the flaw in your thinking. I will teach you that death is the answer we were looking for years ago in that abandoned subway.

I hope that Ex didn't rough you up too much. They are good at their job, but leaving people alive isn't their specialty.

See you soon, Rob

I didn't understand the point of John's notes. He had always been a bit scatter-brained, but it almost seemed like he was desperate to talk to me. At the same time, I wondered if it was meant to be a mind game in some way. Almost a signal that he is in control. The first time was in that nowhere city when he gave one to random guards, and now he had Ex plant it on me while I was knocked out.

Then there were his words. The first note outlined how he started down his path, and then the second seemed like he was just trying to talk to me without giving me a way to respond. He even referenced a conversation from our first mission together and spoke about the end. It just didn't make sense with the egotistical nut job I had come to know for so long.

I pondered the note for a few minutes trying to see any hidden message he might have left, but there was nothing. After recognizing this, I slipped the note into my bag and finished cleaning my staff. The staff was an unassuming weapon, but it could be a deadly force in the right hands.

Blood coated the ends and random spots from the many broken noses and jaws during my short journey. Ever since Gene gave it to me before our battle in that farmhouse, I have felt a connection to it. I don't know if it was a message from him or John, but the inscription on the handle, "Keizoku wa chikara nari," or "to continue is power," just found me at the right time.

"So why don't you use a blade?" Mark asked me as I scraped the blood out of the engraving.

"Sure, now you wake up after I start cleaning," I answered as I collapsed the weapon and unfolded it a few times to make sure it moved correctly.

"You didn't answer the question, you little twerp. It's a simple question, but your avoidance tells me that there is something there." I rolled my eyes, knowing that I couldn't avoid the conversation if he really wanted to know. I just didn't understand why he cared.

"I don't enjoy killing. I have done it many times before, but there was a point where I swore to never kill again. Then John happened, and I became filled with anger. All I wanted to do was hurt and kill those who hurt the ones I cared about, but I thought I could restrain the monster by using this. I thought if I made it harder to kill, I would do so less." I told him.

"But why that thing? You could use any weapon, but you chose a stick. I mean, I even carry a small blade just in case a situation gets tight." Mark said in turn. I was surprised by the response though I didn't know why. I knew he had been alone in those woods. Still, I never considered his fighting ability outside of the intimidation of that bear.

"This was a gift from my old mentor Gene. In Despartian, Gene made a deal with John to protect Iris if Gene became this villain I had to face. But then John did what he does with his pawns. He had Gene kill himself just to break the deal. Now I want to use Gene's tool to fix the wrongs that our brother creates. Plus, it just felt like a nice F-you kind of thing." I answered him. This satisfied his curiosity for the time being. He didn't dig anymore; he just sat back and appeared to listen to the water and skies for a few hours. While I kept the boat from being consumed by the river.

We docked the boat on the shoreline as night began to fall, and we made camp. The nights were growing cold as the northern winds started to trickle down south, so I built a ferocious fire to keep us warm.

As I sat with my eyes fixated on the fire, my mind flashed terrifying images in front of me. At first, it was the Executioner walking out of the flames, then after I shook him off, John stood in front of a burning city. Was it Despartian or some other one? I was not sure, but I could see his silhouette laughing with the fire as his backdrop. My heart began to accelerate while my body started to shiver. I tried to breathe myself into a calm state, but more darkness began to move in as I did. John's presence continued to fight every lesson Mark preached. Though I was getting better sometimes, he was still too mighty of a foe to push out of my mind.

I started to wonder if this had all been planned out since the first time we talked on a rooftop in Despartian or if the plan stretched farther back. If he honestly had that type of foresight, would I be able to beat him? Then you add this new partner of his that fought, unlike any man I had ever met. I wasn't sure if I could beat John. The second foe only added to that doubt. My thoughts were plummeting into those dark places again as I buried my head into my knees.

"What's on your mind, boy? I can hear you shaking despite the glorious fire you constructed." Mark whispered.

"I'm calling bull on that one," I said unconfidently as my head rose from my knees. Even if he couldn't hear the shaking, the desperation was now evident to him.

"You still have a long way to go, kid. When you sit, your staff hangs off your hip, and as your body moves, it clunks the wood you are sitting on, making a unique sound. Why don't you tell me why you're shaking?" He suggested.

"It was John and his new Executioner. I was trying to come up with a strategy, but all I saw was defeat. As you spoke of before, I tried trusting, but historically, things do not just work out when it comes to John. They are manipulated in his favor." I explained as my shakes calmed down ever so slightly.

"Is that so? And what exactly is bending things in his favor?"

"I don't know. His plans just always work."

"Have you ever thought that there is no set plan, but instead a loose plot that he adjusts to the flowing nature of the world."

"What?" Mark had taught me several lessons by this point, but this time I had nothing.

"Poor wording, but let me explain it this way. What if there isn't a plan? There might be a goal, but I don't think he has planned as much as you think."

"Come now. I know you can't be blind to everything I told you. John has had everything laid out from the start."

"See, that's where you are mistaken, Rob. The reason you can't get ahead of John is that he is not a planned road. Rigid and set; instead, he is like this river. He had a set start and finish point, but everything between is a flowing push and pull. Ever-changing and ever-adapting to the world around it while slowly changing the world around it as well."

"No, it's all planned. I've been there during some of his plans and…." As I spoke, I hesitated for a moment. I thought of my experiences with John and the plans he had set. Maybe it wasn't as scripted as I thought. Just perhaps I made a mistake when I read John. Even when we played chess, go, or shogi, he made me think I was playing into his plans, but there was no plan. He was just better at adapting than I was.

"Notice something?"

"How could he adapt so easily?"

"As the great Bruce Lee used to say, 'be like water."

"And that means?

"It means by living in the present moment, you learn to push and pull with the tide of life. You are strong when the moment demands strength, but the awareness to know when to be soft. To take shape when you are put in a role that demands form, but formless when you have the freedom to move."

"I think it is starting to make sense," I informed him.

"I bet it is, but let's practice a fighting form that will drive the point home and make you unpredictable when you fight them." He instructed. Mark rose from his seat and moved into a battle position.

I rose to meet the old man. I didn't want to strike, but I also knew someone had to act for the sake of the lesson. I threw my fist, but instead of blocking it or avoiding it, he moved with it. He shifted like a lily pad as he guided my fist. My momentum carried me towards him, and he accelerated the process with a single touch. By guiding me further than I planned to move, my body was thrown off balance and had he intended to, I would have been vulnerable to a strike. I tried a few more times, but each attempt ended in the same manner until I was exhausted.

I felt like I should've known better, but I tried to hit him again. Unlike the last time, he didn't just avoid my strikes; he used them against me. Instead of blocking, he guided my strikes and pushed me into a position of unbalance. He never landed a blow, but I was growing exhausted with every movement. Eventually, I conceded.

"I yield." I panted.

"Use their own movement against them, Rob. You have become an expert at attacking and countering movements, but it has made you predictable. Instead, I want you to learn to flow with your opponent, become unpredictable like the lily pad you watched. John is not expecting you to move with him. Instead, he wants you to move against him for his plan to work. He is a river and expects you to try to swim against the current. He'll never expect you to flow with it." Mark explained.

"Can we continue our practice on this, but with you attacking this time?" I asked.

"We can, but not tonight. Tonight you need rest. As we will start to combine lessons starting tomorrow and soon we will add the last one." He informed me. I wanted to keep training, but he insisted I rest. I found an excellent middle ground by falling into a deep meditation. I worked on becoming more mindful of the moment and started to reflect on the lessons.

Chapter 16
Storm Brewing

We started our journey as soon as the sun peeked over the horizon like we would do many times afterward. We were unsure where the next step would be, but I knew it had to be somewhere along the river. John was planning something that went deep, and he would have needed time to prepare. He had to have the infrastructure already prepared. That left the final two Ascension strongholds in the Americas as the most logical spots. We were on our way towards Memphis, and if he wasn't there, New Orleans would be my last chance. Luckily both were along the riverfront. Regardless of the final destination, the journey would be long, especially when I accounted for the breaks I took for training.

A couple days passed with little remarkable news, but Mark and I continued to train. Each night we would have a central focus; sometimes, it was mindfulness, concentration, trust at times, and then moving like water. He combined physical training with mental fortitude. He was determined to help me find balance not only within the physical realm but a spiritual one as well. As I grew stronger, I also found that my mind started to find peace. I discovered that the more in touch I was, the more the nightmares seemed to fade.

On top of that, my twisted hatred for John started to lessen as well. It was a freeing feeling. A feeling that I didn't even have before the War. Even back then, I had some early signs of depression that I always had to fight with, but now I was learning to just be happy.

Then one day, just before landing near Memphis, things grew deeper between us. Our bond strengthened from the trust we shared that day. It started just like any other. I steered the boat, and Mark listened for any disturbance that I couldn't see.

"Boy, pull the boat off the river!" Mark ordered. The urgency in his voice worried me. It was rare for him to grow anxious like this.

"What is it?"

"A storm is coming our way, and if we do not reach shelter, our journey is over!" he yelled, pointing towards the shoreline.

"Understood, but can you explain how you deduced this oh wise one," I said. I may have been learning to live in the present, but Mark was still the master. I always wanted to know what I missed. While I waited, I steered the boat to a clear landing on the west side.

"You haven't listened to me once, have you? What do you hear right now?" He asked. I tried to listen but could only locate the sound of the wind and waves moving us through the river.

"I don't hear anything." I finally responded.

"And that is the key, you idiot. It is easy to notice what is added, but we need to recognize what is absent at times. When the weather's nice, wildlife fills the atmosphere. They should be enjoying the day. However, animals have a keen sense of weather changes. They run when trouble comes, and I advise that we do the same." As soon as he pointed this out, I began to notice my surroundings. The lively world around us from earlier in the journey was dead, and that never boded well. I decided to row us in to quicken the pace knowing Mark's prediction would soon be confirmed.

After I tucked the boat safely into the shoreline, we found a small cave hidden in the old Hatchie Wildlife Refuge. We were all alone outside of a couple turtles bopping around in the water. It was peaceful hiding from the storm and taking a break from our rigorous training. As we sat and chatted, I realized that I never asked him the big question about his eyes. I don't know how it never came up beforehand is beyond me, so I dove into it at last.

"So, I'm curious, Mark, how did you lose your eyesight and end up in that cabin?" I asked him.

"Ah, that is an easy one. I got some shampoo in my eyes once and got lost looking for a towel," he laughed.

"I'm being serious. We have been together for a while now, and yet I don't know about that part of your life." I persisted.

"Did you ever think that I didn't tell you because you don't need to know?" He responded hostilely. I was shocked by his anger. Despite all my annoying habits, he had rarely raised his voice like that with me.

"I'm sorry for asking. I just thought that it would be better for us to be open."

"Better to be open. You sound like my wife, you little punk," he started as he paused for a minute, "Yeah, my wife would agree with you, and it does play into our fifth lesson. I guess there is no harm in telling you the brief story." He leaned forward in his seat and recalled the tale as if it was yesterday.

"First, you should know that I had two children a son and daughter. My boy was working at a lab in his college town during the war. He ended up building something that I can't even remember the purpose of. He was so proud of it and invited us to his first public demonstration. Despite the fact it was something peaceful, those brutes known as Reverters thought it was a tool for war and sabotaged it."

"As soon as my son turned on his creation, the machine blew. Tossing me across the room like a ragdoll. Fire and chemicals were spread around the room from the blast. The next thing I knew, I was lying in a hospital bed sometime later. I continued to move my eyelids, thinking I would see again, but my sight never returned. On top of losing my sight, my family and most of the lab crew were dead."

"There were only two survivors of the blast outside of myself. One was severely mangled, and the other was in a coma. The worst part of it was when I could finally be wheeled down to the morgue; I couldn't even identify the bodies. They were burnt messes that my touch couldn't distinguish. I had to trust that the doctors had matched the I.D.s to the correct bodies. I felt their faces that were burned and destroyed. I tried to hold my composure as I had been guided by an attendant but couldn't. I was at my lowest moment being stared at by some stranger just there because the hospital needed bodies to run. I had lost everything precious because the Reverters were so convinced that my son was inventing a weapon. As soon as I was able to walk, I ran. Eventually, I found that shack where I figured I'd die, alone and in peace." He cried as I sat in silence.

I walked over to his side and placed my hand on his shoulder. It was difficult to see Mark like this. So, far I had only seen him as this powerful blind man with super hearing. And now he was falling apart in front of me. I didn't have the right words, but still tried my best.

"I'm so sorry Mark."

"There is nothing to be sorry about. You cannot change what fate that has already occurred." He sniveled as he tried to regain a little bit of his normal composure.

"Fate…fate does have a funny way of working. Especially, when bringing lost souls together. It is perfect timing for the two of us to find each other. We needed normal, and luckily our version of normal is screwed up." I commented as I pulled one of the bullets from my pocket.

It was the one that was never fired. The one that John used to torture me. I was at such a low point, drinking, womanizing, and running from my problems. While also feeling tempted to put the bullet in my head as I had considered it before I was given the shell. Yet, I didn't do it. Then through the destruction, I found peace with Iris. I thought I was bordering on happiness until John took her from me. Usually, I would have lashed out after thinking about it, but I was able to calm myself that day. John wasn't there, nor was Iris' corpse. Why should I have let it consume me?

"We did find each other, but as I sat in that cabin, I discovered something even more important. You have to be able to find yourself. The last lesson we have is on insight." He explained after gaining his composure.

"What do you need me to do?"

"Insight in mindfulness teachings is looking inward. It is about looking at the ugliness as you try to figure out why you are the way you are. I want to talk about John. He killed your fiancé, but you have reservations. I want you to really dig into why that is the case." He lectured.

"I guess we have to go back to the start because that is where it starts. This could be a long one." I told him.

"Don't you know, kid, that when you are old, all you know is long stories, plus this storm is going to keep us down for a few minutes. Open up, young blood." He ordered as I thought back to the first time John and I met. Which was the day we became brothers.

Chapter 17
Invasion

It started seven years ago, and if I recall, correctly it was late summer. The Civil War was two and a half years in and nearing its finish. Thanks to the sacrifices made at the slaughter of Despartian, the northern forces were able to crush the Reverter northern front, which effectively ended organized battles outside of the southwest. Those that based their ideology on hate and racism were nearly defeated. This allowed the Unity army to hone in and crush the rest of the rebellion. However, what we didn't know at the time was that the War was merely entering its second act.

Up to that point, the squad I was a part of was considered elite, but not the legend it would become. We were a rag-tag bunch that was very good at what we did, and we were led by a man who was exceptional himself. Each mission we took part in was suicidal, yet we continued to prosper through it all because we cared for each other and protected each other. We knew no one else would be there for us, so we became family. Unfortunately, during a mission in Texas where we were flushing out a group of the Reverter rebels, a member of our team by the name of Tom caught a stray bullet and didn't pull through. We were forced to find a replacement as our missions were too critical to be down a man.

Now when I say forced to find, I mean we were assigned a new man. As you can imagine, this is where John enters the story. He was a man shrouded in mystery even back then. Typically, the team would have gotten a file on the new member, but all we received was a sheet of paper completely blacked out. All we knew for sure was his name and rank. The rest was a rumor, and no one could confirm where he was during the first half of the War. These rumors about him ranged from convict to spy to soldier caught defecting. Even he refused to tell us his story at the time or any time after. As imagined, when a group is as tightly knit as ours, a man of mystery made integration a challenge. He was just put on our transport as we headed off to L.A.

The ride to L.A. was silent. We tried to chat a bit with a friendly act, but it just felt uncomfortable. He seemed to have a grudge against us before we even fought together. Making things worse was the magnitude of where we were going. The first bullet of the War was fired when Jeffery Irons, the peace activist, was shot in New Orleans. Still, the War became what it was when the first group of Reverter rebels took command of some navy ships and flattened L.A. with them.

Ever since the city had been considered a sacred site, and no one wanted to fight there. However, rumors started to swirl that a group of rebels camping out in the remnants of Fort MacArthur. This raised two concerns as the fort had been resurrected to watch over the Pacific in case of invasion. The second was that we couldn't allow any rebellion to remain. It was all or nothing. Then the rumors seemed to be proven true when communication was cut off the week before we arrived. This loss of communication mobilized our unit and started the mission.

Our transport brought us to the edge of the city. We didn't know what was awaiting us in the city, so we decided to walk into town, assuming it would be easier to sneak in. We trudged our way through the rubble that was the new L.A. Craters littered the ground, and we had to be careful with every step. I couldn't imagine the bombardment that the ships unleashed on the city. I never got to see it before it fell, but I had seen enough pictures and what remained was a pitiful shell.

As we plunged deeper into the city, our marksman Dave collapsed to his knees. We ran to his side, unsure of what happened, but then he began to cry. Dave had often been a rock on the team as one of the older men, but L.A. was too much for him. One of the most brutal men I knew was having a breakdown.

L.A. was his home. He was raised there and raised his own family there. His wife and two-year-old son lived in the city when the bombs started to fall, but he was in Sacramento when the fire fell from the sky without them. He lived, but at a cost, no man should endure.

Now that I have lost the woman I loved, I could empathize with him compared to the sympathy I had at the time. Gene bent down to comfort him the best he could while the rest of us surrounded him. Well, the rest of us except for our newest member. John stood with a scrunched face. He had no need for camaraderie, and something wasn't sitting right with him.

"I don't think we are entering a city of rebels," John claimed while the rest of us assisted Dave to his feet.

"What makes you say that?" I asked him as I started to scan the city for the signs he must have been referring to.

"Do I have to spell it out for you, or are you as smart as everyone says you guys are?" He asked with a snarl. He was and is still an ass, but I scanned harder. He wouldn't have been that arrogant if there wasn't a reason. I looked at the fallen buildings, eventually picking up on movement. However, the idea of people living within the rubbish was not a revolutionary thought, nor did it clarify who they were. The War forced survivors to live wherever was convenient, and this was accessible.

"Are you referring to the refugees? They could very easily be the rebels we are looking for." I started as I continued to study the horizon.

"You guys are supposed to be elite, but I guess I have to spell it out for you. Grab a scope and look closer at those people. All those people are wearing uniforms and are oriental!" He shouted, throwing a spare scope at me!

"Hey, I don't appreciate the term oriental new guy," Chen commented.

"My apologies, they are wearing uniforms and appear to be from East Asia." He replied, though his eyes did roll. It was the first indication of some deep hate in John's soul though it was never consistent. I don't think he intended to spew racism. I think he was just lashing out at his first victims and trying to dehumanize his enemies.

With that said, I started to scan the buildings closer and noticed that he was right. Every man was of Southeast Asian descent while wearing fatigues and looking healthier than a refugee should. As I looked over the buildings, the rest of my team used their own scopes, and when the realization consumed us that these were not just rebels, we grew tense. This was supposed to be an easy mission and hopefully our last one, but we now knew that this was an invasion force. We weren't going to be able to just scare them off.

Feeling the urgency, we all drew our weapons, entered our infiltration formation, and snuck into the first building before we were detected. With me at point, Gene in the middle, Dave in the rear, and everyone else filling out the gaps, we started to formulate a plan.

"Alright, gentlemen, this is no longer a simple in and out mission. We have to be smart about this. John, based on the rumors I heard about you, you should make a perfect complement to Dave, so I want the two of you on the windows. If you see movement outside of the building, shoot at it. Meanwhile, Jackson and Rob, I want you two to clear the building above us. We need a safe base to strike from. The rest of us will protect our marksmen. Move out, men!" Gene ordered as he took control of our situation. John and Dave followed orders immediately. Dave had dropped two before Jack or I could reach the stairwell. Jackson's knife play made him perfect for this situation. Though I didn't have much fighting experience before the War, I learned several fighting styles fairly quickly during it. We were the two best at close-range combat and were often tasked with situations like that.

Dave's shot drew enemies quickly to the stairwell, and they didn't stand a chance. The first one took a blade to the foot from Jackson as I flipped him down the stairs and put a bullet in his brain. Jackson dropped another with his classic dagger throw, and we separated at the top of the steps. I was quickly pinned down, but I was able to put one in the soldier's knee, and as he writhed in pain, I drove my own blade through him. Another tried a chokehold, but a headbutt with the back of my head broke his nose. I followed with two shots to the chest. As I caught my breath, I studied the men I had just killed and saw that they were part of the People's Liberation Army. I couldn't figure out why Chinese soldiers would be in L.A.

I moved cautiously through the rest of the floor as we continued to clear the building. I entered the final room and found a pile of dead refugees. Out of instinct, I shot the door that had been open next to me. A soldier dropped. The building was clear on my side. As I started to head back to the rest of my team, I caught a glimpse of something through the window. I approached it and was shocked. A Chinese tank was cruising down the street next to us. I rushed back to my team to warn them of our threat.

"Is everything alright?" Gene asked, seeing me run back to him.

"Upstairs is clear, but we have bigger problems, Gene. There is a PLA tank strolling down the street next to us." I explained as I caught my breath. He closed his eyes for a moment to formulate a plan and shook his head countless times when a preposterous one came to mind.

"Alright, I have an idea," Gene started as he removed some explosives from his pack, "I should have enough here to take the tank out, but we have to use them wisely. That means for us to pull this off successfully, I need two volunteers to distract them while we hit it with our supplies." He had barely finished before I had raised my hand. It would be a deadly distraction, but I was always up for that kind of mission. The only question was, who would be my partner?

"I'll go as well." John voiced from behind me as he reloaded his weapon. We were all a bit surprised, but there was no time to question our new addition's willingness. Gene nodded and started to draw up a map in the dirt he would reference during the plan.

"So, I need you two to move to the building here and take cover. From there, you need to wait until the tank is near our location. Then start firing on any soldiers escorting the tank so that they are drawn away from us as we make our move. Once they are focused on you, the rest of us will start placing the bombs and blow it sky high." Gene instructed as we each reloaded our weapons in preparation for the firefight.

"Sounds easy enough," I smirked.

"Good luck, gentlemen." Gene wished as we headed out.

The two of us scurried down the street to the new building and slid into safety before the tank convoy could turn the corner. We positioned ourselves next to a crumbling building and hunkered down, waiting for the convoy to inch closer. We lined our shots, and on my command, we dropped two of them. Unsure of what had happened, the rest hid behind the tank and opened fire.

"I bet I can kill more people than you." John quipped as he prepared to return fire.

"Are you serious? Does that matter right, now?" I asked, appalled by the lightness he was approaching the situation with.

"No," he stated as he stood up to fire back and returned to safety, "but just so you know, I'm up to three, and you are at one here." He was egging me on, and I am ashamed to say it was exciting to have him push me like that. That should have been my first warning sign with John. He was trying to turn me into him. He wanted someone else who saw opponents merely as pieces in a game, expendable pieces.

The soldiers of the convoy were nervous. I could tell by their shot patterns, and it didn't take long to have them all focused on us. The next key was keeping them on us. John and I fired on them relentlessly. It was to the point that we had to feel like 100 men, but they still had numbers and could close in on us. This allowed the rest of the team to sneak towards the tank with the explosives. While we fired, we caught our allies out of the corner of our eyes. Their hands were on their guns, wishing they could help, but they knew that their job was to be done in silence. We kept our guns quiet while they worked. We couldn't risk a stray bullet, but this allowed the enemies to grow closer. A few tried to breach our position, but once they were that close, John and I could handle them without gunfire.

Our team placed the charges in position as quickly as they could and scurried off. Once clear, they set them off and destroyed the tank. Then we all cleared the remaining guards. We thought this was a victory until a second cannon fired upon John and me dropping the building around us.

Chapter 18
Separated but Destined

I'm not sure how long I was out cold, but the next thing I knew, I was squirming under a metal beam. My leg was pinned and growing numb. Then I heard John calling my name. By some miracle, both of us survived the ambush of our ambush.

"Is there anyone alive down there?" John called as I tried to free myself.

"Yeah, but my leg is stuck!" I yelled back as I prayed that he wasn't in a similar scenario.

"I guess I should come and free you then! Just keep talking so that I can find you!"

I don't know if I've ever breathed a greater sigh of relief than at that moment. He was not only alive but able to move. I followed his instructions and talked nonsense for several minutes until he found me. When I saw him, he was a bloody mess, and I wondered how broken he was, but first, I had to worry about myself. With the proper leverage and enough intense effort, we were able to pry the beam off. From there, we took inventory of our injuries. I knew something in my right leg was off, and two of my ribs were damaged. John had a gash across his head, which resulted in a mild concussion and a laceration that nearly ripped his left oblique apart. I think that oblique injury haunts him today. Needless to say, we were beaten up, but considering a building fell on us, we were in good shape. We were lucky that the building was already Swiss cheese and could only drop segments on us. Had the city not endured a bombardment already, we would have been crushed by all the steel. Still, by the time we arrived, it was just enough to support some drywall and wiring that shattered when the tank struck it.

Once we had collected ourselves, we started to crawl through the rubble. I did not move very fast, and he had issues turning during our slither. We pushed debris out of the way as we clawed our way to fresh air. We pushed the final piece out of our way and saw that our only light came from the moon. We had been stuck under that building for some time. I limped around looking for my team, but the only things I found were the corpses of the men we had killed and the burnt husk of the tank. Our men had not died there, at least.

"Somehow, your friends made it out of here alive. Unfortunately, I'm going to assume they are now prisoners. What we need to worry about is what we will do? We are broken, outgunned, outmanned, out everything." He pointed out as he pulled a flask from his pocket.

"I don't care what you do, but that is my family we are talking about. I'm not abandoning my brothers." I informed him! I wasn't sure what I was going to do, but I was confident in my conviction. He took a long pull from the flask and offered it to me.

"I can already tell you are going to do something stupid, so have some leg healing juice, better known as bourbon." He offered. Even though he hadn't said he'd come, I could tell that he wasn't going to let me go alone.

"I have always been more of a tequila guy, but leg healing juice sounds good," I answered while taking a swig myself. Without another word, we made our way towards the fort. There was no plan but two stubborn men on the march. A few minutes into our walk, a voice called out to us.

"Hello, strangers!" An old slurred female voice yelled. We turned to see this short, frail old woman of what appeared to be Native American descent waving at us from inside a nearly collapsed building.

"Who are you?" I called back as I started to look for my weapon. I could see John doing the same as we awaited the woman's response.

"I'm merely an old woman who is going to live longer than you two if you don't get out of the kill zone!" She clapped back, retreating inside the building.

"Should we follow her?" I asked.

"Let's put it this way. I have more faith in our ability to fight in close quarters than in the wide open," John explained as he limped towards the building the old woman inhabited. Once inside, we noticed that there wasn't anyone there. The old woman we had both just talked to was gone. We looked over the whole building but couldn't find any sign of her.

"You coming?" the slurred voice called from below us. John and I looked at each other like we were idiots as I moved the shaggy carpet below our feet and found a trap door. Which housed the old woman and a secret path below the city.

"Alright, follow me and stay close. This is not an easy passage to cross." She insisted as she began to crawl through a hole in the wall. I looked at John, hoping he would have some type of wisdom, but he just shrugged his shoulders. Without a protest, I decided to follow. We kept our distance as we still couldn't trust her, but she was almost the one pulling away from us. She moved through the tunnel precisely and nimbly in a way the two of us could not replicate. Between our injuries and larger built frames, the tunnel was a challenge. We kept up, but just barely.

She eventually led us to an old subway terminal that had collapsed outside of a few square feet. Once my feet were firmly placed on the terminal, I studied the square footage that wasn't under rubble. There were metal huts and about twenty scraggly inhabitants walking around, just trying to survive. I studied them and realized quickly that they would neither be a threat or help. Most of them were women and children with a bit of fight in their eyes. Years of malnourishment and difficult living had broken their souls.

"What is this place? And why does it smell like excrement?" my partner asked. I slapped my forehead with my palm after he added the second part. My early impressions of John were that he was skilled but lacked any form of social literacy. He just spoke without caring for others.

"This is one of the sanctuaries that exist for those that lost everything, and when I say everything, I mean bathrooms too." She answered, leading us towards the farthest hut.

"That is a comforting thought. Was it the E. Coli that brought your numbers down?" John insulted. I would learn later in our journey that this was his level of sensitivity, no matter the circumstance. He just prods at a person until they want to kick in his teeth.

"You are a piece of work. Our numbers have declined since the invasion started." She explained as her voice trailed off. The topic of the invasion was clearly one of deep pain.

She led us into her hut, where a much younger woman made dinner over an open fire. Outside of the young woman, the hut wasn't much to look at. There was just clutter everywhere. I don't think I had ever met a refugee that managed to be a hoarder at the same time.

"This is cozy, but can I ask you why you are helping us and who you are?" I asked while the old woman started to search the junkpiles.

She ignored my question as she pulled a black metal tube from her pile. "This thing may be crude, but hopefully it will work, so try it on and let me know what you think." She handed me the brace, and I fidgeted with it until I could make it work. The device didn't help with the pain in my leg, but it did give me extra strength to stand on.

"You didn't answer his question. Why are you helping us, and who are you?" John followed up as I tried to make my new contraption fit comfortably.

"I'm just an old woman who was taught to help lost souls." She said.

"And why do you think we are lost?" I asked, not letting John say something offensive.

"Because of the aura that you two give off." She replied as she walked over to the younger lady at the fire.

"Rob, this bat is crazy. I think we should leave." John whispered as he turned his back to leave.

"What are you running from, knɨy?" The woman asked, stopping John.

"What did you call me?" He asked as he turned back to her.

"Knɨt, it means fox in my tribe's language." She explained.

"Just say fox then, you old hack. And I'm not running from anything. I'm just done wasting my time speaking with you. As it is clear that you speak nonsense." John fired back. He wasn't upset, but her assertion that he was running seemed to trigger something in him that I couldn't explain. He stepped outside, done with the conversation.

"And what about you šaq'?" She asked, turning her attention to me.

"Should I even guess?"

"It means turtle. I like you. It is too bad that your destiny is entwined with that one."

"Why do you say that?"

"Because when I saw you, two, and your auras radiated, I could tell that you are destined to run together forever. More importantly, I could tell that one of you will bring death and the other life wherever you go.”

“Bull! We’re both soldiers and death bringers!” John yelled as he stepped back into the tent. He had just perched himself right outside the door. He was curious about the old woman after all.

“Maybe it is. Maybe everything I say is bull as you say knly. There is no way to tell if the supernatural is real, but I can only tell you what I see.” She responded, not trying to counter John but engaging him.

He was ready to fire back, but I had to interject first, “And what else do you see?”

“Rob, don’t buy into this insanity.” He argued as I said nothing. I wanted to hear her.

“I saw freedom, but two paths that counter each other every step of the way. I saw things much greater than this War. I saw a battle between sin and salvation that will decide whether man is meant to walk this Earth.”

“Bats-” John started.

“Fascinating, but if we will not know more until after the War. I believe my partner is right, and we should head out.” I replied. I wasn’t sure if she was crazy or a prophet, but continuing this conversation would be pointless the way John was behaving. So I decided it was best to end it.

“No, I insist that you stay and eat before your battle. If you are to fend off the invaders, you will need to be nourished.” She invited us as she handed us each a bowl. John rolled his eyes, but I accepted. The young woman poured us some of the stew as we sat with them. After the first step, I understood why everyone in the encampment was malnourished. Don’t get me wrong, she was not a bad cook, but there is no good meal when there are no ingredients outside of scraps and bugs. We all finished our bowls, but it was a stomach-aching experience. I had to clench my jaw multiple times to avoid puking what little nutrition I was consuming.

Given the quality of the meal, none of us spoke much during it. I could see both of them struggling at times as well. We all just wanted it to end as quickly as possible, but some mild, base-layer conversation occurred. Mostly centered around how the old lady had managed to collect so much junk. She was descriptive with some of it and utterly vague with other pieces. I looked for a pattern, but I think she may have just been a hoarder.

"Well, thank you for all your help, ladies, but we should be going," I claimed after I had finished the stew. John started to follow me when the old lady grabbed both of our arms.

"As your current doctor, I advise that you both stay the night. Your bodies and spirits need to rest so that you can be at full strength. Besides, I think my granddaughter wants to speak with kniy." She insisted. During dinner, I noticed that the two of them kept looking at each other but hadn't thought anything of it until she mentioned it. The young woman rose from her silent seat and took John by the hand. They walked out of the tent as the old woman held onto me.

"Did I miss some under the table footsie?" I asked, suddenly flustered by the way events unfolded.

"No, it isn't a physical thing going on between them. However, their souls were both calling out for something like their own. As they locked eyes, they heard each other's cries. Now they will talk to each other, and I think my granddaughter will understand why your friend is running. Meanwhile, he will hear what has been killing her soul in a way that I cannot." She explained in a far more serene voice than she had before.

"Sounds like mumbo jumbo to me, but I guess I lost the vote," I admitted, sitting back at the table.

"You are right. You don't get a vote, but in the meantime, we can talk. Do you know where you two are headed?"

"To the fort was our original mission, and now that our allies are captured, I believe it is even more pressing to get there."

"If you go the straight route, you will never make it."

"And what would you suggest then?"

"There are tunnels from our little subway to the fort's walls. If you follow that, you shouldn't have to fire any shots." She explained while grabbing a piece of paper and a pen. She started to draw a map to the fort and insisted on which turns would get us where we needed to go.

"And how do I know I can trust you?" I asked as she finished her drawing.

"I already saved you once. I don't think pointing you towards death would be beneficial at this point." She replied as she handed me the drawing. I wasn't sold on everything, but she had numerous chances to kill us, and yet we were still alive.

Once she was done explaining the pathway, I tried to listen to John and the girl, but the old lady slapped me in the back of the head.

"Leave them alone."

"Fine, but can you tell me more about the death and life bringing you see?"

"Every person is destined for building or destroying, but it is the choice that decides which."

"So, your prophecy means nothing?"

"No, it means that you will each make a choice at some point, and it will likely counteract the other. From there, you two will have to decide what to do."

"So, I can choose my path?"

"That is the funny thing about destiny and fate. You either choose your destiny, or you were destined to choose. Either way, the person is correct."

"Anything useful to say?"

"No, because me telling you more can affect your choices, or maybe it won't, but I'd prefer to be safe."

After this, John and the girl came in. It was clear from the red in their eyes that both had cried, but neither wanted to speak more. I explained the tunnels to John, and then the old lady suggested we both go to bed. I did not argue anymore. I thought I heard him cry a few more times that night, but I have never been able to convince him to confirm that with me.

Chapter 19
Fort MacArthur

The following morning John and I left before the rest of the refugees had awakened. Neither of us was particularly talkative in the morning. Instead, we began our journey through L.A.'s underground. I tried asking him questions, but he was different. He was still arrogant but not nearly as boisterous as before. He just seemed determined to do whatever was needed. I wish I could have been there to hear everything as it changed him at the time.

The directions she gave me led us through about three miles of various tunnels and pathways. Several of them were crumbling and flooding, but somehow, they were stable enough to use. Once at the end of the tunnels, we found a false dead end, just as the woman described. She had told me that she and the other refugees walled off the areas near the fort during the invasion. They feared that they would be tracked and hunted like dogs. However, she explained that there was an easy way to bust through it, and on the other end, we found a storage room in the basement.

"Do you think they heard the wall falling?" John whispered. Both John and I knew the answer to his question but hoped that no one was near enough to hear it.

"I don't know, but we have to be proactive about this, and I have an idea," I answered as I crept to the door. I grabbed a handful of rice stuffed in a bag and rolled it next to the door as I lightly tapped it. John hid behind some boxes as I hid behind some barrels, while voices started calling outside the room. My plan worked as one mentioned something about a rat.

Two men entered the room, searching the floor. They split up when one finally shined a light on the hole in the wall. It was at that moment John, and I jumped them. A quick twist of the neck took care of our problem in an instant. We were fast and efficient, and more importantly, it was a clean way of doing things. We stripped the men and hid their bodies behind the wall we loosely reconstructed. As we prepared to leave, an announcement came over the P.A. system. Every word was in Chinese, and I was clueless as I looked at my partner.

"Did you understand that at all?" I asked.

"Unfortunately, I did. They said that the execution will be in the courtyard in twenty minutes."

"We have to hurry then!" I exclaimed, mindful of my voice level.

"Hold on. It might be too late for them already; we have to complete the mission we were originally sent to L.A. for. Everyone will be at the execution, which means we'll be able to sneak to the communication center unimpeded. We can send a distress signal and end this invasion." John argued.

"Don't do this now, John. We have come too far, and I am not abandoning my comrades."

"This is a team that goes on suicide missions. Dying was what we signed up for."

"Death is the last resort, not a guarantee. I am saving them; you can do whatever you want."

"You are stubborn," John started as I nodded my head, "Do you at least have a plan?"

"Not in the slightest, but that has never stopped me before," I informed him as his jaw dropped. I don't think he expected me to be so candid with my ineptitude.

"Alright, how about you let me come up with a plan?" John started as he searched the room for anything of use.

"If you insist, but just shooting and stabbing has worked for me this long." John just shook his head. At last, he opened a container and found bottles of baijiu that he started placing on the ground. Afterward, we tore apart several of the empty bags scattered across the room.

I started following his lead and tore up several other bags. We then opened each bottle and placed the scraps inside. We grabbed our cocktails and made our way to the courtyard. We had to be cautious a few times, but there were not enough guards to stop the two of us. Even back then, we were better fighters than most soldiers, especially when we had the element of surprise.

At last, we arrived at the courtyard and a safe ledge that hid us from the guards surrounding it. There were a hundred armed guards and hundreds more spread throughout the facility out of our sight. In the center of all the guards stood five men pointing their rifles at my team. On the other hand, our men were on their knees with hands tied and a black cloth over their heads. They were not tied to the ground, which meant all they needed was a distraction to make a run for it.

"I hope you know this is not a good plan. We could have an army here by sunset tomorrow, but you want to take them all on by yourself." John reminded me as he prepared himself for battle. We loaded our weapons with the diminishing bullets we had. Then laid out the cocktails.

"I know, but it won't fail. It can't fail." I replied as I secured my brace and pulled out a few matches I kept in my shoes for when someone needed a smoke.

"I hate you; I just want you to know that before we die here." He informed me as he lined up his first shot.

"I don't really like you either," I answered as I aimed a couple cocktails at the larger crowd. John and I looked at each other one last time. I used my matches to light the first cocktail and sent it flying. It hit a guard square in the head and spread to several others in an instant.

Meanwhile, John took out the executioners in a blink of an eye. He had put two on the ground in quick succession, and the last three tried to find us, but John was as good as the rumors suggested. Almost as good as Dave.

Chaos quickly took hold as men began to scramble as they tried to understand what was happening. We were able to shoot several more men and launch a plethora of firebombs before the invasion force had found us and fired their first bullet.

While eyes were turning towards us, our team had moved to each other. Gene had taken command quickly as they unmasked each other. As a soldier would aim at them, John or I would make them our priority. They picked up the weapons the executioners had dropped and moved to the cover of one of the doors. From there, they began assisting us in taking out the guards. Reinforcements began to flood the courtyard, and we launched the last few cocktails at them to cut off their paths to us, and the rest of the team moved into one of the doors not filled with guards.

From there, I couldn't see how they were going to escape. Whatever route they took was likely littered with guards, but John and I had our own issues. Our location was blown, and men were going to close on us. We decided that our chances of making it out completely were slim. Hence, we headed to the communication center to try to accomplish the main objective.

Most of the guards had gone towards the rest of the team, anticipating us to run, which opened up our path. We had some light resistance as they had not expected the aggressive maneuver. Unfortunately, my leg began to worsen as we pushed on. I didn't tell John about my situation as I didn't want him to grow hesitant. I decided that I would help him push until I could no longer move.

They had kept only critical crewmen at the communication center. They were quickly dispatched. Once we had secured the room, I locked the door and blocked it with a few pieces of non-essential equipment. Once word spread that the room was ours, the entire force would be at our doorstep. While I handled our preparations, John began to work on the communication systems.

"Well, we made it," I commented as I loaded my weapon with one of my few remaining clips.

"Don't get comfortable. Once I start broadcasting, I figure we'll have about five minutes before this place is crawling with enemies. We have to hope someone responds before then." John responded as he loaded his own weapon.

"Attention any Unity forces near L.A., this is Shadow Squad! The country has been invaded, and we need assistance! Please respond!" John called into the headset. There was no reply. He sent the message again, still no answer. The minutes ticked by with no response, and I could hear the calls coming from outside the room. They tried to break the door in, but the metal held up.

"I don't think it's working," I informed him as I hid behind a barricade.

"It has to. This is Shadow Squad calling any nearby Unity forces! We need an army here now!" He screamed! All we heard was static as the door blew in. I fired on the opening, and John followed suit. We were in a firefight that we could not win. The two of us were in a frail state and low on ammo with no way out of that room. No one was coming to our aid, and we would be dead in minutes, but at least my team was safe.

"Shadow Squad, this is the USS Irons. Your message has been received, and all nearby Western forces are converging on your location." A staticky voice replied. At last, someone had picked up. Unity men and women were coming to end the invasion. We just hoped that we would live to see it.

"The country's counting on you, USS Irons!" John informed them as he returned fire as carefully as he could! The gunshots echoed across the radio frequency.

"Give them Hell Shadow Squad!" The man ordered. John and I smiled. We didn't know how far the ship was from us, nor did it matter. There was a chance that the team would see another mission.

"So, what's the next step?" I asked John as we hid behind the central console. Bullets were whizzing around us as the enemy forces were crashing down on us.

"To be quite honest, I didn't plan this far ahead. With your leg and my own injuries, I didn't think we'd make it this far." He chuckled as he loaded his last clip. I only had a few bullets myself and had to be sparse with my own return fire.

"So you're saying I surprised you." I inferred as I shot another man in the leg.

"You definitely did. You earned my respect, kid. I have never met anyone with the stones you have." He complimented, knocking a man's helmet off in the process. They were closing in on us slowly as they realized our ammo situation.

"You aren't too bad yourself. A bit of a prick, but I don't think there is anyone I'd rather be sitting shoulder-to-shoulder within my final moments. You earned the title brother by standing by me." I told him during the echoes of my last bullet.

He fired his last shot as well, and we were out of options. We were cooked when a large blast rang from behind us. It shook the whole building, and the enemies had fallen silent with their weapons. Another explosion rang. This time it was a little bit closer. All we could hear now were screams. We jumped from behind the barrier, grabbed the fallen soldiers' weapons, and pushed our way out. Something was happening, and we knew we could use the chaos.

Outside of the room, several holes now lined the walls of the fort. Dead or injured bodies were scattered across the floor. As we shot down the remaining guards with the weapons, we picked up along the way. We knew another wave would be coming soon, but we were saved for the moment.

We looked outside to see the source of the holes. There we saw our team next to a tank and a smaller escape vehicle. Gene tossed a rope up to us, and we secured it to one of the remaining pillars. The options were clear, but with my foot, I doubted my ability to climb down it.

"John, with my leg, I'm not going to be able to crawl down this thing. I'm going to stay here and cover you all. You have to..." I started before John pushed me off of the wall. I landed in the surprised arms of Dave and Jackson while John slid down the rope. I rose quickly to get in his face.

"You nearly killed me, you ass!" I screamed as our squad mate Chen started to drive us away.

"If I've learned one thing today, you are not that easy to kill." John laughed. I soon joined him as we remembered the day we had just gone through.

We were able to escape to the coastline where the Unity ships were moving in. We didn't know how many invaders were spread across the city, but our allies landed while more were on the move from a northern land base. Our job was done while the real battle was about to start for L.A.

Chapter 20
Meaning of it All

As I finished my story, I found the blind man was enthralled by it. At first, I thought he might have died. He was so quiet, but then I saw him breathing. As I started to reflect on the story, I realized how long ago that had all taken place. Things were far more straightforward back then, and with the chaos around me, it was nice to remember the easy times.

"And what about the refugees?" Mark asked after he finished pondering the story.

"Once our allied forces drove the invaders out, we went to look for them. Somewhere along the way, the refugee camp was discovered and executed for helping us. When John found out, he flew into a fit of rage. I tried to talk to him about it, but he shut me out. He beat-up several of the prisoners the forces took and had I not restrained him, they would have been killed by him. Whatever the two of them talked about, it was meaningful in ways I could never understand. I saw a shift after that day. When we met, he was at his most arrogant, but I saw him flash hope for a moment. Then I watched him grow more sadistic. He grew to enjoy killing, especially those that reminded him of the invasion force. I tried to talk to him about it countless times, but all he would say was that we all lose what we care about." I replied softly as I remembered how my friend handled the loss. In honesty, it reminded me of how I first reacted when he killed Iris.

"It seems that he lost someone that connected with his soul. Something like that can change a person forever. Something else you two have in common." Mark remarked as the storm continued to rage outside our little hideout. I hadn't thought about it like that, and it worried me. I began to think about the end of the road. After I kill John, what will become of me? Will I merely take his space, or will I be the good man Iris thought I was?

"Is killing John the right thing?" I asked as I tucked my knees tight into my chest.

"There is no such thing as right or wrong, Rob. In a universe, without higher thought, things would just happen. The only difference is we as humans are obsessed with labeling to associate meaning. We crave this meaning even though it only ever creates stress." Mark replied.

"But how can you say that? There seems to be so much evidence to the contrary." I argued.

"Evidence that had been created by man to apply meaning. Have you ever wondered why a herd never attacks alone predator after it picks off a weak link?"

"Can't say that I have."

"They don't retaliate because they understand that death is natural and someone will always die. A deer fears a wolf because they don't want to die but do not resent the wolf for doing what it must to survive, and the wolf is not haunted by the fact that it killed to survive. There is no right and wrong. There are only choices."

"So good and evil do not exist, you are saying. John's killing rampage is not evil because nothing is evil."

"I'm saying that if he wins, it will not be remembered as evil, whereas if you do, it will be. These labels exist because you apply them. However, to worry about how your actions will be interpreted is meaningless. All you can do is focus on what you believe will help you and those you care about survive."

"But how do I act if that is the case?" He smiled for a moment before he answered.

"Take the lessons I have taught you. Be mindful of the moment so that you can act only in the present. Concentrate on what is in front and around you to understand the moment. Learn about yourself so that your actions are always in line with your beliefs. Put forth the right effort to apply the needed action. Finally, trust that no matter the decision, what happens is best for the world." He smiled, trying to bring everything together at once.

"Maybe you aren't as crazy as I thought," I admitted as I stoked the fire. He had worked with me all this time just for this moment. I was already starting to change at that time, though it wouldn't be until later that I truly understood his wisdom.

"Oh, I'm still crazy, just smart too. Now let's talk about something more interesting, like that spark between you and the girl. You've gone on and on about Iris, but nothing about this woman."

"You mean Dani?"

"Yes, unless there is someone else I missed."

"She is my best friend and Iris's best friend. But yeah, I felt something a long time ago."

"And?"

"And I felt it again. There is just something about her. However, there was a complication; she was dating someone else. She was dating someone that she loved deeply. It sucked, but she was happy. Which is all I ever wanted. Then Iris and I got together, and things worked out. The two of them were best friends, and we were all happy." I told him as my eyes teared.

"Love is a difficult thing, kid."

"That might be the understatement of the century."

"Haha. You are right about that, but what is really bothering you about it?"

"When we were alone that night, we kissed, and it felt so right, but also like a betrayal."

"You said 'we,' so it wasn't you that initialized it?"

"I don't know who started it. I just know we both leaned into it."

"So she has feelings for you too, and now you don't know what to do next."

"That would be a good summary of events."

"Well, I wish I had a good answer for you, but this is something your heart has to figure out. However, I will say this. I don't think learning how to love someone again is a betrayal of those that have passed. Those that die want us to be happy if they love us. For some, that means they never love again, but I don't think that is possible when you are young. You can't let it destroy you, kid."

"I appreciate it, Mark, but you're right. I have to figure out how I feel before we see each other again."

"Not necessarily. You have to figure out how you feel about yourself first and who you are, and then the rest will take care of itself."

"Maybe you're right," I suggested as he nodded. There wasn't much else to say, and after some more small talk, we said goodnight. That was the problem. I didn't know what I wanted. I didn't know what I wanted to do when I caught John or when I saw Dani. More importantly, I didn't know how I felt about myself. I had been consumed by other things for so long I wondered if I deserved happiness. I wondered if it was something that I was meant to have, and if I was, what would it look like.

I didn't think killing my brother would make me happy, but leaving him alive the way he was wouldn't either. I didn't want to betray Iris's memory by loving Dani, but I didn't want to be alone either. Then I thought about Mark's speech on right and wrong and the old woman's speech on destiny, and a theme came to my mind: choice. Maybe it wasn't about the consequences or how I think it would make me feel. Perhaps I just had to make a choice and see what actually happened.

Part 5
Memphis

Late October ~22nd

Chapter 21
Devotion

By the morning, the storm had subsided, allowing us to ride the current again. As I navigated the water movement, I thought about the advice that Mark had given me. When I faced John, I felt that I had to do whatever aligned with where I was at that time. After he killed Iris, the mere thought of him would send me into a fit of rage. I was beating the guards in that nowhere town to a pulp because I had been so blind. I acted selfishly, which had never sat well with me. Then by the time I reached that part of my journey on the river, I started feeling the love I had for him once. He was broken, probably worse than I had ever been, but does that justify him. I just knew that hate wasn't going to control me anymore.

I've killed more people than I could have imagined, but now that I have only one I'm supposed to kill, I'm not sure if it is the route. Could I stop the destruction by committing more? I don't know, but the thoughts danced around in my head during our travels.

After a few days on the river, I started to recognize the terrain close to Memphis. I knew that it could have been the final destination. Crawling with people wanting to end my life, but we had to stop no matter what. Our supplies were depleted from the traveling and weather that we encountered.

My path was set. I was going to return to a city that I had left in ruin only a few years prior, and hopefully, it would not be filled with those who hated me.

"Any thoughts on what lies ahead of us?" Mark asked as he packed a bag for himself. We pulled the boat ashore and hid it behind several large branches that had fallen.

"If I'm being honest, I don't have the slightest idea. The last time I was in the city, it was nearly burnt to the ground. It is likely rebuilt around the Ascension headquarters." I explained as we walked down a tree-lined pathway. After walking a few more steps, Mark turned to the trees and stared at them. He had heard something, but what was a mystery to me.

"What's wrong?" I asked as I reached for my weapon.

"It's nothing. I thought I heard something familiar. But it is gone now." Mark claimed though his guard did not drop for some time after. As we continued our walk, he seemed distant, unlike anything I had seen before. Something was in those woods, but for whatever reason, he chose not to tell me.

When we arrived at the crown of the final hill, I was astonished. The city was a dazzling sight to see. This was not the same city I left all those years ago. It looked as if the city had gone untouched by the War as there should have been no way for it to be in such a pristine condition. Anyone who had not seen it during the conflicts would have thought they improved while the rest of the world suffered.

The buildings appeared to glisten when the sun reflected off of them—a stark contradiction instead of the gloom and shoddy workmanship that I had grown accustomed to. As we grew closer, I started to notice something else that I hadn't experienced in years. The town smelled fresh. I couldn't detect the aroma of decay, but instead, the usual smells of an autumn day. I was impressed until I saw the cause of it all. The Ascension logo was branded on every building. Every office, house, church, and market was labeled with that bloody rising star. John may have spent most of his time in Despartian, but he had clearly influenced the rest of his empire. He had turned Memphis into a loyalist fortress.

"Why is it so quiet?" Mark asked, breaking the trance the city had on me. I hadn't even noticed that there was no one but us. There were birds chirping and wind blowing, but not a single voice echoed through the streets.

"I don't know. I don't see anyone anywhere." I answered as I continued to scan the streets we were walking.

"Rob, how many churches do you see?" I found the question odd but decided to count the churches I could find. There were four of them within a half-mile of each other. They were also the only buildings that had their lights on. I wondered if his question was implying what I think he was implying.

"Four."

"That is what I thought. It would appear that the sermon is nearly finished." He informed me as the clocks began to ring and crowds filed out of each church. This was not an isolated occurrence as I could hear the chimes ringing from the other side of the city. It was eerie watching the hordes fill the empty streets. It reminded me of cattle leaving a train for the farm. They would die.

They all looked uniform and moved like robots. Their shapes, sizes, and skin tone may have differed, but each man wore dull grays and blacks, while the women wore white. On top of their clothes, their facial expressions were also matching. It was a toothless smile meant to feint happiness without actually revealing genuine emotion.

It was like a cult of robots flooded Memphis. I knew that John was the master board, but I couldn't understand how he could do this while spending most of his days in Despartian. It was news whenever he left the city, and trust me, he didn't do it enough to oversee what was in front of me.

As I contemplated John's power, I started to recognize that the whole city was moving towards the same place. Afraid that dissent would draw attention, I grabbed Mark by the arm and followed the herd. We stuck out like sore thumbs, but at least we were now attempting to blend.

The lemming-like behavior eventually led us to a large gathering around the central road. After a few nonsensical calls, the crowd split in half, with part going to one side of the street while the rest went to the other. Mark and I moved as quickly as we could with the change, but even during the split, they moved uniformly like it was a preset timer in the back of their minds. From there, the crowd knelt down and bowed. I was never a fan of bowing, but I couldn't blow our cover now after getting this far, so we followed closely. Then things grew even odder as the crowd began to chant and cheer.

"Here comes the Mayor! Here comes the Boss! Here comes Peace at last!" They cheered repeatedly. I looked at Mark, and he turned to me. As the cheering continued, they rose to a seated kneel and raised their arms in the air.

I could feel my spine shiver as I looked around at the madness around me. Then, at last, the source rumbled down the street. Dave and a far chunkier, then I remembered Chen sitting in a car like kings waving to their peasants. I realized that John was willing to make bold moves to ensure things worked in his favor. He had never trusted the two but put them there to become fat happy kings under his thumb.

I couldn't believe it until I saw the ebony-armored figure that rode the white horse behind them. The Executioner I had just met must jump between the cities to enforce John's rule. Ex likely had complete control of the day-to-day operations while he let the other two be the smiling faces. I watched the petite man sit tall on the horse with no fear of being seen. The other two may have been the people clamored for, but I quickly deduced who was really in charge.

Then I saw something I could never have imagined. In his huskier form, Chen pulled an electric guitar out of the car he was sitting in. He played a few chords to warm-up and started to sing:

"Dadum, dadum, dadum. My pretty city, you got me feeling two-fitty. My heart and stomach are full, as you make all our problems null. Some may call this place shifty, but they're all shitty. Dadum, dadum, dadum Let's throw a party, and don't be tardy. This ball is going to rock, don't get left at the dock. I love a good feast, and ladies, I am a beast." He sang. If I wasn't scared enough by the singing, his continuous hip-thrusting nearly made me throw up. Part of me envied Mark, but he had to listen to the singing to a greater degree. I fully understood how brainwashed these people were as they were fist-bumping and dancing to every chord.

After he finished his performance, their car moved farther down the road, where he repeated it several times from what I heard. However, once they passed a section, the crowd would disperse behind them.

Now that there was some variety, Mark and I started to explore. As we wandered around, I began to understand that I couldn't approach Memphis the same way as other cities. Chen and Dave had pictures hanging in every household window. People adored the pair of idiots, and any fight would involve a city, not just three extremely well-trained killers.

I needed a full scope of the city so that I could look for any weak spot. I would need to lay a trap if I wanted to get answers out of anyone. Unfortunately, I started to pick up John's design for the city. It wasn't just uniform. It was one carbon copy after another like a brick in a wall, perfectly made to fit with every other piece. The city streets were his protection. As we marched deeper towards the center, we found the factories that took up more room and created a considerable barrier. Their headquarters had to be in the center of it all, and they likely had points on every block that allowed viewing to protect it from obvious threat.

While we marched into the heart, I would look through the windows of the factories and warehouses. I wanted to know what was in the city worth protecting. Yet nothing seemed worthwhile. There were no illegal stimulants or weapons, from what I could see. It was just assembly lines worked by men and women, making goods. I saw nothing shady in the least.

In the center of the city was a large three-story mansion protected by a red brick wall. Both the estate and wall were covered in ivy, thorns protruding from every inch of the wall. It made it look elegant while also being the perfect hidden defense. Even if you enter what lies beyond them, your hands are virtually useless. It didn't look like the fortress that De Luca had, but it had a better cover.

"You're getting nervous. Your breath is growing fast and shallow, kid. I need you to find yourself and calm down. We are not one match away from an explosion this time. We may not be able to do anything here." He advised. As he talked, I started following up on the first part. I concentrated on my breaths in and out. I took control of myself and adjusted my thoughts back to what was directly in front of me.

"You may be right, but we can't leave without trying anything," I informed him with a long breath. I had let their connection to John raise my blood pressure, but I was in control this time.

"Alright, but we need to leave. There are too many eyes on us right now." He whispered. When I became tunnel-visioned on the fortress, I failed to take in my surroundings fully. Through the windows around us, I could see women, men, and children watching us as we stood where we weren't supposed to be. There weren't guards yet, but if we loitered, trouble would soon follow.

We shuffled away from the fortress and started to wander again. As I walked, I tried to figure out what had happened. How did John build a city like this and inspire so much loyalty while destroying everything else? There was no fear in their eyes or looks of dissension. I just couldn't fathom it as I looked for any sign of Althea's group, but nothing jumped out at me.

We walked into a bar looking for information. The bar reminded me of the ones I used to hop around in during my younger days. Joyous laughter and happy cheers filled the room. There was a jukebox playing, and though the instrumentals were fun, Chen was singing every song. Making it worse, the patrons were singing along. I felt the shiver go down my back but tried to hide it the best I could.

There was no one upfront to seat us, so we found an empty corner and sat down. The service moved at a snail's pace, which gave me time to observe the place. At first, I had thought this place was different from everywhere else, but then I noticed the truth. Every drink and every plate was the same with no menu or checks. People arrived and just sat down. Soon after, a plate of mush and glass would be placed in front of them. As they left, an old poker chip was dropped off with a man who was stamping hands. Then, at last, a waiter approached us, lacking the mush everyone else received.

"You gentlemen are not from around here, are you?" The waiter asked with a sneer.

"What makes you say that?" Mark questioned.

"To put it nicely, you two gentlemen are *different* from anyone else here. Which means you two will not have the required weekly food and drink chips." He explained.

"So that is what was going on at the door," I whispered as the waiter continued to judge us.

"Yes, and without these chips, you cannot eat here. I will have to move the two of you to the back lounge." He insisted as he began to shoo us away from the table. I assisted Mark to his feet and followed the waiter. Something didn't feel right, but this was the only way to avoid a scene.

He led us to a backroom hidden behind a large wooden door that was far tougher than the first half. If the initial room was an after-work hangout, this was more of a pirate mess hall that could erupt at any moment. There were people in all forms of attire and yelling that had been masked by soundproof walls when you were in the other half. As we would walk by groups, we could hear them talking about their travels. Apparently, this is where all outsiders were placed when they stumbled into Memphis. Although there were a few locals, by the way, they were dressed. This was clearly meant to be the ugly side of the city that was not approved by the leadership.

Once inside, a new waiter led us to our seats. We handed him some silver that Dani's group had given us, and he handed us some food. I listened to the patrons around me who had conversations that were in stark contrast to those outside this room. These men and women had a variety of tall tales and stories to tell. One struck me as quite interesting:

"Two months ago, I was over in Europe in old Germany. Doing some trade work for the Ascension office in Berlin when the city fell under attack. It was only a small raid, but it demonstrated efficiency unlike any I had seen before. Twenty people rode in on horseback and burned down several warehouses before the guards were even aware of what was happening. Not a single person was killed, but the damage had been done.

After the raid, I asked the local officials what had happened, but they all declined to comment. It wasn't until I met this little old lady did I get the truth. Apparently, spread across the old country are villages of nothing but women. In what is left of the Black Forest sits the new home of the Amazon." An older gentleman said! For a moment, his compatriots sat in awe before they erupted in laughter. They jeered at the tale he told and called it a fairy-tale. Cities of only women in this chaotic world sounded like nonsense. Still, I had learned that nothing was impossible in the world today. The hollering came to an end when the lights lowered and the spotlight shined on the stage.

"Good evening, my fellow degenerates and hell-raisers! It is time for tonight's entertainment!" Shouted a man as he exited from behind the curtains. The man wore a dark mask to hide his eyes and a large black hat and red jacket. The crowd began to cheer again and chant nonsensically. Whatever was going to happen was not going to be tame.

"Every day, the people of this city stay conformed and stood in unison! Never do they cause trouble or create uproars to upset the order! They are the perfect citizens, just as they are asked to be! However, our masters know that it is a tall task to maintain that level of conformity. So at night, we let them join the outsiders here in this backroom! So, do you all want to be rewarded?" He asked the crowd as he danced across the stage.

"Bring them out! Bring them out," the crowd shouted! The man smiled as he basked in the cheers with his arms fully extended. I started to understand what the story was behind all the conformity. They had been brainwashed into thinking that if they comply, they will have steady work (in meaningless jobs), a house (that was designed as a wall for Ascension), and rewards at night (whatever this depravity was going to be). Then John had placed a spokesman like this to put on performances and entertain the masses.

"I love you, degenerates," he started as the cheers grew louder, "Boys, bring out today's opening act! Tonight we have special entertainment outside of our exotic women. Today we found someone who thinks they are better than the rest of you. He didn't think he needed to go to the mandatory mass this week. He skipped both masses, disrespecting all of you! Disrespecting the laws of this land! He is a criminal and will now be punished for your entertainment!" As the ringmaster outlined the man's "crimes" the crowd would boo. It was deafening, and when the guards dragged the poor man out, they blew the roof off the building. The poor guy was in nothing more than his underwear.

"Please, I didn't mean to disrespect the masters. I was sick and feared contaminating my fellow citizens!" The man sobbed as he was tied to the ground.

"Oh, dear sir, this is a terrible mistake then, you were sick...Do we believe him? More importantly, do we care?" He asked the crowd as servers passed out expired food and mush. The ringmaster's smile gave him away. He knew the man was telling the truth, but no one seemed to care. They took their mush happily while my stomach turned.

"Hell, no!" shouted one of the patrons as a handful of mush flew through the air, hitting him in the shoulder with a plop! It stuck for a moment before slowly sliding down his shoulder like a snail trying to run.

"The people have spoken! Let it, loose folks!" The host yelled as more food flew! He made sure to stand far enough away to avoid splashes but close enough so that he could look the prisoner in the face with his smug grin. I was ready to defend the man, but Mark grabbed my arm to stop me.

"Remember the endgame, Rob. If we start playing hero, then all of this is for nothing, and you are no closer to your wife's killer." He reminded me as his grip tightened. "The best thing you can do is take Dave and Chen down."

I had fully comprehended what Mark was saying and had thought it through, but I wanted to act. At that moment, I didn't care about John. I just wanted to help the man. I resorted to throwing my food at the other audience members' projectiles. If I couldn't stop the throws, I could knock them off course. It worked decently, but there were just too many, so with my final parcels, I knocked the host in the head. He was clearly irritated but had to accept that misthrows happen with drunks.

The final pieces of food were thrown, and the host waved his hands. The public humiliation was finished at last, and I hoped that it would be enough. The host stood over the man's convulsing body. He was weeping uncontrollably as rotten food dripped off his back. I was disgusted by the sight and the cheers surrounding me.

"Are we done?" The host yelled as he grabbed a whip from his belt! I

"No!" the crowd shouted. It was then I realized the final part of John's manipulation. He was not only rewarding the good but punishing to the point of breaking those that misbehaved in this city. They were afraid of him, but the rewards were so great that they never showed it.

The host unrolled the whip and raised it to the air. The memory of what I had been forced to do to Dani was still fresh in my mind, and I couldn't tolerate this. Mark's point was moot now. I had to do something. Before he could stop me, I threw a plate at the one-lit spotlight in the dingy room and shattered it.

Chapter 22
Family

Darkness filled the room as I rushed to the stage to help the man. Mark's teaching made it easy for me to find the ringmaster's arm during its downswing. I caught him mid-swing and had to figure out what to do before the lights turned on again.

I was not fast enough as the house lights flashed on and revealed an intriguing sight. Not only was I standing there holding the host's arm, but there was also a second more petite figure holding a blade to his throat. I was shocked to see anyone else standing up to this madness, especially the petite light-haired brunette next to me.

"Put that thing away and go sit down before you get hurt. The grown-ups are talking." I instructed. I figured that she wasn't much older than twenty, and I feared that she would only be in my way if she stayed there.

"Sorry, gramps, but I think you have things a little reversed. If you push it too hard here, you might pull something, and I'm not carrying you out of here too." She insinuated. Defiant and cocky. I had a hint of respect for her after mouthing off like that. While the two of us exchanged comments, the host stood on the stage shivering with a blade to his throat and a man gripping his arm. He may have wet himself; he was so terrified.

"That made me chuckle somewhere deep, deep down, but do you actually know how to use that knife? It isn't the standard one that came with your toy kitchen sets. This one can create a mess if you use it wrong." I insulted back.

"Hey, butthead, you might think you are all tough, but you're just an idiot. Interfering in matters that you don't understand is the exact way that old guys like you end up dead!" She quipped back. This girl had a loudmouth, and despite my respect for her moxie, she was also becoming quite an irritant. I wanted to handle things with far less hoopla than she was starting, and now I needed a better plan.

"We aren't getting anywhere, are we? How about this? You free the man with your butter knife, and I'll knock the senses out of this guy." I suggested as guards started to replace the guests in the room. She looked around the room and nodded, knowing that she had to do something quick for them to have a chance. She swirled down to the man cutting the ropes while I knocked the host out with a sharp blow to the face. The three of us found ourselves alone on the stage with guards surrounding us from every angle.

The man we had freed was a mess and could barely raise his arms to protect himself. I looked at the numbers trying to figure out how we could get out of there, when a commotion began around Mark's spot, followed by a second one in the corner. My ally had made his move, and it appeared that this girl had a partner of her own. Seeing my chance, I jumped right into the fray, going for knees, necks, and other weak spots. I needed to be efficient as I made my way to Mark, with who I had left my staff and bag. While I was knocking men out, I caught a glimpse of the young girl's progress. She was holding her own in the scuffle. Apparently, the girl had learned how to fight at some point. It wasn't pretty fighting by any stretch of the imagination. Still, she had a toughness and flow to her movements that gave me confidence. I didn't have to worry about her or the sniveling mess that followed her down the aisles.

After knocking a few heads, I reached Mark, who was using my staff at the time. I called his name, and without hesitation, he threw it to me. His throw was so precise that I was able to use the momentum to deliver my first blow. I was able to do some real damage now. Bones were breaking one after another as I struck the guards with speed and power they were unprepared for. The two of us stood back to back as immovable objects. More guards filtered in to face us. Some were coming off the streets while others were off-duties that had taken up arms from the other room. We could not fight the city, so we moved our impenetrable circle towards the young girl. Whoever they were, they were doing their own damage but took our distraction as an opportunity to escape out the back doors. We were able to burst our way out as well and followed their footsteps using Mark's hearing.

"Do you ever think things through?" He berated me as he led the way. After our exit, the guards continued to pursue, but they fell too far back to keep pace with us after knocking over enough trash cans.

"Before I met you, I didn't, but that time I knew what I was doing. I understood the consequence and decided that I would prefer to protect that man over hiding in the shadows." I responded as we drew closer in our own pursuit. It was faint, but I could almost hear their footsteps on my own now.

"You have either grown beyond my expectations, or you have just improved your lying abilities." He admitted. He waved for me to slow down as we were near the young girl and her partner. If our voices or footsteps were too loud, it would blow everything.

"I hope I am growing. I'm tired of acting so rashly and watching everyone else pay for it." I whispered. I didn't say it then, but I could only think of all the actions I had committed with little thought. I ran to war without talking to Iris, I ran to the drink after it ended, and I ran around Despartian chasing Gene without trying to investigate anything. I just followed John's plan without pausing to think, and I ran around that nowhere town blinded by hate. I was tired of running recklessly. I wanted to move out of thought, not passion.

We rounded the corner to the sight of two lovely young women standing in our way. There was the first woman I met with a smart mouth and petite body. The second had a far more athletic build with broad shoulders and more muscle definition. They each had light brown hair with the first's shading towards blonde. The first also tried to maintain a serious look, but she came off a bit goofy. In contrast, the second kept a straight face and clearly didn't trust us.

"Why did you two buttheads follow us? And why did you make me run that much?" The petite one commented as she tried to catch her breath.

"We just want to talk," I responded in an apologetic tone.

"We don't talk to strange men who start bar fights." The sterner of the two explained. She was a lot more direct than the bubblier one, but her voice was mellow rather than intense, as I expected.

"Not a bad philosophy. I apologize for my reckless compatriot. If you are worried, then let's not be strangers. My name is Mark, and my idiot here is named Rob." Mark explained in his normally soothing tone.

"Good enough for me. My name is Samantha or Sam for short." The first smiled.

"Dude, I thought we talked about this." The second started shaking her head.

"What they obviously helped us out back there. Not many people would have done that." Sam argued. The second let out a sigh.

"Fine...my name is Morgan." The second answered reluctantly.

"Well, it is nice to meet you, fine ladies officially." Mark smiled as he began to walk closer to them. Sam seemed receptive to Mark and me, but Morgan backed away from us. Rightfully, she was more hesitant in the beginning.

"Sam, stay away!" Morgan ordered when she saw how close her friend was to us.

"Come on, look at this one. He is a cute old man. He is helpless, and this one is an idiot!" She commented, pointing at Mark! Her eyes were large like a puppy's, and her lips were puffed out.

"That helpless man and idiot escaped the bar all by themselves. Then they managed to follow us all this way. That means they are either extremely powerful or working with those monsters. So, stop being so damn trusting. The Boss will kill us if we bring them with us." Morgan explained. There were valid points in her concerns, but she slipped up. Hearing that there was a third person in the crew was important. Hearing that the third person was their boss was monumental. These girls suddenly became more exciting and possibly useful.

"So, what brought you to that bar?" I asked, trying to break the ice wrapped around Morgan.

"We wanted to stop a loser from hurting innocent people because no one else will," Sam answered with a bit of pep in her step.

"That seems like a bold strategy for someone so young. Who is pulling the strings?" I asked, trying to dig deeper.

"Just shut up! We aren't going to tell you anything until we can trust you!" Morgan shouted as she raised a gun to Mark's face! Sam backed away, instantly shocked by her partner's behavior. I didn't move much but shifted my feet just enough to attack if she provoked me.

"I'm not going to say this twice. Put that thing down and step away from the blind man!" I ordered as I lined up for the disarmament. In turn, I received an icy stare that made me nervous. I was ready to lunge when Mark raised his hand to stop me.

"Enough antagonizing Rob. You want to know if you can trust them but have yet to give them a reason to trust us. These fine ladies and their boss could be valuable allies, and I will not allow you to harm them." He insisted. I backed off, hoping that she would do the same. He could disarm her himself without hesitation but was playing the long game.

"The old one is a lot wiser than you, isn't he?" Morgan smirked as her arm stayed unwavering.

"That he is, so how do we convince you ladies that we have similar goals here?" I asked as I lowered my guard.

"Nothing too complex. You just need to trust us first, put these blindfolds on and earplugs in while we lead you to our next destination." Morgan grinned as Sam pulled out some earplugs and old fabric. The earplugs were not clean, but I will give the ladies credit. Most people only use blindfolds. These girls were a little bit smarter than the average street urchins that I had met.

I placed the blindfold over my eyes and earplugs as instructed. The next thing I knew, I was being led through streets and down to the sewers. Based on the amount of walking, we traveled for over two miles though there was a lot of unnecessary turning to throw us off. I'm sure Mark was as aware of where we were as I was. When the ladies reached their destination, they sat us down. Then proceeded to tie us to chairs while removing our earplugs. We were now interrogation-ready.

"What brought you two to Memphis?" Morgan asked in a softer tone than I was expecting.

"I'm chasing a man who I have to kill," I answered, wary of how much I should reveal.

"That's great, but it doesn't answer my question. Who is this man?" She asked. Her voice was growing loud, but more importantly, was the rate of her breathing. My answer was unsettling, and despite her attempts to fake confidence, she wasn't sure about my honesty.

"Remember, we need them to trust us. Just tell them the truth." Mark ordered quietly. He was right, but still, I sighed before answering.

"His name is John Kore. And he is the former, maybe current depending on what people are told, owner of Ascension. He is the one that put Chen and Dave in charge of this city. On top of that crime, he is also the man that killed my fiancée." I responded after a long silent pause. I could feel the fire on my tongue just from speaking his name, yet there was a doubt for the first time in my journey. When telling the story about him, something happened that made me question my own convictions and realize why Iris told me not to chase after him.

"What about you, old man?" Morgan asked. This time I could hear a quiver in her voice. My answer was unnerving, and now she was shocked.

"My answer is not nearly as fun. I was just bored. You see, I was old and alone in a cabin in the woods when this guy who was nearly eaten by a bear showed up. I was impressed by him, and I decided that he would be an interesting companion. I've now followed him this far, and he has lived up to expectations." Mark explained. I did prefer his explanation of our meeting over the truth. Staring a bear down is more impressive than cowering and hoping for a miracle.

"That is such a ridiculous explanation. It almost has to be the truth." Morgan claimed as she began to pace around us, "Okay, so why here? If someone as powerful as John was here, we would know about it." As I listened to her pace, I also listened for her compatriot. However, there was nothing, not a breath or a footstep. She was alone with us.

"You're right John isn't here, or at least I am unaware of his presence. In fact, us being here is pure happenstance. You see, we have been sailing the Mississippi tracking rumors when we started to run low on supplies. We decided that we could listen for rumors while refueling as this had been an Ascension headquarters and a city. Once we arrived, I noted how strong his influence truly was on the city. I also knew we would have to do something. Especially after seeing the idiots, he put in charge." I informed her. She knew our intentions, and despite the fact I could escape the bonds she had me in, she was effectively in control.

"You came from the river. That means you are the outsiders the boss spoke about. She told us that the old one could be trusted, but there is more to our story than you know." She told me as she removed the blindfold at last. As my eyes blinked back into focus, I was able to absorb the surroundings. We were being held in a collapsed sewer. It was a real eyesore, along with being a damp, dark holding place. The darkness was finally shed when a door opened behind Morgan. Out of the opening walked Sam and an olive-skinned black-haired young woman.

"She is right. You two cannot just come barging into our city, causing havoc. There is more going on than you are prepared for." The new woman affirmed as she grew closer to our seats.

"It can't be...that voice sounds like." Mark began to quiver as his head rose towards the stranger.

"What's wrong, Mark? Who is this woman?" I whispered. Mark was visibly shaking, and I was worried about him.

"It's me, Dad...it's Vicky." She cried, caressing Mark's face. She ran her hand over his scared eyes. She wiped a tear from his eyes along with one from her own at the sight of the reunion.

"Vicky, how are you here? I was told you all died in the attack." Mark questioned as his tears turned into a full-blown sob. The pure joy he was experiencing became overwhelming.

Vicky's left ear was damaged beyond saving from the fire, along with several other scars. His blindness was a blessing that allowed him to remember his daughter as she was not as the disfigured woman she was now. She used a glove to caress him, covering further damage caused by the explosion. The parts not scarred by fire were still Greek goddess-like, but it still would have done him more harm than good to see what had happened that day.

"You see, Dad, they misidentified some of the bodies. When they brought you to 'my' corpse, it was just another technician who was found next to my I.D. badge. I had been tossed into a coma for several months. When I woke up, I discovered that in a blind fit of rage, you had run, and everyone else had died."

"Unsure of how to proceed, I decided to become someone new. I was doing my best to help people who, like myself, were left behind in wreckage. About eight months later, I found these two struggling to survive. Both of them were barely seventeen and all alone. I didn't plan on staying with them this long, but there is something about them that I couldn't leave. It has been difficult, but we have survived this long as a family." She explained as she wrapped an arm around each of the girls' necks. Mark cried after the story. He was so proud of his daughter's ability to survive and saddened by her need to do it without him. Unfortunately, I couldn't allow the touching moment to continue as both Morgan and Vicky hinted at something more extensive. I needed to know what was going on.

"This has been very touching, but according to you and Morgan, there must be something far more urgent occurring here." I interrupted. I was a bit coarse, but Vicky turned to me, realizing the truth in my words. The reunion was pleasant, but after the mission, she could catch up with him better.

"You're right. This city is in a crisis that it is not even aware of yet. This situation is hard to explain, so follow me, and I'll show you." Vicky ordered. Sam and Morgan tried to untie us but found the two of us had already undone our binds. The ladies were surprised that we had escaped so easily.

Now that we were free, we followed the trio through the winding mess that was the sewer. We followed them down the dark corridor until we arrived at a room that had a small screen and microphone set up. It was a crude set-up they had placed there, but it was just enough for them.

Now it was the content of the screen that terrified me. On the other end of the feed was a pair of men sitting in front of hundreds of screens. The men's eyes moved from screen to screen as they scribbled notes constantly. It didn't take me long to piece together what I was watching.

"I'm sure you have figured out what is going on, but Dad, I'll weave our story for you. Memphis was flattened during the War to the point that even ghosts couldn't call it home. It was once a beautiful city that turned into a disaster zone like most of the world. The people who called it home and lived were devastated until John brought Ascension to this pit. Soon after, he placed Dave in charge of the city to build it in his image."

"The first thing was the mansion in the center of the city. Then the factories that wall off the mansion from the rest of the city. The next phase was rebuilding the living quarters. Under what we presume was John's orders, Dave oversaw every construction and placed bugs with cameras across each one. There is no privacy, and the people know it. However, no one is willing to challenge the corporation. Recently a masked figure appeared at the daily parade, and with his arrival came disappearances. Then I heard rumors from the guards that something else was planted along with the bugs, something dangerous. I worry that this masked figure is bringing a disaster to the city." She explained as I looked at the monitor. I was disgusted by this. This was over the line even for John, and I couldn't help but wonder what the plan was.

"That masked figure you speak of is death personified. From what I was able to gather, he must be John's right-hand man, and he goes by the name the Executioner." I informed her.

"A little on the nose, but it is nice to have a name for the newest threat. How do you know about them?" She asked.

"I fought him in St. Louis," I answered.

"And what happened?" Morgan followed up with concern on her face.

"I lost...I lost badly. He put me down for a couple of days. However, that is irrelevant right now. The only thing that matters to me is interrogating Dave or Chen. They are how I finally get to John. You three want those fools out of the way, which means we have a common goal." I pointed out. Vicky nodded her head in agreement.

"So, do you have a plan to accomplish these goals, or are you just going to run around busting heads, as you did in the back bar?" She asked.

"Initially, I was going to run around swinging my stick at anything that moved, but I met you three. I'll defer the plan to people who know this city." I responded as I turned to the old man smiling.

"I guess my Dad does choose good company. Alright, this will be quite the turnaround for you, but with you two here, I'm more confident we can pull this off. Tomorrow night Ascension is hosting their annual masquerade ball to celebrate the re-founding of the city. If you were at the parade earlier, you heard that loudmouth sing about it. I obtained masks and several invitations from members of the guard to get us in. The guards will be too busy to focus on us as we begin our surveillance during the party. Between the four of you, we will need entrances and exits that can yield the best results, weak points in the security, and the most likely positions for the daily guards. Meanwhile, I will be placing bugs across the mansion to gather further details. Then we'll party the night away to avoid suspicion and return here around one the following morning as the party winds down. Then the final preparations will be made." She explained. It wasn't much, but it was more than the two of us had earlier in the day.

I leaned against the table the monitor sat on and thought for a moment. I wondered if the plan was sustainable. She wanted to take us inside the lion's den to take pictures of it, hoping we wouldn't become snacks. Dave and Chen were not the types to just sit around if they discovered my presence, making this far riskier than Vicky knew. However, this was the best plan we had. More importantly, this was Mark's daughter, and he was going to follow her over me any day, so I kept my protest quiet.

"Alright, the plan sounds reasonable to me, but there are other preparations we need to make before tomorrow. Namely, neither Mark nor I am equipped for a party, and I don't fit into a size four or two." I pointed out as I grabbed my blood-stained shirt.

"Understandable, none of my outfits go with your eyes anyways. I will have Sam take you to one of the local stores using the dead zone map." Vicky ordered as she motioned for Sam to come over.

The young girl had proven to be quite an interesting case. Her moxie was both admirable and irritating, but she seemed to be a scatterbrain most of the time. I couldn't imagine why someone who seemed as collected as Vicky would assign her over the other one. First off, she didn't know me. Second, Morgan was far more equipped to handle me. Thirdly I thought that our lives would be more important to protect. Yet she trusted Sam, and I wondered if there was more to her than I had anticipated. Then the girl started skipping down the tunnels, quite an interesting case.

We crossed through several sewer blocks before coming up for air and then several more hugging the alley walls. Despite her earlier motormouth, she had fallen silent for the journey. Apparently, there was an off switch for the chatty Cathy I had known up to that point. However, that did not last much longer as someone like her never stopped talking for long.

"Alright, my dude, I need you to stay close to me. There is no rope; if you go rogue, I run. There are cameras plastered over almost every inch of this city, and if you don't move in the dead zones that the three of us mapped out, you will be caught. Please don't get caught. Vicky would be upset with me." She explained in the quietest tone I had heard her speak in. She was precise in her movements and led me past several guard checkpoints. It wasn't until the last alley that we met an issue where guards didn't belong there.

"Damn, we were so close." She whispered, frustrated by the bad luck. We hid behind a set of garbage cans to figure out a plan.

"I don't see the problem. If we are in the safe zone, I can easily take the two of them out before they know what happened." I told her as I drew my staff.

"This is why I was sent with you dumb-dumb. Guards at night always travel in groups of three. One of them always stays back at all times to ensure the safety of the group. He will be hiding somewhere to alert the rest of the watch if we make a move." She informed me as we heard a sudden click from behind us.

"Good observation, girly." A guard commented as he pointed a gun at her head, "Now get up and follow me before I have to shoot you." I wanted to lash out, but the gun was pointed at her head, and she was already surrendering. She couldn't risk the plan falling apart if we caused a disruption.

"Boys, come see what I found!" the guard yelled, "We have a couple of stray dogs breaking the curfew."

"Don't you dare call me a stray dog!" Sam yelled.

"Do you want us to call this in, or are we going to finish this here?" One of the other guards asked as he reached for his own weapon.

"I think we can handle this ourselves." He chuckled as he knelt down next to Sam. "So, what brings you to this side of town?"

"Just trying to survive." Sam mouthed back.

"I'd say most people are doing more than surviving, so what's your issue, girly?" He asked.

"You pigs." She answered as she spat at his feet. As to be suspected, he did not take kindly to this. He slapped her to the ground, which is when I decided to speak up.

"So I'm in a bit of a hurry. I'll give one chance to walk away without any broken bones." I threatened, keeping my voice calm and collected. The guards started to chuckle at my comments. Given my situation, they were not intimidated in the slightest. However, the one was a bit irritated by my comments, so he pointed the gun at my head while Sam worked her way back to her feet.

"Who the Hell do you think you are?" He yelled with nostrils flaring.

"I'm the man who is going to break your arm and nose. Then take out those two." I smiled. His eyes grew intense as I remained calm. He licked his lips and started pulling the trigger, but in a swift movement, I took control of his wrist. Then aimed the gun at each of the other guards and put a bullet in their shoulders. I followed it up with a twist of the arm and a knee to his elbow. I heard the snap instantly. That would have been enough, but I am a man of my word, so I took the butt of the gun and smacked him in the nose.

While the man screamed, Sam grabbed my hand and whisked me away. We hit a dead sprint to avoid any more guards. This girl was fast as I struggled to keep up with her. She may have been a goofball, but she was also part gazelle. Now I don't know if anyone was actually chasing us. Still, we covered a substantial amount of ground, reaching a small clothing store at last. She picked the lock as fast as she had run, and we ducked inside. A few moments later, I heard guards rush by with zero ideas about our hiding spot.

"Well, we made it." I chuckled as I tried to catch my breath.

"You nearly got us both killed, you butthead." She scolded, hitting me in the arm as I continued to laugh.

"Lighten, we made it. Besides, if you and that guard kept arguing, we were going to die anyway." I insisted.

"I had everything under control."

"You were on the ground."

"I had him right where I wanted him."

"Sure you did."

"I did!" She insisted, letting her voice raise a little. I worried about the guards outside and decided that this was no longer an argument worth having.

"Okay, you did," I admitted to her. "And I must compliment you. You are quite fast."

"Thanks, dude. Now shall we do what we came here for?"

"Let's." I agreed as I motioned towards the clothing that lay before us. We started to scavenge around the tiny shop, picking at the different tables and racks to find something for Mark and me. We each grabbed a few things at a time and then consulted with one another. I was concerned about whether it would be practical if we ran into a fight, while she wanted to make sure it fit the event. Unfortunately, the two looks did not go with each other well, and we had to find a few compromises. As we hunted the store for the right look for the ball, I started to grow curious about her and her partners. I hoped that her bubbliness would cause her to slip more than Morgan or Vicky would.

"So, what do you think of Vicky's plan?"

"It's the best we have."

"Wow, the confidence is astounding."

"Sorry, it's just that this isn't our first try at these guys, and things have not gone well."

"Then why do you keep following her?"

"Because she is all Morgan and I have."

"I get that. I'm the same way as Mark, but why here. There are several cities less dangerous than this one."

"I don't know. I just know she wants to help this place, and I will fight with her until the end." Sam shrugged as we threw a few outfits into a bag at last. "Anyways, let's get back before she gets worried." I had more questions, but it didn't appear like Sam was the one to ask.

Outfits in the bag, we headed back to the hideout. This time we faced no resistance as the guards we had beaten earlier were forced to tend to their injuries, and the replacements were patrolling elsewhere. Back at the hideout, Sam took me to the section of the sewers that was more of a catacomb. There was a large area that consisted of several floors. Sam took me down a couple of flights to some paths with curtains pulled around sections. This was where they slept, and Morgan was asleep on her cot while Vicky and Mark were catching up.

"Did you get lost, Sam?" Vicky asked, surprised that we were just now returning from such a simple task.

"No, but we did encounter some guards that strayed from their routes." She admitted, ashamed of what had transpired.

"You took care of them?" Vicky assumed.

"Rob kicked their butts pretty easily, and then we were able to get the outfits.

"Good. Now go off to bed. You have had a long day." Vicky suggested. Sam nodded her head and headed to her own cot.

"I think I will do the same. I'm getting too old for these late nights." Mark claimed as he headed to the bed Vicky prepared for us. I threw him his outfit for tomorrow and let him be.

"Did you guys have a nice chat?" I asked, turning back to Vicky.

"It was good. So many families were broken apart by the War. It is nice when one is reunited." She explained, taking a seat back where she was with her father. I strolled over and took his spot at an old ragged picnic table that should have been firewood.

"It can be, but it can also be a painful reminder for others," I told her, thinking about my own life.

"I guess, but at least for the two of us, it was good. Did you and Sam have any good conversation?" She asked, placing her head on her propped-up hand.

"A little bit, and I must ask why this city if you've failed so much already?"

"Because this city needed someone to help it, and my father always taught me to help those that need it."

"You'll never be appreciated even if you succeed."

"That's not why I do it."

"You might get those girls killed."

"We could die anywhere, but at least this way, we die for something." The way she said this felt off to me. I didn't know what it was, but the way she answered that question was not what I expected. Given how Sam was talking, I expected hesitation when I suggested they might die, but she fired off the response instantly.

"That seems pessimistic." I pointed out. She chuckled at my response and sat up straight.

"I've nearly been blown to pieces and live in a sewer. Optimism is for those that haven't seen the reality of the situation."

"But how are you not more concerned about those girls?" I asked with harshness in my voice I did not intend. She did not appreciate the question as she bit her tongue for a moment to think about her response.

"I love those girls. Never doubt that." She looked over to where their curtains were drawn, and I could see that her face was in agony. She was acting tough, but there was more to it. I could feel it.

"Then why?"

"I don't know. I guess I just thought things would be simpler than this, and now that I'm in this deep, it isn't." She admitted with a slight quiver. She was clenching her fist and retreating her body language. I could question her more, but that no longer felt right.

"This time, it will be different. Mark and I will make this a success."

"And how can you be sure?"

"Because if we fail, we'll die, and to entertain that thought is useless. I might as well believe that things will work, and if they don't, it won't be our problem anymore. But we will have at least tried." I assured her.

"Maybe it will be different, but I think we both need our rest now." She suggested as she rose from her seat.

"If you insist." I agreed as we said our goodnights and headed to our beds. Before we pulled our curtains, I called to her one last time, "It'll work out." She had no answer, but she stood still for a long moment before she closed herself off.

Chapter 23
Party Time

Given our late nights, the five of us slept for most of the morning, with only Morgan waking before noon to patrol for any breaches. After she finished, she began to wake the rest of us up one by one, with Sam being the last one up.

Once awake, we talked about what the day would look like and how we would be expected to act. Vicky informed us about the mood of the ball while I suggested strategies for hiding in the crowd. Along with critical points that people should look for while they are dancing. We changed into our outfits as the start of the party neared.

Mark had an owl mask to go along with a silver wool robe that encased his figure. Sam had a sterling silver dress that fits tight to her petite figure and complimented her rabbit mask. Morgan had a dazzling black and white striped dress with sparkle on the black stripes along with her zebra mask. Vicky had acquired a two-piece sun-yellow dress to match her leopard mask. Lastly, I had a basic gray and black suit to go with my...monkey mask. Our masks did not cover our whole faces, but enough to maintain anonymity.

"Before we go, remember this is just a reconnaissance mission. No one is to engage unless absolutely necessary." Vicky reminded us. Though it was a statement to the group, I felt like she was looking at me in particular.

When the hour struck eight, the ladies led us to the compound. We handed the guards the invitation that the ladies had obtained earlier in the week and entered the estate. We were lucky that Vicky brought several extras. She explained that Sam was known for losing things. Thus, extras were always an advisable option.

Once inside the gate, I began to study each guard and door that I could locate on our way to the main event. Inside the ballroom, it became obvious that the ladies we were with would draw a crowd. Men started swarming us, trying to buy the young ladies drinks. All of the men seemed oblivious to my presence. However, the crowd surrounding the girls was only the second-largest as another was surrounding someone at the food table.

"It would seem that you ladies are causing quite the disruption," I whispered to Vicky as we tried to pull away from the crowd closing in on us.

"It would seem that way." She responded by pushing one of the men away from her.

"Well, to complete our missions, I suggest we spread out. You and Mark will be best together while Sam and Morgan can protect each other while being on the lookout. Besides, they can act as a distraction for the rest of us to move freely." I suggested. Vicky nodded as she relayed the plan to the other three, but he had one more piece of advice before Mark left.

"Don't do anything stupid, kid," Mark advised as Vicky grabbed his hand to guide him.

"Never." I smiled as I started to prowl around the party. I enjoyed a few drinks as I looked for weaknesses. To my surprise, there were far fewer guards than I expected, but after looking at the crowd around me, I deduced that they didn't see this crowd as a threat. They didn't keep many guards around because the people of the city were guards. Messing with Dave or Chen would mean war.

"Well, well, monkey boy, what brings you down to Memphis." A familiar voice called from behind me. I turned to find a black-haired woman wearing a fox mask standing just behind me. The mask covered her face, but the dagger eyes peering through were a familiar sight. I also knew that she had been the one drawing the large crowd at the food table earlier.

"I take it that you've kept re-dyeing your hair while on the run, Trisha." I pointed out as we circled one another. I couldn't believe that John's niece was standing in front of me. Though John was the one that shot Iris, it was her that led the two of us into the trap that got Iris killed. It was this eighteen-year-old that manipulated me while her uncle played dead. Her presence worried me, given Vicky's assertion that something was going to happen soon. There were four players in John's game, all in the city at once, which was not a good sign.

"Who says we were on the run Rob? The two of us have just been moving from one city to the next this whole time. I've used it more as a vacation than anything. Now, will you dance with me, or should

I call the guards and cause a scene?" She threatened with eyes that reminded me of her uncle's. Cold and calculating, yet unassuming to those that did not know them better. I looked around and weighed my options. Despite my detest, I had to think of the others this time. I took her hand as the band began to play some salsa classics.

"Fine, I'm chasing, but you two aren't running. Regardless, what brings you here?" I asked as we began some simple warm-up steps.

"My sweet uncle wanted me to deliver a message," she began as we each took a spin and brought ourselves into a closed position. "He says he is waiting for you and the army that will follow you. He has high hopes for you, Rob." As she finished, the music picked up the pace, and so did our own intensity. She was quite the fluid dancer as I led her from one combo to the next.

"I don't know what army he is expecting, but you can tell him that the message has been delivered and I am coming for him. However, I have business here to take care of first, unless you want me to bring you down with Chen and Dave. I'd get out of here soon." I informed her as I tightened my left hand around hers in an attempt to intimidate her.

"That isn't proper etiquette." She remarked, digging her claws into my back.

"How about we finish this song and part on friendly terms," I suggested as I spun her twice more to the rhythm and loosened my grip.

"We are going to finish the song, but continue on for a few more, Rob. I have more I want to talk to you about." She commanded as she retracted her claws. I couldn't imagine what she would want, but we hit our big finish and posed to the sound of applause. As I released her, I noticed that we had accumulated quite the following. I'm sure the others were upset with me, but at this point, my only option was to roll with it. Trisha turned to the band and signaled for the next song.

"I hope you know how to samba." She smiled as the music started again.

"I do, but it isn't quite as fluid," I answered as we began our solo portions of the dance. Early on, I let her pick the routine as she danced primarily with her hips. After a few moves, we came together and began our conversation again.

"Now that you understand empty threats are useless, you can listen to my proposition. None of this has anything to do with the idiots in charge here. In all honesty, John and I say kill them if you desire. Hold that thought, and let's do a lift and twirl here." She commanded.

"So what is the devil's princess scheming?" I asked with our pace increasing with the tempo of the song. During our next move, she leaned in close and placed a kiss on my cheek. I tried to react, but she laced her fingers behind my head to hold me still.

"Don't worry. This is just to keep our little show going. In fact, just so I can put your mind at ease, I'll let you in on a secret only my uncle knows. I don't play for the team you think I do." she whispered with the song coming to an end.

"I'm sure all the men staring at you will be devastated, now. Can we do something slower for when you explain this proposition of yours?" She nodded as the sweat dripped from her brow. This time she clapped at the band as they tuned up for something slower. I grabbed her hand and waist to begin again.

"Better?"

"Indeed, now what do you want?"

"It is simple. I will help you kill my uncle if you agree to a fraudulent marriage." She admitted. Her openness nearly brought me to a complete stop. What she had just suggested was treason.

"Do you realize what you are saying?" I asked, trying to keep my composure. She just smiled as I led her through a slow turn.

"Oh, trust me, Rob, this didn't come easy, but my uncle has left me with little choice. A few months ago, something changed in our plans. They suddenly accelerated beyond what we had discussed. Then he threw them all out of the window—making a new one that started back with Hope Tower's destruction and the killings perpetrated by Gene. Originally, none of that was supposed to happen. He was slowly going to spread Ascension and groom me to take over the world. I was going to build a world better than anything ever seen. Now he wants to destroy it all. He wants complete and utter devastation taking away my promised world." She claimed with an icy glare.

"If he is causing you such distress, why not slip a dagger into his back and save me the trouble?" I asked, trying to ignore her proposition.

"Rob, Rob, Rob, you know, killing him isn't that simple. He is not like most men that show weakness. He is strong at all times, stronger than anyone except for you. You are the only man that knows his weaknesses. You are the only one that he will be vulnerable around. Any other attempts in his life would lead to disaster and my end. On top of that, my uncle put in certain safeguards to ensure I couldn't take control of Ascension without his approval." She explained as we swayed from side to side with the music.

"What do you mean by that?" I asked.

"To ensure a smooth transition, he wants a male figurehead. He fears that the world would reject me and my sexual orientation. He fears that there are still those with power who hold strong prejudices attempting to undo me. To compensate for this, he placed an order to all of Ascension's affiliates that I could not ascend without a husband to act as my scapegoat." Trisha explained while the slow song finished up.

"That is quite the story, but it doesn't mean I have to help you. Don't forget you lured Iris and me to that alley. You are a target just as much as John is." I informed her. She walked around me for a moment, grazing her hand over my shoulders. She knew I couldn't fight back right now and used that to her advantage.

"Oh, sweet Rob, you know that I was only following orders. Uncle had a plan, and I was just trying to survive." She claimed as she winked to cue the next song.

"We both know you are not some helpless little girl in all of this. Hell, you are scheming to kill him right now. You don't get to play the scared girl this time." I was thinking back to the girl I held in my arms while covered in the 'blood' of her 'dead' uncle back in Despartian. She had fooled me, and I wasn't going to fall for it again.

"Fine, I'm not some helpless little girl, but I'm your best shot. If you decline, then blood will be shed, a small war will be fought, and people will die on your conscience." She threatened as we began to dance again. This time we went big, and I gave all I had to the performance. Trisha gladly obliged and gave all her energy as well. We moved from one step to the next with precision, and I tried to act as nothing had occurred between us. It was an elegant performance, and at the end of the three-minute song, the room applauded us. I had failed to maintain a low profile, but I think they all figured I wouldn't.

"I'm stopping Dave, Chen, and you tonight. Originally, we were going to wait, but you can't be allowed to escape." I whispered, bowing to the applause.

"You are right that this is going down tonight. That was settled as soon as I decided to show up. Dave and Chen are not aware of this. When the city was being rebuilt, my uncle placed a safety measure in each home in case of trouble." She panted.

"You little witch, what do you have planned?" She licked her lips with a smile before answering my question. Whatever it was, it was going to be paramount.

"You see, every house has a bomb placed in the foundation that is waiting for detonation. Ex and I each have a switch that will blow up one at random each time it is pressed." I wanted to wring her neck right there and then, but the chance that she wasn't lying was one I couldn't take. She began to head to the stage and pointed to a stairwell opposite us. I followed her direction and found Dave's gaze resting on me. My cover was blown.

I only looked towards Dave for a mere second, but Trisha had vanished on me. She had made her way behind the band and disappeared to some back room. I wanted to follow her, but Dave was the more critical target right now. I had to figure out how I was going to get to him now that I was marked. He started to descend the staircase towards me when suddenly the room began to shake. A majority of the room began to scream, but I stood my ground as I knew what had happened. Trisha had detonated a building and signified the start of the end game.

Chapter 24
Chase

Dave was shocked by the sudden tremors. He looked at me in fear and clearly thought I had something to do with it. Just when the room finished shaking, a second explosion went off. This time, it was far closer as I could see the fireball consuming the sky just outside the window. This time the patrons knew what was going on. They screamed louder as they ran for the nearest exits. I tried to fight the flow of traffic as Dave ascended the stairs. His tail was tucked between his legs as he hid behind the crowds. It was now, or never I had to make a move.

I fought through the crowd knocking out guards that tried to stand in my way. I had hidden my staff under my shirt for just this sort of occasion. Now weaponized, I cut through the crowd like butter. More guards tried to stop me on the stairwell, but I threw one off the stairs after another. These men were pathetic. I was severely disappointed in what Dave had selected to be his guards.

"Boy!" Mark yelled from behind me. I turned to the blind man and the three women who stood on the lower level.

"I know Mark. I screwed up!" I shouted.

"Yeah, you did, but we'll adjust. Just catch him while we look for Chen!" Vicky ordered. I agreed and returned to my chase. I busted through the door that Dave had left behind.

"Dave!" I yelled down the hallway in front of me with no reply, in turn, just the slamming of a giant metal door at the end of it. Unfortunately, my yell did attract some guards that were shaking in their boots. I smiled and charged ahead. A few tried to draw their guns, but the quarters were too tight, and I could make their weapons obsolete. I closed quickly and was on top of the gunmen.

It was a nice warm-up, but the group of men was merely a delay so Dave could get into a position to strike. I strolled through the hallway stepping over the bodies I had knocked out. Making my way to the door at the end of the hall, I knew a trap was most likely waiting. I kicked the door open, expecting gunfire, but was only met by the sound of footsteps descending a staircase.

"Dave!" I called again. This time my yell was answered with a bullet from below. Dave ricocheted the shot off the spiral staircase and nearly took my head off.

"That is your warning Rob! You know I do not need a clear sightline to end you, and I don't miss!"

"Fine, then give up, Chen! You never really liked him, and he can give me the same information!" I bargained. He denied with an exclamation as another bullet flew towards me. This time it hit the railing next to my left ear. Dave's marksmanship hadn't declined at all, and this wasn't going to be easy. Most men fire in a straight line, and that is the end of it. On the other hand, Dave had mental capabilities that allowed him to calculate trajectory in an instance. He could bounce a bullet twice and still hit his marks with a high level of accuracy though there was some error that had already saved me.

Dave didn't want to be anything he wasn't already, nor did he really care for the morality of the War. Dave liked shooting things, and he picked the side that hadn't killed his family. He was out for revenge, and he was really good at it.

During our boot camp days, Dave told me the story of the first time he killed something, and it was an accident. He was out hunting with his father when he was eight years old. The two of them were hunting wild pigs in Northern California and had no success the first three days of their trip. Dave had seen two pigs over that time, but both times he couldn't pull the trigger. On the last day, another pig walked into his sightline. He raised his gun but couldn't look. He closed his eyes and fired. At first, it appeared as if he had missed. He heard the sound of the bullet hitting the tree and figured that was it until the pig squealed. The shot had bounced off the tree right into the pig's head. It would be a move that Dave would become fond of and studied how it worked endlessly from that point on.

Now he was using that skill against me, and I never wanted to be at the other end of Dave's gun barrel. Only one man had ever survived a battle with Dave. There was a legend that a man named El Cazador once outdrew him in Colorado, which is why he is missing the tips of his left hand's fingers. However, none of that has ever been confirmed. Despite it all, I gave chase avoiding a string of bullets from Dave below. I never knew where they were coming from, but I knew they'd be close with him.

"Just give-up, Rob. You know I eventually hit my mark!" Dave called as his footsteps stopped. So far, he had been firing on the move, which had increased the error, but he was lining up his next shot. My only shot now was to become unpredictable and hope my ears could track the ricochet. It rang out, I swerved, and it grazed my shoulder.

"You know I can't do that, Dave! John brought me down this rabbit hole, and I don't think there is a way out without going through him and you!" I grunted, trying to shake off the wound. Complicating matters was the ankle that was bugging me from the last city. I could feel it acting up throughout the fights and dance. I couldn't swerve nearly as much as I wanted with Dave firing.

"I figured that was why you were here, and the Executioner came to warn me of your arrival. However, blowing up buildings is quite theatrical for you!" Dave admitted, firing his next shot. I tucked and rolled down several steps to avoid this one. I nearly popped out my shoulder in the process.

"You are clueless, Dave. I didn't blow up those buildings. Trisha pressed that button!" I revealed.

"Trisha isn't here. There is no way! I've only seen Ex!" he yelled with hesitation in his voice. I could tell that he was telling the truth. He hadn't seen her, but how was that possible? She was at the party dancing with me, and yet she had not talked to him prior.

I prepared for another bullet but heard nothing until the door at the bottom of the steps swung open. With the steps unguarded, I hurried after him, but the damage was done. A small bullet wound, my reaggravated ankle, and bruises from the tumble slowed my progress.

I reached the bottom of the steps but halted at the door. I could hear something, so I dropped to the floor quickly before a series of bullets sprayed through the door. After the clip was empty, I charged out and tackled Dave. We wrestled for a moment. Dave had been an excellent shot but was terrible in hand-to-hand combat. I had the upper hand quickly and was ready to knock him out until a pair of guards ripped me off of him.

A kick to the side of one's knee and an elbow into the other's nose was all I needed to free myself. At that moment, I was able to observe where I was entirely. Dave had led me to the garage under the mansion. He was in a dead sprint towards a running jeep that Chen was sitting in. I began to give chase until I noticed a scuffle by some other vehicles. I tried to ignore it until I saw Mark clobbering one of the guards. I had to assist them first. Regardless of how much I believed in them, I couldn't abandon them, especially since I had blown our plan.

I jumped into the fray to find the four of them were handling things well. Mark was knocking out guards one after another. I was impressed, and I was ready to chase after Dave again when there was a click. It is quiet in those seconds after a gun fires. You hear the shot and the ringing while the rest of the world slows down. Mark began to fall to the ground while Vicky's screams pierced through the ringing. I turned back to finish the guards while the others attended to him and joined them once the grunts were handled.

I knelt down to my teacher, who had just taken a shot to the abdomen. At first, I hoped it was a simple entrance and exit shot, but this was dashed when I saw the amount of blood flooding out. I put pressure on it the best I could and had the two younger girls assist me while Vicky cried for her father.

"You're going to be alright." I lied, examining his injury closer. It was ugly. Dave must have used a hollow point bullet as there was no exit wound. Instead, his insides were bleeding profusely.

"It's alright, kid. I can feel the damage. Just go stop them for the sake of this city." He ordered, gasping for air. I looked up from my dying mentor to see Dave and Chen driving away in their jeep. I didn't want to chase them at that moment. I had spent so much time pursuing people out of anger. This time I just wanted to be with the person that mattered to me. I didn't want Dave occupying my thoughts in Mark's final moments. Yet, I couldn't disobey a dying man's wish.

I looked around and saw a set of old motorcycles behind a group of guards trying to regather themselves. I instructed the girls on how they could assist Mark in his final moments and keep him comfortable until I got back. Then I charged the motorcycles. I was delivering moral breaking blows. I stole one of their guns and a bike to begin my chase. Before I even knew it, I was being followed by Vicky. I wanted to call her off, but I knew that look in her eyes. It was the same one I had when I lost Iris, and there would be no sense talking to her. All I could do was protect her by taking Dave and Chen down first.

Typically, catching Chen is near impossible. However, they weren't expecting us, and with his stomach pinned to the steering wheel from all the excess eating, we gained ground. Once we were within firing distance, I took aim at the tire. Unfortunately, Chen detected my presence just before I could fire.

Despite being out of shape, he was still a superior driver, with perfect knowledge of the city's layout. On top of those bits, he also had no moral quandary with driving through crowds. He knew that I wouldn't fire wildly in a crowd, but Dave's moral compass was more in line with Chen. Dave pulled out a rifle hidden in the jeep and opened fire. The first shot missed the two of us. However, a pedestrian took it to the shoulder.

We needed to push them towards an empty street. All the weaving and zigzagging to avoid Dave's shots meant nothing if they were just going to hit innocent people. I accelerated to pull closer, but Dave bounced a bullet directly off the bike's front, nearly blowing the tire. Vicky began her pursuit only to take a shot to the right handle of her motorcycle, causing her to swerve. We couldn't hang back as it would risk the lives of civilians, and we couldn't approach without giving Dave a direct shot.

Chen took a turn down an alley at last, which gave me a few free shots, but Dave could also line up his shot better. I could feel his scope honing in on me. If one of us couldn't take him out soon then, I would be dead within a minute. We continued our fire, and there was a moment that he looked away. He glanced at Vicky as the muzzle turned ever so slightly towards her.

What happened next, I can't really remember. All I saw was a flash from our surroundings, and I thought I saw the light from Dave's muzzle. I was lying on the ground with a road rash running up my left side the next thing I knew. My ears rang louder than my thoughts as I tried to straighten my eyesight out. The building to our immediate right was nothing but flame and debris. I couldn't find Vicky in the smoke but saw the jeep overturned ahead of me. I tried to crawl towards it, but my left arm was bleeding badly. I tried to stand and kept falling. I pulled out my staff and used it to rise to my feet, but I could barely move. I saw Dave helping Chen out of the wreckage, both men were breathing, but they both kept falling.

That was until a figure approached them from behind the fires. I could not make out who it was as the fire was the only light left after the numerous explosions. I had hoped that it was Vicky, but I knew better. It was in the wrong direction, and suddenly the figure pulled a gun on the pair of men. They looked like they were begging for their lives. Two shots, that was it, and then the mystery figure stabbed one of them with something. Before the mystery figure left, it turned towards me. In the flickering light, I saw the mask of the Executioner.

"No." That is all I could mumble with, the ringing still drowning out the noises around me.

I limped to the crash site. After several agonizing steps, I reached the jeep and had support to lean. I looked over the carnage seeing both men dead with a bullet hole in each man's head. The casings sat next to them with an "I" and "T" etched in them. Dave had a knife plunged into his heart with a letter on the blade's end.

It was addressed to me, but now was not the time to deal with it. The men I was after were dead. I picked up the letter and casings as my hearing started coming back just enough for me to hear the screams. The screams were just enough to bring me back to my senses. It had to be Vicky screaming, and I had to find her. I swung myself around and looked for the other fallen motorcycle. It took me a few minutes for my eyes to adjust, but I limped to it the bike and her when they did. She was lying on her stomach, moaning in pain. When I rolled her over I, found a bullet wound similar to her father's. I had seen the muzzle flash, but the blast knocked Dave off course. She was not long for this world.

"Vicky, you need to stay with me. You can't die here." I ordered as I stood her bike back on its wheels. I placed her on the front and held her the best I could as we drove back to the garage. We arrived to find Morgan and Sam keeping Mark alive the best they could, but his willpower was all that kept him going. The girls saw Vicky and me in rough shape and rushed to the bike. Morgan carried Vicky to her father while Sam assisted me in limping to the site. The guards were cleared out for now as they were spread thin trying to deal with the fires, but we still didn't have long.

"Hey, Daddy." Vicky grimaced.

"Hey, baby girl," Mark replied, gripping his daughter's hand. The girls began to tear up, knowing that the end was near. I held them tight, trying to stay strong for them.

"I wanted to catch up with you some more, but I don't think it is going to happen." She coughed with blood dripping from her body.

"It's okay...we'll have time later with Mom and your brother." He cried, holding her hand tighter, "Now Rob, I know this is another life you have seen extinguished, but it is going to be alright. You are a better man than you know. I have taught you all you need to know. The rest is in you." With that, I saw Mark's life flicker off for good.

"Bye Dad." Vicky whimpered, "Sam, Morgan, I told you that I wouldn't leave you, but something has come up. Rob is going to take care of you from here on out. Trust him; he'll get you to safety." Vicky reached her free hand to Sam and Morgan. They each gripped it tightly, and she was gone as well. As the ladies wept, I overheard the guards calling. Our time was up, and it was time to move.

"I'm sorry to rush the process here, but the guards are coming. We need to run, ladies!" I ordered, grabbing their arms. We found another nearby vehicle and headed towards the boat I had stashed at the riverside. Our exit went smooth, given the chaos of the city. The guards were not trained for emergencies such as this. The people had become so complacent in the mundane that a cataclysmic event such as this rocked them. The city was about to spiral down into madness and chaos, but I could not focus on the side effects of my actions. The girls were all that mattered at that moment.

Chapter 25
Three's a Crowd

We arrived at the shoreline and ditched the vehicle. They assisted me to the boat I had covered in leaves. I could hear the guards calling from nearby, but it was too late. We entered the water and sailed off under cover of the night sky. The Mississippi would guide us away without a sound or disturbance. I am not blind to the irony that both times I came to Memphis in my life, I came to save it, yet both times left in the cover of night as the city burned.

Once we were far enough downstream, I signaled to the ladies that we were safe. Upon the confirmation, the two of them began to ball their eyes again. Vicky was their mentor, hero, and sister who made sense of the craziness of the new world we inhabited. I felt for them, and it was hard to keep my own eyes dry given what Mark had done for me. However, there was no time to focus on what had already occurred. The river could be dangerous, especially when I could not see, so I turned my attention to it and focused all my energy. I would let myself break later when the time was right.

The ladies continued to grieve as I steered the boat to safety a few miles down from Memphis. When I thought we had entered a safe area, I pulled the craft aside to gather the troops. I had rushed them away without any say, but they had a right to make a choice.

"Okay, ladies, we're safe for now. That means we have to talk." I said as the boat came to a stop on the shoreline.

"What are we going to do?" Morgan moaned in the first audible words she had spoken in several minutes.

"You two are going to have to make a choice. Memphis is no longer safe, which is why I have brought you this far, but you don't have to keep going if you don't want to. We are far enough from the city that you can run and never see me again. I know Vicky said I'd look after you two, but you are grown women. The path I'm headed down is dangerous, and you have to make a choice to stay on it. I will honor Vicky's wish if you follow me, but what do you want to do?" I explained. It was a harsh truth, but they had to make a choice.

"I'm tired of losing people and being left alone. I want to go with him." Sam proclaimed, wiping her eyes dry. In every word, I could hear the hurt that accumulated over the years. I heard the War ripping a young girl from her family and Vicky being torn away from her just as she had a new family being formed.

"Okay," was the only word Morgan could utter. Though do not let her simple answer fool you. She was only capable of a single word at that moment. I could see her emotions nearly bursting, and if she had said anything more, she would have fallen apart.

"Alright, if that is what you girls desire." They both shook their heads as I moved to sit next to them in the boat. "This isn't going to be easy. You know that, right?"

"Is anything easy these days?" Sam asked. I had no good response because she was right. No matter which way they went, things would be a challenge. They were two young women all on their own in a virtually lawless land.

"I guess not," I said as I turned my eyes to the sky. I looked at the stars poking through the clouds and the faint smoke that trickled from Memphis. We made camp for the night as the girls curled up to each other and passed out from the day. They were exhausted physically and emotionally at this point. I did hear a few more tears, but no matter who started to cry, the other would wrap their friend tighter in their arms.

I could not fall asleep yet, so I stood guard and pulled out the note that the Executioner had stabbed into Dave. As I figured it was from John:

Rob,

This will be my last letter to you, and I must say I have enjoyed this little chase of ours, but the next time I tell you something, it will be to your face. You will be on your knees before me where all of this chaos started. I will show you that this world is lost and deserves to be burned. Then I will become death. I'm sure you've always wondered why and you asked me several times what I told that young woman in L.A. The answer is one and the same.

I had been a good soldier for years when I met my wife. I had thought that I was meant to be a killer until I met her. She was my world, Rob, and I was going to leave the military for good when I was sent on a mission that went against my conscience. However, I was still the good soldier who followed orders. I completed my mission. The person I killed didn't deserve to die. The world would be better off with him alive. What made matters worse was that the people who ordered the kill had me arrested secretly for it and claimed that I was a danger to the world. I lost everything, my love, my freedom, everything that mattered was ripped from me by men who sat in an office. I lost my wife after that. The person who made me feel human again, then in L.A. I found someone to connect with again, only to have that person ripped from me.

The world turned me into a monster Rob. The world put me on the path of destruction, as the old lady predicted. That is why I took everything from you. I want you to see what I lost so that you can understand me. And I hope that now that you have lost everything, you will stand by me as I set this world on fire one last time.

I will see you soon,
  John

All these years later and he was finally telling me the truth. John began to make sense to me. He had survived a lot in his life, and he was angry. He hated the world as I hated him, but most of all, I saw his weakness in the least bit. John was alone, maybe not physically, as Trisha was always with him. However, on a deeper level, he had no one and had this hope that in the end, I would be standing by his side. I guess that was the difference between him and me. He was damaged and alone, while despite my damage, I continued to find love from others. Iris stood by me, Gerald never turned away, Anna kept me strong, and Philip was a constant rock. Then even when I ran from them, I found others. Mark sensed something in me and taught me before he was ripped from me. I reunited with Dani, which brought back a piece of Iris that I had lost. And now I had these two. Maybe my greatest salvation would come in watching over Sam and Morgan.

Part 6
A New Beginning

Late October to mid November 10 A.L.A.

Chapter 26
Sam and Morgan

The following morning, we began traveling again, making our way to the end of the river. I now knew from the letter that John waited for me in New Orleans. The home of the last Ascension headquarters in the old U.S. and the location where Jeffery Irons was shot down, sparking the end's beginning. It had to be what he meant by *"where all of this chaos started."* The destination was set. Now I just had to join my dance partner in a confrontation that would decide the fate of many beyond just the two of us. I was more unsure now than ever about what I really wanted.

The first few days on the river, the two of them were silent as they grieved for their lost comrade. However, each day their personalities slowly started to shine through. There was more to them than I had first expected. On about the sixth day after Memphis, we stopped to start training, and I got to see the girls in their full display. I decided that, given their loss, meditation would be an excellent place to start. I learned quickly how frustrating it can be to be a teacher.

"Alright, girls. Vicky trusted me with you girls, and I think it is time to start our lessons."

"Sounds good, bro." Morgan said while Sam made an "ugh" sound at the word lessons.

"So we are going to start with a meditation where...yes." I started calling on Sam, who had raised her hand.

"If your goal is to protect us, shouldn't our lessons be more bam, bonk, sploosh, and less ohmmm," Sam said, motioning out the different sounds she had just made. My jaw just hung for a moment at the words this girl had used to describe a fight.

"Yeah, I think we could also throw in some kapows, whaps, and thunks just to spice things up when sploosh gets old." Morgan smiled. If I was shocked by Sam's use of the cartoonish onomatopoeias, Morgan floored me. I thought she was the serious one, but she was just like Sam after all.

"I guess I can teach you kapows...but first, I think a meditation would be good given our recent losses," I said, not believing I had just said the word kapow.

"Don't forget the splooshes." Sam insisted.

"Of course not. Now, let us start by taking a seat and just starting to breathe...What is it this time, Sam?" I asked as she raised her hand again.

"Were we not supposed to be breathing this whole time?" Morgan laughed at Sam's question as they were both realizing that they could get under my skin this way.

"It would have made things easier for me," I replied with tongue in cheek. The girls laughed at my comeback and finally started to take it seriously. This serious behavior lasted a good two minutes before Morgan began to hum, and Sam followed closely. I tried to direct them back, but I failed miserably as they started to have a...sing-off that lasted a good half hour. I had started a lesson on mindfulness. Suddenly, I judged a singing competition with lousy pop songs that came out just before the War began. I could have thrown the hammer down, but they were still new to me, and I was trying to understand them better. Later that night, each girl came separately to me and actually took the lesson seriously. After Morgan's lesson, I decided to talk to her about what occurred earlier that day.

"So, what was that all about?" I asked as she uncurled from her meditation position.

"Oh, that's just something that Sam and I like to do from time to time, you know." She replied.

"How often are we talking?" Honestly, I was worried about what her answer would be. I didn't know if I could handle that as an everyday thing.

"Let's put it this way, you'll know a lot of songs by the end of this journey." She smiled. Already that day, I had seen her smile more than I had in the previous days. It was a lovely smile that I wished would come out more.

"Maybe singing lessons should be next then," I suggested as I pictured my sanity slowly slipping away already.

"I'll let you try and tell Sam she can't sing. It will end wonderfully." I didn't know what Morgan was implying, but I had a hunch that it wasn't the first time that suggestion had been made.

"Noted, have a good night." Morgan went back to her blankets. I heard the two of them just chatting the rest of the night as I tried to do my own meditation.

The next day we floated farther down the river until we reached another stop. This time I decided that physical training might work better. It started off with fewer questions, but as I would demonstrate, the girls would be dancing. Sam had this weird movement she would do with her hand and a pouty lip. Though they goofed off during my demonstrations, their actual practice was crisp. Each of them picked up the maneuvers quickly and helped each other when there were questions. Sam was a bit more fluid in her movements, while Morgan was more powerful.

During one of the more intense patterns, Sam was able to pick it up quickly and started to dance around. This irritated Morgan, who was trying to work through the motions.

"Hey, can you take this a little more seriously!" Morgan hollered. She was frustrated with the moves and her inability to master them the way she wanted. I would learn quickly that Sam was more natural, but Morgan held herself to a standard almost as high as mine.

"Sorry, I can try." Sam whimpered back, knowing that she had upset her friend. With Sam restraining herself, I assisted Morgan with the movement. After about ten more minutes, she had mastered it enough to satisfy her standards for training. That night after my meditation, I went back to the campfire we had made and found Sam alone.

"Where did Morgan go?" I asked, slightly concerned that she was on her own.

"She went to practice those moves some more."

"And you didn't want to join her?"

"I did, but she really wanted to work through it on her own. That is pretty standard for her, my dude."

"And how does that make you feel?"

"Fine. Morgan has always been driven like that. She works really hard, and sometimes I join her. Other times I just wish there were still places I could get great waffles at." I placed my hand to my face at her comment. I was trying my best not to laugh, but her face, as she said it made it near impossible.

"And what do you want right now?" I asked, afraid that the answer would be waffles.

"I want to be really good so that I can protect her and you, my dude." Not the answer I anticipated. I went and sat next to her after that one. She was a goofball, but you could see it once she took the training seriously the last two days that she did care. She wanted to be great at what she did but didn't want to lose herself in it.

"I like that answer. And I'll do my best to get you there. Until then, I will protect you two. I promise." I said as I gave her a side hug.

The next few days followed a precise pattern. We would wake up, eat any leftovers from the night before and then shove off. We would sail a few hours downstream and then pull back ashore when we were growing weary. From there, we would fish using simple tools we had made or hunted around the area for any food. After we ate, I would attempt to train in some manner. Often it degenerated about an hour in, but some days were better than others. Then we would eat dinner and go to bed to start the process over again.

Then after several more days passed, I finally thought it was time to talk to them about deeper topics. During our training, I had gathered a little information. Still, I avoided the big one knowing how fresh Vicky's death was in their mind, and the reminder would be ill-advised.

As we sat at the campfire after one of our more successful meditations, I decided that it was time, "So how did you two end up on your own?" I was blunt with the question, and it took them a minute to think about it.

"Well, my brother and I were the only ones to survive when our hometown was decimated. He helped me escape but fell into drugs during our time on the run. Soon after that, I was by myself, lucky to be found by this girl and then Vicky, my dude." Sam responded as she looked long into the fire. She leaned against Morgan as Morgan thought over her answer.

"I'm sorry to hear that. And I hope you know that I will be here for you." I responded. Morgan was quiet while she looked at the fire. Her hands gripped the ground beneath her tight. I could see the veins popping from her forearms as she grabbed the grass and dirt.

Whatever she was thinking about, it was much more than the simple, "I was the only survivor from a battle."

"After my family was killed, my boyfriend and I went on the run. Then one day he was killed protecting me from this sick freak who tried to...who wanted to...." She couldn't utter the last word. It was killing her inside as the tears choked her up. There were only a few options based on the context, and I didn't need her to say it. I went to sit by both of them and held them tight.

As I held them, I forgot how young these girls were. I had never asked, but it was clear by their development that they had been young teenagers when the War started. A whole critical stage of their life was ripped from them, and they had to learn how to be adults in this world, which was nothing like the world they were a child in. All while having no stage to adapt. I had to help them. I needed to give them a life beyond war. Unfortunately, they would have a few more battles to fight, but I would get them to the other side. That was my new mission. It was no longer to get revenge. It was to give them hope that was robbed from them when they needed it the most.

After that conversation, our bond continued to grow tighter and our conversations deeper. They still goofed off during some practices, but it was reduced. They saved most antics for afterward. Even pranking me a few times. I was able to get my revenge, though, so it was fun. It felt like I had a family in these two. This continued for a few more days, then after one challenging practice session, I sat the two of them down at the campfire again. I wanted to make sure they understood what was going on and what may be expected of them. I also wanted to allow them to jump off the wagon before we entered the swamps of Louisiana.

"So, before we enter the point of no return, I want to talk about what we are approaching," I explained as I stirred the firewood.

"What do you mean by that?" Sam asked. She was munching on a fish that we had caught earlier and had a tilted head with a look of confusion.

"You see, as we get closer to New Orleans, we begin to enter John's territory. Once we enter his territory, we enter his trap, and it becomes impossible for you two to escape." I told her.

"Just tell us what you want us to know," Morgan instructed. I smiled at her boldness as it was refreshing to see her start to take control. Sam had the highest ceiling talent-wise, but Morgan was going to be a leader someday. She was the one that I'd have to trust in case of emergency or my own untimely demise.

"John is different from anyone that you have faced before. The men in Memphis were willing to kill you, but they were both untrained and unmotivated. Even if they had caught you, they would have just killed you. John's forces will be merciless. Worse off, John is a monster, unlike anything you have met. He will torture the two of you just to dig his claws deeper into me. Everything going on right now is a game to him. Memphis was a test, the drugs that filled St. Louis were for laughs, and his weapons factory in Illinois was a hobby." I explained. I tried to convey the terror that awaited them, but John has always been a difficult one to describe.

"You can't face him alone then." Sam smiled, scooting closer to me, and Morgan did the same on the other side.

"Yeah, and besides, what is the point of all this training if we don't use it. They'll never see the kapow and splooshes coming their way." Morgan added as I smiled. The two of them were so naïve, but it was refreshing. Mark was realistic, which I needed before to help me understand what lay in front of me. However, their optimism kept me going now.

"I appreciate the support, ladies, but this is not a decision that you can make recklessly. John is responsible for the state of our world right now, maybe not the War, but everything Ascension has been a part of. His hand guides the world and all of us. He manipulated my old mentor to force me into this game, killed the woman of my dreams, and has led countless more to their deaths. He lives to see destruction." I told them again.

"And like I said, we aren't going to let you do it alone, you stubborn butthead," Sam reminded me. "I told you I wanted to be good enough to protect you and Morgan. And now I have to do it." I couldn't have found a better set of students. They might have had me worried that first day, but they were full of surprises.

"Besides, based on what Mark told us and what we saw happen in Memphis, someone should be chaperoning you at all times." Morgan joked as she finished her own meal. Sam laughed at the comments.

"I much preferred it when I thought you were the silent type," I commented, glaring at the chuckling young ladies.

"You love us," Morgan commented with a smug as she looked at Sam, barely holding it together.

"I do indeed," I announced as I threw my arms around them again.

"On a different note, can I ask you something?" Sam asked, breaking up the seriousness of the moment.

"You are going to ask me regardless, so go ahead," I replied, turning to face her.

"Do you remember the day this all started? I was so young, and most people I've talked to shy away from it, but I've always wanted to know about that day." She admitted looking down at the ground. She seemed ashamed of the question. I could tell that others had made her feel like it was taboo and not worthy of conversation. I also realized that no one ever did talk about the day L.A. was attacked. They talked about Mr. Irons and the riots, but never that day.

"I do, and let me tell you, Sam, it was eerie." I began as I thought back to that day. "Whenever I had pictured the end of the world, I always figured it would be an obvious ending. You know those dramatized moments in a movie, T.V. show, or book where the rain poured for three days or an eclipse happened unexpectedly. There was none of that. It started as a beautiful morning with a gorgeous sunset and mild temperatures. I don't think there was a cloud in the sky across the U.S. It was just one of those days. Nothing felt like the end to any of us when the day started. I think it was a Thursday if memory serves, and I was treating Iris to a special lunch that day. We both had a fondness for Mexican food, so I took her out to celebrate as she had finally finished all her graduate school applications."

"As we sat on the restaurant's porch and ate our lunch, I remember the birds singing as the sun blinded my eyes. Iris would laugh at my futile attempts to block it out. I, in turn, threw a few pieces of rice at her. The usual for our relationship. Then we heard a scream from inside. We ran inside to see if everyone was okay. All we saw were fixated eyes staring at a T.V. screen with a caption about L.A. being under fire. No one knew who had fired upon the city until later in the day when war was announced, but I remember standing there. I remember the quiet. That was the scariest part about it girls, it was like a painting. Not a sound could be heard, the scenery was perfect, and no one could move a muscle. That was the end. It was as if the world wanted one last moment of peace before it no longer existed." I finished searching for the right words, knowing nothing could genuinely encapsulate the moment where a city was flattened, and a war began.

"Hm," Sam muttered as she sat there looking towards the stars above us.

"Not satisfied?" I asked. She just shook her head, though I wasn't quite sure what it meant. Morgan just shrugged as she was confused.

"I don't know. I guess I expected something else. I guess I had hoped that there was something more than that. You know it was the start of all this, and I hoped that there was something that could help make sense of it all." She admitted.

"Unfortunately, there is no sense in destruction, and people have an aversion to the topic. Though it wasn't anything substantial, I'm sure whenever you asked people about it, all they could think about was the War itself. Thus they refused to talk about it out of their own personal fears." I answered, knowing it wasn't the answer she wanted, nor the one I wanted to give.

"That's depressing," Morgan commented. I just laughed at the simplicity of her response.

I told them stories from the War while they recited their own experiences the rest of the night. They talked endlessly about Vicky while I sprinkled in small bits about Mark, who I had known only for a fraction of the time. On occasion, we would throw in a couple jokes or tall tales. It was nice to just enjoy that moment with them. It was meditative. My mind was free from the trouble that often fluttered through it. As the night grew late, we began to wind down when I heard a rustling from the leaves around us. I drew my weapon only to have a possum waddle out of the bushes. After looking at the staff, Morgan had one last question for me.

"So, what is the story behind that thing? You could be using anything, but choose a powerful stick." She wondered as I retracted it back to its travel size.

"Obviously, I'm compensating." I laughed though neither girl found it as funny as I did. "Alright, I guess I can tell you. The weapon's official name is a Japanese Bo. Basically, a big stick, like you said. However, I find it has more versatility than most weapons. It fits who I am as a fighter and complements my style while also allowing me to fight multiple enemies at once." I spun it around in my hand as I talked, thinking of all the fights it had helped me through since the first one with Gene.

"Does that one have a story of its own? I noticed the engraving on it." Morgan pointed out. I handed the staff to them so they could see it as I talked.

"It was given to me by my mentor Gene Unvek. The engraving roughly translates to "to continue is power" in English. It would be closely related to practice makes perfect, but I prefer the literal. I prefer it because there was a point that I was ready to end my life and found the strength to keep moving forward. After that, every day reminded me that I was stronger than the day before, and every day I realized that by living, we are powerful." I explained.

"Now that is deep," Sam said after a long silence.

"It is, and now we should sleep. Tomorrow we will enter the Louisiana bayous, and who knows what we'll find. Think about all we've said tonight and be ready for a new world starting tomorrow," I told them, resigning to my sleeping space.

Chapter 27
Museum

It had been a few weeks since we left Memphis, and finally, we were entering Louisiana. I had heard rumors throughout my years that the northern part of Louisiana was hotly contested between opposing forces and could be treacherous for us. I kept my eyes open and ears in tune with the world around me, preparing for any danger that we could encounter. The training had been good for the two of them, but at the same time, I had made strides of my own. Teaching them forced me to sharpen my own technique and helped me return to my soldier shape. I was more ready now than when I began this hunt back in Despartian. Plus, the extra weeks had given my body to heal from all the damage I had inflicted on it.

Early in the afternoon, I could feel the winds shift and pressure start to change. A storm seemed to be on the way, so I pulled the boat ashore. As I hid the boat, the girls wandered around the shoreline, and Sam stumbled upon something.

"Hey Rob, come look at this." She called. I ran towards her voice, unsure what they had found. When I arrived, I saw a sign that directed us towards a museum.

"It's not going to be open," I assured her, trying to avoid any extra delays.

"You don't know that. Come on, please." She begged with her large piercing blue eyes. I just shook my head, trying to ignore them, then Morgan chimed in.

"It looks like there is smoke coming from somewhere in that direction." She pointed out, leading my eyes over the tree line. It didn't feel right, but I didn't think there could be any harm in a slight detour like this one. Plus, if there was trouble, it would allow me to see what the girls had learned. We began the long trek towards the billowing smoke. We made it about half a mile when a tree branch snapped to my left.

"Triangle formation, ladies!" I barked as they responded to the sound themselves. All of us prepared as practiced. Our backs were tight against one another, and there were zero blind spots in the formation.

"Do you think it is John's men?" Morgan whispered. Her eyes continued to scan the bushes just as I had trained her.

"I don't think so. He's never been much of a cloak and dagger type of fighter. He would just send his forces at me, but let's find out." I answered, "Show yourself whoever you are!" There was no answer at first, but then the bushes began to rattle again.

At last, something began to rise from the shrubs. A man came into our sight, he wore very little, but a goat mask covered his face. I could not make much out about him as swamp moss dangled down his body. He was smaller in height, yet there was the power behind that mask. I could tell just by the weapon he carried, a sizeable medieval maul that could crush skulls like glass.

"Any thoughts?" Morgan asked this time.

"Definitely not John's men," I told her. "Identify yourself and stand back, or you'll give me no choice!" He approached us closer and closer, drawing his weapon with a single hand. A maul like his probably weighed 15 to 20 pounds, and to hold it in one hand was a mistake. It was intimidating but impossible to swing.

"I told you no choice," I informed him, but I soon realized it was my own hubris in the way. Just before I could launch my counter, nets flew towards us and caught us like wild animals. I should have seen it, and more importantly, I should have heard the others surrounding us. I was an idiot getting my girls caught like this by a man in a goat mask. Soon after the nets flew, a crowd of ten to fifteen equally disguised enemies surrounded us. I had far more spears in my face than I was interested in at this point.

"On second thought, I think we can figure out an alternative." I smiled as the silent goat-man knocked me out.

Chapter 28
Consequences

The next thing I knew, I was sitting inside the museum, which was an actual museum dedicated to pre-war topics and post-war life. Though I might have been able to break out of my binds, it wouldn't have mattered. The girls would have been vulnerable, and there were too many enemies to take care of before they could harm the girls. I went through every possibility, but none of them ended with us all alive unless I did nothing. The girls were still alive and close to me, which was a win to me.

"You three will now face the judgment of our leader." The goat man explained as another man entered the room, wearing an alligator mask over his own face. He was taller and leanly built compared to his pudgier follower, whose frame I could now make out with his swamp dressing removed. The alligator man carried a longsword on his back that hung from his leather armor.

"God. I was caught by a furry cult." I mouthed as I took a blow to the back of the head. My sarcasm was not well received.

"Take the girls away. Our business is with him." The alligator claimed as his masked underlings surrounded us again. I couldn't let them separate us, and I lunged towards them, but the goat threw me to the ground. As he threw me down, I caught a glimpse of a tattoo on his thigh that wasn't fully covered by his swamp apparel. The tattoo was of a pan flute. These men were allies of Dani's and Gina's.

"Wait...Wait...Wait," I pleaded as they tried to grab the girls. "We are on the same side. I know Dani and Gina. She said you guys would owe me one." The goat man paused for a moment as he waited for instructions.

"If only Gina knew what trouble you'd be, she wouldn't have made that promise. Take the girls, but do not harm them." He ordered. It wasn't much but was enough of a guarantee for me to sit quietly.

"Rob, what should we do?" Sam asked as they both looked for my guidance.

"Keep out of trouble and survive," I instructed as the men took them away, leaving me alone in the room.

Once the girls were in a different room, both of the men removed their masks and armor. The man who had worn the goat was pudgy but was battle-worn with scars stretching across his body, including one from his left ear to the top of his shoulder. The gator man was a tall blonde who had scars littering his own body. Bullet holes covered his left arm, and I was amazed it was functional. On top of this, his tall body held muscles on top of muscles. He appeared stronger than anyone I had met on the journey.

"What you did for Gina was important, but since then, you have caused huge stress for the army. That cannot be ignored." Gator informed me as he crept towards me. "Stand up and follow me. You will be tested by the best the revolutionaries have to offer." He began to walk down the hallway as the goat man stood close to me, waiting for me to follow. I graciously followed him.

As I trekked down the hall, I began to notice the exhibits that lined every corner of it. Every exhibit represented a different battle from the war with in-depth details that should have been confidential. On top of the battles, several secret missions were on display that only a few people were aware of, myself included. With that being said, I should have known everyone who had access to the files but had no idea who these men were.

"Who is the curator of this museum?" I asked, trying to untie my hands.

"This place was established by the man elected president of the outcast, ruler of the forgotten, and leader of the freedom seekers. Pan is the shepherd of peace and built this place as a memorial so that we do not forget the folly of men." He explained, pointing out the different exhibits.

"That is fine and good, but how did he get access to the data for these missions? I was a part of several of these that were classified, and about ten people knew of the mission." I informed the man who had not yet given me his name.

"You forget a simple fact...someone has to clean up the messes you make. Someone stands in the background and puts the pieces back into some shape for the rest of us. He knew because he was there to count the bodies after your classified missions." He informed me as we entered another room. This room had a pair of chairs and a single light bulb hanging from the ceiling. The goat man sat me down in the nearest chair as the other man took up a seat in the other spot.

"You are dismissed, Diego." The gator commanded. The goat nodded and left quickly. "So, Mr. Doran, what brings you here?"

"Accident, the winds started to change, and the girls I'm traveling with saw the sign. I was stupid enough to not say no." I responded, trying to free myself again now that there were no eyes on my hands.

"It's amazing how many accidents you seem to stumble into. More amazingly, I can't believe how many of these accidents seem to disrupt our plans throughout the different regions. To the point where you have earned the nickname Rob 'the Meddler' Doran."

"Well, that's a nice name. Which reminds me, who the hell are you?"

"Dirk Mattson, the 1st Division Commander of Pan's Army. The right-hand man to the people's shepherd." He announced with pride that bellowed from deep down in his barrel chest.

"Well, it is nice to meet you, Mr. Mattson, now. Can we do something about these binds?" I asked. I could have freed myself but figured it would be more diplomatic to let him do it.

"I don't think so." He responded. I was not a fan of his response and decided to do it myself. Diplomacy was no longer my focus. "Is the baby happy now?"

"No, your men kidnapped me and took my friends. I think there are a few things to take care of first."

"I do apologize for that, but I needed to take precautions. You have a reputation for being a loose cannon. I needed assurance that when this conversation got real, you wouldn't just start bashing skulls. My men don't need this right now."

"Point taken, but know if anything happens to them, I will bring you all down. John is my main target, but you can become my current one."

"No harm will fall upon them, Rob, but we need to talk. I need to know what you are planning on doing once you reach New Orleans." He demanded as his demeanor shifted.

"Well, I haven't thought about all the details, but in summary, I sneak in, bring down John, and subdue Trisha."

"That is why we stopped you. You see, that plan ignores collateral damage. I had hoped that your travels had changed you, but it is clear that it hasn't. You have always been a soldier, scorching earth ignoring those affected by your decisions, but that has to stop here. As evil as John might be, a sudden removal from power would create a power vacuum that would send what little stability we have into turmoil." He lectured. It was clear that what I had told him had triggered something. Though his words had remained calm, his grip tightened around his chair, nearly breaking the arm of the chair within his grasp. I wasn't quite sure how to respond to his comments.

"I don't know what you want. My goals have been consistent, and I'm sorry if that disrupts your plans, but that isn't my responsibility." I told him.

"It is clear that you don't understand yet, and need some more convincing. Follow me." Dirk ordered as he led me back down the hallways again. I wanted to argue with him, but I knew it would be better for the girls if I played nice. As we walked, Dirk would point at the statistics of each exhibit and let me read. Hundreds of photos and thousands of bodies were counted. To say the least, it was terrifying knowing how many of these bodies were due to my failures.

"Are all these numbers accurate?"

"Unfortunately, these are just healthy estimates. Many of the bodies were dismembered and burnt beyond recommendation, which means these are likely lowballed estimates. If you don't believe me look at this exhibit." He motioned towards one of them. I made my way towards it and noticed its name, at last, Battle of Despartian.

My eyes grew large as I became consumed by it. I had to know what these people knew. I didn't just need to know how accurate the numbers were. I had to know if they had eyes within the strategy room. The exhibit read as follows:

The Battle of Despartian was one of the final battles of the second United States Civil War. The sleepy city of Despartian was home to around 51,000 people before the War started.

It was the final words of that statement that sent a shiver down my spine. They knew that someone had given the order to use Despartian as a diversion. However, it was not clear if they knew I suggested it. On top of that, I knew these numbers had to be close to accurate. Only about fifteen thousand people still resided in the city despite being one of the largest remaining ones on the continent outside of the other Ascension-run cities.

"Is this all you know?" I asked, hoping that Dani did not know about one of my darkest moments.

"Yes, but it doesn't matter who gave the order. It wasn't the person who led to the destruction. It was the system that didn't care about people. It was the system that led to no other option." Dirk explained as he leaned against the wall next to me. This was a different take than I expected, but I was happy that if Dani discovered the truth, it would come from me.

"Why build this place?"

"Simple, people often forget the ugly side of history. People forget that collateral damage is people."

"Okay, but what does this have to do with my pursuit of John?" I inquired.

"I need you to see what it is like for those of us who weren't soldiers," he began. "Did you ever ask who buried the bodies that were littering the streets behind you? Or have you ever wondered who sweeps the rubble away so that supply trains can plow forward? What happens to the babies who need feeding when their parents are cut down next to their cribs? Have you ever thought about who has to deal with the aftermath of the disaster named you?" After each question, Dirk's voice rose and grew more intense. I started to understand his point.

"I mean, I have, but it isn't something that I could control."

Dirk smiled as he led me into the next room. Above the door sat a sign labeled 'Toy Room.' Inside was the most gut-wrenching sight I could have imagined. Every corner was covered in old toys. Teddy bears ripped to shreds, dolls missing half their faces, action figures melted, and children's books shot to pieces.

My heart ached at every turn; all I could think about was how many of these were my own fault. How many children lost their lives because of my allies? How many children lost a parent because of me?

"That is exactly why we built this place, because no one thinks about it, and for the sake of the world, you need to start thinking about it when you pursue John. If the men in charge had seen the things Pan and I had, there would never be another war. They would all realize that peace always fades, power erodes, wealth is spent, safety vanishes, but death is forever." Dirk told me as he stared at a picture of some kids.

"So, what do you want me to do?" I sighed.

"We want you to stop making messes for our forces to clean up!"

"What messes are you referring to?" I asked, insulted by his comments.

"St. Louis and Memphis! When you were a soldier, you learned how to destabilize an enemy stronghold by taking out the head. You were very good at it and continued doing it today. However, that is a messy way of doing business that leaves a city in turmoil even if a plan is in place. This is a mess you keep creating."

"In St. Louis, there was a plan to overthrow 'The Family,' but because of your presence, Dani accelerated her plan. Now our forces are hunting down leftovers that should have been squashed in a single sweep. On top of that, you threw Dani for a loop which left a vacuum in our own organization. Meanwhile, you left Memphis in the worst state. We had deemed the city as a low priority because it was stable. It needed to be overthrown, but the risk to innocent lives was low. Then you arrived and blew up several buildings while killing the heads of the city. Suddenly, we needed to divert hundreds of our soldiers to the city, which took them away from towns and cities near their own disasters. We can't allow you to do that in New Orleans as well." Maybe I should have been ashamed or felt pity for his forces, but I felt nothing. Instead, I felt insulted that he was blaming me for all of their issues.

"Memphis wasn't my fault. Let's start there!" I replied as I began to grow irritated by his accusations.

"I don't care, and neither does Pan. It wasn't an accident that everything happens when you are around!" He yelled with the vein on his forehead beginning to pop.

"I get it. I'm the bad guy because you guys have failed to take care of business. 'The Family' is pumping a deadly drug into the streets and shipping it to John by truckload, but it could have waited a month. Memphis is a low priority because all Chen and Dave are doing is brainwashing a city to do John's bidding without question. On top of it all, you seem to be ignoring John and letting him operate without opposition. At the same time, he funnels in super-soldier drugs, weapons, and mind control devices patented by Rick in Despartian. However, I am the one acting rashly/" I defended, pointing out all of his failures.

"You misunderstand Rob. We don't think you are a villain. You are just a wild dog. You can be a great help to us, but first, I am going to domesticate you and suppress your wild nature." Dirk told me as he led me to one final room.

"I'm not that easy to tame."

"Well, let's see if we can change that." He replied while pulling my staff from behind his back. He threw it at me, and I reacquainted myself with it. I spun it around a few times.

"Taming me through battle is a bad choice and one where you will get bit."

"Oh, I think you'll find this fight to be a lot more revealing than you'd expect." He suggested as he strolled through the room.

As I prepared myself for battle, Dirk just walked. I started to move side-to-side, but there was no reaction. He had just talked a big game but seemed uninterested in fighting me. Then it hit me, and I mean, I was literally punched in the back by someone when I said that. I turned my head as I was lying on the ground and saw Diego from earlier. He was holding his hammer with the butt end of it pointed towards where I was standing.

"Heh, not playing fair, are we?" I commented, standing back up while rubbing my back.

"We're soldiers Rob, there is no such thing as fair in war." Dirk smiled as he finally drew his weapon.

"Alright, no holds barred then. Just my style." I replied as I prepared myself for whatever else he had planned.

"That is good to hear. You see, I've been looking forward to this fight for some time. During the War, I was housed within a testing facility that was destroyed by your team. I was left for dead by your team with deadly chemicals coursing through my veins. I'd be dead if it was up to you, but Pan found me in the scorched facility and gave me purpose again. Now I'm going to beat sense into you for him and myself." Dirk explained as he charged towards me. We locked horns as he drove his great sword closer to my body. He was going to change me or kill me. It was clear that it didn't matter to him in the end.

I pushed him back despite his overpowering brute force. He hadn't specified which facility he was in. Still, it became evident that it was one of the super-soldier facilities set up across the world. As we moved from move to move, I watched Diego, who stood watching us. I tried to reason out what was going on, but Dirk was skilled beyond my imagination. I figured he was just a brute like everyone else I met these days, but he was highly skilled.

As our clash continued, I took a few slices and dealt out several crushing strikes. Just as my advantage reached its paramount, I saw Diego moving out of the corner of my eye. He swung his hammer as Dirk locked up with me. I ducked and rolled as quickly as I could. Just when I thought I was safe, a kick came flying towards me, sending me skidding across the floor. I looked up, wiping my brow to see a woman standing there with her leg outstretched.

Three on one, not an ideal circumstance, but I believed that I was capable of winning that fight. The blow was followed by a string wrapping itself around my neck. I threw the assailant over my body and saw a fiery red-headed woman standing there with a snarl and a thick piece of wiring. The odds were definitely shifting out of my favor as we moved to four-on-one.

Unfortunately, the surprises didn't stop there. Just when I thought I was safe, a small knife was thrust into my abdomen. I screeched and flung myself to the center of the circle. The fifth opponent was another Amazonian. Her eyes were dead, unlike anything I'd seen before. She hated me, and I had no idea what could have prompted the feelings.

"I think I may be outmatched at this point," I admitted, looking around me.

"Not just that you are out motivated. Diego came from Argentina and was in one of the villages you burned down during the South American campaign. Thanks to your team, despite his imposing presence, he is missing three fingers and his left shank. The first woman who kicked you is named Mindy. She is one of our newest recruits hailing from Memphis. She had a bit of a rebellious spirit, which cost her house when others had been destroyed. That thrust her onto the streets, where she was taken advantage of. She was raped because Memphis had lost all order." He informed me as he moved from one soldier to the next.

"The woman who tried to strangle you goes by the name Arya Strong. She was sixteen when you destroyed Minneapolis, and since then, she has become one of the fiercest fighters in our army. I would be nothing without her by my side. Lastly, there is Alayna, who was favored by Rick De Luca. When you destroyed the Family, she was chased from her home like a rat. Until we saved her." He strolled across the entire room and gathered the five soldiers against me. I was unfamiliar with the odds, but these five were far superior to most I had faced in recent memory. Particularly with Dirk's enormous strength leading the charge.

"Shit." That was all I could muster at the moment.

"Well put, Rob. This is where action meets consequence, and you die or become domesticated." Dirk boasted as they all scattered around me again for another assault.

I laughed in defiance, unsure of what else to do at that moment. Dirk did not enjoy my laugh. My options were diminishing. At this point, there was no running, no strategy, and little hope. I had to make my move before they had a chance. One light illuminated the room, and it was my only shot. I used my staff to break it and darken the room, though it limited my own abilities. My time with Mark had sharpened my ability to fight without eyes. Everyone else in that room, however, would be negated.

As soon as the room was dark, I charged to the spot where Dirk had been and attacked him first. I had to neutralize him before they restored the light. If I could do that, then maybe there would be a chance. During our conversations, I noticed his loud breathing pattern and used that to hone in on him. I went for his knees to start off, which dropped the massive man down. He tried to retaliate but could only swing wildly, making it easy to dodge. I slid around his swings with a few precise dance moves and struck him over the head with my staff.

As I turned my attention to the other four, the lights flashed back on. I had hoped for a little more time. Still, at least the most significant threat was incapacitated laying on the ground behind me. The room was heavily tilted in their favor; however, I had a fighter's chance again. They charged me all at once, and I did everything to defend myself. I mainly stuck to defensive tactics using counters to turn them around. However, the numbers were overwhelming.

Arya and Diego were fierce fighters that could have fought me for some time on their own. At last, Arya had gotten behind me with her wire. She wrapped it around my neck, choking me out. I thought I was finished when Diego raised his hammer, but just before he could deliver a blow, a whip wrapped around his forearm, stopping him in his tracks. It pulled him backward and distracted Arya enough for me to free myself.

I was unsure what was going on, but someone had turned the fight around in my favor. I did not waste the opportunity afforded me. With Diego distracted, I took care of Arya. After she was down, I moved on to the other enormous woman. As I fought her, I saw the masked woman twirling the whip around and taking on Diego. The mask was pointless. Dani's moves were unmistakable. She commanded the room like she always did.

"Enough." Dirk coughed while raising himself from the floor.

Chapter 29
He Did It

Each side stopped fighting as he stood up. He was still wobbly, but his forces had no interest in disobeying him, and the two didn't want to fight in the first place. I was glad that he had called it before I had to do any more damage. Dani was still fuming.

"About time you stopped this madness, you moron. We are fighting a war, and you are fighting a man on our side, wasting time on a battle that has no winners." Dani lectured while walking up to him. She helped him to his feet just to slap him across the face. "And you. How do you constantly end up in situations like this?" I quickly received a slap of my own.

"This man has to learn, Dani. We cannot let him run loose without a plan!" Dirk argued.

"I'm not going to argue with that. He is a lot dumber than his reputation would lead you to believe, but trust me, he doesn't respond to physical threats. It just makes him more stubborn." I was offended by the comments, but she was correct.

"Dani, I still rank above you." He reminded her with a deathly stare.

"But apparently, I'm still smarter as I realized that neither you nor Pan can beat John, but he can." She sassed back. He stayed silent for a moment as he took in his surroundings. Two people had taken out his best soldiers, including himself. He had to accept facts.

"Alright, Rob, you win this round. Not because you defeated me, but out of respect for Dani and our duty. I now know that I can never beat you because you are not a dog to be trained but a wolf made to roam free." They assisted the rest back to their feet, with Diego and Arya bowing to Dani after removing her mask.

"Now that this is settled, we need to talk about the girls," I informed Dirk after the room was cleared.

"Don't worry, your friends are being released as we speak and should be joining us shortly." He responded, leaving Dani and me alone.

"Oh, good, I kind of liked Mark and hoped he wouldn't leave you alone." She smiled, leaning against the wall.

"Unfortunately, he has since passed," I informed her, avoiding eye contact.

"What...what happened?" She asked, moving closer to me.

"He was shot in the line of duty," I said.

"I'm sorry to hear that. So who are your friends?" She placed her hand on my shoulder, trying to comfort me the best she could.

"A pair of lost souls that I found when I lost Mark," I replied with a smile. She was confused by the smile, but the mere thought of those two just brought that reaction out of me.

"Lost souls?" She asked as the doors swung open and the girls ran to me. We hugged each other and felt comfortable that we were all alright.

"Yeah." I looked at Dani. She started to realize that I had grown in the weeks that had passed.

"So, who are these two?" She asked me, turning our conversation for a minute. Deep down, I knew she still wanted to talk about my loss, but it wasn't the time.

"This is Samantha, but you can call her Sam, and this is Morgan." The girls turned and shook Dani's hand.

"Is she one of them?" Morgan asked as she turned to me.

"Sort of. I work for the same group, but I was a friend of Rob's first." Dani responded for me.

"Friend?" Sam asked with a raised eyebrow. I could tell by her tone and look she was trying to imply something more profound.

"As of now, yes, just a friend," I answered, leaving the answer open for the conversation Dani and I had to have at some point when we had more time.

She was uncomfortable at this and clapped her hands together, "Well, I think that is good for now. We can catch up more later."

Dani's face was red as she exited the room. I led the girls out after her. Once outside the room, we saw Dirk, who beckoned me over.

"I want to show you the rest of the museum." He informed me. I was hesitant at first but felt that it was the least I could do. Most of the rooms were just as haunting as the first few and brought back many memories that were best left as memories. Then, at last, he brought me to the exhibit they had for Irons.

It brought back many sour memories, but there was something there I had never seen before. Irons was killed by a sniper that was never identified that much I knew, but there was a shell casing. The shell casing had an "I" engraved in it. It looked identical to the other two that I had found. I went pale as the realization hit me. I grabbed my bag from one of Dirk's men, who had brought it to me. I found the other five bullet shells and lined them up in order of appearance. A "D" from the bullet that hit the fake John, an "I" given to me for suicide, the second "D" on the shell that killed Iris, and the last "I" and "T" that were fired at Dave and Chen. Now, this is an "I" before all of these.

"What are you doing?" Dani asked. I hadn't seen her following us, but once she was there, I had to explain it all or at least everything that I had figured out.

"It is a confession. John's mission he wrote about, the one that cost him everything, was killing Irons. John did it." I stammered.

"You've got to be kidding me." She responded. Dirk couldn't even muster words. The whole idea was preposterous, and yet it still made some type of sense.

"John, how could you keep this secret?" I whispered to myself. We wondered who could have done such a horrific thing all this time, yet it was the man who saved my life many times. It was the man I was chasing.

As I realized what had occurred, I started to piece together another conversation I had with him. One that I should have remembered way back in Despartian with the first engraved bullet. He told me once that he always liked to engrave the roman numeral on his bullets to symbolize one shot, one kill. He didn't know why he did it but enjoyed knowing they would know he did it when the shells were found. I looked at the other bullets and saw that each started as an "I" but had additions made to it for his little game. He knew how the sentence would start, and he wanted to ensure I got the message, which is why he left me the casings. He wanted me to know that it was him, but it was not just him.

"So, does this actually change anything?" Dirk asked now that he could formulate the right words again.

"No, but it completes the puzzle that John wanted me to solve, and now that it is finished, he will want me to make a choice," I informed him as I placed the bullets back into my bag.

"And what are the choices?" Dirk asked.

"To stand against him or with him as he tries to destroy the world."

"And what do you choose?" Dirk followed up as his hand reached for his weapon.

"I will stand against him, but I fear that I am about to cause you and Pan more issues," I informed him as my wheels turned.

"What do you mean by that?" Dani asked before Dirk had the chance.

"In Memphis, they told me that they are expecting me to come with an army, and the way John has been phrasing things, I think we are moving into the end sequence. This means I don't have time to wait as I'm sure you'd prefer." I explained. I wondered if Pan's army was the one Trisha was expecting me to march with. It made the most sense, but there were no guarantees that they would follow me.

"Army? End sequence? What in God's name are you talking about?" Dirk asked as he tried to comprehend my comments.

"Yes, from what his forces have told me. He has something big planned, a total world reset, but he also expects me to fight. He expects me to lead men against him to stop it."

"I'm not sure about you leading, but I will follow Pan if he chooses to battle with you," Dirk commented.

"And I'm not sure if we have time to wait for him," I responded, unsure if I was qualified to lead them.

"Well, what would you propose then?" Dirk asked.

"I'm not sure, but can we stay the night? I will let you know in the morning." I suggested.

"That works for me. I will think about options myself. I will have my men set a room for all of you." With that, Dirk left and had his men prepare a space for us. Meanwhile, I went to find Sam and Morgan, who had wandered off.

I eventually found them in a weapons room. They were ogling over the different tools. I had not introduced weapons into their practice yet, but I wondered if it was time to do so. Especially with the final battles looming, they would need every advantage possible.

I confirmed with the guard who watched over the room to take a weapon for each of them. He had no arguments.

"Girls, let's get you something, but I get to choose," I informed them as I waved them over.

"Just no lame sticks," Sam said as she looked at my weapon. I chuckled as I picked up a pair of nunchaku and handed them to her. She sighed as she looked at the sticks chained together. "Why?"

"The nunchaku works for people with your fighting style. They move and can slither with your style of fighting. Trust me and for Morgan a pair of twin sai." I handed Morgan the small blades. She was much happier than her partner. I didn't need to justify my choice to her. After they had their weapons, I led them outside to practice. Sam was reluctant at first, but she started to understand her weapon better after a few demonstrations. She liked Morgan's better but accepted my choice.

A couple hours passed as we practiced. I finally dismissed them when Dani approached me. "Want to go for a walk?" She asked. I was panting from the training but agreed.

Once we were clear of the museum, she finally asked me a question, "So what are you going to do?"

"I think the three of us are going to infiltrate New Orleans and try to delay John the best we can until an army can get there," I told her. It wasn't much of a plan but was all I could muster in the hours since I spoke with Dirk.

"And if the army doesn't come?"

"Well, then I go out swinging." I smiled as she paused for a moment. She was in deep thought, but I couldn't tell what she wanted to say, until it came out at last.

"I'd join you if you asked." I nearly laughed at the way she phrased her statement. I figured if anything she was going to demand to come, but this was different. She wasn't sure and she wanted me to make the choice.

"Dani, do you want to go to New Orleans and risk your life with me?" She chuckled at the way I phrased my own question.

"Yes." She replied once she was done chuckling.

"Fabulous. Now we have four suicidal idiots banded together. With that settled, do you want to talk about that night?" I asked, shifting the conversation.

"Do you?"

"I do. Trust me, I'm as surprised as you are by that." With this conviction to face a night I normally would have run from Dani turned to look me in the eyes. We each stared deeply for a moment before she spoke.

"We're adults, Rob, and we both felt a moment of passion, but I think that is all it was. Momentary passion." She stated with a lack of conviction. I wondered how truthful she was being, but regardless, I would say what I needed to.

"Well, I think that I cared for you before I cared for Iris. Then I loved her, and I was content with us living our happy separate lives, but now she is dead, and I don't think she would want me to spend my life alone." Dani was struck by my admission and what I was implying and said nothing at first. I decided to continue, "That being said, I just want you in my life. It doesn't have to be in any romantic way. Hell, that just complicates it. I just want to stand with you and fight. If that is all that happens, then so be it, but it is what will make me happy."

"I...I don't think I feel as strongly, Rob, but I like that last part. I like the idea of standing with each other. If something else happens, then it happens, but I think we can cross that bridge when we get there." She responded. Before, I didn't think she was honest, but now I knew we had opened up our hearts. Neither of us really knew what we wanted from one another, but we knew that we cared. We knew that we had spent a good portion of our lives separated from the people we cared about, so now we wanted stability. We wanted someone that would be there when we stood at the gates of Hell ready to fight the devil. Eventually, we made our way back in for the night. I went to meditate on the day and clear my thoughts for the following morning.

Chapter 30
Final Details

When I woke, I didn't have a good answer for Dirk. What I told Dani the night before was the best my brain could muster, but I wasn't sure it was enough. The whole point of the day before was to teach me to slow down, but here I was, running in again without thought. I knew it wasn't right, but John was leaving me with little choice. On top of that, I had to wonder about Trisha. She seemed eager to gain my help, but I wasn't sure if that was genuine or just an act.

My mind raced the whole morning as I ate breakfast. I tried to meditate, but my mind grew more consumed by the decision each time I did. As I finished my food Diego came and found me. He informed me that Dirk wanted to speak and that any more delay would not be appreciated. Not wanting to upset him before we had an upsetting conversation, I made my way to the meeting room, where I was first introduced to Dirk. He sat at a table with another chair perched, waiting for me.

"Sit." He suggested as he waved his hand at the open spot.

"I appreciate your hospitality up to this point."

"My pleasure. Now have you thought about what you are going to do?" He asked, leaning over the table.

"I have. I think it would be best if Dani, Morgan, Sam, and I infiltrated the city and delayed John for as long as we could. If you can bring Pan here, I would appreciate it, but if not, I will adapt."

"So there isn't a real plan?"

"No, but with John, our plans don't matter. We just need to learn how to adapt to his, and this is the best method right now." I explained, trying my best to justify the poor idea I had given him.

"I don't know much about John, but from what I have seen, I understand your point. Now I don't agree with your idea to sneak in there, but it is also the safest option."

"So you're going to help me?" I couldn't believe what he was saying.

"I will approve your idea and send for Pan. I cannot guarantee that he will come, but I will keep you updated via Dani. Now, what do you think you'll need to be successful?" I hadn't thought that far ahead but was able to quickly form a list. I wrote several items down on a piece of paper and slid them to him. He looked it over then called for a guard. He passed the guard the note and whispered something to him. Then he turned back to me. "Your supplies and horses will be ready within the hour. I will also give you a map to the city, but know we have no idea what it looks like from the inside and will require your help with that in case Pan agrees to help."

"I understand. I will go grab the ladies and have them start preparing." As I left the room, Dirk stayed seated and twisted his pen in his hand a few times. He disapproved, but it was clear that he saw no other option at this point. He had to trust me even if it killed him on the inside.

I rushed to the ladies and informed them of what was occurring. They prepared themselves the best they could. They grabbed food and cleaned themselves up one last time before we left. We had no idea when our next meal would come in peace or when the next shower would be. Once they were ready, we headed out front, where they were finalizing the loading of our horses. We mounted our horses and prepared for New Orleans. I looked around at the ladies. Dani wore her scarlet blood-stained armor from the fights that prepared her for this. Morgan sat in an entirely ebony outfit looking like nightfall with her twin sai strapped to her waist. Sam had some difficulty mounting the horse, but once she did, she sat elegantly in a white shirt that once belonged to Vicky. Her nunchakus were strapped to her legs though she was not as proud of them as Morgan was of her own weapon.

Meanwhile, I wore a pale green swamp suit that Dirk had made for me. If I was to lead them from the front, I wanted to blend into the surroundings. I wanted to be unseen so that I could strike and deliver a quick end if need be.

Once we were in formation, Dirk finally left the museum to talk with Dani. I assumed it was regarding the communication about the city's layout and Pan's army. The only thing I heard him say was, "Fortuna favet fatuis" or "Fortune favors fools." Not the most positive message he could have delivered, but one that I understood. Once he finished, he wished the rest of us luck as we started our trek towards New Orleans. It had been a long journey, but it was coming to its end. All roads led south and the destiny I felt I had was coming to its most pivotal moment. However, to my surprise I wasn't going in alone, I was going to face it with three people I cared for deeply. I wished that Mark and Iris could have been there with me, but I knew that they rode by my side even if their bodies were gone. John I am coming for you and the army you created.